PRAISE FOR

SNOW BLACK

"*Snow Black* is a classic horror thriller about a small, isolated town, a fierce blizzard, and a monster. It calls to mind stories like *Dark Was the Night*, *Phantoms*, and *30 Days of Night*. It has all the creepy shocks and fun you'd ever want! Thom Erb sticks the landing on this spooky tale!" —Jonathan Maberry, *New York Times* bestselling author of *NecroTek: Cold War* and *Red Empire*

"Erb's *Snow Black* is a thrill-filled blast full of arctic chill. With a classic small town set-up and a cast of flawed but believable characters, it's a love letter to the action-packed, gore-filled horror movies we know and love. A quick, supremely enjoyable read." —David Moody, author of *Hater*, *Autumn*, and *Shadowlocked*

"Thom Erb's *Snow Black*, like the winter blizzard at the novel's heart, will blow you away. It's old-school creature-feature horror that combines native folklore, extreme violence, realistic characters, and a killer ending, but more importantly, it's a well-constructed story with a hell of a lot of heart. I was super impressed. Highly recommended!" —Gord Rollo, author of *The Jigsaw Man* and *The Dark Side of Heaven*

SNOW BLACK

A Monster Novel

THOM ERB

JOURNALSTONE
YOUR LINK TO ARTIST TALENT

ISBN: 978-1-68510-168-8 (trade paper)
ISBN: 978-1-68510-169-5 (ePub)
The Library of Congress Catalog Number has been applied for.

First printing edition: December 5, 2025
Published by JournalStone Publishing in the United States of America.
Cover Design: Drew Brayshaw and Thom Erb
Edited by Sean Leonard
Proofreading and Cover/Interior Layout by Scarlett R. Algee

JournalStone Publishing
1400 North Wood Rd.
Murphysboro, IL 62966

JournalStone books may be ordered through booksellers or by contacting:
JournalStone | www.journalstone.com

For David Somerville, Clayton Pelton, Jesse Pyron, Tim Deal, and Mom, Dad, Brian, Lisa. I love and miss you all everyday!

For **Mom** – Thank you for always making sure I marched to my own drummer. And thank you for always believing in me and I hope I make you proud.

For **Dad** – Thanks for all the things you taught me—and even more for the things you didn't.

For all of my **"Sterling Point"** friends – We had some great times, didn't we?! I miss those days—and I miss you all:

Clayton Pelton, David Somerville, Chris DeGelleke, Raymond Pelton, Jesse Pyron, Rob and Petra Zajak, John Cossaboon, Robert Cossaboon, Laurette Cossaboon, Dawn McCullough, Chris Ward.

For **Rask** – You were my best furry, four-legged friend and constant writing companion. I hope Dad is keeping you happy, playing fetch with your favorite tennis ball. Love ya, Bubba (Pablo).

And never last…never least…as always, for **my Roxane Marie** – Though the storm may have raged, we shall embrace the calm of our ever-after. Thank you for being my guiding light—my lighthouse in stormy seas.

INTRODUCTION

When the storm came… it didn't come alone.

That's the tagline for this book—and yeah, I'm proud of it. It's been seven years since my last novel, which still feels surreal to say. But *Snow Black* is finally here, and I'm grateful to be sharing it with you.

Like many of my stories, this one has been haunting the corners of my mind for over a decade. It's taken on many forms—different drafts, different intentions—but it always circled back to the same chilling core. Originally, it was an eco-horror tale about climate change and the consequences of ignoring nature's warnings. But over time, it evolved into something more personal. Still dark. Still monstrous. But grounded in grief, memory, and the quiet horrors of real life.

A lot has happened since I first started writing *Snow Black*. The kind of life-altering stuff that shifts your perspective: losing both of my parents, saying goodbye to beloved friends and pets, going through a divorce, moving from place to place, and letting go of the family home. I'm not sharing this for sympathy—just honesty. Life throws storms at us, and whether we realize it or not, those storms find their way into our stories.

I'd already lost my mom when I began this book. My dad passed not long after. I don't like saying I "lost" them—I know exactly where they are—they're just not here anymore. Writing *Snow Black* helped me process that absence. It helped me wrestle with grief, with memory, and with my deep-rooted dislike of winter and cold (which, as you'll see, plays a major role in this story).

This book became a kind of therapy—raw, emotional, and honest. It helped me work through the darkness, and I hope, in its own strange, snowy way, it resonates with you too.

The air here in Lot 13 is turning colder. The leaves are falling. The holidays are creeping closer. And who knows—maybe the storm is already on its way.

Live Life Full,
Thom Erb
Lot 13, New York

SNOW BLACK

A Monster Novel

PART ONE

"He realized that much of his torment of the years past had been self-inflicted, and an inevitable part of growing up."

— Thomas Wolfe, *You Can't Go Home Again*

PROLOGUE
If We Make It Through December

RHODES HOLLOW, NY.
DECEMBER

Darkness slumbered for thousands of years.

Its origin was unknown, even to itself.

Only that something. Some creature had summoned it. But unknown by whom.

And the cave contained it.

But it was the humans—long-haired and dressed in animal skins—who fought to imprison the Darkness within this stone chamber. Their crude magic and salted weapons weakened the entity until the shamans arrived. These cloaked figures, tribal magicians of the Ononciawa'ga:'Gawe:no, spoke in an ancient, powerful tongue and unleashed their rituals against the foul, skin-clad humans. Using sacrificial blood, they painted wards and warnings across the stone walls and floor—signs meant to be honored by all. And in the end, they bound the Darkness here, sealing it away forever.

The Darkness fought and clawed at the bright, flickering light of the cave. again and again, it failed.

Its captors, broken and decayed bones, and pitiful weapons filled the dark lair in their desperate attempt to contain its growing power.

It tore viciously at the mystical veil that kept it tormented and bound, the primordial growls and howls echoing as the Darkness prayed to its great-elder to be set free for what seemed like eons. But alas, it was for naught.

Until…

***

A moose-sized buck stumbled into the cave. It snorted as steaming blood spilled out from its side.

It was broad, strong, and in its tenth season.

Its blood-soaked hooves slipped on the rock, and it crashed into the darkness, its labored breath lost in the frigid air as it fought to survive.

It struggled with the fresh wound on its side as blood continued to pour onto the ground.

The ancient, smooth sandstone seemed to glow and drink every drop as if it had never drunk before. The struggling deer's heart pounding, ushering more blood over the strange cave floor.

A harsh voice broke the cavern's silence, announcing, "It's in here," as two hunters entered.

There were five of them but only two came into the dimly lit chamber.

Two-leggers. An unseen force kept the gust of snow from entering the cave as the dying buck's fleeting thoughts flickered.

"Shut the fuck up." Another gruff voice. "Next time you shoot, boy, check your sector. Ya damn near took my ear off, for Christ's sake!" A drop of blood from the human fell onto the earth.

"Sorry, Pops."

The trembling buck tried to rise, but it failed; It only whimpered and bled.

The old two-legger stood above it.

He grinned and spat a wad of brown goo onto its blood-covered muzzle.

"You can run, but ya can't hide, bitch. Look at all the bones. There must be hundreds of them.

"Hot damn. The guys are gonna love all this."

A shotgun blast echoed through the cave.

* * *

"What's that?" Denny Pritchard said, kneeling, still filming with his smartphone, pushing some bones aside.

The older hunter pushed past his son. "Outta the way, boy." Royce Pritchard dabbed a gloved hand at the fresh wound on his cheek, then stepped around his son's big frame. He lost his footing on the piles of bones and something else and nearly fell, but reached out to the stone wall, balancing himself.

A soft glow on the wall caught the old hunter's attention. He squinted and tried to angle his bifocals to see in the dim light. "Hmm.

What the hell?" he murmured as Denny continued to rummage through the pile of bones and junk.

In the dark haze of the cave, it appeared to be writing or something painted on the walls. It wasn't in a language Royce had ever seen, but then again, English was barely even his first language. *War leaves little time for study; he pondered the peculiar scratches.* The dim glow on the words seemed to intensify where the blood from his glove touched them.

"Might be losing your shit, old man," Royce said, chastising himself as Denny called to him.

"Pops, look!" Denny exclaimed, clearing away bones and debris.

"What have we here?" His knees cracked and popped as the old man knelt and reached for something shiny amongst the animal remains.

It was an intricately hand-carved box. It appeared to be bone, shaped like a small brick. As Royce uncovered it, he noticed the same faint glow as the paintings on the wall. Inside were various small stones, jewels that emitted the same odd glow, along with an unexplainable warmth.

Royce hastily shoved the box into his pack and saw the entire floor lay covered in more of the same treasures: arrowheads and spearheads, knife blades, along with other bits of what he guessed were Native American artifacts.

"Whoa…" Denny stood up and made his way around the cave, moving more bones and leaves. "Dad, there're all kinds of stuff in here." He reached down and lifted a handful of what seemed to be old jewelry: necklaces, bracelets, and hairpins. "It's like a treasure horde in that D&D movie!"

"Or a lottery ticket," Royce mumbled, shoving two handfuls of the gold and silver coins into his pockets. The old hunter—a tracker of over forty years—examined the area his son had kicked clear. Royce's breath caught in his chest—this time, it wasn't from his many years of smoking. No. Two things almost knocked him to the ground.

The same weird, glowing symbols were painted on the floor by someone. This time, a large, glowing white circle encompassed them. He felt a drop of warm blood from his cheek roll down and drip onto the floor, and he dabbed it away.

The second was what he saw in Denny's hand.

Wow, this is huge!" Denny held a long, thick bone in one hand, still filming the whole bizarre scene with his cellphone in the other.

The pristinely preserved bone was not from a deer, bear, or cougar. No. It was a human bone—a femur.

A flood of panic washed over the war-hardened veteran. "Not our concern, boy. You carry this deer back to camp. We'll talk about this later." Royce grabbed his son by the scruff of his jacket. "You don't say a damn word to any of those assholes, hear me?"

Denny nodded, lowering his head. "Yes, sir."

Royce turned and mentally cataloged all the treasure—lying undiscovered until now—littering the cave floor. He knew he could make a killing with some museum or tree-hugging college for the old Indian artifacts, so he shoved a few more handfuls of treasure into his bag.

Thousands, maybe millions, of dollars might be unclaimed. His military and Kodak pensions would only take him so far. This would change his retirement plans and offer him a whole new life.

A tiny smile curled on his mustached face, and a few more drops of blood dripped from his cheek and onto the treasure and the cold stone floor below.

"Let's get outta here, boy." He turned as Denny hefted the big deer, spewing its own blood on the floor. "Not a word to anyone, capice!"

They left the freezing cave, Royce calculating how he would cash in his newfound lottery ticket.

* * *

A bright flash of white light swelled inside the cave with swirls of obsidian.

The Darkness had awakened.

It drank deeply of both animal and human blood, aching for more of their living essence. It wanted more.

Its gigantic form rose from the darkness of the ancient cave, whirling and black, with burning red eyes and filled with razor-sharp talons. The ancient spirit shifted between forms, finally settling on the immense shape of a furious, ravenous bestial cloud.

It let out a guttural, ethereal laugh.

At long last, it could break free from its prison for the first time its memory would allow.

BAD MAN WALKING

The strong wind battered the centuries-old pines and birches of Carrigan's wood against the backdrop of a cloudless blue sky. Heavy snow fell in biting sheets, and Royce Pritchard cherished every crunching step he took through the dark forest floor.

He dabbed his still bleeding cheek, and he sure as shit, planned on giving Denny a refresher course in how not to hunt like a goddamn idiot. But now he dabbed at his face, and while he wanted to slap the shocked expression from Denny's face, he was also beyond happy with his kill.

What made the day even more glorious was that it wasn't far into day two of their hunting trip, and he'd bagged his second deer. With it being daybreak, he was hoping his luck would continue, as his aching body and other things were not-so-gently reminding him that this trip might be his last.

The bulging bag on his hip might have just been holding the secret to a lavish tour in his golden years, filled with warm weather and cold beer, far away from New York.

They left the strange cave and made their way back down the windswept ravine, toward the old Pritchard family cabin compound, leaving Denny to lug the over two-hundred-pound deer.

Not a terrible start to the two-day hunting trip, huh, ya ol' jarhead? Royce thought as he stood on the crest of a steep rise, stopping for a drink. Despite being seventy, he felt like he was in his forties today. Down the slope, he saw only his son clodding across the frozen swamp. He checked the bag on his hip.

Royce pulled down his balaclava and drank from his silver flask. The whiskey warmed his gums and continued down to his stomach as he watched his lunkhead of a son trying not to break through the ice of the marshland while carrying the big buck, leaving a dripping trail of blood in the deep snow and ice.

"Dumbass." Royce shifted the shotgun from his left shoulder to his right, bitching to the snowy woods. Denny, despite being as dumb as a box of rocks, was Royce's firstborn and strongest genetic hope to raise a real man, not a weak individual. That's what the youngest son, Mikey, provided. He'd tried, but some dogs just don't hunt.

Royce, needing to urinate, scanned the pine undergrowth. Down the hillside, the bog's edge trapped Denny's boot on the bank. He'd at least have plenty of time to relieve himself.

"Candy-ass sonsabitches, you're killing me, for Christ's sake. Thanks for popping out such Nancy-boys, Joanie. Good job," Royce said, heading deeper into the thickest part of the woods.

The biting wind whirled through the lush spruce trees, and Royce hesitated to pull out his penis, afraid frost might claim it in seconds. Finding just the right spot in the center of a cloister of full pines, he let himself free; steam rolled from his piss and weaved with the sharp snowflakes flitting into the woodland.

Royce exhaled and enjoyed the peaceful moment, at one with nature. The old hunter needed a good catch this year. The medical bills were piling up and the disability and retirement payments from Kodak weren't cutting it. However, bearskins fetched a high price, and he had been hunting these woods since he was a boy, barely able to hold a rifle.

Looking out through the trees, he could have sworn he could still hear his father's stern voice and his ex-best friend Gordie Roberts' mocking impression. The old man laughed, remembering a bittersweet moment. The sounds startled him, and he snapped up his Carhartt hunting bibs and returned his focus to the woods.

"Come on. What's it gonna take, a goddamn written invitation? Royce wheeled, hearing a sharp scream. "I'd like to get this big sumbitch back to the cabin and gut 'em before Christmas."

He froze in the deep, snowy ruts he'd made. Watching. Listening.

Briefly, only the northeastern wind's deep gusts and distant hunters' curses were audible.

The violent wind whipped through the dense pines and cedars, causing an almost wailing sound to fill his ears.

Turning to the vast wood before him, he slid his rifle free and hesitated. Should he wait for his incompetent son and the hunting party or strike out on his own? He mulled it over for a millisecond before he made his way to the edge of the hill, back toward their hunting cabin.

As the hunters were almost to the top of the hill, Denny was lugging his prized ten-point buck, and Royce swore he could hear the guttural growling again.

"Nah. You're hearing things. It's just this storm whipping up. Dumbass," he said, chiding himself. "That's all."

"Come on, boys. Jesus Christ. Y'all are slower than molasses in January." Royce's voice echoed through the snowy valley, back down toward the cave, over the frozen swamp, and back to him.

A sharp twinge of regret immediately overcame him. Though he didn't understand why, a primal urge to be quieter consumed him.

Shaking his head, he drank again as the other hunters caught up.

"About damn time, fellas. I was about to leave ya to the wolves and bears."

"Sorry. It's damn cold out here," the first hunter grumbled.

"Snow is getting bad, boss," bitched another.

Denny and the deer made it up the steep hill at last, and Royce eyed the bleeding beast with pride.

"Hot damn, he's a beaut," Big Bob Babcock, the jolly, heavy-set hunter said and clapped Royce on the shoulder.

The soft, distant wailing flitted on the harsh winds.

"Thanks, Bobb-O. My knees and the clouds are telling me we should get back down the the cabin." But something in the old vet's gut told him something wasn't right.

"What the hell? We just got out here. Come on,"

As Royce and the hunters made their way down the knee-high snow toward their cabin, Royce could have sworn something was following them.

"Quit your goddamn bellyachin', boy, or I shoot you and leave you out here for the wolves. 'Sides, the damn storm whooping up," he mumbled to himself again, and continued down the hill.

"Bobb-O, you're on lunch duty. Best make something mighty yummy, or it's your fat ass pulling KP, too."

The hunters' laughter filled the valley as something colder whispered back in the freezing winds.

Royce didn't like it. He reached into his ammunition pouch and swapped out his buckshot for rock-salt shells.

"Boys, switch to rock-salt slugs," he said, loading the white shells into his Mossberg 500 12-gauge.

1

Hello Brooklyn

Grey Pilgrim Books
Brooklyn, NY

Mitchell Roberts' arms ached from the familiar weight of new books. But it was his favorite kind of ache. It was a familiar and agonizing, yet invigorating pain.

Sweat gathered underneath his Navy peacoat, and his glasses fogged.

As he scoured the many rows of books in this literary Nirvana, his earbuds played the catchy rock guitar intro to Foreigner's "Luanne" for the millionth time. He hated and loved the song from his fellow Rochesterian. He felt his chest tighten, and a dark cloud slowly crept over his inspired mood.

Beth. He let the song play until the chorus, because Mitchell Gordon Roberts was a lifelong glutton for punishment and self-flagellation. He would be damned if he let her and that time and place in his young life rob him of his happiness—again.

The burning and throbbing in his arms took away those memories, which were replaced with a stack of the one thing he treasured most in the world—books.

While he shamefully frequented the big box bookstores, Brooklyn was the home to many of Mitch's favorite bookshops, and he preferred the cozier, more personal stores like this one and a handful of others.

He'd spent the better part of his days since Halloween holed up in his cramped apartment, putting the final touches on his latest novel and researching his next. Tonight, he planned on finishing it.

This was one of the myriad reasons he loved the path he'd chosen since leaving his Podunk lake town.

"Great to see you, Mitch," Shannon, the curly-haired co-owner of Grey Pilgrim Books and Curiosities, said with a wide smile. Her long, black-painted fingernails punched the yellowed keys of the register that must have been new when the first Bush was president. "We have a new batch of your books in the back. Might you have time to sign them?" She shot him a hopeful wink.

"Of course." Mitch grabbed his big bag of plunder and headed toward the back room, but not before leaning over the heavily stickered counter and chat at Shannon's five-year-old daughter, drawing in a sketchbook. "Hey, Dragon kid, I didn't forget."

The little girl with a crazy head of hair, like a toddler-Medusa, jumped to life, letting her book fall to the floor, and screamed with excitement. "Mr. Mitch, yay!"

"You can leave your bag here. I can cash it out for you, so you don't have to lug it in the back?" Shannon offered.

"Oh great. Thanks," Mitch over-dramatically rummaged through his jacket pocket and produced a small, well-worn object. It made the girl squee in joy as she held her chubby hands out.

"Now, promise not to lose it, okay? This is magic!" Mitch said with a wink.

"I promise. I promise!" She shouted, catching the twenty-sided die in her shaking hands.

Shannon called after him, "Thanks so much. Alice is going to be so happy."

Mitch loved the shop owner. She always treated him well. A near celebrity. A bizarre thought, that, and far more than he deserved.

"How's the writing going?" Alice asked with a bit of a wince, and Mitch began signing a stack of his books.

He cocked an eyebrow and peered over his black-framed glasses, accentuating his faux-annoyance with the question. "It's almost done. Tonight's the night, good lady. Stay tuned. I think you're gonna dig it."

"I'm sure I will." She bagged the books into Mitch's prized Monty Python quotes canvas bag. "Wow. Maberry, Melton, MacDougall, and Steiger, huh? Digging deep into monster lore, are ya? What do you have cooking in that twisted head of yours, Mr. Roberts?" Alice teased.

"Indeed. Big, evil monsters threaten to devour an entire small town, kinda thing. It's going to differ vastly from my other stuff," Mitch said, cashing out.

"Sounds fun."

"Death and destruction with lots of gratuitous blood and gore is always a good read," Mitch said.

Alice chuckled and said, "I'll put this week's purchase on your tab. You can pay next time you come in. Looks like the line is getting long out there. And we don't want to keep you from finishing your book."

"Ah, sweet. Mucho appreciated. I'd best get signing. Need to get going. Mother Nature is brewing up a good one out there."

"The weather prognosticators have been on full blast the past few days. So, we shall see."

Mitch began walking toward the black curtain that separated the storeroom from the store when he tentatively turned.

"Oh, hey, is there any chance of holding a book release party here when *Temporary Saint* is published?" Mitch had always hated the sound of his voice. And asking anything of anyone was even worse.

"Of course. Let us know when, and we'll get the books in and make it a big thing." Alice's bright smile always made him feel better.

"Groovy. When I get all that fun stuff from my publisher, I'll let you know," Mitch said. "Have a Merry Christmas," he added, and walked out into the blinding snow and icy streets of Brooklyn.

The weather had gotten worse.

The brutal wind nearly knocked Mitch off his sneakers.

He didn't care. Being on the verge of finally completing his novel kept him warmer and protected him from any storm the world had to throw at him.

The street was crazy busy as always, and while the bright sun was the ruling king now, the brooding storm clouds off the coast to the east were threatening a nasty snowstorm. Just in time for Christmas. So the crowd was even more insane. But Mitch didn't care.

His apartment was only two blocks away, and even though his books were heavy, they made his soul and mind lighter, as they were passports to his creativity.

Gov't Mule played in his earbuds, and that made him even happier.

Mitch, lost in a creative euphoria and plotting his monster novel's opening chapter, ignored the slippery sidewalk and his soaking sneakers. When he was in that mode, the outside world was just a necessary annoyance.

But he was happy.

As he reached the intersection, he noticed a guy in an overstuffed jacket and hoodie who seemed to be lost in texting on his cellphone. Mitch shook his head. It annoyed him to see everyone so lost in their stupid phones. Texting, Facebook, Instagram, or the bullshit social media-du jour. All were time-sucks, and Mitch hated every one. He watched this twenty-something guy talking into his phone with his earbuds in, about to walk out into the slushy street. Then he saw an NYC snowplow coming the man's way, and he wasn't paying attention.

"*Idiot!*" Mitch said into the icy air.

Without thinking, he dropped his heavy bag of books and ran toward the oblivious guy, one foot onto the road. The snowplow driver's horn filled the bustling street.

He snatched him by the hood of his jacket and violently yanked him back from the curb, sending the guy crashing to the snowy sidewalk.

The snowplow's blaring horn echoed off the surrounding buildings and startled the guy with wide-eyed clarity.

Mitch offered him a hand. "Wow, you okay, man?"

The guy glowered up at Mitch. His eyes were wide with confusion, which quickly, unexpectedly, turned to anger.

"Whoa, bro. What the fuck?" the guy shouted, struggling to get to his feet, still holding his iPhone as he got in Mitch's face.

"I was good, bro. How dare you touch me?" The guy shoved Mitch hard, causing him to trip and fall into his bag and a snowbank.

"I-I'm sorry. But you were about to walk in front of a—"

"I don't give three shits. You don't lay your grimy hands on me, you fat piece of…" The guy kicked some of Mitch's books down the snowy street.

"Jesus Christ. Stay there!" the pissed-off guy yelled.

Amid a maelstrom of instant emotions, Mitch clenched his fists in rage. But the stranger loomed over him, and a flurry of feelings rushed through his mind. Shaking, he reactively held his hands up in surrender.

"No, no. My apologies. I'm sorry. I didn't mean to—" Mitch tried.

"Of course you didn't mean to. Stay down there." The guy glared at Mitch, leather-gloved fists clenched, nostrils flaring with rage and disgust.

"Fuck you very much and Merry Christmas," the guy said, then walked away, resuming his phone conversation. "The city should really do something about…these people. It's been going downhill every day, I swear. Anyway, we can make the party by five…" The conversation trailed off as he disappeared down the snowy street.

Mitch sat in the snowbank for a minute, trembling, trying hard to find an ounce of sanity within the incredibly insane moment.

The all-too-familiar weight of shame covered Mitch, and his stomach roiled. And the world felt as if it were closing in.

Despite the numbing cold, sweat poured down his face and body, and his heart pounded in his ears.

His mind drifted back to age ten, when his father erupted in rage after discovering he'd used American Legion stationery to write a comic book story. The beating that followed still echoed through him, the memory casting a long, unshakable shadow.

Mitch finally got to his feet.

The snow poured down in heavy sheets, and he made the short walk back to his apartment as though he were walking with a thousand-pound weight upon his soul.

He just wanted to get home.

2
Of Wolf and Man

The appetizing scent of copper was in the air.

The pack leader sensed the changing temperature and smelled the fresh blood.

Her stomach ached, the pack was hungry, and it was her calling to feed them.

She howled, calling the rest of the hunters in the pack to follow.

The heavy snow was piling up, threatening to bury the tracks of the two-leggers.

She howled, and the pack tracked the blood trail through the thickening snow.

Even with the biting wind, the pack eagerly followed the deep trenches the humans had made.

Onward the pack ran, their growling stomachs pushing them on.

They made no sound, they took no chances, as they drew closer to their unsuspecting prey.

The pack master growled low, signaling to the pack to fan out and surround the group of humans and the pack's food, blood still steaming and dripping from its fatal wound.

Her hackles rose as the pack entered the clearing.

***

Royce spotted the twisting smoke tendrils rising from the fieldstone chimney of the cabin below. He smiled widely at the warming, woody smell filling his nostrils.

He could almost taste the cigars, the freshly grilled venison, and the soothing whiskey, all chased with a cold beer with each step he took into the knee-deep snow.

"Step lively, boys. It's gonna be a good night," he said, turning to face his fellow hunters.

Huge lake-effect snowflakes fell, nearly blinding all movement around the hunting party.

Royce paused. "Rock salt!"

Within an instant, all the hunters—save Denny, who hefted the heavy deer—swapped out their buckshot rounds for rock salt.

Royce knew he was a miserable bastard, but he wanted to keep the wildlife ecosystem healthy for the next season. Slaughtering bears or wolves was not what he had come here for.

The hungry howls of the scavengers filled the clearing, and Royce thrust the last rock-salt shell into his Mossberg.

"Scare 'em off," he shouted into the freezing air. "Boy, get to camp!" he shouted to his son.

The wolves leapt from oblique angles into the clearing, and the sound of gunshots echoed through the trees, chasing the crows, cardinals, and sparrows from their roosts in the tall pines and elms.

The first gunshots took down three of the pack, sending them into a red-and-white spray of the rock salt.

The rest yipped and howled, running back into the safety of the thickets, leaving their pack members dying or bleeding out onto the snow.

Doing as he was told, Denny trudged down the hill toward the cabin as the rest of the hunters scared off the scattering scavengers.

* * *

The Darkness did not ask to be disturbed.

It had been held captive in that cave, its prison for nearly a thousand years. It had not been asked to be brought here, this desolate, hopeless place.

It was the blood, the life-essence that had awoken this ancient entity that didn't even quite understand its own existence. Filled with a twisted mix of rage, hunger, and curiosity, it now moved and followed the bloody trail that the two-legged creatures had clumsily left in the deep white.

It knew now that it was alive.

The Darkness held no ill-will toward the unwitting creatures of this realm, yet an unbridled, gripping drive for flesh and blood filled the ancient, flowing force, which seemed to conjoin with the raging snowstorm, and twisted and corrupted the natural force into a supernatural weapon. As for the vile creature had stolen from it. Desecrated all that it owned in this forsaken realm. Now it had its freedom.

The scent of death and life was on the frigid air, and the Darkness followed with a violent frenzy, commingling with the biting wind that raged down through the old valley, tearing through the hundreds-of-years-old woods. Relentless, it left a ravaged landscape in its wake.

The increasing snow, jagged and deadly as whipping sand, tore into the bark, exposing the soft flesh of the trees, and any living creature in the Darkness' path was unapologetically devoured. Their flesh, blood, and soul now belonged to it.

With the raging winter storm came a set of glowing red eyes, surrounded by a sea of gaping, hungry maws. With it came the Darkness, slathered in fresh blood and the ragged flesh of its victims.

An apocalyptic cacophony of death, mixed with a deep, bowel-shaking growl, reverberated through the large valley, spilling over into the hills and toward Millstone Glenn.

This brooding nor'easter, gaining strength from the Atlantic Ocean windstream, melded as one with the ancient force. It now had focus and purpose, and with every ounce of its otherworldly being sensed its prize.

It would have blood and flesh. Someone would pay the ultimate price. And it did not understand why it was pushing onward with such a bottomless bloodlust, yet it tore and dug over acre after acre in search of its prey. From black bears to deer, from foxes to rabbits—and even the unsuspecting fowl that once lived in peace with the then-dormant Darkness, lying deep and silent in the isolated valley.

Now the world of Man had awakened it and set it free.

And now that it was awake, the two worlds—the ancient and the new—would blur, and the force would be unable to rest until it had retrieved its golden purpose and had retribution.

It was on that path now. It sensed the living. Their blood and flesh. But it was a far greater sense that filled its mind and body.

3

Down and Out in New York City

Mitch's shivering body felt every biting gust of the unforgiving winter wind, which effortlessly ignored his multiple layers and well-worn peacoat. The shocking incident with the angry jerk who almost died a brutal death took up valuable space in Mitch's mind for the duration of the short but emotional walk home.

After he had stacked his new and still somewhat wet book haul in its proper place, the to-be-read-shelf of his massive wall of books, Mitch sat at his computer desk, which he had scrummaged from a nearby school that had dumped it on the curb. He thought of the hundreds of hours an exhausted teacher must've sat at the worn desk and imagined Mrs. DeVolt, his favorite English teacher from high school back in Sterling Point. And how she was the first to acknowledge he had at least an inkling of creative talent. And she told him it was okay to read Tolkien, King, Matheson, and Shirley Jackson.

The harsh, growing winds and pellets of snow took turns rapping at the window and slapping the glass, waking him from his daydream.

Long gone were those troubled days back home, as well as the two-bit hipster bully that tried to ruin his day earlier.

Now he sat at his happy place: his writing sanctuary. The desk stood in vast contrast to every other apartment in the building that lay slathered with garish, blinking Christmas lights and glittery decorations. But this room was dark, save the soft, red glow of a burning incense stick and the bluish haze of an iMac screen. Behind the monitor sat a figure of stout stature, casting eager shadows on the wall behind him. Like a mad conductor commanding an imaginary orchestra, Mitchell Roberts let out an evil laugh as he typed two words that made every writer worth his salt shout in ecstasy:

The End.

"Oh, hell yeah!" Mitch clicked *save*, smiled, and let out a deep breath, cupping his hands behind his head. It had been a long and torturous year and had taken everything he had. "Labor of love" wasn't the right term for the experience. While his first novel, *About to Rage*, and its sequel,

Beautifully Broken, had flowed from his soul as if he were a man possessed, this book had completely kicked his ass six ways from Sunday.

But *Temporary Saint,* the third novel in the *Lonesome Abyss Trilogy,* was complete, and he would send the manuscript to his agent after one or two more passes over the still-hot manuscript.

Mitch sipped the bitter-tasting iced drink that had begun its life as steaming hot Earl Grey tea; due to his hyper muse, *Grace,* he'd forgotten all about his favorite beverage. He looked around his small apartment, bookshelves filled with his favorite reads and movies and other nerd-loves, and he tried to come up with a way to celebrate this galactic accomplishment. Nothing was forthcoming. He'd watched all the seasons of *The West Wing, Doctor Who, Justified, Hap and Leonard, The Witcher,* and *Kolchak: The Night Stalker.* Sure, he could have thrown on a Rush or Gov't Mule CD, but he wasn't in the mood. He tried to think of someone he could call to brag to, but there weren't many people on his speed-dial list. His mom might still be up, but his dad would flip his lid if he were to call the house this late. The old man was in bed by seven this time of year. Mitch felt a deep chill run through him, and he shivered.

"Ah, more splash of the herb is what you need. And hot tea you shall have," he said in his best Sean Connery voice, and made his way to the kitchen. He snatched the empty kettle from the stove and filled it with water, shuddering as he caught his reflection in the window above the sink. It startled him how much weight he'd gained. He'd always been a big guy, but the lonely, sedentary lifestyle of a writer seemed to have taken its toll. That, and the daily doses of fast food and pizza. He hadn't shaved in weeks, and he was beginning to look like a homeless recluse.

"Good god, man, this isn't a good look for you, sir. No…not at all," he said to his ghostly reflection. He wouldn't hit thirty until July, but he was looking every minute of forty. Thoroughly disgusted with himself, he shut the water off and set to work on another batch of tea.

"From hero to zero in forty seconds. That just might be a new world record, Roberts."

The apartment suddenly felt cold, and the faint vibe of victory scuttled off into the shadows, the soft hiss of the kettle the only sound. Mitch leaned against the counter, trying to wash the horrific image of himself out of his tired mind.

"Dude, you just need some sleep," he told himself, really wanting to believe it. He should have been happy. The constant demons of self-doubt aside, he had all the reasons in the world to be ecstatic.

His first thriller was selling well, especially considering the traditional publishing industry was circling the drain in the new digital age. He was finally making good money and didn't have to worry about rent, heat, food, or keeping his car on the road. Yet, he still felt like a failure. In the ever-changing publishing business, you were only as good as your latest book. He could hear his mother's words softly echo in his mind: "Smile, Chief Thundercloud... Be happy, better days are coming." And while he cherished those words, some days they felt hollow. Mitch only wished he could heed them. It was at times like this that he would have liked the taste of alcohol, but his abusive drunkard of an old man had fixed him of that slippery trap at a young age. He was more than happy with tea. Hot or cold, it was just perfect for his taste. He had worked hard to put his Podunk hometown of Sterling Point in his rearview, and the gods willing, he'd keep it that way.

A tall pile of unopened mail sat on the kitchen table, and Mitch figured he could celebrate by poring over a sea of useless mailers from local politicians and car dealerships and seemingly never-ending pleas from his cable company, begging him to come back.

Underneath the stack of wasted paper sat a package he vaguely remembered being delivered, and which, due to the intensity of his writing sessions, he had completely forgotten about.

The familiar writing filled the label and stated that it had come from Mrs. M. Roberts, Sterling Point, NY. His mom. It made Mitch smile. He fetched the small Buck pocketknife his dad had given him on his tenth birthday, which he had dutifully named *Mack*.

Eagerly cutting at the thick tape, he ripped the box open. Sure, his mom was good for a few care packages throughout the year, but when it got to around Christmas time, the clever old lady always turned it up a notch or two.

In a fit of childlike glory, he laughed at the glorious bounty his dear mother had beset upon him. A delicious Grandma O'Brien's fruitcake; her ever-so-carefully frosted cut-out cookies; a thick, hand-crocheted scarf with matching hat and mittens, all in his favorite colors, orange and black.

Mitch quickly wrapped the scarf around his neck with glee and tried to ignore the fact that he felt like Harry Potter or Tom Baker and kept digging, tossing aside a sea of multi-colored packing paper to reveal a box of socks and underwear, cleverly wrapped around a bundle of paperbacks: mostly M.R. James, Dean Koontz, and Peter Straub. Mitch let out a small chuckle. She was always pushing her favorite pen-masters on him. His tastes were closely aligned with hers, but they were at an impasse when it came to the king: Stephen King, that was. Mitch thought the Man from Maine walked on bloody water, while Mrs. Marguerite Allen-Roberts thought his talent, which she admitted was great, was sadly a bit long-winded at times. But she always bought him King's latest offering.

Digging at the bottom of the box, he found another object: a single book. Taking it out and removing its tightly wrapped butcher paper, tied in a white string, Mitch pulled off the note attached to the top.

Dear Mitchie,

Happy Holidays! We've been trying to get all the decorations up and the snow has come early, which hasn't made it much easier. If you remember from my Thanksgiving letter, we weren't very thankful for the eight inches of white stuff Mother Nature brought to the holiday dinner. But your father and I made the best of it.

We sure wish you would come home this year. It's been so long since we've seen you. And you know the house just isn't the same around this time of year without you. I sure could use your help decorating the house, and the tree and all. It's been a challenging fall, with your father being so busy with work, so it's been just me, and I've been feeling under the weather lately. I can't get around like I used to. But I'll manage, you know that.

So, how is writing? I tried to buy your book at Somerville's Drugs, but they didn't have it. I called them to ask, but no one answered. I guess you can't get good help these days. I'm hoping it was all sold out. Anyway, I'm sure it's wonderful. Your stories have always been delightful. Nothing like that creepy Stephen King. Thank God. I don't know why he's so preoccupied with women's times of the month and all that. Anyway, keep following your dreams and marching to the beat of your own drum, honey. You have it in you. I just know it. I'm so proud of you.

I hope you like the gifts I sent. The hat and mittens should fit you fine. I was going from memory, but you know how that's been suspect from time to time. Did I get the colors right? I think I did. Now, I know you're probably complaining about the socks and underwear, but you know as well as I do, you can never have too many. Enjoy the goodies too. Don't eat them all at once, make some last at least until Christmas morning...unless you're here, that is.

I'm really excited about the last package, and I hope you are too. Last time we talked, you were all excited about your next book project, that monster one, and you were doing what you've always done and getting lost in reading and research. You always did love having your nose in a book. I guess I raised my boy right.

So, I was browsing the internets one night while your father was at his poker night down at Yowner's Tavern and I came across this website that had all these neat, autographed books on monster histories and some such. I knew it was meant for you. I do hope it can be of use and hope you enjoy it.

Okay, I have to run now. I have to make your father's birthday cake and get ready for the Fourth of July parade. Your dad is marching in it again. No rest for the righteous and all. Hope your writing is going great, and I cannot wait to read more.

I miss and love you, Chief Thundercloud, and if you can make it home for Christmas, I would really love to see you.

Love you,
Mom.
P.S. I'm sure your father would like to see you too!

A hitch gripped his chest. However, something glaring jolted him as he reread the letter and the date on it. It caused him to pause. April 11, 1956. It was in his mom's handwriting, he was certain. Mitch felt a sour pit in his stomach. It wasn't just the date that had him flummoxed. It was all the small-time discrepancies that worried him. She'd always been on the eccentric side, which was one of the million things he loved about his mother. But this was extremely odd. A maelstrom of concern and wondrous thoughts filled his mind.

He fumbled with the package and cut it open, revealing two hardcover books inside: the first one, he knew very well. He still had the heavily dog-eared copy his mom had given him for his birthday years ago. It was Stephen King's *On Writing-A Memoir of the Craft*. The cover, with its yellowish hue and comforting image of a set of basement doors, brought back many happy memories, but he wondered why another copy. Had she forgotten she had given him one before? He felt a lump in his stomach grow, as did his concern for her faltering memory.

But he flipped the cover open and saw a big sticky-note on the first page that read, *Merry Christmas, to my favorite writer! Love, Mom.*

Mitch gasped as he gently removed the note and saw what was underneath.

It was signed and addressed to him.. *"To Mitch—keep going. The world needs stories."*

He stared in silent disbelief for God knows how long, and his cheeks ached from smiling.

The book had inspired him so much when he first started writing. He'd made a tradition of reading it once a year since. He held the book close to his chest and felt warm, then finally set it aside and picked up the second book.

This one was much older, and one he'd neither seen nor heard of before.

Mother Lorelei's History and Guide to the Greater World – A Handbook of Wards and Magic. From the binding, it must've been from the early 1940s, Mitch guessed.

He made more tea, and with a book and mug in hand, he plopped down on the sofa and dug right in.

It seemed to be an encyclopedia, or a how-to-book of creatures and beings not-of-our-world, written by the mysterious Mother Lorelei. He would surely need to investigate this author more.

It was a heavy book: nearly six hundred pages. Mitch's mom must've spent a fortune mailing it to him. But as he thumbed through it, his mind flitted with ideas and curiosities, inspired by the monsters of mythology and urban legend contained within its yellowing pages.

Whoever this enigmatic Mother Lorelei was, it seemed she knew her stuff. Granted, some of that stuff was common, everyday information grifted from mythology, horror novels, and television shows. They all seemed to hold the same advice when it came to using salt as a ward against all kinds of evil, devils and demons alike.

He flipped more pages. Werewolves. Vampires. Of course. Everyone and their cousin know about those, and how silver would make the undead meet their unholy makers.

Iron. That was the one that caused Mitch to pause. But as he read on, it began to make sense.

Graveyards are surrounded by iron fences. Throughout history, iron horseshoes have hung inside, or even more importantly, on the outside of homes and barns to ward off evil spirits. Mitch's creative juices were in full flow now.

Without knowing, his mom was once again a genius and an inspiration. Both books would arm him with all he'd need to start his next novel, *Of Wolf and Man.*

Mitch was five pages in and engrossed in the use of various elements, such as salt, silver, and iron, when the ringtone of his cellphone startled him.

Home.

He hadn't spoken with his mom in months and couldn't recall the last time he had talked to his father. The thought of either of his parents ringing his phone at almost midnight was jarring.

Charley Pride's "When I Stop Leaving, I'll Be Gone" ringtone rang again, sending the cell bouncing about the worn desktop. Shaking, he reached out.

Was it another guilt trip to get him to come home for the holidays? That had been an annual battle since he'd left after graduation. Mitch loved his mom's annoying yet somehow endearing persistence.

He looked out the window at the snow coming down, and the red and green lights from the building next door and wondered if he should stop being stubborn and go home for Christmas. He grabbed the cellphone, causing a picture frame to crash to the floor. The sound of shattering glass was lost in the continual ringing, and he pressed the answer button

"Hey, Mom."

A long pause. "Mitchell, it's Dad. We need to talk." The cold voice stirred up years of bad memories and Mitch nearly dropped the phone.

"Hey, Dad. Is everything okay?"

Another long moment passed. The snow battered the windows.

"No. It's your mom…"

"Is she…okay?"

"No… She… She wasn't doing good at all, and I had to take her to the E.R." Gordon Roberts coughed and cleared his throat. "And, well…she died, son."

Mitch froze.

"I'm meeting with the funeral home in a day or so."

"Dad?" Mitch's voice came in a whisper.

"It's up to you, if you wanna come or not. I'm only calling because your mother made me promise I would. But if you are coming, ya best get on the move, boy, a big storm is coming in. The weather yahoos are calling for a nor'easter."

Mitch stared out the window. "I… Of course. Why would—"

The line went dead.

"Fuck!" Mitch felt the word tear from his throat in such a primal scream that it scared even him.

The cellphone hit the floor mere seconds before Mitch did. Sorrow engulfed him, stealing his breath and his heartbeat, every part of him shuddering in denial. He had known she was sick, but had no idea it was that bad. Typical of her to protect him from worry.

"Damn her," he cursed, and cried.

He sat on the worn linoleum floor for a long while. He needed to go home. But he'd sworn he'd never, ever set a sneakered foot back there. His mother was dead; his father, he'd had no connection with ever; and the painful memories of Beth and Tony washed over him like a poisoned lead veil. Add that to the freshly open wound that was the whole of Sterling Point. They were feelings he'd worked damn hard at pushing to the back of his mind.

"Mom," was all he could say as he wiped away the tears and forced himself off the floor. The weight of the stunning news seemed to pin him down.

"No. No. No!" he shouted into the silence of the apartment, his various Funko Pops and signed movie posters staring back at him with an apathetic silence that only amplified his dread of returning home.

Home… What an absurd word that was for him. He'd never felt at peace or comfortable in that simple-minded collection of old, decaying buildings and fake people. Mitch always thought of Sterling Point—and even all of Wayne County, for that matter—as a place where dreams and hopes go to die.

The one thing that had been holding him to that place was gone.

It was obvious that his father didn't give two shits whether he came back or not. Sure, he missed a few friends with whom he randomly exchanged pleasantries on Facebook, but other than that… His mom was dead. It might have been the final nail in his proverbial coffin for that tiny lakeside town too.

Mitch stood in his apartment. Not a mere ten minutes earlier he had been beyond happy, excited that he'd finished the book. It was an addiction he hoped he'd never get used to.

Now…the apartment shrank. The lights dimmed, and with the encroaching shadows crawling closer, it stole away any happiness he had mustered to finish the novel. There was to be no celebration now.

No more of his time-honored tradition of lighting some incense and pouring one shot of Tullamore Dew, followed by a rewatch of *Twin Peaks*, or a reread of Joe R. Lansdale's *The Drive-In*.

"Goddamnit! I have to go," Mitch heard himself shout into the nothingness of his apartment.

As if on autopilot, under some otherworldly control, Mitch found himself poring through his closet to find his suitcase.

A tidal wave of conflicting recollections overwhelmed him as he coughed through the dust-covered debris that was his closet.

Old concert t-shirts, beat-up photo albums, which were so old-school, pelted him. But it was the drinking horn that got his attention.

Falling to his ass in a heap, all his past rained down upon him like an avalanche of nostalgia.

It was the last summer before their senior year. He, his Dungeons and Dragons crew—Chris, Clay, Ray, Dave, Jesse—and after enough begging and pleading, Beth and Tony, had come to the Renaissance Faire in the nearby town of Fair Haven.

Mitch had never been a big drinker, but his friends were, especially Tony.

They'd been playing through one of Dave's epic Norse mythology-inspired D&D campaigns, and of course it made complete sense to buy a drinking vessel made from a bull horn.

After coaxing from the crew, and a kiss on the cheek from Beth, Mitch relented, and here he was, eleven years later, with the damn thing nearly poking his eye out—which it might have done if not for his glasses.

He tossed it aside and finally unearthed the dusty suitcase. A lost relic he hadn't used since his Camp NECON convention nearly eight years earlier. It was a great trip to Rhode Island, and he'd wanted desperately to attend again, but when you take up the mantle of starving artist, reality loves to keep you in your station. *The best laid plans,* he thought as he yanked the case free from the closet.

"Man, I don't want to go," he said to no one as he lugged the large case into the bedroom and tossed it onto the bed.

His arms felt as though they were made of lead, and the suitcase was the size of his Honda downstairs, collecting snow.

Mitch stolidly marched back and forth from his dresser to the suitcase, tossed a bunch of clothes inside, took them out, then tossed them back in again.

"Dammit." The exasperated word dripped with grief and panic. His breathing, again, grew labored and shallow.

"Mom, god," he said. One pair of socks in, two shirts out. Then back into the case they went.

It took him nearly three hours to pack.

Despite the snowstorm raging outside, he had soaked through all his clothes and smelled as if he'd run two marathons and crawled through a ditch by the time he'd completed the Herculean task of packing to go…home.

The snow was really piling up outside and it showed no signs of clearing.

He would get the car ready tonight and leave at first light, trying hard, as he was, to ignore his guilt and deny his procrastination. It was at least a six-hour drive, and with the storm coming, Mitch knew he'd need a few hours' sleep to make it back home.

Sterling Point. Just thinking about the place, the people, the life he'd left behind, made his stomach ache and his heart race.

The weather alert app on his iPhone chimed with a warning, and the overwhelming sense of sorrow made sure that sleep wasn't going to happen, but he needed to try.

He needed to rest.

First, he'd read a bit more, try to fall asleep, then pack and head out.

The book's pages became matted with his tears as the snow rapped at his frost-covered windows.

And then his mind turned to the sadness; the loving thoughts of his mom, and of course the only other woman that ever mattered to him, Beth Connolly, all pulled him into a worried sleep.

He was certain the brewing nor'easter wasn't the only storm about to rage.

4

Flowers on the Wall

The loud clamoring of the receiver on the telephone echoed off the cold walls and the dark corners, which were swallowed up by the darkness of the kitchen. Gordon Roberts felt his aching knees give way. Whether it was due to the heaviness of the conversation with his estranged son, or the loss of Marguerite—the love of his life—he wasn't certain, but the overwhelming need to sit took him and he hurried to the bench in the breakfast nook, sending a pile of unread mail and newspapers skittering to the floor.

The streetlight broke through the window, casting mocking shadows on the once-pristine kitchen, which now resembled that of a homeless shack. If his dear, sweet Marguerite could lay her soft, gorgeous blue eyes upon such a mess, she would have been mortified. A dark wave of grief and guilt swallowed Gordon up as he fought back the jolting sobs brewing inside his tired body. He'd been through many tough spots in his sixty-seven years on the planet: an abusive childhood, polio, Vietnam, but the one strong-as-iron tether he'd always had was now gone. The compass that had pulled him back to true-north whenever he'd veered too far off the reservation was gone.

He clumsily fumbled about the table to find the can of Genny beer and let out a victorious grunt when he found it. As he lifted the can, he saw a hardcover book with a fresh, wet ring on its cover. Mitch's book.

Staggering and fighting to see properly without his bifocals, Gordon picked it up.

"*New York Times Bestseller*, huh? Hmm. Look at you, boy." A slight smile broke across his face. "Still don't know how to talk to you. What do I say to him, Maggie?" Gordon tossed the book down and turned his attention to the can in his hand. Taking a long pull, finishing the foamy contents, he said, "Damn you, woman. Goddamn you, Maggie-girl. Why the hell did you leave me? Leave me alone with him? Leave me here in this miserable piece-of-shit world?" Gordon shouted at the shadows and the worn wallpaper and shakily got to his feet. He staggered to the fridge, yanked it open, and peered inside, leaning heavily on the door.

He snatched a fresh soldier from the fridge, popped the top, and drank deep. He wiped the excess on his sleeve and slid down against the open door, slamming it into the wall. "Jesus H. Christ, honey bunny, ya know damn well I can't do…" His words choked off in deep sobs and a vicious ripple of grief bore deep into his body, tearing at every fiber of his being, and he gave in to the unforgiving darkness. He drank the entire contents of the fridge until the alcohol-fueled undertow swallowed him whole.

5

Monday Morning Meltdown

"Tony, look, I don't have time to talk about this. I have a class starting in five minutes," Beth Connolly-Severt said, hanging up her cellphone, making sure none of the other teachers in the lounge could see her crying. Her knees grew weak, and her head was spinning. She caught herself on the bookshelf in front of her and held on.

The final chorus of Bing Crosby's "White Christmas" faded out of the desktop radio in the teacher's lounge. Beth felt exhaustion coming over her in waves, and her emotions were like exposed wires, sensitive to the touch. She knew it was crazy, but she swore she could feel her ring finger burning. She grabbed it and tried to shake the feeling. It didn't help. The past few weeks had been at her like a vampire, nearly draining her completely.

"You okay, darlin'?" Felicia Dixon whispered, placing a hand on Beth's thin, quivering shoulder. She had been a great friend to her since she had begun teaching at Sterling Point Elementary School, and especially supportive since the separation.

"Oh, yeah… I…am okay." Beth took a deep breath. She was sure all the other teachers at their lunch break were staring at her.

"Is he piling on the pressure to let him come back…again?" Felicia asked as she moved to shelter her friend from the nosy busybodies, who, for the past few months, had reveled in the drama that was Beth's life.

Beth glanced over Felicia's broad shoulders and watched the once glaring eyes hide behind their newspapers and brown bag lunches.

"Yes, he's relentless and just doesn't get it," she said, pushing her blonde hair from her face.

Felicia, in her motherly fashion, took Beth in her large arms and comforted her.

"Oh, Bethie, he should just leave you be. It's almost Christmas, for goodness' sake," Felicia said, her hand now on her hip. She dabbed an escaped tear from Beth's face with a handkerchief—she always seemed to make it appear out of thin air. "You aren't letting him, are you?"

"No. Oh, I…uh…don't know what to do." Beth exhaled and turned her gaze back to the bookshelf.

"Now, Bethie, listen to old Auntie Felicia. This isn't the first time, honey, and you know darn well it won't be the last." Her tone had changed, and her pudgy forefinger seemed to command Beth's attention.

"He's a dog, and once a dog, always a dog, honey. There just isn't any way of teaching an old dog new tricks."

Beth turned toward her, and fresh tears flowed down her flushed cheeks.

"I don't know how to thank you for being here for me," Beth wheezed from within her friend's comforting embrace.

"Oh, darlin', it's all going to be okay. I promise. Someday, a good boy will come along and make you forget all about that…that low-down, dirty skunk." Felicia gently rubbed her back.

Beth supposed it was what a mother's touch might feel like.

"Hey, Beth, did you hear about Mrs. Roberts?" Missy Ralston peeked over her cat's eye-shaped glasses while coyly pawing at her cellphone. Beth was more than certain Missy was doing all she could to hold a smug grin at bay. "She's not doing well at all, it seems."

"No, I didn't. Oh my god, no… What happened?" Beth's thoughts turned to Mitch, as they often did, and she welled up again. Felicia gave her a gentle touch on her shoulder.

"Um, yes," the haughty math teacher said. "I have a good friend at Newark Hospital, and he told me Mr. Roberts brought her into the E.R. last night and it seems really bad. Guess it was because of pneumonia or linked to her Alzheimer's, or some such thing. That's too bad."

"I didn't even know she was sick." Beth felt weak again and used Felicia to steady herself.

"Oh really? You don't talk to Mitch anymore?" Beth knew full well that Missy already knew the answer and that she meant it as a low blow, seeing how they had all graduated high school together and that Beth had broken Mitch's heart their senior year and married his best friend. She loved watching Beth squirm. And seeing her reaction, it quite satisfied her, as she took a sip of her Fuji water. Beth wanted to reach out and strangle her, but she loved her job and it was the only bright spot in her life. Justifiable homicide would have to wait.

"Oh, no, I don't, and you know damn well I haven't in a long time. Thanks so much for your *help*, Missy." Beth tried to feign sarcasm and strength, but that's all it was. Faking it was all she had been good at for the past few months. She felt nauseated, her head spun with uncertain emotions, and she needed to sit down. She leaned on Felicia again. But there was only so much even the god-sent mentor could do.

The overhead speaker crackled to life and everyone in the faculty lounge stopped talking.

"Attention all students and staff members—because of the storm that's been forecast, we are erring on the side of caution and we will be dismissing students and all staff at one-thirty. The buses are on their way, and all teachers must prepare their students for early dismissal."

"Okay then. Let's get these little darlings home and then we can start an early Christmas break, what do you say?" Felicia winked and escorted her out of the lounge and into the bustling hallway, giving Missy Ralston a death glare she hoped would freeze her thin behind in her seat.

6
Hiding Place

The Darkness followed the clumsy trail the humans had left behind.

It heard loud sounds and recoiled for a moment.

But its intense hunger drove it forward.

It rushed through the dense forest in the dying afternoon light, when it found the shivering, whimpering creatures, huddling under a large rock outcropping.

It relished in their delicious fear, lapping it up with every baleful cry and yelp.

Blood steamed on the white ground. And its body whirled, and it wailed as it slowly, teasingly surrounded the trapped animals.

All those wide, yellow eyes stared at it, and it engulfed every drop before it tore at the feral creatures in a savage, hungry rush.

Their short-lived death-howls filled the biting air and echoed off the gore-splattered rock.

It fed. Yet it was still starving. Angry.

The blood trail of those who had awakened it led down the steep hillside.

It followed.

PART TWO

"Scars have the strange power to remind us that our past is real."

—Cormac McCarthy

7
Man in Motion

The last hour or so was a light snowy blur as Mitch awoke from his restless slumber while reading his mom's Christmas present. He loved to read, yet often fell victim to falling asleep halfway through an engaging tale. And the nature of rereading the *On Writing* book had made him even more enraptured—yet not too enraptured to stay awake. He chalked it up to the obvious fact that it was also mixed with the shocking call from his dad.

Mitch's hazy mind felt like an unfamiliar hangover wrapped in a grief-laden nightmare; he hoped more tea would help.

Giving up, he forced himself into the shower. He felt as though he weighed a thousand pounds and was a hundred feet under the ice-cold waters of Lake Ontario, not even half a mile away.

Despite the pressing dread weighing him down, Mitch made it a quick shower. And then, an even faster packing job that he so monumentally failed to do the night before. Next, he loaded his car and made more of the hot liquid salvation in a to-go mug for his drive.

He didn't plan it. He was in too much of a hurry to think about it, or even care, but as he waited for the car windows to defrost, his tired, stinging eyes caught the battered, well-used and loved *Stephen King Rules* travel mug. A nod to one of Mitch's favorite cheesy monster flicks of the eighties, *Monster Squad*.

It had been a birthday present from Beth, right before graduation.

Even through all the bitterness, hurt, and anger, he had not been able to bring himself to throw it away.

He had tried several times, but something had stopped him each time.

He filled it up with hot tea and covered it.

"Wolf-man gots nards!" he chuckled, a hollow, feeble attempt to lighten the stormy mood that filled his small car.

He thought about calling Beth. Or at least texting, letting her know he would be back in town. Even grabbed his phone.

Even started to dial her number.

Then he hung up.

"Enough, Roberts." Mitch let out a long breath, placed an old mix CD in the player, and began the five-and-a-half-hour drive home.

A pit in his aching stomach reminded him why he'd never wanted to go back. The encroaching storm was close in his rearview mirror now.

"Swell," was all he said as he drove northwestward. "That's that last thing you need right now." Mitch knew he would regret even dialing Beth's number. "'Cuz it ended so well the last time you talked to her, or that jackass."

He cursed his weakness for the next twenty miles, as the wipers thumped their mocking tone and the snowfall began to worsen. And all the while, he fought the overwhelming urge to turn around, back to the safety and solace of his apartment.

8
Word on the Wind

As Beth made her way back to her classroom, she tried to make sense of the tragic news, peering out the large windows that overlooked the playground and the brooding storm above Lake Ontario.

She had spent a good portion of her childhood at the Roberts' family house. She and Mitch had been friends since kindergarten and she considered them family. There was that, and then there was the way things had ended with him.

Her cellphone vibrated in her pocket, and she ignored it, knowing full well it must be Tony.

The halls raged in a sea of commotion, and she was lost in her own mind as she entered her room. Beth closed the door and collapsed into the chair behind her desk, hoping everything would all just blow away with the coming storm. She'd never meant for any of it to happen. They were just kids.

The years came rushing back to her. Good and bad. Tony and Mitch had been best friends, and she loved them both. And Mitch's parents too; even Mr. Roberts. He was always kind to her and welcomed her into their home. He may have been an obnoxious functioning alcoholic, but he was still kind to a stranger when he had no cause to be. Beth had grown angry and filled with guilt; after she'd married Tony and Mitch had left town, she'd subconsciously—or perhaps consciously—cut off contact with the Robertses. She regretted that. Especially now. But having shattered their only son's heart, how in the world could she face them again? She didn't have an answer, so she'd pretended they didn't exist and had gone on with her life.

"Shit," she said, and prayed for help and a bottle of wine to appear out of the ether—neither of which seemed to be forthcoming.

Grief filled her and she crumbled under the weight as a rush of anxiety won out. The realization that Mitch could come home and that she would have to see him after all these years added to the claustrophobic moment.

An icy darkness fell over her. The sleep that had been evading her for weeks gave way, and Beth fell into a deep slumber—

Her sleep was short as a harsh knock came upon her door.

"Hey, darlin', you need to be at the bus circle in five minutes," Felicia said through the half-opened door. "Go. I'll meet you down there."

Beth jumped up. "Yeah, yeah. Okay, sorry. I'll be right there." She gathered herself and donned her winter coat, hat, and mittens, and ran to the bus circle, only to find the last of the buses leaving.

Like a pepper speck amongst a blanket of salt, Beth stood alone in the snow.

"Shit." She shrugged in defeat. No sign of Felicia.

A small voice cut through the chill wind. "Mrs. S?"

Beth turned to see a shivering Sheldon Hendricks wearing only a worn Buffalo Bills sweatshirt and a thin knit cap and lugging a beat-up BMX. "You don't have an air pump, do you?"

Smiling, she put an arm around Sheldon and pulled him close. "No, I don't, Shel. But I can do you one better. Leave your bike here and come with me. We'll warm up my car and then swing around and put your bike in the trunk and give you a ride home. A flat tire doesn't do much good in all this white stuff, don't you know." Beth offered a chilly giggle.

"I know, I know. But it beats trying to walk home." Sheldon laughed.

"Where's your mom?" Beth knew the answer before the same old, painful question had left her chapped lips.

The sullen look on the boy's face spoke volumes.

Beth nodded and grabbed Sheldon's thin shoulder. "I'm sorry, kiddo. The storm's coming, young sir. Let's get you home, okay?"

Beth secured the bicycle on the roof rack and got into the driver's side and turned the heat up.

"I think your tire is complete toast, Mr. Hendricks. You wouldn't have gotten very far on that flat thing." Beth smiled at the young boy drawing monster faces in the fogged-up window.

"I know, but I had to try." Sheldon shrugged. "Had to get home somehow."

Beth buckled her seatbelt and headed out of the school parking lot.

The car's radio aired: "*Well, good morning, Sterling Point and all of 315! It's your friendly neighborhood morning guy, and I certainly hope you kept your brass monkeys in last night. Whoa, boy! The word from the National Weather Service is that we have one humdinger of a nor'easter headed our way, just in time for the holiday travel time."* Dean-O, the habitually upbeat DJ, joked, and the rest of the Morning Crew laughed along.

Beth turned down the radio as they drove, and after a long minute, she asked, "How's your mom?"

"Eh, she's the same, I guess." His monotone answer told Beth all she needed to know. She knew he had it rough, and his family life was not much to speak of: an absent father doing time in a downstate prison, and a mom fighting a losing battle with severe mental health issues and substance abuse. Beth had spoken with his mother on a few occasions, and she liked her. Her heart melted for the woman. She loved her son and had been fighting her persistent demons for a long time. Sadly, the darkness seemed to win out more often than not. Not a very warm support system for a twelve-year-old.

"Ah...okay. Is she feeling better?" Beth continued her usual inquiry. She worried about her favorite student. He was a bright kid. A good head on his shoulders and a good soul. Surprising, after all he'd been through.

The large lake-effect snowflakes pattered at the windows and the brutal Canadian wind pushed the car from side to side as Beth drove through downtown Sterling Point.

Sheldon shuffled in his seat and wiped his artwork off the window with a swipe of his worn-out glove. "Come on, Mrs. S. We both know the answer to that one."

"Same old, same old," Beth and Sheldon said in unison.

"I'm sorry, Sheldon. I know it's been a rough time. But she is trying, you know that, right?" Beth said, squinting to see the snow-covered street.

Sheldon flipped through the radio stations as Christmas songs played through the speakers. "What the heck? Why does everything have to be stupid Christmas tunes? Not one Jimi song. Geesh."

"I don't think Jimi Hendrix wrote any holiday songs, buddy."

"Well...he should've. Jimi would have rocked any of those lame tunes. You can bet your ass on that."

Sheldon nodded and stopped on the Kinks' hard guitar-riffing "Father Christmas." "Hey, this ain't too bad."

Beth knew all this music talk was a diversion, a way for Sheldon to avoid the uncertain reality of his young life. And her heart broke for the poor kid every time. Despite all the cards being stacked against him, Sheldon Hendricks was a gentle, generous boy who lived to make people happy and to play his guitar. He'd tried to bring it to school but had landed in trouble for it. But Beth had let him keep it in her room. He had so little, and the guitar brought his soul alight. *Rules be damned,* she thought, *for a kid with so little light in his life.*

"The Kinks are a good band. At the same time as Jimi, so check them out. I think you'll like them. They have your kind of attitude."

"Hey, what does that mean?"

"They have your special perspective on life. Plus, they have kick-butt riffs."

"Really? Nice!"

"So, speaking of Christmas—and don't give me that look, young man!—did you and your mom put your names on the Angel Tree at the hospital as I told you to?"

Sheldon lowered his head, pulling at the frayed stitching on his winter coat. "We did."

"Good. There's no shame in doing so, Sheldon. There are many families out there that are having a rough go of it this time of year. Good folks who work their butts off and still have a tough time giving their loved ones a good Christmas. And you, Master Hendricks, are no different. You get me?"

Sheldon sat silent for a moment, staring out at the snowy streets.

"I know, Mrs. S. It's like...I don't like how I feel."

"What do you mean?"

"I don't like how everyone looks at us. If they even take the time to look at us. But when they do...they look down at us like we're...*less.* Pathetic, like something stuck on their two-hundred-dollar shoes." Sheldon pulled his battered jacket around him and stared out the window.

Beth wasn't sure how to respond. They were almost at his house, and with Christmas so close, she didn't want to leave him like this. She slowed the car down, hoping it would give her time to figure out the right thing to say.

"You've been through a lot, Sheldon. You and your mom both. Never let that other stuff get to you. I know it's hard, but we all go through shitty times, and there isn't anything wrong with asking for help."

"I just...I wish I could run away. Take my guitar and go. I love my mom and all, but sometimes it gets so...just so..." Sheldon dabbed at his eyes.

Beth turned onto Water Street and felt her car slide in the deep ruts. The front wheels spun, and she fought to straighten out just as a huge plow truck came along. A familiar face honked their horn and waved: Mr.

Gordon Roberts, Mitch's father. Beth's mind raced as she got her car under control and pulled into Sheldon's unplowed driveway.

She let out a breath and put a gentle hand on his shoulder.

"Well, kiddo, as much as it sucks, there are some things we can't run away from. No matter how far we go, or how hard we try."

Sheldon cocked his head, giving her an odd look. "Thanks for the pep talk, teach."

Beth laughed. "Now, hold on, *Snarky Snarkleson*. I would add, thank you very much, you're a great person. And I honestly believe your circumstances will not dictate your outcome. You, Sheldon, my little doubting Thomas, have complete control of your future. Whether you believe it or not."

The harsh wind whipped and tossed the car around and the thick flakes caked the windows.

"You know, you keep telling me that, but I'm not sure if I believe it. Don't get me wrong, I want to. I do. But my mom needs me, and I have zero chance of getting any kind of scholarship and college. I've got be realistic, Mrs. S."

"What about your music? That's all you ever talk about."

Sheldon thought about it. "I love it. But there ain't much call for what I want to play. It's all the same old, twerking over talent, and over-computerized crap. Nobody plays instruments anymore. I know I'm good. Really good. But what chance do I have?" His words trailed off and fogged up a small dot on the window. "Living…here?"

"I know what you're saying, but you have just as good a chance as anyone. Remember, what's old is new again."

"What's that mean?"

Beth pushed play on her CD player and Meghan Trainor's "All About That Bass" came through the speakers.

Sheldon scrunched his face up.

"Now, listen. Really listen."

After a few measures, his head bobbed to the beat.

"Not too bad, huh?" Beth prodded.

"Yeah, it's all right," Sheldon said, tapping his fingers against the window.

"Now, what does it remind you of?"

Sheldon leaned in toward the speakers.

"It sounds familiar."

"Does it sound like everything else on the radio today?" Beth asked.

"No. Not really. I mean, it has the same really produced sound, but there's not too much overproduction or anything… That's kinda cool."

"Exactly. Now, does it have that same feel as the hip-hop, rap, and pop sound like the other stuff?" Beth asked, grooving to the song.

Sheldon shook his head. "Nope. It reminds me of some of that old stuff. Ummm. That dead British chick, with the big hairdo."

"Amy Winehouse?" Beth chuckled.

"Oh, yeah…yeah. That's awesome." His head mimicked the rhythm of the song, and his grin sparkled with the magic of his musical epiphany.

"Yes… Yes." Beth bopped up and down with the beat.

Sheldon laughed at her and joined in and they both sang along.

"I hope you and your mom have a very merry Christmas, Sheldon." Beth hugged him and he didn't resist. He even hugged her, stronger, cracking her back.

"Yes, Mrs. S."

"I'm sure your mom has something special planned." She felt like an idiot as she noticed no signs of Christmas anywhere around the dilapidated house. Sheldon kept a tight grip on her and she thought she felt him sob. She patted him on the back.

"Doubt it." Sheldon coughed and squeezed tighter. At that moment, Beth was glad to have done a little Christmas shopping for one of her favorite kids. She knew it wasn't appropriate for a teacher to buy gifts for their students, but if there was one kid she could identify with, it was Sheldon James Hendricks. The boy lived and breathed guitar—and everything guitar-related. He would often proudly proclaim he was descended from the rock-and-roll legend Jimi Hendrix. Beth never had the heart to tell him there wasn't even a small chance of them being related, but she knew Sheldon already had enough cards stacked against him. Why not let him embrace something positive rather than all the real-life negativity he was facing?

Beth broke the heartbreaking embrace and gave him a wide smile.

"It's good to have faith, Mr. Hendricks." She winked. "Hey, isn't that what Christmas is all about?" She cringed at the trite phrase and broke into a chuckle.

"Yeah, thank you, Linus." Sheldon turned away, but Beth knew he was crying.

Beth turned the music down and reached into her bag in the back seat.

"Thanks for the ride, Mrs. S. I really—"

"Hold on, mister," Beth said, bringing her bag onto the console.

She offered a small, square package wrapped in Christmas paper, covered with Peanuts characters. There was an envelope taped to the top, underneath a purple ribbon.

"Merry Christmas."

He paused, gazing at the gift as though it were a trap, just waiting to strike at the greedy kid who was foolish enough to snatch it.

Beth laughed. "It's okay. It's not going to bite you, sheesh."

The snow intensified as they sat there.

"Sheldon, it's cool. Honest. You don't have to open it now. Save it until Christmas, if you want." Beth undid her seatbelt. "It's getting nasty. Let me help you with your bike." She thought it sounded like the perfect diversion and got out of the car.

Sheldon met her at the back of the car as she lowered the bike onto its flat tire.

"Okay. Here you go. Want me to help you get it to your house?"

Sheldon stuffed the gift into his backpack and launched himself into her arms again.

"Thanks, Mrs. S." His voice was barely audible through the biting, whipping winds.

"Tell your mom Merry Christmas for me, okay?" Beth said, and forced herself away.

Sheldon whimpered and pulled back too and snatched his defunct bicycle.

"I will. Merry Christmas, Mrs. S. And, hey… You deserve better." With that, he threw his backpack over his shoulder and trudged his bike toward the dark house.

Beth sang out, "Because I'm all about that…"

A shrill wind tore through the chain-link fence around the house and Beth waited for a moment, but as she was growing cold, she got into her car.

"… that bass," she heard Sheldon sing. Beth headed home. He was a good kid, and she would worry about him until after Christmas break. At least at school she could see him and at least a dozen or more at-risk children who needed help. But she needed to take this vacation for herself. Even during the most idyllic times, being a teacher was challenging. But when added to the stress of a horrific separation and a possible divorce, it only made things a million times worse.

Beth grew thirsty and couldn't wait to dig into the stash of wine in the cellar. While they weren't rich by any stretch, the one thing Tony was good for was his taste in high-quality wines.

Regardless of price, it all did the job. Especially now.

Beth turned onto Abts Street, and she could spot her house immediately even though the heavy snowfall had created a veil of white. The entire street glowed with red, green, yellow, and blue Christmas lights. Each house had a shiny, well-lit tree on display in their picture windows. *Like something out of a Norman Rockwell painting,* she thought, as she pulled into her unplowed driveway.

The sad bungalow looked like a missing tooth in an otherwise beautiful smile. It reminded her of the *Sesame Street* game she used to watch as a young girl. *One of these things is not like the others. One of these things just doesn't belong.* She put the car into park and stared at her empty home. The emotions punched her in the stomach, and she collapsed onto the steering wheel and sobbed.

Bruce Springsteen's "Merry Christmas Baby" flowed out of the car stereo and made her chortle. She caught her breath and tried to regain control. Control was something she hadn't had for a long time. A very long time. The bitter wind shook her small Hyundai and whistled through the windows. She pulled some Kleenex from her canvas purse and blew her nose.

"Why bother?" she whimpered.

The song finished and a friendly voice came on.

"That was the Boss, friends. Ya know, I gotta say, I love me some Christmas tune——" DJ Dean-O in the Morning proclaimed just as she turned the radio off.

"Ugh, bah humbug, Dean-O."

She gathered her purse and bright orange satchel and got out of the car. The powerful northern winds knocked her back in and she fought to stand back up.

After a few moments of struggle, she climbed out of the car and plotted a course to her front porch.

She'd made it halfway when her cellphone rang.

"Ah, dammit," she said, pulling herself onto the slanted, rickety porch with her free hand.

Yet another thing that would never be crossed off Tony's to-do list.

She caught her balance and let out a tired breath. "Tony, for Christ's sa——" She paused.

Beth didn't recognize the missed call's number. It wasn't Tony or Felicia. No, it was a New York City number.

Her breath caught in her chest.

"Mitch?"

9

Million Miles from Yesterday

Route 81 north was like riding on icy rails as Mitchell Roberts fought to turn onto 690. After a few tense minutes of treacherous driving through downtown Syracuse, he thanked the gods as he made it through the tollbooth to Route 91 East.

Mitch was grateful for having beaten the snowstorm on the Thruway as he cautiously headed west. But with every aching mile, it took every bit of energy not to turn around. He'd much more gladly face that storm— and the even more brutal one waiting for him in that hellhole he bitterly called home.

He finally made it off the NYS Thruway and headed north on Route 14. It was a long drive from Manhattan, and he half-welcomed, half-dreaded the sight of Sterling Point. He hadn't been home since graduation and he was damn happy about it. Gov't Mule's "I'll Be the One" was blaring from his speakers when his cellphone rang. Fumbling with the cell and turning down the stereo, Mitch swerved all over the road. After a few panicked seconds, he finally brought the car under control and searched for a safe place to pull over.

The screen read *Bridget Holly*, the literary agent who signed Mitch for his first book. He answered the call.

"First, Mitch, I received your email, and hey, I'm really so sorry about your mom. How are you holding up?"

"Thank you. I appreciate it. Yeah, it sucks… But I…I'm doing okay. But you didn't have to call me. I know you're set to head home. It's the holidays, don't you know," Mitch said, in his best North Dakota accent; he knew it sucked, but it drove her nuts.

An audible sigh came over the phone. "You still can't pull the accent off, pal. Keep working on it." Bridget laughed sarcastically. "I'll be heading out to the airport within the hour, if the weather holds out. Thanks for your concern. And good attempt at ignoring my question, Mr. Roberts."

There was a brief, heavy pause.

"You betcha," Mitch said. His agent responded with another sigh.

"I know it must be hard...going back home, your mom, dad, and all that." Bridget's voice filled the car yet sounded a million miles away. "I just want you to know that I get it...and I am so very sorry."

An even longer, ten-ton weighted pause filled the car and the miles between Mitch and his concerned agent from here to Manhattan.

"Anyway... How're the roads? I hear it's getting nasty up that way."

"Not great. It's like driving on rails. A white-knuckle ride for sure." Mitch frantically turned up the wipers and cleared the gathering condensation from the inside. He needed a new car. This one had seen better days and was the same vehicle he'd left home with ten years earlier. "I really appreciate you calling, Bridget, but you know me, I can't multitask." He let out a small, forced chuckle.

"Okay, okay. You're right. I'll make it quick. I am the bearer of good news, Mr. Roberts." Bridget's tone grew upbeat.

"Oh? Well, please tell me fast, before I put this piece of junk into a snowbank or worse." He laughed nervously and slowed down as a blue Kenworth truck sent its white wake all over his much smaller windshield.

"All right, all right. Sorry. You know the new book you spent over three years worrying so much about that you got an ulcer?"

"Ha! Yeah. How could I not?"

"You will be happy to know *Beautifully Broken* has just joined *About to Rage* on the *New York Times* bestseller list."

"No goddamn way."

"I'm not kidding, Mitch. It was just released. You are a bestselling author again! How does that make you feel?" Bridget paused. "Well, in spite of your mother passing away and all."

A tsunami of conflicting emotions rushed over him. Not even twenty-four hours earlier, he'd received the call from his father. He'd thrown a duffel bag together and headed upstate immediately, although he wasn't sure how to feel. He'd sobbed all the way from Brooklyn until he reached the west side of Albany. Now he had a bestselling book. He felt guilty. He wasn't looking forward to coming home. With his mom gone, there was no buffer between him and his father. But still, *a bestselling author!* Mitch's mind was swimming.

"You still there?" Bridget asked.

"Um, yeah, sorry. I am. That's so...so incredible. Thanks so much! Thanks for everything you've done. I can't thank you enough, Bridget. Thanks for calling me!"

"No problem," she said.

"I'll definitely call you when I get to my folks' house, and thanks again for calling, I needed the good news. Talk soon," Mitch said, trying not to sound like a snot-gobbling fool.

Another pause. This time, it weighed a bit lighter.

"Hey, B…"

"Yeah, Mitch?"

"It's hard… I…I don't want to go."

"I understand, Mitchell. Remember. Your mom would be so proud. Be safe, and congratulations. Please take time out to celebrate and really think about how far you've come. It's been a long road, my friend. Enjoy it. At least a little. Merry Christmas. Later, gator."

Mitch tossed the cellphone onto the passenger seat and the emotions washed over him. Losing his mom right before his first book went bestseller cut deep. He had seen no one from high school since graduation night. He hadn't thought about home in a long time, apart from Beth. It was her he missed the most and he had always wondered how she was. He tried not to think of unpleasant people and memories; instead, he pushed up his black-rimmed glasses and tried to shake it all away for now. He never had forgotten how nasty the western New York winter storms were; he needed to focus on the worsening roads.

Seeing the sign for the small Wayne County town of Lyons, he knew he needed to take a short break. Pulling off into a Kwik-Fill gas station parking lot, the flurries of happiness, grief, and guilt filled him. Once he collected himself, he continued along Route 14 north toward home, Sterling Point, one step closer to the place he'd sworn never to set foot in again. All around him, the snow picked up its intensity as he headed straight into the blinding white wall of blowing snow.

10

I'll Be Home for Christmas

"Give me another one, Sal," Gordon Roberts ordered, slamming the empty Genesee Cream Ale can on the bar and wiping his mouth. He hoped his hand would mask the tears flowing down his face. A well-deserved liquid lunch was in order, and he placed the much-hated cellphone, which the Sterling Point highway superintendent had mandated he carry at all times, onto the bar with a sneer of disgust.

"Howie still busting your balls?" Sal Yowner asked from behind the worn bar.

Gordon shook his head and drained the can. "Hell, that young fatass ain't never stopped. I have hunting socks older than that snot-nosed punk. I've been plowing these streets and fixing broken water mains and patching together sewer pipes longer than Howie's been sucking on his mama's teat." He held up his large, callused hands in a *far-be-it-from-me* gesture. "But I'm at that useless age and the town is looking for any reason to send me off into my golden years." Gordon motioned for another beer.

Sal nodded as he tossed Gordon's empty into the bin beneath the bar and let out a sympathetic sigh.

The tavern was dark, except for the multi-colored glow of Christmas lights and the lone shaft of daylight creating a path to the long oak bar that extended all the way to the back, which seemed to escort the patrons to the bathrooms at the end of the tavern. It smelled of stale beer, fried food, and a lifetime of hard times and good times, all mixed together in a Norman Rockwell-meets-*The Deer Hunter* scene.

"It Came Upon a Midnight Clear" filled the place. Assorted animal heads, decorated with Santa hats and Christmas bulbs, hung from the walls and stared down upon the two human occupants with a stoic sadness.

"Here ya go, Gordie, it's on the house." Sal popped the top of a Genny can. "I know it's been a rough few months." His old friend poured himself a draft and leaned against the bar.

"You ain't shittin', Sal." Gordon took a long sip. Shaking his head, he continued. "I just don't get it. You try to be a good man, take care of your family. You bust your ass, and where does it get ya? Goddamn nowhere." Gordon drained the can and slammed it down.

"Nah, Gordie, you did good. Marguerite loved you like all get out, and I hear Mitchie is doing good. You can't think like that. You can't focus on all that negative shit."

Gordie knew he was a hard-ass and hard to console. He also knew Sal had run out of things to say as he reached into the under-bar cooler for another beer and placed it in front of him.

"Thanks. You're a good man, Sal."

"Now don't let that nasty rumor get around, pal." Sal winked. "Now, um, when's the service?" His voice quivered at the painful question.

"A couple of days, I guess. I got to meet Dave over at Murphy's tomorrow, and I'll know more after that. I'm thinking nothing too fancy. It'll be a small thing. Maggie didn't want anyone to be fussin' over her. You know how stubborn her Irish side could be." Gordie tried to force a smile.

Sal nodded solemnly. "Ah, yeah, that's true. She was so gentle, but ya piss her off, may God have mercy on your soul," he said, too nervous to look his friend in the eye.

"So, not trying to toss a match on an already simmering inferno, but is Mitch coming home?" Sal wiped the same spot on the well-worn bar and waited.

Gordon waved the nosy barkeep off. "Yeah, yeah, um, Mitch…" he mumbled. He popped the top on the beer, hoping Sal hadn't noticed his eyes welling up.

"Ah, yeah. I called him and he said he was gonna be here today," he said, still staring at his faraway place.

"Well, damn, I sure hope he makes it before this damn storm kicks into full gear." Sal stepped out from behind the bar and crossed the old plank floor that creaked and moaned beneath his booted feet. He reached the door and looked out at the winter wonderland that was brewing over the lake, beyond the icy window. His breath caused the window to fog.

The jukebox crackled with the sounds of the vinyl, bringing memories of better days rushing into Gordon's mind. Images and sounds of the holidays spent in Vietnam with his friends, who were all now long-dead or far away. Images of their wedding night and how Maggie "had to have it" on Christmas Eve. He'd only had a few days home before heading for Camp Pendleton, then onto Vietnam. And looking into her beautiful blue eyes, he couldn't say no. He never could and never did, even right up until the very end. Watching the doctors and nurses pull the plug was the hardest thing the war-hardened old man had ever had to do. He knew she would always bitch at him about his drinking, and even he— begrudgingly—admitted she was right. He'd tried several times over the years to stop or even slow down. But why now? What would be the reason? He had nothing left. He knew he should, though. He held the can in his hands, wondering if now this time would do the trick. Pushing the beer away might finally stick for good. Would it?

"This was Maggie's favorite." Gordon hid his tears and stared up at the chipped drywall ceiling.

"I know, buddy, I remember how we used to tear it up at the VFW Christmas party. Phew, we had some good times back then, didn't we?" Sal dabbed a tear and smiled.

"Ha, yeah, we sure the hell did, brother. We sure did." Gordie pulled out a cigar. New York State's no-smoking law didn't pertain to Yowner's on Christmas.

"Got one for me, you stingy ol' bastard?" Sal laughed and slid over a beer from the cooler.

"For you? Ah, what the hell, it's Christmas, right?" Gordie's flushed cheeks were coated with tears as he slowly turned the beer can in his large callused hands and stared at it. A small smile appeared as he pulled another stogie from his inside jacket pocket.

The phone erupted and thrummed on the bar.

"Are you gonna answer that, or are you waiting for Howard to have a stroke?" Sal raised an eyebrow.

Gordon's shoulders dropped. "Yeah, yeah, yeah." He opened the cellphone and read the text.

"Bad news?" Sal asked, an open beer in his hand.

"Fuck me runnin'." Gordon slapped the phone shut and tucked it into his shirt pocket. "Yeah, the nor'easter is a quicker mover than the eggheads thought. I need to get back to the town barns and load up with rock salt. Howie wants all hands on deck out there, salting the roads."

"Merry Christmas, peckerhead." He tossed it to Sal. They both filled the otherwise empty bar with solemn silence and drank.

"Merry Christmas, jackass."

Gordon tipped his old friend and made his way out to his awaiting plow truck, cigar still smoking into the frigid air. His thoughts turned to his beloved bride, their troubled yet love-filled life together, and then to their son…Mitchell.

11

Wine and Blood

After dropping Sheldon off, Beth's mind raced with thoughts of Mitch. The only light in the disheveled living room was the flickering fire inside the old stone fireplace. The twisting flames cast desperate shadows, causing the room to appear in constant, tortured motion. Beth sat amongst a collection of empty wine bottles and boxes stacked with their lids wide open like crying baby birds. All around her lay images and keepsakes, ten years' worth of scattered memories, splayed out like ashes in a hurricane: their wedding day at Sterling Point Lighthouse; their honeymoon in St. Thomas; their graduations; the day they bought the house. The weight of the past weeks pressed down upon her small frame, surrounding her like a suffocating coffin. The house had been so cold, so empty, so silent since she had kicked him out.

Outside, Pablo, her best friend, a massive Alaskan malamute, bayed at the night sky and offered Beth a little comfort.

She drained another glass and refilled it, flipping through another stack of photographs. She paused and snatched a picture from the pile. Their August wedding at the historic Sterling Point Lighthouse. They had their reception at Foreman's Park—it was the perfect day. Not a cloud in the sky, and Lake Ontario had never looked so beautiful. Tony was so handsome in his gray tux with tails, and her dress was like something out of a Disney fairytale. The lush, calm waters of Lake Ontario behind them, the orange-yellow sun setting behind them framed it all perfectly. She sipped from her glass and glared into Tony's brown eyes. Those gorgeous, lying eyes.

There had been dozens of texts from Tracy Smith on Tony's cell about a month earlier, and Beth had tried hard to pass it off as just something fleeting. Tony was a good-looking guy—and a cop—and he talked to dozens of people every day. Although the 1,383 square miles of Wayne County lay spread out, it was still a small community. And boy, how the county lived for drama. Like redneck vampires that thrived on spreading pain—there was never a shortage of rumors.

Beth sipped the wine as she rubbed her thumb over her husband's face. The smooth finish of the photograph meant nothing; the only image that kept rushing through her mind was of Tony and Tracy in the last text she'd seen.

She guzzled the rest of the wine as if she was dying of thirst. Everything was a lie: the vows, the lovemaking, the promises of a family. All of it. All bullshit. Somehow, betrayal wasn't a good enough definition of the hell it had thrust her into.

Beth felt her heart race and forced herself to her feet. She staggered as the alcohol took hold and the dark room started to swim with a muddy image of her memories, accompanied by the crackling sounds coming from the fireplace. She smashed the large picture against the wall. The glass inside the solid silver frame exploded over the mantel. She let the broken frame drop to the floor with a loud crash, ignoring the blood forming on her hand.

The room spun as she kicked, punched, and screamed. Boxes tumbled and spilled open, vomiting bittersweet mementos all over the living room.

Fractured glass mixed with blood as she stared at the picture on the hardwood floor. The wine tasted good—fantastic—but her world was spinning out of control.

Along with the glass, she felt her heart splinter into a million pieces, her stomach churning as the rage and bitterness overwhelmed her. She let the blood streaming from her hand cover her lying, cheating husband's handsome face. A raging sea of mixed emotions fought a war inside her that had always been there. Beth's head and heart were at odds; she loved the asshole and they'd been together since high school. But the thought of him screwing or even touching another woman made her skin crawl and ignited a rage inside her she hadn't felt in years.

Barefooted, she kicked around a pile of pictures and something caught her eye.

Pablo huffed at the back door, and she tried to ignore him.

Beth pulled the image close and covered her mouth as an unexpected bolt of laughter echoed off the walls. The precious old moment came rushing back at her, as if tethered by a short string.

She was with Mitch.

They were in his parents' basement and other people were there. All of Mitch's friends: Chris Delaney, Dave Somerset, Clay and Ray Felton, Jesse Pierce, Dawn McCormick, Rob Jenkins, and Petra Salinger. The whole crew. Beth knew most of them from one class or another, but it wasn't until after months of Mitch harassing her to come to one of his Dungeons and Dragons games that she decided she should finally get to know them. They were fun, and good people. While she was certain the rest of Sterling Point High School wouldn't think so, she liked them. And it was through that silly fantasy dice game she understood what Mitch and his friends were all about.

The picture captured her and Mitch in a hug and the rest of the gaming group mugging it up in various Halloween costumes and making devil-horn gestures. Beth laughed again at the embarrassed face Mitch had made while she'd kissed his baby-faced cheek.

A loud bang at the back door startled her, followed by a demanding bark.

"In a minute."

The warm memory wrapped itself around her and enveloped her in a thick blanket of nostalgia and better days. His smile was always contagious. Mitch had always been there for her. Even when she knew she was just being a bitch and perfecting her drama-queen persona, he never judged her. Never tried to lecture her. Other than the time she'd mentioned to him about her going on a date with Tony Severt.

Beth winced at that memory and wished she'd listened to him.

She smiled looking at Mitch's blushing face. She missed him. And now his mother had died, and he was coming home. And she felt the temptation to call him.

She grabbed her cell and hit the call button, and it rang. She waited and wished she could climb up off the floor and get more wine, but she was certain her legs would fail her. So, she waited.

After a few messages about the caller not being available, she heard Mitch's voicemail response.

"*You've reached Mitchell Roberts. I'm too busy working on my next brilliant novel or just avoiding your call. So please leave a message and I will try to get back to you as soon as possible. If you're a Hollywood producer looking for your next hit script, I'm your huckleberry. While I don't work for scale, I'll still be on the first plane out to L.A. If you're a bill collector, I'm sorry, you have the wrong number. Sayonara, sucka!*"

She felt a wide smile grow on her face and she hesitated for a second. Should she leave a message? Would he be pissed off at her? Would he even care? Erring on the side of caution and taking advantage of a momentary flash of sobriety, Beth hung up and lay back against the couch.

"I miss you, you nerdy bastard." She felt guilty as soon as she'd uttered the words. Beth was excited and terrified at the thought of seeing Mitch again after all these years, especially considering how he had left. She still felt guilty about how he'd found out about she and Tony, and she knew she'd been a bitch to him and pledged to apologize after the graduation ceremony. But he'd taken off and left Sterling Point that night. She hadn't spoken to him since, although she'd tried. A few phone calls, e-mails, even letters, went ignored.

Pablo barked and loud thuds echoed through the kitchen.

"All right, all right. I'm coming for you, ya big fur ball. Hold on. Sheesh." Beth got to her feet and the effects of the wine hit her again. Giggling, she staggered to the back door, unlocked and opened it. A brutal, biting wind tore into the house, slamming the door against the wall, nearly shattering the glass. The large dog leaped up to her shoulders and loomed over her. It took all she had to not tumble to the floor.

"Easy, now. Your mama isn't feeling too good, big guy," she said, fumbling with the latch on his collar. Finally free, Pablo hopped down and ran to his food and water dish and set to eating.

Beth pushed hard on the door and finally forced it shut, then locked it.

"You're welcome, sir!" She ran her hands through his thick, icy fur, and the big dog let out a happy huff as he kept chowing down.

She found her way to the small wine fridge Tony had gotten her for Christmas the year before. "Sure put that sucker to good use, didn't we?" she said, using the wall, then the dining room chair for balance. In a flash, she had picked out another bottle and had it uncorked within thirty seconds, and she did the drunken dance back to her spot on the floor, carefully avoiding the broken glass.

"Now, where were we?" Beth plopped down and took a swig. "Ah, yes. Mr. Roberts. Where the hell have you been, darlin'? Man, I hope you don't hate me too much." Delving back into the stack of old photos from high school, all the innocent young faces welcomed her back, and then her cellphone vibrated and rang, startling her.

Was it Mitch calling her back? Should she answer it? What in the world would she say? What could she say? *'I'm sorry,'* didn't seem enough. She put the bottle down and frantically searched for the phone. With her one good hand, she flipped through a sea of pictures, papers, and other random memorabilia, the phone still ringing.

Finally, she found it under a picture of herself and Mitch, with his mom and dad, at their sixth-grade graduation. Beth couldn't help but notice Mr. Roberts' more-than-obvious *I would rather have an icepick shoved into my eye than be here* face. She laughed, that was Mr. R—a nice man, but he and Mitch had never really had a great father-son relationship. The annoying ringtone reminded her of what she was doing, and she checked the screen to see who was calling.

Tony.

"Ah shit." Beth tensed and all those good feelings became shattered and replaced with a sudden rage. She took a long pull from the bottle and hit the hang-up button.

"Just leave me alone!"

It rang again. Tony.

A deep, guttural, primal scream began in her stomach and rushed through the rest of her trembling body. Beth didn't recognize the sound emanating from her and echoing off the walls.

In a white-hot rage, she threw the phone with all her strength, and it shattered against the wall.

The ringing stopped.

The last person she wanted to talk to tonight was Tony, with his tired excuses and false apologies. Forcing him from her mind, she snatched up the bottle and Mitch's picture and leaned back against the couch and fought to breathe.

After a few quiet moments, with her blood pressure and heartbeat back where they should be, she sipped from her glass.

"Ah, another good reason for wine," she said, her sobs echoing amongst the dark corners of the old house.

Tomorrow she would have to replace her phone, but that was something a sober, more put-together Beth could deal with. Right now, she had a sea of rushing emotions to wash down with a nice bottle of pinot noir.

INTERLUDE

J & J DEGELLEKE STATE CAMPGROUNDS
RHODES HOLLOW, NY

"Best hurry up, this shit is about to hit the fan," Marty Dowd shouted through the howling winds and pelting snow.

"I know. I know," Jimmy Dowd bellowed back as he fought to bury the tent's stake into the nearly frozen ground. It had taken them both nearly two hours to dig through the three feet of snow just to get to the hard earth.

The two brothers had been living off the grid for a year or so, having had enough of the "bullshit, corrupt system" controlled by mega-corporations and fat cat billionaires like Musk and Bezos. They had been dividing their time from state camping sites and open land all through New York. They had planned to be in the South by Halloween, but when Marty had some health issues, they were forced to stay longer than they'd planned.

Now, knee-deep into winter, and with money running out, the brothers were fighting to hunker down until the storm passed; then they could head to Florida to join their brothers.

A wicked gust took the side flap of their tent, nearly sending it off into the dying dusk.

"Got it!" Jimmy shouted, tackling the line and hammering it even deeper into the ground.

Standing up, Jimmy and Marty chuckled, as they had conquered Mother Nature's unrelenting brutality again.

"I'm thinking a hot toddy or two once we're settled," Jimmy said, opening the tent's flap and tossing his backpack inside.

Marty stared at his brother wide-eyed. He, too, dropped his backpack. It landed at his booted feet.

"What?" Jimmy asked, shrugging. "Come on, man. We nee—"

That's when his brother's chest exploded into a bloody, gore-filled miasma of rent flesh and bone, as a savage blackness with razor-sharp talons nearly a foot long split the Dowd brother in half.

Shards of breastbone and splintered ribs were sent like blood-and-guts-soaked shrapnel into the air. Marty watched in heart-stopping disbelief as his younger brother was devoured by a soulless Darkness that ripped Jimmy limb from limb and swallowed up his blood, flesh, and bones.

The ghostly cold night and the swirling Darkness howled, and Marty stood stiff, frozen as the horrific arctic world around him.

The deep swaying pines and birch trees stood witness as the ancient Darkness fed, and the Dowd brothers were devoured.

Only the bitter snowstorm heard the last of their agonizing death screams.

The baleful howl followed as the Darkness continued its path toward those who had awakened it, growing hungrier and more insatiable with each soul it devoured.

12
Christmas in My Hometown

Through flickering snowflakes, the headlights caught the old sign: *Welcome to Sterling Point*. The words were nearly obscured, the snow piled up so high that all Mitch could read was *Welcome to*. And the snow had shown no sign of letting up since he'd left the city. Mitch had a hard time keeping his compact car on the road. The only good thing was that there weren't many other vehicles on the road, except for the large yellow county snowplows and the police and tow trucks. Dread washed over him at the sight of the trucks.

Mitch followed the curvy road that followed the lake into the small town. Not much had changed. All the same small businesses were there. Some had different names now but looked untouched. All the closely grouped houses seemed no worse for wear. The good ol' Salacia's Marina had all the boats wrapped up nice and neat, waiting patiently for the next summer to come and set them free to sail the waters of Lake Ontario. He couldn't see anything out over the lake; a wall of white covered everything from the iced-over water to as high as the eye could see. It seemed to Mitch as though a glacier the size of the moon was blocking all paths northward. The thought unnerved him. He turned up the CD player to drown out his overactive imagination. The slide guitar of "Railroad Boy" filled the Honda, but it did little to settle his queasy stomach, stopping at the one and only stop light in the small town.

Instead of taking the quickest route to his house, he turned left, preferring to save the sightseeing for another time, and took the back streets home. Most of the sights were already ingrained into his patchwork quilt-like memory of a few enjoyable moments stitched together with large swaths of sadness, pain, and anger. So he subconsciously avoided the easiest path to his old house. And consciously, he had hoped he'd drive full-circle and be right back on the Thruway and headed back to Brooklyn before he'd even realized he'd left.

Only one soft yellow light in the picture window greeted Mitch as he pulled up to his parents' house.

The stout two-story structure sat on the front portion of the long stretch of the Roberts' not-so-palatial estate. Two flags mounted on either side of the wide porch were both lit up, and they whipped and swirled about, the American flag on the left pillar while the flag of his father's beloved Marine Corps fought off the sub-zero winds on the right. That struck Mitch as odd. His dad was a stickler for correct flag etiquette, and here it was well after dark, and winter was in full rage.

A long driveway was set off to the right and led behind the house to a two-car garage. There was a set of covered big tire tracks leading up the drive to where Old Blue sat, gathering the piling snow.

He gave the car more gas to make it up the short but steep rise so as not to get stuck, but it seemed that even the car didn't want to come home. The tires fought for purchase on the snowy driveway. After a third try, the compact car made it up the drive.

His dad's old Chevy pickup with the even older rusty Western snowplow hanging from it sat parked sideways in front of the garage.

Mitch pulled up next to the big blue 4x4. Good old Gordon "Gordie" Andrew Roberts was well known for his expertise in snow plowing. He took great pride in it, almost as if it were an art form. The downside of it was, once the old man finished work, he would then get plowed down at the bar and then park creatively in the small drive. His mom used to get so mad, but his dad would ignore her; if she got too lippy, the old man would backhand her and send her back to the kitchen.

His stomach churned, and he shook the old memory away and got out of the car, a biting gust of wind tearing at his face and stealing his breath. He'd forgotten just how much he hated the winter in Sterling Point. Reason Number 232 why he'd never wanted to come back.

The garage light was off, but the ambient light from the snow cast a warm glow. Grabbing his laptop and his backpack from the back seat, he shoved the car door shut and made his way to the back door. The truck sat covered in snow and there weren't any footprints. Mitch's sneakers were getting soaked as he trudged through the white mire. He climbed the covered steps and knocked on the door, which opened without resistance.

"Dad?" Mitch peered in. Nothing.

He opened the door into the kitchen, the dim light from the range hood casting a strange yellow light. Without thinking, Mitch kicked off his snow-covered shoes and fought to close the door, fighting the strong lake winds. *Old habits die hard,* he thought, seeing his father's worse-for-wear black boots sitting neatly in the boot tray.

"Hey, Dad. It's me, Mitch." Only the loud humming sound from the old furnace welcomed him.

He went to set his bags on the kitchen table and stopped short as he noticed it was littered with empty beer cans and pizza boxes. The entire kitchen resembled something from a college fraternity house. He set his bags down on the only clear spot and crossed to the dining room, which was pitch-black save the light from the snow coming through the two tall windows. The fast-food typhoon had spilled into this room. Mitch could now hear music coming from another part of the house.

Reaching the living room door, he pushed it open. "Dad?" A wash of light from the ceiling flooded in, and he squinted to see the room.

"What the——?" As if the unplowed driveway and the garbage dump of a kitchen weren't enough, this new sight made Mitch step back. The fast-food delivery massacre had filled the living room too. His father had passed out in his old, worn-out leather La-Z-Boy, still wearing his blue work shirt and pants. Mitch remembered his father used to have his mother iron them. Peaked creases on the legs. "Sharp enough to cut a finger off," he would brag. But these were stained, and as wrinkled as the deep lines of the old man's unshaven face. A beer can sat crooked in his hand, almost as crooked as its drinker.

On his chest, an open book, as if he'd fallen asleep or passed out while reading. Normally, his dad reading an old Zane Grey or Larry McMurtry paperback wouldn't have been strange, but this particular novel caused Mitch to pause; it was a worn copy of his first novel, *About to Rage*. It must've been the one he'd sent to his mom.

The thought of his stoic, take-no-bullshit, war veteran dad sitting down and actually reading something he had created startled Mitch. There was a lot of creative writing therapy in that book. And a lot of—as the title suggested—rage in it. Anger and resentment aimed at his father. His head began to swoon a little at the thought of what kind of conversation that could inspire.

Shaking that panicked thought from his weary mind, Mitch looked beyond the book and next to his snoring father, where on the table sat his mother's old record player. On it, Charley Pride sang about burgers and fries and cherry pies.

The soft hissing of the needle on the vinyl brought back a rush of childhood memories. Mitch's breath caught in his throat when he saw a pistol sitting on the side table. He hated guns, he always had. The old man used to try to get him to join him on his hunting trips, but had eventually given up asking. Mitch felt guilty enough about eating a hamburger or a steak, much less going out in the pre-dawn and killing a living creature. Another thing he and the old jarhead didn't have in common.

His head began to pound, and a sharp pressure grabbed his chest. Mitch fought to breathe as a tidal wave of adrenaline coursed through him. *I don't want to be here*, he told himself over and over again.

Go! Go! Go! I don't belong here, Mitch's rattled mind repeated like a scratched record. As he knew damn well, his fight-or-flight lizard brain was taking control, telling him to run as fast and as far as his old Honda would take him.

Freezing to death in a snowstorm would be an easier death than staying in this decaying museum of decades-old scar tissue, slowly, brutally being ripped open with each step he took into the world of his youth.

In the faint distance of his racing mind, he heard the calming voice. His mother.

She would want him to stay. His father needed him. The old man had nothing, no one else.

With his heartbeat slowing, and the sweat abating a little, Mitch wiped his forehead and continued his tour of Château Hell.

Mitch's socked foot kicked something, and he jumped. It crashed into a sea of empty Genny cream-ale beer cans littering the worn-out shag carpet. His father shifted in the rickety chair, then began snoring like a grizzly bear. Mitch didn't move for a long moment, fearing his father's old war nightmares might cause him to freak out and shoot. He let out a morbid, uncomfortable chuckle as he considered how ironic it would be for him to come back to the last place on earth he'd ever wanted to visit and catch a bullet from the last man he'd ever wanted to see.

Mitch watched the all-too-familiar scene before him. The only thing missing was his mother, on the couch in front of the picture window, crocheting or reading and sipping coffee, or her afternoon favorite, Diet Coke. He wanted to blame it on the wretched stench of rotting Chinese food or his father's swamp feet, but no, the tears pouring from his eyes were coming from the halting realization that his mom was gone.

Forever.

It all felt like a bad dream. Or a *Twilight Zone*-tainted nightmare. As though he'd wake up any moment and she'd be there, smiling at him from her usual perch. It was the only space in the room that didn't have a food or beer container covering it. Even her wooden box of yarn and needles sat untouched alongside the couch. His chest squeezed, and he fought the tears away.

The real vision in front of him was his drunk, disheveled father. Mitch felt his grief tighten into an overwhelming rage. He wanted to shake the drunk. Punch him into an even deeper unconsciousness. Hell, the cruel, abusive bastard deserved a fate far worse than that. All those torturous years living under his brutal yoke and having to watch what he did to his mother. He hated the man. A deep-seated loathing planted with painful absence and watered with the scars of rage. He heard his mother's voice in his head. "Never use the word *hate*, Mitchell. It's a strong word and will consume you if you let it."

The beer can toppled to the floor as his dad twitched and jerked uncontrollably, fighting off an invisible attacker.

"No, you fucking bastard. Get away from him! Joey, Jay-Co, Ferg, man, you guys okay? DAMN YOU! Charlie's run the wire. Run… Go. Go. GO!" The rest was tear-filled gibberish.

Mitch took a breath and walked around the chair to grab the pistol. Setting it on the windowsill, he felt much safer.

"Dad, Dad, it's me, Mitch," he whispered. He'd forgotten how powerful his father's nightmares were.

A small grumble came from the chair.

"I'm home, Dad." Mitch edged closer.

"Grr…rah… Wh… What? M—Mitchie?"

Mitch knelt and took his father's hand. "Yeah, it's me, Dad."

"Oh, good. Glad ya made it." He tried to stand. "There's a bad mother coming. That peckerhead weather broad on thirteen says it's gonna be a bitch." The lines on Gordon's face turned into sinkholes as he looked up at his son. A crooked smile abruptly cut the scar—running from his right cheekbone down to the left side of his chin—in half.

He fought for the strength to stand and held out a hand for help.

"Give your old man a hand, would ya?"

"Sure," he said, stunned, the sound of his own voice sounding foreign, as strange as everything else that had transpired in the past twenty-four hours. He grabbed his father's upper arm and helped him up.

His dad placed an arm around Mitch's shoulder, patted him on the chest, and they made their way to the stairs.

"Packed on some pounds, eh, boy?" A cold chuckle followed.

Mitch felt eight years old again. The words escaped him as the room seemed to close in around him.

As always.

After a slew of colorful expletives and a tough few minutes of navigating the stairs, Mitch managed to get his inebriated father to his bedroom.

He tried to steer him onto the crisply made bed, but he shoved Mitch's hands off him and staggered toward an old, stiff-backed chair in the corner. He collapsed into it and pulled a nearby blanket over him.

"Get yer hands off me, boy. I don't need to be handled like a…" His words came out in a slow, low mumble, trailing off into the corners of the room.

Mitch stood there in his parents' bedroom, the hallway light casting a pale yellow wash over his father.

"Leave me be." He motioned to the doorway with a floppy arm. "Your ma left your room…" The slurred mix of words morphed into a deep snoring.

Mitch felt as though he was watching himself in a David Lynch flick. Nothing was making sense and his emotions raced and spun. The tightening in his chest returned, and as he stood in the doorway, a rushing wave took him.

He looked down the dimly lit hallway to the stairs that led back to his car. Back out into the December storm. Back to Brooklyn. His true home. Away from this old, yet grotesque new world.

Run now! Get the hell out of here! Mitch told himself.

He needed to sleep. There would be plenty of time to figure all this shit out. He turned, wiping the sweat from his face again, and caught a picture on the wall by the door.

Mitch and his mom at graduation night. Outside the Sterling Point High School auditorium.

Mitch's father couldn't have taken the picture because the old man wasn't there. It wasn't a big deal to Mitch, as that had always been his father's modus operandi. He had never come to anything Mitch had ever done.

Then he remembered it was Chris Delaney who must've taken the picture. His old friend was an avid photographer and was always shooting.

And while it took him a split-second to recall the photographer of the image, the vivid memory was so ingrained in his mind, he could still feel the scorching stage lights as he and fellow classmates sat for what felt like forever. Beth was on his left, her breath-stealing smile wide upon her pale face. Her hazel eyes sparkled under those bright lights. Her long, strawberry-blonde hair was styled just perfect. And Mitch knew she must've spent at least two hours staring into the mirror and cussing at herself until she got it just right.

He still felt the tug on his right arm. It was Tony Severt, his best friend, who'd spent the entire ceremony making extremely inappropriate yet hilarious comments about the principal and guest speakers' speeches.

Mitch knew Tony was trying to get him to laugh out loud. He almost did when Tony said something raunchy about Valarie Bronski's panties while she gave her beautifully written speech. Tony was always good for a laugh and a fun time. Mitch had always admired Tony's strong and confident personality and, in many ways, looked up to him. *I wanted to be like him.*

And when Tony leaned in, gave a look over Mitch's shoulder at Beth, and whispered to him, "Tonight's your chance, dude. Tell her," Tony smiled wide, all teeth, and his deep brown eyes bore into his. "Go for it, man." Tony winked and patted Mitch's knee. "You only live once, brother."

Mitch was going to finally let Beth know how he felt. All those long years of wanting to be with her.

But that was a long, long time ago.

In the picture, behind Mitch and his mom, he saw something he'd never noticed before. Or at least never acknowledged... In the background, amongst a thick crowd of orange and black graduation caps and gowns, there they were.

Beth and Tony. They were standing behind a brick pillar that led to the gymnasium and doing a bad job if they were trying to hide.

Mitch stared intently at the photograph. This was the first time he'd seen it. His mom had sent him a few from graduation night, but not this one. And now...he knew why.

Tony had his arm around Beth. He was leaning closely, as if to whisper into her ear.

That's when the old photo jerked Mitch's thoughts from vivid memory to real-time remembrance, and he went back in time and recalled that just after the picture was taken, he'd seen a strange look on Chris's face.

What happened next was one of the many painful reasons Mitch had packed up and left Sterling Point the next morning.

Mitch had turned around to see Tony hugging and kissing the girl he'd pined for. No...*loved* since pre-school. Beth and Tony were in a tight embrace and kissing deeply, and with each gut-wrenching second, Mitch's world was torn into a million tiny, jagged shards, ripping the air from his lungs and tearing his world to pieces.

The old thickly scabbed wound burst open, as if on fire in his chest, his heart pounding like a sledgehammer. A knot grew in his gut, and acid roiled in the back of his throat. Fists balled tight, Mitch's nails dug into his palms.

Two of the most important people in his young life. He loved them both deeply. Tony knew things he'd never dare share with anyone else. Especially his love for Beth.

A loud clunk from below shook Mitch back to the cold, dark hallway.

He was no longer in his old high school. But he certainly felt as if he were.

Lord knows the bone-aching pain and stinging tears were brilliant proof.

The furnace clunked again, sending out a rush of cold air from the large metal vent below his feet.

He yanked the picture off the wall and slowly made his way down the dark hallway until he reached the frosted window at the end, the weight of the past twenty-four hours pulling him down. He opened the door to his childhood bedroom—his old sanctum sanctorum, the only place he'd felt safe and free from the alien planet he had lived on as a teen. The soft light from the hallway shot a path leading to his bed against the far wall.

Stepping inside and closing the door behind him with a light squeak, he noticed the same annoying sound it used to make, and he smiled as he reached for the light switch.

Nothing happened.

"Ah, swell. Nice to see nothing ever changes here at Casa Roberts. Thanks, Dad," Mitch said, using the soft moonlight to show him the way to the nightstand where a lamp sat. He kicked something and cursed out loud as he stumbled into the night table, nearly knocking it over.

He regained his balance, fumbled for the lamp, and clicked it on.

Still cursing, he turned to the obstacle he swore he'd sprained his big toe on: a large banker's box. "Jesus, the hits just keep on coming." He'd mess with it tomorrow; he was tired and needed a good night's sleep. And there was a damn good chance he would leave in the morning. The next few days would be hell, and he needed all the energy he could muster.

Turning to the bed, Mitch stopped, startled to find it was neatly made and turned down.

He looked around the room and couldn't see one speck of dust. His dad was a stickler for cleanliness, but he didn't think the old man would have cared about his room, especially after his mom passed. Trembling, he touched the cool handmade comforter.

His mom must have made the bed before she... *Before.*

Sorrow washed over him and he slumped onto the bed, grabbing the neatly placed blankets. With his eyes closed, the house, his room, the sheets all smelled of lilacs. Like his mother.

The graduation picture slipped from his hand easily, as if its callous and vindictive purpose was done.

Its glass shattered harshly on the hardwood floor. A violent snore echoed from his parents' room down the hall.

It was all so surreal; she was really gone. A stark reality he wasn't ready to face. Pulling the heavy comforter over him, he snuggled into the bed and let the sadness take him away.

Mitch wearily mumbled into the lilac-scented pillow. "I wanna go home, Mom."

In a few cold moments, the growling sounds of his snoring joined those of his father down the small hall.

Outside, the howling wind battered the Roberts' home and large lake-effect snowflakes assailed the small town, as if trying to get inside.

13

Bad Little Doggie

After a restless sleep, Mitch got out of the warm bed. He paused and realized that he had been under a heavy patchwork quilt. He didn't ever remember moving a muscle, let alone getting up for a blanket. His drowsy gaze turned to the half-opened door and the dark hallway beyond.

Shaking his head in hopes of shaking last night's torturous stagger down memory lane and this morning's sleepy cobwebs, he went to stand and suddenly recalled the shattered glass from the frame and yanked his legs back up.

"What the?" he said, as he saw that the shards of glass were gone. Cleaned up.

His father.

Mitch shook his head in an effort to wake up and to gather his wits about him.

His bags, which he'd left downstairs, and which he'd forgotten all about, were now on the side dresser that bore a sea of Marvel Comics stickers he'd stuck to the drawers as a kid.

Man, his father was pissed when he'd seen what Mitch had excitedly thought was cool and close to a piece of art. The Hulk, the Fantastic Four, Wolverine, Daredevil, and Iron Fist tumbled down the worn, laminated drawer fronts like animated morning cartoons.

Closer to a piece of shit, he could almost hear his father say.

He staggered to his bags, and sitting on top was a small sheet of yellow paper. Immediately, Mitch both smiled and grimaced.

It was from the same notepad his father used every morning before he left for work, to leave a note for Mitch.

As he picked up the hastily written note, a loud snowplow roared down the street, shaking the house. A distinct memory Mitch found both comforting and unnerving.

The yellow paper always had his father's orders on it, along with a promise of a heavy-handed reprisal.

Back in the day, it ranged from mowing the lawn, which Mitch could never do right, to weeding their small vegetable garden or washing the

Oldsmobile for whatever American Legion function was happening that night.

This time, the orders were simple:

Need milk, bread, peanut butter, sugar, coffee. Maxwell House. None of that fancy, pansy latte shit you city kids drink. Toilet paper and a twelver of Genny Cream Ale. I'm sure you can afford it now, Mr. New York Times Bestseller! - Dad

Mitch shook his head. "Of course." He tossed the note onto the bed and dug through his bags and set to taking a shower. But not before he dug through his laptop bag and forced himself to get at least a few words down in his new book. When he wasn't writing, it always left him feeling…off. Like an annoying itch inside him that could only be scratched when he put words to paper, or on his MacBook.

After all, writing was the only thing that had gotten him through all the crappy times in his life. How many times can you hear your drunk-off-his-ass father scream like a lunatic and slap your mom around, blaming her for every slight that had fallen upon him?

Mitch's passion was creativity. He found peaceful, inspiring neutrality in art. Art of all kinds. The written word, the visual arts, music. All of it spoke to him in ways that no living creature ever had or ever could. Art and creativity had saved him many times from tying a cinderblock to his sneakered foot and tossing it into Lake Ontario.

"Yay me," Mitch muttered as he got dressed and made his way downstairs, scribbled note in hand.

The house didn't look any better in the daylight. In fact, it was much worse.

It all seemed far more real now in the harsh, nearly blinding white light of the snow piling up outside.

The once pristine floors and countertops were now a grimy, muddy shadow of their former selves. What wasn't covered in take-out containers and empty beer boxes was under a layer of filth.

This wasn't the home he'd grown up in, nor one his anal-retentive father would have put up with. The old man was lost without her. Mitch knew he would be. Hell, so was he.

Pushing himself on, he threw his still-damp sneakers and jacket on and fought the snow to get out of the porch and onto the deep-covered sidewalk. Wherever it was.

The sun was barely a suggestion in the dark, brooding snow clouds, and his father must've been gone a while, because as Mitch walked out into the blowing and drifting snow, he spotted two deep snow tracks being slowly swallowed up.

"Bright and early, like always," he thought as he began the nearly forty-five-minute daunting job of excavating his car. Another reminder of why he hated living in western New York in the winter. After several harrowing attempts, one where he nearly ended up crashing through Chauncey's fence and burying his car in their front yard, he finally made it out of the driveway and onto the snow-packed street.

"For the love of God. That was fun," Mitch mumbled as he fought to stop the car from veering into the front end of an oncoming minivan that was driving too fast for the conditions, and which nearly took him out as it passed.

"Well, Roberts, now's your chance. You should go back, grab all your shit, toss it in the car, leave a note for your father, and get the hell out of Dodge before the really bad weather hits this dying town," he complained. "Swell."

Before the ink of his oscillating thoughts could dry, he found himself driving toward downtown, certain he could remember where the supermarket was, praying he wouldn't kill himself along the way. Or maybe hoping he would.

Turning on the radio, a familiar voice came through the crackling speakers:

"Hey, you kats and kittens. Dean-O here. How are you holding up out there in our winter wonderland?" The ever-cheerful voice of DJ Dean-O worked hard to over-sell his happiness. *"Yup, that was "The Season's Upon Us," another holiday classic for your Yuletide spirits. This groovy version was brought to you by the Irish stylings of those Celtic punks, Dropkick Murphys. Gotta love it. So, we've just received an update from the National Weather Service and it's not sounding too good, folks. Looks like the Lake Ontario snow machine is gearing up to join with Lake Erie in the next few hours, and by all accounts, we sure will be having one heck of a White Christmas all around western and central New York."* Dean-O chortled lightly.

"Dean-O, huh?" Mitch's mind pondered the voice. Maybe he's the guy he'd known back in school? He couldn't remember, and he gave up as the already slippery roads grew worse as he turned onto Main Street. It was packed and bustling with activity. Mitch wiped the inside of the fogged-up windshield and did his best not to ram into the bus in front of him.

"Note to self: if the royalty check is big enough, buy a new damn car. This sucks." Mitch struggled to see but caught bright lights on his left and a traffic jam of vehicles fighting to get in and out of the parking lot.

"This should be the P&C," Mitch said to no one, as he finally reached the parking lot and paused at the storefront. While there was a supermarket at the old P&C location, it was now Wegmans, a Rochester company that had been expanding for years in New York, Pennsylvania, and other parts of the country. "Huh, at least some sign of progress, I guess."

After an annoying eternity of shopping inside *The Hunger Games* meets *The Walking Dead*, Mitch had all the items on his dad's list and a little loose-leaf tea and pinwheel cookies for himself. He was pleasantly surprised there was any bread, milk, or toilet paper left. That never happened back in the day when a big snowstorm was forecasted. He was happy not to have run into anyone he knew, and let out an audible sigh as he reached his car and loaded everything inside.

"Nothing ever changes in this damn town," he said, shaking his head as he drove by the throng of people rushing in and out of the small grocery store. "If all else fails, buy more pizza, chicken wings, lottery tickets, and beer. That's bound to make your life better. Jesus Christ."

Mitch impatiently made his way through the tangled parking lot of oblivious white-hairs, unaware soccer moms, and self-absorbed idiots, and prayed for a zombie apocalypse as he shouted a world of obscenities inside the safe confines of his late-model Honda.

Now that he'd made it out of the pre-Christmas madhouse, Mitch tried to get his bearings and chastised himself for not remembering where Yowner's Tavern was. He should have had the route burned into his tortured psyche, especially after the black Christmas Eve of 1988, where his dad had taken him Christmas shopping for his mom, and they'd stopped into Yowner's for a quick holiday beer and ended up missing Christmas Eve dinner with Mitch's grandparents.

He thought back to how upset his mom had been, and how his father, drunk as a skunk, had blamed her for planning dinner too early and then stormed back out into the wintry night. Mitch had spent the rest of the night in his room, reading and crying into his pillow as his poor mother wept while she cleaned up and prepared for Santa's visit downstairs.

A loud noise came from the left. Something ran in front of him, and he slammed on his brakes and cranked the wheel to the right. His car spun sideways and crashed into a four-foot snowbank. His head smacked into the driver's side window and a bright flash of white light filled his vision.

"What the…?" Mitch tried to clear his head, and a throbbing pain rose in his temples. "What the hell was that?" He heard a dog barking loudly and looked around to find a huge dog sitting on top of the large snowbank. It looked like a wolf with its pointed ears and shaggy long black-and-gray fur. It wore a large collar, from which hung a long leash. It didn't seem mean; in fact, it sat on top of the snow pile like a king, but its long pink tongue hung out as if he were smiling at Mitch.

"What the hell?" he said through the windshield, as if the dog would answer him.

A young woman with long strawberry-blonde hair and an ankle-length wool coat came rushing toward him from across the street. "I'm so sorry, sir! Are you okay?"

Mitch opened the door and stumbled out of the banged-up car.

"I'm sorry. He's just so strong and he loves this weather and…" Mitch heard her gasp, and he looked up, still trying to clear his aching head.

"Mitch? Is that you?" The woman's voice and face seemed familiar.

Then it hit him with a ferocious punch to the gut. He knew exactly who she was.

"Um, Beth?" He slowly made his way toward his old school friend.

She ran over and grabbed him in a deep embrace. She squeezed him so tight it took his breath away and almost hurt. He returned the hug, and it felt good. After all these years, he'd forgotten how much he had missed her.

"It's so good to see you!" Beth whispered in his ear. She continued to hold him as the snow poured down as though a million bags of flour had been opened above the earth.

"It's great to see you too, Beth," he said, squeezing her tighter.

"I'm so sorry about your mom." She pulled her head back to look at him and smiled wide. "I take it you just got into town?"

"Thank you. Yeah, I got the call from my dad, and I left straight away." He had forgotten how beautiful Beth was. Standing there in the snowy street, with cars honking all around them, he felt himself slipping back in time.

A long, silent moment passed as they stared into each other's eyes and a loud, deep bark shook them from their trance. They both jumped and laughed.

"Pablo, get down here," she said through laughter, letting go of Mitch and motioning for the dog to come.

"Ah, so that behemoth belongs to you, huh?" Mitch watched as the dog hopped down from the snowbank onto the hood of his car, then ran over to its master. The dog jumped up onto Mitch, knocking him down into the road.

"Oh, Pablo, get off of him," Beth laughed, and the dog started licking Mitch's face.

He noticed a tenseness from Beth, as though she was afraid to laugh. As if someone were watching. Mitch lay there as the dog's tongue-lashing continued.

Mitch said, "It's okay. It's the most action I've gotten in decades." Despite the betrayal and the pain from that night, he felt a wide smile grow on his face and an old, familiar warmth grow in his chest.

"It's really so good to see you. I wish it wasn't such a horrible occasion," Beth said.

Then their reunion was cut short by an all too familiar voice.

"What's so funny?" Tony Severt stepped out of the sheriff's car and walked toward them. His confident swagger changed to one of hostility once he realized who it was that Beth was helping up from the ground.

"Swell," Mitch mumbled, all the air and energy draining from his body. It was a voice he'd hoped never to hear again. Even worse, that lying, stupid face.

Yet, here he was.

Mitch started praying again; this time, he hoped God would strike him dead right there on the spot.

"Well, well, well, look who finally decided to grace this old nowhere town with his big city presence," Officer Anthony Severt said, eyeing Mitch up and down.

Beth lowered her head and shifted away from them.

"Uhm…oh, Tony." Mitch fumbled for words, getting to his feet, wiping himself down. His smile and laughter fell away with the falling snow. "It's good to see you too," he lied.

Tony's broad face offered the same old arrogant smirk that Mitch remembered well.

Large lake-effect snow was piling up on his "Smokey the Bear" trooper hat, and Mitch desperately fought the urge to knock that damn arrogance off his face.

A sudden, overwhelming rage rekindled within him, like an old furnace kicking on for the first time, and he could feel his face and ears grow hot. He swore he could almost hear the melting snow hiss as it fell onto his skin. But, as the nearly six-inch taller shadow stood over him, the fire was pushed down as the familiar old blanket of self-doubt and insecurity quickly replaced the anger.

"So, it took your mother to die to finally bring you back here? Pretty sad, Roberts, but hey, that's always been you." He leaned in, the hard brim of his hat pressing Mitch's wet forehead. "Predictable, and just damn sad."

Clenching his fists into tight balls, Mitch turned his face away as his old friend's coffee-and-whiskey breath filled the air.

As they stood there in the freezing, snowy street, Mitch realized he'd envisioned this moment many a time. Nightmares, in fact, of what he would do if he were ever to see his old best friend again.

Would he man up, as his father would always demand of him, and finally confront Tony for the damage and hurt he'd caused? Try to beat an apology from him? Or would he at least shout and scream at Tony, unleashing all those years of anger, confusion, resentment, and betrayal from his soul, finally finding closure?

The memories and nightmares, the wishful thinking lasted several minutes in Mitch's pressurized, racing mind; in reality, it was mere seconds.

Mitch just stood there, his typical man-of-inaction thoughts ever oscillating, once again, letting fear win the day.

"Tony, come on, knock it off. Don't you have a job to do?" Beth finally said, stepping between the two men. They continued to stare at one another over her head.

"Please, just go," she pleaded.

"No worries, Beth. I'm… I need to find my father," Mitch said through gritted teeth, finally shaking himself free of his thoughts. Turning, he saw the big dog rush between Beth and Tony, and he began growling, glaring up at the big cop.

With an all-too-familiar burning anger inside him, he walked to his car and got in, slamming the door.

Mitch didn't even look back at them. The walls of the small car shrank and the vise-like pressure in his chest combined with the pounding of his pulse in his temples, telling him to leave. And leave now.

"Oh, I'm sure you can find his drunk ass over at Yowner's. It's about time for his liquid lunch. Practically lives there anyway," Tony said, almost laughing at the words. He pulled his gray hat down and winked at Mitch. "And hey... You don't get to call her that anymore. Should have stayed in the big city, buddy. Nobody wants ya here anyway, *best friend*." Officer Severt's sarcasm dripped from his tongue like poison from a blade. And the words found their target.

"Why don't you shut up?!" Beth let out, and many of the scurrying townspeople stopped at the sound of her shouting.

The car clunked loudly in reverse, and it lurched from the snowbank. Mitch cranked the wheel and looked out the window at Beth and Tony standing there together, and his heart wept. *Nothing has changed in twenty years,* he thought. *I should have stayed home.* He jammed the car in gear and drove around them, catching a glance at Beth. For a second, he thought he could see tears streaming down her cheeks, but he blamed it on all the snow carpeting the town.

Mitch made his way to Yowner's Tavern. His father's second home.

He remembered the way all too well.

14

Seeing Things for the First Time.

"But, babe, he's a piece of trash. He was back in school, and he still is now. Why do you still defend him?" Tony's imposing frame loomed large before her, as always. Beth ignored him and stepped back toward Pablo, who was fast approaching.

"Don't you dare '*Babe*' me! Just… Go… Just go, I need to get some things before the storm fully buries us." She glared at him with a fiery stare that could've melted a tank, grabbed Pablo by the leash, and headed for the bustling supermarket. The crowd was ebbing and flowing like the evening tide on Lake Ontario's beaches.

Pablo's howls filled Main Street as all the panicked shoppers made their way to their homes to await the storm.

"Whatever. You know I'm damn right about him. I don't want you to talk to that loser. You hear me?"

Beth kept stalking toward the store.

"Whatever. Shouldn't you be out keeping the roads safe? Or banging your whore?" she added, losing herself in the crowd.

Some fights just weren't worth fighting.

Seeking to catch her breath, warm up, and process what had just happened between Mitch and Tony in the street, Beth walked through the violent, wind-whipped parking lot and into Wegmans Supermarket, where the final refrain of Mariah Carey's "All I Want for Christmas" welcomed her and Pablo as they entered the madness of the store. Beth shopped quickly, Pablo at her side. It wasn't too difficult, considering most of the "staples" were already wiped out. In truth, she didn't need much in the way of supplies; it was more of an excuse to get away from her jerk of a husband. Pablo had been her best friend in the world since she'd brought him home from Lollypop Farm. He'd kept her safe and from feeling completely lonely when she found out about Tony's "extra-curricular" activities. She walked aimlessly through the crowded aisles, looking at nothing, and absent-mindedly threw a few random items into her basket. Pablo began to growl, and his hackles stood up on end. He froze.

"What is it, buddy?"

He continued to growl and stared directly behind her. She turned to find Tony standing there, glaring at her.

It took all she had to keep the dog from going after him. "Pablo, back!" she ordered, and he backed off. But only a little.

"You best get control of that damn thing before…" Tony slowly reached for his sidearm.

"Before what? You'll shoot him just like Boots?" Beth's words could have cut the state trooper into pieces. "Oh, that's right, you're a big bad cop, nobody can mess with you, isn't that right, Tony?"

She caressed Pablo's head and muzzle and he let out a low growl.

"Come on now, babe, let's not go backward. I told you that the old lab had distemper. You know damn well I was sorry, now let's just get you home and we can…" Tony stepped closer, and Pablo lunged at his groin. He jumped back, grasping at his service revolver again. The nearby customers scattered as fast as possible to other parts of the packed store.

Beth rushed forward and shoved a thin, pale finger in his uniformed chest. "Again…stop with the '*babe*' bullshit, Tony. You've been screwing around on me since high school, and I looked the other way. I'll be damned if I will be made a fool of *ever* again. You are an arrogant piece of shit!" Pablo gnashed his huge white teeth and tried to get to the cause of his human's pain. She held him back. This battle was hers, and hers alone. She pushed forward, jamming her finger repeatedly into her husband's chest. Tony stepped back, taking all the verbal and physical blows. He backpedaled into a pyramid of toilet paper, and it came crashing down around him. Beth stopped, stared at all the tissue piled up around him, and began to laugh.

"Wow, how fitting." She tugged on Pablo's leash, and they made their way to the checkout. Pablo wagged his tail, and his long, pink tongue seemed to laugh at State Trooper Severt, standing knee-deep in Charmin.

Beth and her furry best friend suddenly felt much better as they walked out into a wall of white. The parking lot and Main Street were slowly being devoured into looming darkness. Suddenly, Beth knew she needed to get home. Her first thought was…

Mitch!

She tugged Pablo's leash, and they headed south toward Yowner's. The snow kept coming, and night was coming with it. Pablo stopped and tilted his wolf-like head. He cocked his ear upward and sniffed the early evening air.

"What you hearing, P?" Beth asked, kneeling in the deep snow on Main Street. As she concentrated, her already pale face grew white as bone. She could hear it too.

"Let's get going."

Yowner's Tavern was just down the street a little way. Sterling Point wasn't a big town, and despite the horrific weather, she and Pablo could make it with no problem at all. But she estimated that at least one foot of fresh snow had fallen since they'd let school out.

Pablo had a fun time running playfully through the deep snow, but Beth's feet were getting cold. The temperature was dropping more and more as the storm clouds crept closer, and it seemed like the tavern grew farther away as she went.

As she crossed the slick street, she saw the headlights of a black-and-gray police car of probably the last town cop in all of Wayne County. The car came slowly up and slid to a stop at the intersection.

The tinted window slid down. "Afternoon, Mrs. Severt." The chilled chin and nearly perfect smile of Sterling Point's only police officer greeted Beth. A tiny shadow beside the big cop popped his head through and immediately Beth felt exhausted.

Pablo barked and let loose a small snarl.

"Officer Notebaert." She bent a little to see the small man in the shadow of the car. "Mr. Mayor." Beth felt the slack on Pablo's leash tighten, and she tried to pull him back.

"You should be careful on the streets. They are getting a bit greasy," Officer Notebaert said with a slight smile.

"I will," Beth said, yanking the big dog away from the car's window. "You doing escort duty for the mayor now?" She realized that may have come across more uncouth than she'd intended.

The mayor laughed and said, "Well, as a matter of fact, yes. My old eyes aren't quite what they used to be, I'm afraid. That, and we're taking some holiday presents over to Sunnyside Manor for the old folks, then heading over to the American Legion for their Toys-for-Tots fundraiser."

Uh huh. "Holiday" gifts? Beth noted the smarmy politician's word choice, trying hard to ignore the almost unbearable weather.

"Are you going to Mrs. Roberts' funeral?" The gaunt mayor's face broke into a cordial, yet very creepy wide grin—as if the Joker had devoured the Cheshire Cat. "Of course we are, dear Mrs. Severt. It's the very least we could do to honor such a wonderful woman. After all, she was a saint to be sure, enduring life with such a grumpy curmudgeon such as Gordon. Am I right?"

The sheriff shifted in his seat, growing more uncomfortable by the frozen second. "Good. That's nice to hear, Mayor. You too, Sheriff." She pulled the furry hood closer to her face, as Pablo was fighting to eat the tasty morsels inside the police cruiser.

"Is Mitchell coming home?" The mayor's question was obviously orchestrated to elicit a response. "It would be so wonderful to see Sterling Point's own Stephen King come home." His harsh, angular face looked as if it could slice into the sheriff's thick leather jacket, as the old mayor leaned in to look at Beth.

Pablo yanked her hard into the cutting wind; the furry beast was obviously done with them. "Coming, boy," Beth shouted through the worsening storm. "Last I heard, yes. Gotta go, gentlemen. It's not fit for man nor beasts out here." She nodded and tromped away in a gallop and the ninety-pound malamute was about to take her for a ride into the wild white yonder.

"Happy Holidays, Mrs. Severt!" She barely heard the mayor's screechy words as she briskly tromped through the deep snow toward Yowner's Tavern.

Once she entered the bar, she knew she had to call Mitch. He was surely freaking out after Tony pulled his typical macho, tough guy with a gun and badge routine. Mitch deserved better, and after seeing him in the flesh after all these years, a strange warmth filled her, and she felt herself smile, genuinely, for the first time in a very, very long time.

15

Blue Christmas

"Fucking asshole!" Mitch screamed, punching the steering wheel as he drove slowly down the snow-covered Main Street. His body shook and his heart fluttered as if it were melting. The windows fogged up and blocked his visibility even more. The white wall surrounded him and appeared to be closing in. "'Oh, I'm a big tough cop now.' Who the hell do you think you are, you…?" His words caught in his throat. Sweat ran down his face, his knuckles turning white as he strangled the steering wheel. "She was your mom too, you backstabbing prick! Hell, you practically grew up at our house!" The car seemed to shrink, and the spasm of pain came in a burst that felt like fire, burning him from the inside out.

"Okay, Roberts, get your shit together. This storm's coming. Fuck Severt, fuck Christmas, and fuck this Podunk town." He gulped for air, and he finally felt his lungs expand and the tension in his chest wane. "You just need to get through the funeral and get the hell out of here. Go *home*, where you belong. You are a bestselling author, you dumbass." He let go of a small chuckle. Mitch knew something had forced it, but he didn't care.

He absently took one turn after another, feeling the need to just *drive* as his body shook with spasms and tears streamed down his face.

Absently again, he took a right, then a left-hand turn, not caring where he was going. He needed to get as far away from Beth and Tony as possible.

INTERLUDE

Even in the harsh daylight, the Darkness' emanating power swallowed, consumed all around it, its immense twisting, deadly, evil form devouring all living things within a half-mile radius and growing unforgivingly, exponentially with each unfortunate soul it assimilated.

There were no signs of wildlife. Not anymore.

All gone. Eaten. Their souls, no matter how small, tiny, barely detectable, now part of this ancient, malevolent creature that the once-brave Seneca tribes' most powerful shaman and warriors had sacrificed their lives to entrap in that cave.

But now it was free and still starving.

The Darkness sensed the flesh and blood and the souls of the humans who had freed it.

And stole what belonged to it.

And it wanted to thank them for its glorious freedom.

The Darkness' insatiable hunger drove it on through the winter storm.

16
Family Tradition

Millstone Glen, NY

"What's with using the rock-salt shells?" Caleb Oque asked amidst the raucous laughter of the hunting cabin.

"Wolves..." Royce said.

Caleb chewed on that for a moment. "Why not just kill the damn things?"

Royce sipped his whiskey. "Son, we were hunting deer, not those scavengers. No need for killin'. Rock salt just hurts them a bit and scatters them away. No use in wasting good buckshot."

"Ah, I see." the kid nodded. "Smart."

"I didn't live this long, son, being stupid." Royce winked.

One of the hunters joined in. "Hell yes. Did ya see the way the furry fleabag flipped ass-over-tea-kettle when I hit the bitch with the rock salt? Funny as shit." His slurred words told Royce all he needed to know about the young guy.

"Ah, come on now, you couldn't hit a bull in the ass with a snow shovel if you were inside and the goddamned door was closed!" Royce Pritchard laughed and took a long sip from his Jack Daniels bottle. The rest of the hunters erupted in raucous, lemming-like laughter at Caleb's— the newbie's—expense, as the old patriarch held court.

The kid fell silent and shifted on his rickety chair at the long table and sipped his beer, hoping his blushing cheeks weren't showing. The rest of the hunting party carried on drinking and laughing.

"Hey, kid. Don't let ol' Royce bust yer balls too much. He's got more shit than Carter had liver pills. Hell, I remember back when we were kids and went out deer hunting for the first time..." Big Bobb-O Babcock chortled, his rotund belly bouncing. "We were camping out in old Wickham's orchard. Oh, lordy. When he spotted his first buck, he nearly pissed himself." He could barely finish as he broke into a laughing, coughing fit. The hunters all burst out laughing, until Royce shot them a fiery glare of warning.

The group abruptly fell silent, letting their attention turn to their drinks, and gazed at the worn pine planks of the cabin as Denny Pritchard let out a little chuckle. The elder Pritchard responded with a quick backhand to his stunned son's face.

"Watch your sass, boy, and you shut the fuck up, fat man; I can still whoop your big old ass all over these here woods, five foot o' snow or not," Royce said, never leaving his perch at the head of the table. He glared at his youngest boy, who was holding his red cheek, but addressed everyone at the table. The old man was making sure they understood his message.

Gently sipping his whiskey, Royce looked around the table, gauging the reactions from all the other hunters. This was the kid's first hunting trip, and these guys were all well known for their grand hunting exploits, and he could appreciate that. But he didn't want the kid getting any crazy ideas on the pecking order here; Royce Pritchard demanded respect. Even though he and Babcock were the old timers and the same age, Royce's sons, Mike and Denny, had been hunting since they could barely walk. Then there was Johnny Cadigan, the wise-cracking blackjack dealer, Royce meet years ago down in Jersey. Alicia Samms was Bruce's niece and more manly than most of the rednecks sitting at the table, Royce had always thought. He didn't know much about the other hunters—Ken O'Cleary, Lucas Briggs. They sat drinking at the far end of the table and laughed whenever he made some kind of joke, good or bad—mostly bad.

Royce took a long sip of his whiskey and continued watching over his inebriated flock.

"That was one helluva shot ya had on that big sumbitch today, Roy," Kenny said, raising his whiskey bottle in salute.

"Thanks, Ken, like a fish in a damn barrel." Royce sat back into his tall-backed chair. He let out a loud belch and wiped his mouth with his sleeve, his oversized dentures glistening in the light from the fireplace.

"Hell yes!" came a wail from the table.

"What about that weird cave it went down into?" Denny's voice nervously cracked.

"Yeah, I dunno." Royce paused.

"Maybe it was an old bear den, or some shit, up top that ridge." Big Bruce leaned in, a huge grin on his wide, rosy face.

Denny added, "It was really weird, man. There was a shit-ton of bones and a bunch of jewelry, arrowheads, and other India—"

Royce shot a sharp glance at his son over his thick bifocals.

"Oh, damn, boy. Ya gotta be pie-eyed already. Not one of ya would know a goddamn bear if it jumped out of a tree and bit ya in your sorry asses. But yeah, it looked like a dumping ground for asshole poachers. I sure as hell wish I'd caught those bastards. They left the meat and just took the furs. If I'd had the chance, they'd be paying in the lead-price, I fucking tell ya. So why don't y'all quit flappin' your gums and get to drinking." Royce never took his eyes off Denny.

"Hey, son, why don't you fix your old man another whiskey?"

"Yes, sir." Denny got up and headed for the kitchen.

Royce felt a deep rage burn inside his gut and grabbed his glass.

"Um, yeah, Roy, are ya sure that was a—" Jim started to ask.

"Keep drinking, boys. Don't listen to 'em. Boy never could handle his booze anyhow. I'll be right back." Royce stood and followed his son into the kitchen. The old alpha male's gait was purposeful and swift for a man his age; Jim and the others knew better than to ask any more questions about Royce Pritchard.

Once in the kitchen and out of sight and earshot from the other half-drunk cabin mates, Royce approached his son, who was reaching into the lower cupboard for the whiskey. He grabbed his son by his long ponytail and jerked him around, pinning him against the cupboards. Royce grabbed him by the throat and squeezed.

"Now listen here, I don't want those motherfuckers knowing anything about what I found out there. Do you understand me, boy?" Royce brought up a ten-inch Bowie knife to Denny's throat.

"P-pops, I…didn't say—" Denny tried to squeak out.

"No more talking. Just listen. Hear me? Just shut the hell up and let me make this perfectly clear. Just in case you can't get it through your thick head, nobody can know anything about all the bones, jewelry, and coins, or any of that Indian bullshit. Understand?" Royce pulled his son down onto his knees and lightly slipped the shiny blade across Denny's quivering throat. A light trickle of blood ran down onto his brown flannel shirt. His son shook his head in agreement with wide, tear-filled eyes.

Royce wiped the blade on Denny's shirt, grabbed the whiskey bottle out of his hand, and leaned in close.

"That's a lot of money to be had. And ya know, I need as much as I can get. And if there's anything left over, I'll give you a little. But if you ever say one damn thing to anyone about *my* treasure, I will gut you like that buck hanging from the tree outside. Comprende, boy?" Spittle landed on Denny's nose and mixed with his blood as it ran down and crept under his shirt.

Royce left his trembling behemoth of a son crying on the kitchen floor like a blubbering child, nothing new for the Pritchard family. The laughter resumed as Royce entered the main room brandishing the new bottle of Jack.

"Come on, ya pantywaists. Who wants to do a shot with the old man?" Royce's tone and mood shifted as quickly as the biting winter wind outside, and he was met with a rousing round of laughter and cheers.

Except for Denny's cute but pissed-off-looking girlfriend. Alicia had been giving Royce a heavy stink-eye all the way into the kitchen and stayed right fixed on him as he made his way back to his captain's chair at the head of the table.

"What's wrong with you, girl? Ain't never seen a father having a moment with his boy?" Royce chuckled, glaring.

Alicia didn't respond. She glared at the old man as he sipped his whiskey.

"Whoa, girl, don't get your pretty pink panties in a pinch, I ain't keepin' his big ass. He's all yours, honey." Royce topped off his over-the-top misogyny with a sharp wink and a wry smile. Then he took a long, teasing pull from the bottle.

Alicia ignored him and kicked her chair back and joined Denny in the kitchen.

Royce's analyzing gaze followed the hot young woman as she went to tend to the boy. *He could do better. But if I were thirty years younger, and not married...* He took a second to imagine the things a much younger Royce could do with a piece of meat like that. He chuckled into the bottle as he took a small sip and turned his attention back to the hooting and hollering hunters drinking before him.

Just then, the radio had just finished Charley Pride's "White Christmas in my Hometown" when the National Weather Service broke in.

"Attention all occupants of the Western and Central New York region. This is a severe storm warning in effect for the next forty-eight to seventy-two hours. We advise everyone to stay indoors. A no unnecessary travel order will be in effect. Expect heavy snowfall over two feet an hour. We expect the temperatures to be in the single digits working well into the minuses: twenty below zero. Do not go outside, and bring animals indoors."

The radio made the shrill alert signal; then a sultry female voice came back on. "Well, here we go, my friends, looks like a snowed-in Christmas for us. I hope everyone stays safe, and you might as well enjoy the cozy family time. Now, before I'm out of here, let me leave you with one of my favorite holiday tunes. Be safe." The opening note to "Grandma Got Run Over by a Reindeer" was cut off as Royce turned it all the way down.

"Well, boys, looks like we're gonna have to cut our trip short. Normally shitty weather doesn't bother me, but something tells me this is a snowstorm of a different kind. Drink up now, but we had best get a couple hours of shut-eye before we head back to Sterling Point in the morning. We should get there just before this sumbitch hits us full-on." He didn't wait for a response and headed to the only bedroom in the cabin, taking his bottle with him.

* * *

"Good night, asshole," Denny murmured from the kitchen. He sat on the cold floor and sobbed. He never could please his old man, no matter what he did. He pulled another bottle from the cupboard and took a long swig. He nearly spat it out as Alicia walked around the corner.

"What the hell ya doing on the floor, Den?" Alicia came to him and squatted down, grabbed the bottle from his hands, and took a massive gulp.

"The old man up to his old shit again?" She wiped her winter camouflage sleeve across her face and took another sip, then handed the bottle back.

"Yeah, no big deal." Denny tried to force a tone of confidence. He drank. She could see right through it and sat down next to him.

"When are ya gonna grow a pair and kick the shit outta him?"

"But he's my dad, Alicia." He turned toward her slowly and leaned into her.

"I know, ya big pansy, but one of these days he's gonna be the death of you. And I wouldn't want to kill the old piece of shit." She kissed him deeply and wrapped her arms around him. They both laughed and fell into one another, and before long, slipped into a deep sleep.

A few drunken hours later, the rest of the hunters decided Royce was right and went to their cots, which lined the walls, and climbed in their sleeping bags without a word.

Snow piled up outside as the bottles piled up inside. The half-drunk, slumbering hunters didn't care. This was a once-in-a-lifetime hunting day and would keep them warm for many years to come. The victorious glow lit up the entire cabin.

Meanwhile, Royce wrote down on a pad the exact location of the cave and his awaiting lottery ticket. He fell asleep with a warm glow all his own and dreamed of how he was going to spend all that glorious money waiting for him up in the cold cave.

17
I Need to See You Again

The house smelled of freshly brewed coffee and home-baked sugar cookies.

Beth was on her third cup and second batch as the soft refrains of Norah Jones' voice filled the warm kitchen.

It'd been a rough night of sleep; the old house was cold, and the turbulent thoughts of the day's events with Mitch and Tony caused her once-expensive mattress to feel like a bed of poisoned needles.

So, she did what any exhausted, confused over-thinker would do: get up way too early and make Christmas cookies and nearly overdose on delicious baking and breakfast blend.

As she put the next round of holiday goodies into the oven, she looked out the picture window in the living room, where they usually set up the Christmas tree.

The once warm and inviting room, lit up by all her favorite tree lights and the glowing fire in the hearth; now the ambient blue glow of the early morning snow piling up outside was the only light coming into the dark room.

As she sipped, Norah finished and Billy Squire twanged about how "Christmas is the Time to Say I Love You," and Beth nearly snarfed the coffee.

It was one of Mitch's favorite songs from back in the day.

She recognized the irony.

Sure, he has issues, but who doesn't? she thought.

He made her laugh. More than anyone ever had. And he had a quirky outlook on life and would always tell her, "Get out of this Podunk town. You're better than it. We're better than it! I have to live life full, ya know!"

Beth thought he was speaking more to himself than to her, but she understood.

The inspiring sentiment had Mitch's mom's writing all over it. She was an amazing woman.

The slideshow of memories sent her down a nostalgic rabbit hole, from which only the smell of burning cookies and smoke alarm could awaken her.

"Oh, shit!" She yanked the cookies from the oven, tossing the sheet onto the stovetop, frantically fanning the smoke away and trying to remember where the damn smoke alarm was —

Her new Wally World cellphone rang.

Mitch?

It was Sheldon—her wayward student. She had her hands full, opening the window to let the smoke out, and then nearly breaking her neck climbing onto a chair to shut off the smoke alarms. She'd call him back later.

It was awfully early. Beth hoped the lonely boy was okay.

With the baking fiasco under control, she reached for her phone and listened to the young boy's low voice. Thankfully, he seemed safe. Just sad, lost. She would call him back once the smoke had cleared, and she'd let Pablo back in, who was frolicking in the deepening winter wonderland.

Dumping the burnt cookies into the garbage with her iPhone still in hand, something came over her. She wasn't sure what it was, but it came in a flurry.

The tangled feelings that had been brewing up inside her. Increasing since she kicked Tony out. Since she heard about Mitch's mom's passing, and him coming home. Seeing him.

His goofy smile and sillier laugh. Those dorky Buddy Holly glasses that he'd worn way before they became one of the hipster trademarks.

Within seconds, she called Mitch.

He answered in a groggy, yawning second. "Hey."

She froze.

"Hello?"

"Hey, sleepyhead. It's Beth. I hate to be calling this early, but..."

Mitch coughed. "It's okay, I got my usual four hours." A zombie-like giggle came through.

"Sorry. It's just that I feel terrible the way things...with what To—"

"It's okay. I get it."

"Well..." Beth took a breath. "How about a Christmas peace offering?"

"What's that?"

"Remember that old Italian restaurant we used to work at back when we were at school?" Beth's words rang apprehensively.

"Ummm…uh, yeah. Bonetti's, right? Up on Lake Road still?"

"Yeah. I'm going to treat you to dinner…tonight. If you're free, that is?"

A cold pause.

"Uh, yeah, sure. Let me check with my dad first. Just to make sure he doesn't need anything," Mitch said. "Lord knows I don't need to piss him off again."

Sharp "It's too cold even for me" barks replaced Pablo's playful howls.

"Is that your Sasquatch of a dog I hear?" Mitch asked.

Beth forced a little chuckle. "Yup. Guessing he's finally ready to come in."

"Best let Chewbacca in, then."

"I will. Is seven good tonight?" She hated the excitement and neediness she could hear in her voice.

"Should be. Again, I'll get with Dad this morning. I'll text you."

"Sounds great. See ya then, Mitchie." She disconnected.

Her heart and mind were starting a war inside her. Anger and resentment versus laughter and warmth.

"Bethel Marie Connolly, you sound like a silly seventh-grade schoolgirl. Jesus." She admonished herself and let the mountain-sized snowball known as Pablo inside.

18
Back Where it All Began

The out-of-nowhere phone call from Beth left him adrift on a rolling sea of confusion and bewilderment.

Waking up from a fury of dreams in his old bedroom after more than a decade and all the nightmarish dreams of the day before with his dad, Beth, and...*Tony*. It was a lot to wrap his head around.

Mitch's fight-or-flight response had already been on duty since he'd fought to pack his suitcase back in Brooklyn. A nasty battle he'd nearly lost many, many times. And the jury was still out.

The anger, the hesitation, caused him to sweat, and his muscles tensed with every mile his old car took westward.

He'd told her that yes, he'd go to dinner with her, without any thought. A gut reaction. Just like it used to be. Always was. Mitch hated that side of himself.

He was a lifetime people-pleaser. The very thought of disappointing someone was unbearable. His mom, his dad, were people he never could please. His friends, Tony, Beth. It didn't matter.

Mitch was sadly very aware of his multitude of unsympathetic foibles.

It was that nasty, curled up, omnipresent gargoyle on his shoulder, making sure he never forgot his place.

Now he wished he'd let the damn call go to voicemail, like he did all the annoying calls he didn't want to deal with.

But, alas, the early light crept through the thin veil of curtain his mom had sewn on the three windows dominating the room. And he called Bonetti's-on-the-Lake and made the reservation. Like a good boy.

Then Mitch got up. Despite the night-owl habit he'd loved for the past...since forever, he gave in.

The old wooden floors were cold, nearly painful; they sent stabbing chills up his legs.

He went to the windows and peered out into the darkness of Sterling Point. A few faint streetlights offered a little light, but the whipping wind and snow made the tall, thin lamps seem meek and defeated.

The snow pelted the old lead-glass windows, reminding Mitch that he really hated it here. And why he desperately needed to take care of things and get back to Brooklyn as soon as humanly possible.

But as he took in his old bedroom, everything began to overcome him.

The maps of Middle-Earth and the Forgotten Realms intermingled with his own bad gaming maps and character sketches. "No wonder I stuck with writing." Mitch shook his head.

The heavily detailed, colored-pencil map of X-World that their hyper-creative dungeon master, Chris, had played them through from seventh grade to their senior year.

It wasn't those amazing memories that caught Mitch's attention.

It was the heavy old Olympic typewriter hidden under a Rush t-shirt and a thick layer of over a decade's dust that pulled his teary eye away.

For one brilliant, brief flash of time, he wasn't the Mitch of nearly thirty; he found himself in the fantasy land of his youth, filtered by his best wishful thinking.

On the well-worn desk that his mom had rescued from a local school sat the typewriter she had given him his first writing lesson on.

His fingers impulsively twitched as if typing, and he chuckled aloud. The echo startled him in the pre-dawn darkness.

Maybe it was reading the book on monsters, maybe it was being back home again, but there was something he'd learned early: when that pesky blessing and a curse of a plucky and cantankerous muse—which he'd named *Roxy*—whispered to you, you heeded the temperamental mistress's call.

In a flash, he rummaged through the drawers of the weathered old desk. Old comic books, notepads full of truncated ideas. Unread hate notes to his father. He flipped past them but paused when he found a thick manila folder filled with a stack of unsent love letters to Beth. They filled an entire drawer, wrapped in papers filled with lists upon lists and day-to-day monotony. In the third drawer he found a stack of his father's old American Legion stationary and set it up against his lost cast-iron friend, the Olympia.

The wind outside howled and fought to penetrate the old Roberts' house, but Mitch paid no heed. No, within minutes, he was lost in the overwhelming rush of creation. The first chapter of the new novel appeared out of thin, albeit freezing, air.

"Huzzah," Mitch said low. It rarely happened like that… It was usually a pulling teeth or cutting his metaphorical wrists and letting them stain the blank page kind of thing, but not now. The words came as easily as the falling snow outside.

The new book, like a gift from the literary gods, appeared to him in bright flashes and inspirational violent pulls. Witches in North Carolina. Native Americans and Civil War broken allegiances and demons. Mitch felt as if on fire as the spirit coursed through him, as if he was just the lucky conduit.

He needed some words in a foreign language—Latin—as well as something in one of the indigenous languages. He didn't dare stop typing, but knowing his creative time at Chateau Hell was limited—gods willing—he feared forgetting before returning to Brooklyn.

Frantically reaching for his iPhone, he found it and opened the *LinguaScan* application and input the words he was trying to add to the novel.

He laughed out loud as within seconds, the $1.99 app he'd read about in a Horror Writers Association blog saved him hours of research and provided an exact translation, which he quickly added to his first draft.

"Hot damn," he spouted, and for one split second, he was happy.

In a heated, old-school exchange of fingers flying, Mitch typed out ten pages in the blink of an eye. They came out in a nearly erotic bliss as his words filled the blank paper, only stopping when a hard, three-pattern knock on the door nearly caused him to fall off his rickety office chair.

"Hey, Mitch, it's Chris."

"Damn it!" His words bounced off the icy walls. "What? Damn it!" Mitch scrambled for an answer, finding his footing and composure again. Going back to this world after being in the "zone," as he called it, was like dreaming fiercely within a pitch-black room, then being yanked—or better yet, thrown—into a dazzlingly bright room.

The voice came from the other side of his bedroom door again.

"Hey, it's me, Chris Delaney…Your dad let me in," came an old voice through the worn door. "If it's a bad time, I can come back later or text you?"

Mitch staggered to his feet and shook his head to transition from the sometimes overpowering and creative mind to the mere muggle life of the mundane. "Hey, man," he said, opening the door and smiling at the sight of his old friend. "No. No. It's okay. Give me a second."

"Took you long enough. Are you looking at *Lord of the Rings* porn again?" Chris said, a smile on his face.

Chris looked about the same he had when Mitch left: his ever-present digital camera was hanging around his neck and he still wore the same beat-up, second-hand leather jacket with the Iron Maiden, Tool, Rush, and Slayer patches sewn on it, but today, his friend was sporting a vintage Britney Spears t-shirt.

"Britney, huh?" Mitch shook his head and offered a wide embrace.

"Always got to represent, yo," Chris laughed, taking Mitch into a powerful hug.

"Always? Really? Guess if ya *got* to. So great to see you again!"

"Always, man," Chris said, letting him go and stepping into the room. "Damn, you could use a shave. You look like Seth Rogen on a two-week bender of Red Bull and cocaine."

Mitch didn't know how to respond. He absently scratched his thick, scruffy beard.

"Thanks. That's the exact look I was going for. I tried the rugged superhero look, but I guess it wasn't for me," was all he heard his stupid mouth respond. He felt like he always said the wrong thing. He knew—or at least hoped—he was a smart guy, but there were times, more than he dared admit, when he felt like maybe he'd taken too many beatings from his father, and his engine wasn't able to fire on all cylinders, or at least they were firing in the wrong order. It took him a bit to connect things sometimes and made him feel…inept.

After a moment, Mitch let go. "Come in, man."

Wide-eyed, Chris took in the old room. "Wow. Not much has changed, bro. It's like a time capsule."

Mitch left the door open and forced a laugh. "No. I guess not."

"Some heavy, high-end geek shit went down in your house, man," Chris said, spinning, taking it all in.

"Indeed. Hard to believe it's been so long," Mitch said.

"How are you holding up, man? I am so sorry about your mom." Chris's words slowed as he found a place to sit on the old, short dresser against the wall. "How the hell are you? I mean really?" His arms fell to his sides and Chris gave him the look that had always cut to the chase, even through the deepest lines of bullshit.

Mitch ambled to the bed and sat down, feeling his face flush and the old knot tighten in his stomach again.

"Like an orphan. You have no idea how hard it is to be here, man. I mean, after my father called, I just wanted to lock the door and tune the whole damn world out. The very thought of stepping one foot back in this shit-filled town made me sick." Mitch shot Chris a look. "No offense."

Chris held his hands up in a *no worries* gesture. "None taken. Sterling Point is a kinda shitty place. But you got away. Bless ya. And all the crap with your dad and Tony and Beth. I really can't say I blame you for bailing on your old close friends. You might even have called us brothers...family." He shot Mitch a teasing wink.

"Nice." Mitch laughed. "I'm not even back in Hellhole, USA, for a full twenty-four hours and you're already busting my balls like I never left."

"Hey, what are friends...*family* for?"

"True enough. But, man, I'm not kidding about not wanting to come back. I hate this place. Sure, I miss you guys and all, but the minute I got in my car and started driving here, my chest felt like an elephant was taking a nap on it, and my stomach had more knots in it than you can count. I know, I know, I probably sound like a whiny bitch, as my wise and ever-so-poetic father would call me. But, Chris, man. Every mile of the agonizing drive was like getting punched over and over again."

Mitch stared out the frosty window again at the pure white nothingness. "And now, without mom here...her being...gone..." Wiping a small tear from the corner of his eye, he said in a small, quiet voice, "I really felt like an orphan. In so many ways."

The startling words echoed off the walls.

"So, the other ginormous elephant-sized question in this cozy nerd van for ya: Have you run into Beth or Tony yet?" His coy smile betrayed his intention. Mitch knew Chris was avoiding talking about his mom's death, as Chris had horrible, first-hand knowledge on the sober subject of being an orphan. As a child, he had lost both of his parents to a drunk driver.

Mitch found himself standing next to the old typewriter, slowly running his fingers over its cold metal keys, as if to comfort himself.

After a long moment, he responded.

"Yeah, I did. Literally," he mumbled.

"How's that?"

"I damn near wrecked my car trying not to hit Beth's woolly mammoth of a dog outside of Wegmans." Mitch laughed. "Oh, nice to see Sterling Point stepping up in the world and finally getting their own Wegmans, by the way. Kudos!"

"Yeah, well, you've been gone a long while, Mr. Big-Time, *New York Times* bestselling author. There's been lots of upgrades here. Yup. We have our very own Weggies now, no longer having to drive all the way to Carrigan Springs or Newark. And, if your fancy city-boy ass can believe it, we actually have two stoplights now. Count 'em. Two." He held up two long fingers and smiled proudly.

"Wow. Most impressive. What's next? A third pizza joint or another drug store?" Mitch teased.

"Hey, rumor has it we might be finally getting a Taco Bell. Crossing my fingers for that one, let me tell ya."

"I bet."

They both laughed. Then they stared out the frosty window and let the whipping wind outside take the moment.

"So, anyway, you almost killed Pablo, huh?" Chris finally said.

"No. Actually, that cute Wendigo on four legs almost took out my Honda. Thank the gods for the large snowbank that broke its fall."

"Damn, man. Well, at least nobody got hurt. And how did the other…ummm…potential accident go? How'd it go with those two?" he asked with a raised brow, reminding Mitch who he was asking about.

"Much as you would imagine. Beth hugged me. Told me how much she'd missed me. Kissed me on the cheek and then…"

In unison, Mitch and Chris echoed, "Asshole showed up."

The once shadowy room erupted into light laughter.

"Tony, huh?" Chris said, a sour look on his face. "Wow, he must've had an APB out on you, so he'd know the minute your old rust bucket crossed the Wayne County line."

"Yeah." Mitch let the word hang for a second. "Must have. Was kinda odd that he showed up oh so conveniently. He hasn't changed much at all."

"No. No, he hasn't. If anything, the guy's gotten worse. We haven't said two words to each other in five years or more. And, dude, we live in the same town," Chris said.

"Guess neither of us is missing much."

"Nope," Chris said. "I can say the same thing about this town." A few places closed down or became something else. But not much has changed. You might not have missed it, man. But believe me, brother, we miss you. "Again, so, so sorry about your mom. She was aces in my book."

Mitch wasn't a touchy-feely person by nature, but he hugged his old friend tighter and for longer than he normally would. "Missed you too. This town, not so much."

They both chuckled.

"So, since I've been incommunicado, what's the old gang been up to? Anybody still around here, or…?" Mitch asked, finding himself sincerely curious about his old group of friends.

Chris rubbed his goateed chin, which was showing tiny grey flecks amongst the deep black hairs. "Clay is the only one left in town. We get together once in a blue moon. Other than the aforementioned Officer Dickhead." He smiled. "Ray is driving over-the-road trucks from Walmart. Robbie and Petra got married—go figure—and he's doing some IT shit and Petra is a veterinarian over in Henrietta. A couple of kids, I believe. Dawn moved right after graduation, kinda like a certain enigmatic word-scribbler I won't mention."

"Nice." Mitch grinned.

"What about Jesse and Dave? How're they doing?"

"Believe it or not, Dave is one of the head game-and-story developers for Archworld Games out in California. Can you believe that?"

"Wow. Man, that's awesome. Talk about the perfect job for that guy."

"It is. We exchange occasional e-mails, and he's invited me out to Gen Con every year, but damn, man, who's got that kinda cash, ya know?"

"Amen to that." Mitch nodded. "Jesse?"

"Well, hell. Let's talk about enigma. Jesse joined the military the summer after graduation. The army, I think. After that, he just fell off the earth. Clay thinks he ended up in the CIA as a spook or something. I'm thinking of some kind of military intelligence. But no one knows for sure. I've run into his dad a few times down at Yowner's or at Walmart, but he's been tight-lipped about good ol' Jess."

"Yeah, I could see that. Great dude, but he was always planning, plotting, and reading people, so it wouldn't be a stretch. Sure hope he's okay, though. The world's getting crazy out there."

"No. Not at all," Chris agreed. "No shit. Crazy everywhere, my friend."

"Well, I miss them all. And I was hoping to see them. But at least most of you guys made it out of here." Mitch shot Chris with a kidding wink.

"Yeah, well, man. Not all of us have your wanderlust, I guess."

"I know. I know. I got it. And to tell the truth, I don't think it was ever the whole town, per se, it was the people."

Chris laughed. "Yeah, I remember your old adage, 'The world wouldn't be such a terrible place…'"

Mitch joined in chorus, "'If it weren't for all the people.'"

They both laughed, and the room fell silent for a moment. The old furnace clunked alive, sending a rush of cool air as it purged itself, then sent heat through the old house.

"So, when's the calling hours and stuff?" Chris asked.

"Umm. Christmas Eve, if you can believe that. I never thought funeral homes would do such a thing." Mitch shrugged. "But I guess they do."

"Hmmm, who'da thunk it? Do you have plans tonight? Maybe catch a bite to eat, grab a beer, or whatever tea *du jour* you're into?"

"Well, funny you should mention dinner."

"Wait… What?" Chris stood.

"Beth called me a while ago and—"

"Beth Connolly-hyphen-soon-to-be divorced-Severt asked Mr. High and Mighty, bestselling author, out on a date?"

"Ass," Mitch said. "As a matter of fact, smartass, yes, she did." He shook his head.

Chris clapped Mitch on the back as he made his way to the door. "Oh, so let me guess. You two messed-up, it seems, lovebirds are going back to Bonetti's-on-the-Lake, just like in the old days? Well, well, well." He laughed.

"You really are an ass, you know that? I almost forgot that about you," Mitch chided, opening the door. "As a matter of fact, we are. And I made the reservation."

Mitch walked Chris downstairs, and before they reached the front door leading to the porch, Chris stopped.

"Hey, I almost forgot." He reached behind his back and pulled out a heavily dog-eared paperback and handed it to Mitch, a wide smile on his face. "I've been meaning to get down to see you and have ya sign it for a long time now, but, well…ya know."

It was *About to Rage*. All beat to hell. That made him smile. A beat-up book meant a much-loved and well-read book.

"Did you like it? I know it was… It hit pretty close to home…literally."

Chris paused for a second. "Yeah. I dug it a lot. Must admit, it was heavy, brother. But you were, hell, probably still are, dealing with some heavy shit. And I can see why coming back here was something you never wanted to do."

Mitch nodded while he pulled out a pen, which he always carried in his shirt pocket, and flipped the book open to the title page. "I… Honestly, Chris, it took all I had to come back. But it was for my mom. I know she would have wanted me to be here. For my father. Still, every second I spend in this place eats at me like…"

"I know."

Mitch signed the book, let the ink dry for a second, and handed it back.

For Chris, you can go home again…but you're damned better off if you don't. Thanks for always being a loyal friend. It means the world to me. All the best, Mitchell G. Roberts.

"It was so great seeing you. Thanks for coming over," Mitch said, and this time, he initiated the hug.

Chris embraced him. "I missed you, brother. We don't talk enough."

"I know. We're going to have to remedy that from now on, huh?" Mitch said. And he meant it.

"Me too. Let me know when you find the exact times for your mom's calling hours, okay?"

"Of course. It'll be at Murphy's, of course," Mitch said.

"Where the hell else are you going to go? Arcadia Falls or Carrigan Springs are the closest funeral homes, for Christ's sake."

"Gotta love Sterling Point."

Chris stepped out into the blowing snow and turned back. "No, you don't."

Mitch laughed. "True. We'll talk soon."

Mitch watched Chris as he opened the door to his truck. He stopped, opened the paperback, and read what Mitch had written.

His old friend paused…then smiled, shaking his head.

The Dodge roared to life, and now Mitch watched his friend drive down the slippery driveway.

Mitch really hoped he'd see him again soon.

Now, he needed to get ready for tonight.

But first, he headed back to his room…his typewriter…his words.

"Just a few hundred more…or so," he promised his muse, and shut the bedroom door behind him.

19

Scenes from an Italian Restaurant

After getting lost in a mad rush of writing, Mitch arrived at Bonetti's-on-the-Lake almost forty-five minutes late and found it difficult to locate a parking spot. After nearly ten minutes, he lodged his car between a pair of pickup trucks. "Oh, hell's bells. This bodes well." He locked his car and cautiously made his way to the front door of the historic restaurant. He marveled at the quaint old lighthouse-turned-eatery, which reminded him of the hours he'd spent as a waiter and washing dishes.

Bright white Christmas lights illuminated the entire perimeter of the parking lot. From pole to pole, the pathway was lit, leading the customers into the grand foyer. On the whipping wind, instrumental holiday music filled the crisp night air. Mitch chuckled, stopping at the granite steps that led up to the entrance. Large boughs of evergreen leaves and sprigs of holly and mistletoe rested around the doorway. "Sure is awfully romantic to show up so late for someone you've hated for a decade, Romeo." He cursed himself as the words slipped through his paper-thin veneer.

"I know. I know, I'm so, so sorry. I got caught up writing, and before I knew it..." Mitch did his best, but Beth stared at him, and her apple cheeks forming into a stunning smile made him realize it was all for nothing.

She took his arm and pulled him close. "Lighten up. It's okay. I just got here myself. There's a storm coming, don't you know?" She winked.

A young man stepped from the doorway, decked out like a tin soldier. Long red jacket, gold-covered epaulets, and all. "Good evening, sir. How may we help you?"

Mitch stammered, "H-hey there."

"Ah, hello. Good evening, Mrs. Severt," the young man offered.

The air felt thick and uncomfortable as Mitch felt his shoulders sag.

"No. No. It's Ms. Connelly now, Mathew. Thank you. How are you?" Beth stepped to Mitch, grabbing him by the elbow.

"Oh. I'm so sorry. Well, welcome to Bonetti's." The young man opened the door and waved them inside. Christian, your maître d', will be waiting inside for you. Happy Holidays!"

"Merry Christmas," Beth replied, stepping inside with Mitch, arm-in-arm.

A tall, thin man stood behind a wooden podium with a tiny lamp perched atop it.

"Good evening, and welcome to Bonetti's-on-the-Lake." The maître d' smiled.

"The reservation is under Roberts. You know, the *New York Times* bestselling author." Beth squeezed Mitch's arm and winked. Again.

"Oh really? Well, we are so honored to have you dine with us, Mr. Roberts."

Mitch nodded. "Thank you," he whispered.

"It's the least I could do, old buddy."

"Follow me, please. Your table is ready." Only a half-dozen tables lined the outer wall that offered a floor-to-ceiling view of Lake Ontario and the historic lighthouse. "I'm a huge fan. I knew you were from our quaint little town, but never imagined meeting you here." Many heads turned, and Mitch heard several comments referring to Beth and Tony and even his own books. Nothing like a bittersweet symphony filled with razor blades and roses.

"Yeah, um, me neither. Thank you. I'm glad you dig my work." Mitch's voice cracked like a pubescent teen. He winced at the sound of his warbler-like voice.

Mitch tripped down the step, nearly taking out the entire table, but caught his balance.

"Here we are." The maître d' pulled out a chair for Beth. "My sincerest apologies, Mr. Roberts. If we had known we were being honored to have a celebrity here at Bonetti's, I am certain we would have made your accommodations much more…special. Although, as you can see, there is quite a splendid view of our beautifully restored lighthouse."

They sat as a different waiter pushed in their chairs.

Mitch jumped. "Oh, okay. I guess we're doing that."

Beth giggled.

"Sorry. Not a big fan of strangers touching me."

"I remember," Beth said. "Lighten up, nervous nelly."

"Holy crow!" Mitch said. Even though it had been many years, he knew exactly the cost of such a hot-spot table. Not to mention the cost of such a highly in-demand location. "No, this is fine. Thank you."

"Ah, yes. Excellent. Well, Lola will be your waitress tonight. You'll love her to death. She's the best. I hope you enjoy your meal. Oh, my name is Christian. If you need anything at all, please don't hesitate to ask."

Beth offered the clingy host a wry grin. "Thanks so much. I think we're good." She winked at Mitch. "Are you going to stand there all night, looking like a doof, or are we going to get our grub on?"

A short, slender woman approached the table, a weary but warm smile upon her face. "Happy Holidays. I'm Lola. I'll be serving you tonight. Can I start you off with any drinks?"

"All of them," Beth jumped in.

"Iced tea, please," said Mitch. "Straight up, lemon. None of that raspberry stuff."

"Really? Iced tea?" Beth asked.

"What?"

"Even after all this time. Not one beer… One cocktail?"

"You have met my dad, right?"

The waitress asked, "So, drinks?"

Beth glared at Mitch. He tried to shrug her domineering stare off, but relented.

"Just make it taste like an iced tea, okay?"

Lola said, "Two Long Island iced teas coming up," and walked away into the crowded main room behind the maître d'.

"Merry Christmas," Beth said.

Mitch looked nervously around the packed restaurant.

"Mitch?"

He wanted to push it all aside. Hell, he'd always been paranoid and filled with social anxiety. But he knew this was different.

"Are we going to have a nice dinner, or are you going to be Captain Anxiety, like in the old days?"

Mitch held his hands up. "I know. I know. I'm sorry. It's been a long time, you know."

"I know it has." Beth reached out and grabbed his hand. "But it's okay. Nobody here will hurt you, silly. After all, you're a big-time celebrity now."

"Whatever."

"Come on, dude. You must admit, this is kinda cool. Sterling Point has had no one famous escape out of here."

Mitch gave it a thought and peered at her over his glasses. "Oh, what about Bobby Allen Eddings?"

Beth gave him a blank look.

"You know, that sick bastard they caught after ten years with two dozen half-eaten bodies buried at the bottom of his swimming pool?"

"Oh, yeah, that creepy kid out on Centenary Road."

"His parents and sisters included," Mitch added with victorious delight.

"Yeah, yeah, yeah," Beth said. "Well, at least you're better than he is." She laughed.

Mitch joined her. "Yeah, that's true. At least I only make that stuff up. Geesh."

Their laughter died out, and a heavy moment hung between them. The white noise of patrons talking, the soft drone of Christmas music, and the clinking of dinnerware acted as a soundtrack. Mitch spent his time staring at the extensive and far too fancy menu.

"Anything look good?" Beth asked after a minute.

"I don't see any McNuggets here."

Beth glared at him over her menu. "Ass."

"Guilty as charged."

Finally, the waitress returned with their drinks.

"Sorry I took so long. As you can see, there's a big holiday crowd tonight."

"It's fine," Mitch replied.

"So, our holiday specials are Alask—"

"Mr. Roberts will have the turkey special, but he'd like to replace the mashed potatoes with fries and gravy," Beth said, handing her menu to the waitress. "And I'll have a large—"

"She'll take extra fries with extra gravy, to go, along with *my* fries and gravy."

Lola looked dumbfounded, which caused Mitch to break into laughter. Maybe it was the two sips of alcohol he'd had, but the old memories of their long chats at the long-defunct Perkins Restaurant still held fresh in his mind.

"Sorry. Inside joke," Beth said. "I'll have the cacio e pepe with garlic bread and a beet salad."

Mitch and Beth let out a loud belly laugh and even snorted a time or two. The patrons all around stared in shock, and their panicked looks only made Mitch and Beth laugh louder.

"Okay. I'll place your orders. Umm, I...I. I'll bring more drinks, yes?" Lola said sheepishly.

"Of course. It's Christmas, isn't it?" Beth said.

"Right. I'll be right back with your drinks." Lola scampered off like a scared mouse.

While some people in the crowd shot them daggers of derision, there were far more people who smiled and pointed at Mitch, and that made his skin itch and his heart race. He never had known how to deal with attention, good or bad. And the last time he was in his hometown, it was mostly bad. This was like walking into a bizarro-world on steroids. Mitch did his best to deflect the attention and sipped at his drink.

"I haven't thought about those Perkins days in years. Oh, my god. That's great," Beth said, drying her eyes on her linen napkin.

"I have. Friday night, *Rocky Horror Picture Show*, then all of us grabbing chow. It was fun." The words slipped through Mitch's lips before he even knew he'd spoken. *Great way to play the pissed-off old friend, jackhole!*

"Take it easy." Beth reached across the table.

Two women approached with pens and napkins in their hands.

"Oh boy," Beth whispered.

Mitch loved and hated this part of his career choice. But whenever he caught himself getting pissy, he realized that without readers, he'd probably be working at Walmart or living in a cardboard box somewhere. So, if this was the cross he had to bear, he was more than fine with it. Just not at dinner with his best friend-turned-dream-girl, who he'd had a crush on since fourth grade. While Beth shot him an aggravated look, he shrugged and smiled.

"Excuse us," said a lanky blonde woman. "We really hate to bother you, but Tammy here bet me a shot of Tullamore Dew that you are Mitchell Roberts, the writer. Is that true?"

"Oh, boy." Beth rolled her eyes, but Mitch knew it made her happy, if not jealous. He hated the way his brain twisted reality into something he wished to be. He had bailed from this town after letting himself believe in something that had never existed, and now, here he was again, naïve, buying into the same definition of insanity.

"I hate to cost you a shot, but yup, I am." Mitch's skin prickled with a sea of needles, but he kept a friendly smile on his face.

A shorter blonde with glasses laughed and pointed at her friend. "I told you. Pay up, girlie." She turned to Mitch and laid down a dog-eared copy of *About to Rage* on the table. "Oh, I have to tell you. This book got me through some tough times. My divorce, losing the house and…and I…I just love it."

"It's true. She's been through the wringer turned up to ten, and then some," the third woman added, stressing her words with several adamant nods.

"Sound familiar?" Mitch said under his breath. He knew Beth had caught the cutting words from her snide expression.

"Funny," Beth muttered.

"Thank you so much. I'm so sorry you had such a rough go of it. But I'm happy you dug it. Would you like me to sign it?"

Suddenly, he caught sight of a bunch of people heading over and the anxiety pushed in around him.

Beth winked. "That's your cross to bear, *Mr. King.*"

"I'd be happy to," Mitch said. "Who should I make it out to?" He gave Beth a small smirk. She giggled.

"Oh, um. You can sign it to Gidget," the woman said. "That's, G-i-d—"

"That's not a name you hear every day," Mitch said, writing on the front page.

The women exchanged whispered words and giggled. "It's an old nickname from high school. I like it."

"Me too. It's cool." Mitch added the last flourish on his signature and handed the book back.

A small vibration echoed on the table, and Beth rushed to pick up her cellphone.

Mitch guessed who it was, and Beth's flushed face only confirmed it.

"Do you need to take that?" Mitch tried his best not to sound annoyed. He was certain it didn't work.

"Thank you so much, Mr. Roberts," Gidget said, shaking his hand. "It's such an honor to meet you. And Tammy and I were wondering, if it's not too much trouble, could we get a picture with you?"

Beth shook her head *no*, placing the phone back down on the table, her long dark hair surrounding her pale face as she did. *Damn, she's still beautiful. Damn it, Roberts, knock that shit off.* Mitch chastised himself and realized the woman still had hold of his hand.

"Oh, uh, yeah, sure. I'd be happy to." He stood, and the women surrounded him, holding up their smartphones, and snuggled in close to him.

"I'm so sorry to hear about your mother. It's so sad," Tammy offered as she snapped her picture.

Gidget hugged Mitch closer. "Me too, Mr. Roberts. I work over at Turn the Page Books, and she would come in every week asking if you had a new book coming out. Such a sweetheart."

Mitch felt a sob catch in this throat. "Thanks, ladies. Yeah, yeah, she was."

Gidget snapped five or six pictures and finally let him go.

"Thank you again, and I'm sorry to have interrupted your date," Gidget said.

Mitch's gaze flashed to Beth, who sat there with an uncomfortable look on her face.

"It's okay. I'm always happy to meet folks who like my work. It keeps my butt in my chair. Thank you. And Merry Christmas," Mitch said, and sat down.

"Merry Christmas," the women said in unison and walked away, arm-in-arm and giddy.

"Wow. I never thought I'd be having dinner with a celebrity. I'm all a-flutter," Beth teased.

"Oh boy. Please tell me they aren't coming over here." Mitch motioned toward the group of at least ten people, all headed in their direction.

"I hate to say this, *Mr. Koontz,* but I don't think we will get a quiet meal here," Beth said, slyly checking her phone.

Mitch ignored Beth's preoccupation with her phone and took in a deep breath. "Yeah, methinks you're right there."

"Wanna bail? I mean, we don't have to stay."

Mitch appreciated the fact that Beth remembered his social anxiety issues, but he had to weigh the circumstances. Marie, his agent, had sent him article after article on marketing and how to spread his author brand, and while he was a very nice guy, he was also very introverted. He hated crowds and never knew how to handle positive praise or appreciation. It was the negative responses he understood, and that, sadly, was his depressing comfort zone. It was an innate response to cut and run, but he was a writer now and needed to be able to handle the attention. The thought filled him with a racing panic and indecision overtook him.

The smiling crowd gathered around their table; most had cloth napkins and pens. Mitch knew he needed to do something, and that scared the hell out of him. But suddenly, without premeditation, he stood and smiled at the gathered patrons.

"Merry Christmas, everyone. I hope you're having a wonderful evening. I tell you, I've missed a lot of things about Sterling Point, but Bonetti's has to be mighty high on the list."

The crowd cheered and clapped.

"I don't know what to say. I am moved to see you all."

The crowd hooted and raised their glasses to him, and that only caused Mitch to freeze.

A long, uncomfortable moment passed, and he jumped as Beth stood up and spoke.

"What our humble homeboy is trying to say is, thank you so much for showing your support in his time of grief and that he really, truly loves you all."

Mitch lowered his head, running a hand through his thick hair. *Damn, Roberts. She should be your publicist.*

A rush of condolences filled the room, and Mitch felt a knot growing in his stomach.

"So, while he'd love to meet you all and sign things tonight, he has to leave, but wanted you to know he will be doing a book signing at Turn the Page Books on New Year's Eve, and you're all invited to come and celebrate with him there." Beth's voice sounded different, and it scared Mitch a little. But he didn't disagree with her tactic. It saved a lot of face.

A hush of disappointment mixed with more support and cheers as Beth grabbed Mitch by the arm and led him out of Bonetti's.

"I'm so sorry, everyone. Merry Christmas," was all he could offer.

As Beth led him out of the restaurant, only stopping to drop money for their drinks at the maître d's podium, she said, "Stick with me, kid, and I'll make you a star."

Mitch chortled and felt a ton of self-imposed weight being whisked away in the snowy night air. "Funny as a crutch, Beth. Funny as a crutch."

"Well, somebody had to do something. You looked like a deer in headlights, Mr. Straub. And I couldn't let you embarrass yourself in front of your adoring hometown crowd now, could I?"

"Yeah, you're a trooper." Mitch laughed. "Now what?" he asked, his head feeling slightly fuzzy as the effects of the drink started hitting him.

Beth led him to her car and opened the passenger side door. "Get in, H.P. I think we can find some grub where you aren't so high in demand."

"You're just full of 'em, aren't you?" Mitch said as Beth slumped down into the seat. "How long have you been saving them up?"

"Oh, Mitchie, my dear, you have no idea." She laughed and closed the door.

Mitch's head was spinning. The past twenty-four hours had been a smorgasbord of emotions. His mom, his father, Tony, Beth. The alcohol didn't help him find any kind of safe footing. Part of him was grateful for the respite from the same obsessive-compulsive insistence of control. Another part despised the damage booze had inflicted on his life. But right now, outside Beth's car—the girl...the *woman* he'd first loved and the reason he'd left Sterling Point to begin with—he would let it pass.

"I have some tasty leftovers at my place," Beth offered as she started her car. "Follow me, Mr. Poe."

Mitch turned, looking for his car. He'd come this far. His mom was dead, his dad was drunk somewhere. Why not throw all caution to the wind? After all, his dad hated him. He was stuck in a town he despised and was hanging out with Beth. *To hell with it. It's Christmas.*

"Sure," he finally said. "Wait... Your monstrosity of a dog isn't going to eat me, is he?"

Beth drove out of the parking lot into the heavy snow.

"Not unless I tell him to, Mrs. Jackson."

Mitch laughed. "Nice. But what about—"

"Tony?"

"Yeah. That big, muscle-headed elephant in the parking lot."

"We're just catching up, Mitch. Hell, we haven't seen each other in years. Besides, the hell with him. I don't answer to him anymore."

"I see," Mitch said, continuing to watch the half-dollar-thick snowflakes fill the tire tracks as he got into his car and fired the engine.

They drove out of the snowy parking lot, as the violent nor'easter was slowly making its way over Sterling Point and the rest of Western New York.

20
Eating the Cannibals

A soul-wrenching roar woke Royce Pritchard from his drunken slumber inside the main bedroom. Staggering to his shaky old legs, he tried to focus in the dark. He fumbled for his thick glasses on the nightstand, shoved them on, and shuffled toward the door. Screams and the overwhelming stench of iron and urine filled the large hunting cabin. Royce entered the main room, and the aged gray walls were splattered with blood and ripped flesh. He cupped his mouth and nose to stifle the smell and the bile building in his throat.

At first, he thought it was the after-effects of all the Jack Daniels he and his hunting buddies had guzzled hours before, but as Royce forced his feet forward into the room, his boots landed on something sticky and chunky. Looking down, he realized he was standing on Kenny Tompkins' open chest. He heard the crunch of bones as he slipped back into the doorjamb. The bile in his throat won its battle, and pure brown liquid and half-chewed pieces of venison steak splattered the coagulating, eviscerated remains of his friend. His knees knocked together as he wiped the vomit from his gray beard and tried to regain control. It had been years since he'd seen such gore, but it brought the powerful images of the ward flooding back like a black veil of panic and horror.

Splintered furniture and piles of ripped-apart bodies filled the rest of the large room, and blood filled the slats of the pine floor. He tried to tear his eyes away from his friend, but he couldn't. A scream echoed from the cabin's entrance. Royce heard himself gasp as he stared ahead. The front door and window were destroyed, floor to ceiling. Snow filled the opening and a horrid, freezing wind howled through the cabin. He kept his composure, following the blood trail into the darkness beyond the damaged entryway.

The screams and the yelling grew louder as he reached the opening. He saw a shotgun among a deep pile of intestines and blood. He reached in and took it, wiping off the sinew and bits of skin and intestines, and stepped outside on shaking, creaking knees.

The deep red blood became lost in the heavily falling snow. But the screams and ungodly growls sliced through the white veil like razor-sharp claws into flesh. Royce wasn't sure if it was the minus-ten wind chill or the cries of his friends that made his blood freeze. He followed as fast as his old body and the knee-deep snow allowed. He briefly considered stealing "The Prize" and fleeing. A shrill cry caused him to turn back toward the infernal sounds.

Royce discovered the gory trench; his heart pounded, imagining what had lured his friends. He couldn't feel his hands anymore and his face was raw from the harsh arctic winds. He trudged onward toward a cluster of tall, sprawling pine trees. From there, the sound of gunfire and panicked screams tore through the stormy air. He crashed through the low branches of the pine, the sharp needles piercing his hands and face as he stopped mid-stride, unable to comprehend what lay before him.

The snowstorm seemed alive, and blood covered the entire cluster of pines. His friends were there: well, some of them, and some others. Everything was a blur of blackness and shotgun blasts. The crimson blood trail led into the circle, where a large man-sized shape flailed its limbs in defense. His heart stopped.

"Denny?" Royce yelled. His mountain-sized son was fending off whatever attacked him. He saw tears rolling down the young man's bearded face. He was shocked and even more embarrassed at the sight of his son's cowardice. Lying between Denny's legs was a writhing body. Royce squinted through his bifocals to see it was his old drinking buddy's Carhartt. But what was inside looked nothing like Bruce Babcock anymore. The tan overalls were ripped into pieces, exposing the flesh and bone underneath. A piercing wail filled the air. It sounded like a dog being beaten to death. Royce knew that sound well. This time, it brought immediate tears.

The vilest, angriest, most unnatural howl he had ever heard in his sixty-two years drowned out his dying friend's cries. He raised the shotgun and tried to take aim. *Conserve your ammo, you old fool.* He calmed himself. A colossal black mass appeared both ubiquitous and intangible. It would emerge with its many large talons and razor-sharp teeth to strike and then disappear into the snow. He saw others emerging from the nearby woods. He raised the shotgun and took aim, his numb hands shaking with fear.

Royce could make out Mikey, Johnny, and Alicia. He lowered the gun and forced his way through the deep snow around the perimeter of the clearing. He dropped into the snow as a shotgun blast obliterated a heavy branch beside him.

"Sonofabitch," he let out. The dying wails of Big Boy mixed with the howling winds and the agonizing growl of the unknown beast. Royce waved his hand violently, and someone grabbed it and yanked him out from the snow.

"You okay, Pop?" Mikey Pritchard knelt before him, with Johnny and Alicia in tow. His breathing was ragged; tears marked his face.

"I raised a bunch of fuckin' pussies, for Christ's sake," Royce growled. Getting up on one knee, he took inventory of the three and tried to remember who was missing, but his whiskey-filled memory wouldn't relent. He shoved his son's hand aside and stood.

"That thing—Jesus H. Christ?" Royce said.

"Don't know, man. They, it, whatever, killed Karl, Jim, and Kenny. Just ground 'em up like they were in a fuckin' blender! Not sure where anyone else is," Johnny said, and looked about, checking his shotgun. "Let's get the hell outta here." His dark pupils seemed to swallow the whites of his narrow eyes.

"What about Denny?" Alicia said. Her tears caught the quick glint of moonlight. Her voice broke. The girl didn't take shit from anyone except Royce. He disliked her intensely and wished they had butchered her instead.

Royce thought for a second and rubbed his beard. He wanted to leave Denny's stupid ass there; it would give them a head start. He looked over and saw his son turn and flee from whatever was attacking him, leaving a light blood trail behind.

His eyes revealed a terror exceeding any fear he'd instilled in his son. That scared Royce even more. It was time to move.

"Mikey, you guys shoot the shit outta that big fuckin' thing and grab Denny, and meet me at my Hummer," he said, not giving them a chance to respond. He ran back toward the cabin through ankle-deep snow. They followed orders and ran toward Denny.

Reaching the cabin, Royce's lungs burned. Emphysema was catching up with him. He felt the bile rise again in his throat. He spewed out more venison and whiskey. The smell made him double over and retch into the snow.

He wiped his beard clean and reached into his pants pocket for his keys. Struggling with his stiff hands, he found it hard to grasp them, and they fell into the deep snowbank in front of the doors to the old shed.

Royce shoved his aching hands into the snow and retrieved the keys. He shook them off, then unlocked the padlock and chains, sending them into the snow. With great effort, he squeezed through. He didn't need a light to find what he was looking for. He found the cave's treasure exactly where he'd placed it. His old warn large green canvas bag sat atop the pallets and looked like a million dollars in the early morning light.

"Mr. Pritchard," Carl Walker called out; the greenhorn's voice echoed through the snowstorm and into the small shed.

"Newbie, give me a hand," he said, grabbing hold of one side of the heavy sack. Carl leaped from the truck, secured the other end, then helped load it into the SUV. The snow turned sideways and picked up its pace and intensity. A white curtain formed all around them.

Royce covered the bag of loot from the cave with a small tarp and hopped into the driver's seat. Carl jumped in and closed the door. The heat from the burning cabin was a welcome sensation as he started to feel his extremities again.

"Hang on tight, kid, this could get ugly." Royce shoved the truck in gear and headed toward the pine clearing. "Make sure you got ammo, so when we find them, you lay down suppressing fire."

"What's suppress—" Carl's voice shook as he buckled his seatbelt.

"Ah, fuck, shoot at anything that fuckin' moves, kid," Royce said, as he stared ahead and the truck plowed through the snow.

They hadn't driven too far when they saw Denny and the others. The blackness wasn't far behind them. And it was spreading.

Royce brought the truck to a stop as the headlights shone on an immense, swirling form: glowing red eyes set deep into the darkness glowered at Royce and the others, while many ebony tendrils tipped with razor-sharp talons whipped and tore at the freezing air.

"What the hell is that?" Denny shouted.

"Get in, goddamnit." Royce watched Alicia help Denny into the back of the Hummer, while Mike and Johnny climbed into the passenger side. Carl hopped out and let loose six shots into the blackness closing in on them, his hands shaking the entire time. Royce hoped to give his sons enough time to get inside the truck and get the hell out of there.

"Go!" Carl climbed in and slammed the door. The entire truck surged to the right as Royce cranked the wheel and stomped on the gas pedal. A painful growl followed them as the 4X4 forced its own path north-westward, away from the burning Pritchard cabin. They didn't look back. The going was slow, and visibility was turning to zero as the storm licked close at their heels. And it had company.

21

The Nearness of You

"Hey, I didn't know you bought the old Felton place." Mitch peered out at the house. "I spent a lot of time hanging out here."

"Well, maybe if you called or wrote occasionally, you would have known."

"Yeah, yeah," Mitch said. "Works both ways. Mrs. Severt."

Beth continued, "Anyway, we bought it shortly after Mr. Felton passed. I felt so bad for his widow. She couldn't afford the house anymore and her sons had no interest or means. So, she was all on her own."

"I guess that happens. Sad, to be sure," Mitch said.

"Wow. I'll be damned," Beth said as she pulled into the neatly plowed driveway.

"What?"

Beth stared at the clean blacktop, her face frozen in a look of astonishment. Mitch thought it was odd, but played along.

"Well?"

"It's the driveway."

Mitch scratched his head. "Um, you didn't have a driveway when you left earlier?"

"Smartass. Of course. It's just that I've been on Tony to plow the driveway and he's been blowing me off."

"Hmm, I see."

"What does that mean? 'Hmm, I see'?" Beth mocked.

Mitch got out of the car and pulled up the thick collar of his navy peacoat to cut the biting wind.

"Come on, Dr. Freud. Please enlighten me."

"Oh, Christ inside a sidecar going down Main Street. Can we please go inside? In case you haven't noticed, it's damn cold out here."

Beth laughed. "Okay, come on, you big baby. The city life has made you soft." She took his arm and ushered him toward the side door of the house.

From the backyard, a guttural howl echoed off the garage door and held long in the chaotic winds.

"Um, what about Cujo?" he asked.

"Take it easy, you're fine. I told you, Pablo is nothing but a big, furry baby. Kind of reminds me of you." Beth laughed and closed the heavy, worn door behind them.

Mitch was finding an old familiar comfort with Beth and felt the bond they used to share coming through.

"Ha ha. Hilarious." Mitch looked around the large living room and smiled. "You should take your show on the road. I'm sure that the Sodus Hotel has an open-mic night."

Beth took her jacket off and held out her hand. "Give me your jacket, kick your boots off, and I'll see what I can rustle up." Her wide, warming smile struck Mitch deep, out of the blue. He'd forgotten just how enrapturing she was. Her rich hazel eyes sparkled, and then there was the way her freckled nose twitched when she laughed.

Beth hung their jackets on the coat rack. "You okay? I was only joking about the Freud stuff and all that."

Mitch couldn't break his enthralled stare.

"Mitch?"

He reactively stepped back.

"Hey, I didn't mean... We can always call it a night. I just..." Beth's warm gaze bore into Mitch, as though he'd never left.

"No... No. It's okay. I'm sorry. I'm sorry for being such a—"

"I understand, Mitch. I do. It's been a long time and... Hey, have a seat. I'll start the fireplace up and see what magic I can work in the kitchen. I'll be right back." She kissed him on the cheek.

Mitch recoiled and instantly felt like complete shit.

"Okay. I'll just stand here and try to not look awkward," he joked.

Beth laughed and shook her head as she picked up a small remote and lit the fireplace.

"Just chill out. I'll be right back. With drinks."

"Tea, please," Mitch said as Beth disappeared into the dark kitchen.

"You got it, Mr. Hemingway."

"Funny as a crutch, Mrs. Severt," Mitch said to the warming fireplace. "You should do stand-up."

"I heard that."

"Oops." Mitch sat down on what he could only assume was a very expensive suede sofa. He guessed it might have been worth more than the entire house.

Staring into the crackling flames in the once-wood-burning fireplace that now fed through the town gas line, Mitch recalled many summers helping Clay and his brother Ray, splitting and stacking cords upon cords of wood so they could heat their house throughout the vicious winters. And now he inhabited an entirely different world, not knowing if he should run back to his folks' house or risk freezing the water pipes or worse. He felt torn and yet drawn to his town…his past. He hated every second he'd wasted on it.

Sounds of a squeaky door, rattling chain, and deep bark echoed through the house.

Followed by the thundering of large paws against the wood floor.

"Heads up!" Beth shouted. "Incoming."

"Oh, holy hell."

Before Mitch had time to turn, a blur of fur and pink tongue swallowed him whole.

Pablo was on him, and there was no way of denying the Alaskan mammoth his will. Mitch rolled with the dog and laughed as he petted him.

"Whoa, whoa, easy, Tex," Mitch's muffled call came through thick fur.

Beth's infectious laughter broke into the room and merged with Mitch's pleas. He couldn't help but laugh.

"Okay, okay, Pablo. Easy, mister. Let our guest breathe, please." Beth's tone dripped with half-assed admonishment, and it only made Mitch giggle harder.

"He's fine." Mitch spat out dog fur and let the Alaskan behemoth pin him to the floor. "You win, Nanook. I surrender."

The beast got off him, with a little help from Beth, and sat next to Mitch as they leaned against the front of the couch. Both tired, both panting.

Beth entered, carrying two glasses, and quipped, "Looks like you've made a new best friend, Mr. Roberts."

"Yeah, turns out, old Chewbacca here ain't so bad after all." Mitch scratched behind the dog's ears, and he returned the show of affection by lashing his enormous tongue against Mitch's face…his entire face.

Beth nearly snorted her drink. "Good thing."

Mitch did his best to fend off the slobbery assault with one hand while he took a sip from his glass.

"Hey, hey." He stared incredulously at his glass. All the while, Pablo continued his show of affection. "This, my good lady, is not Earl Grey. Not by a long shot."

Beth blushed and Mitch gave her the dirtiest look he could muster.

"I'm sorry about that. Seems we're plum out of old man beverages, my good man."

Mitch normally hated the taste of all kinds of alcohol, but this wasn't so terrible. He tasted it again; it was better.

"Is it okay?" Beth asked with a sincere, apologetic look on her beautiful face. Mitch hated himself for even noticing. But how could he not? *And so it continues*, he chastised himself and took another sip.

"All right, big guy. Enough is enough. I'm sure Mitch needs a towel at this point." Beth set her glass down and pulled Pablo away. The big dog whimpered as Beth helped him to the kitchen. "Let's get you some chow and water. What do you say, buddy?"

"Catch ya later, Nanook," Mitch said.

A curt bark came from the kitchen, followed by Beth. "Mitchell Andrew!"

Mitch cringed. "Sorry," he said, then laughed.

Absently, he took a sip, recoiled at the bitter taste, and then took another. These past twenty-four hours had been like one long *Twilight Zone* episode, and it was freaking him out. Part of him wished he was back in his apartment, starting a new book from his ten-foot-tall to-be-read-pile, or even watching another season of *Doctor Who*. Even in his wildest imaginings, Mitch had never thought for a second he'd be back home, let alone sitting on Beth's living room floor and feeling what he could only assume was a slight buzz, as the kids called it these days.

"When in Rome," he said.

"What's so funny?" Beth said as she returned with two bowls of steaming food.

Mitch choked on his drink.

Beth gave him the old familiar expression she used to use whenever he was being a gigantic dork.

"Ah, never mind. What do we have here, oh, Ms. Giada?"

"Well, first, let me apologize. I had little in the fridge to work with. But, then I remembered that I had made one of your favorite dishes for the St. Gregory's potluck dinner last weekend, and after giving it a quick sniff, I guessed it was still good, so… Yeah. Here you go."

"Dutch lettuce?" Mitch nearly shouted. "Holy hand grenades. Are you freakin' kiddin' me?" Not even caring for an answer, he shoved a huge bite into his mouth and savored the nostalgic flavors of the artery-hardening meal.

"Is it okay?"

"Hells yes. I haven't had this in…well, forever." Mitch nodded with each bite and didn't stop until the entire bowl of the Pennsylvania Dutch delight was gone, the bowl wiped completely clean. Suddenly realizing that he had wolfed the food down in a matter of minutes, Mitch froze and looked up at Beth.

With his mouth half full of delicious Dutch lettuce, he said, "I'm sorry. It's so good." He shrugged and finished chewing.

Beth sat on the ottoman, laughing and taking her third bite. "It's fine, Mitch. I kind of figured it was a dish tough to find in big-time Manhattan and thought you'd dig it."

Mitch finished and set the bowl on the coffee table. "Brooklyn, actually. There's no way I could afford a cardboard box uptown. Not that I'd even want to." He washed down the meal with a gulp from his glass.

"Well, excuse me, Mr. Big. I just thought with you being a *New York Times* bestselling author and all, you'd have a lavish Manhattan apartment overlooking Central Park and a vacation home in Martha's Vineyard." Beth shot Mitch a teasing wink.

"I wish." Mitch drained his glass and set it down. "I can barely afford the apartment I have now. It's kind of neat, actually. It comes with an honest-to-goodness Murphy bed. I dig it."

"What's a Murphy bed?"

"Oh, come on. You don't know what that is?"

Beth laughed. "I'm sorry, *Professor Dictionary*. I must have been sleeping during the bed part of class."

"Not during all of it, apparently." Mitch winced and instantly regretted the words. He prayed Beth had missed what he'd said. Judging by the hurt look on her face, he was certain she'd caught it.

"Shit, Beth. I'm sorry. I didn't mea—"

Beth waved him off, stood, snatched up all the dishes, and headed for the kitchen.

"Hey, why don't you turn on the stereo? I have XM Radio. I think you might like the channels I have programmed," she said. Mitch tried to pry both of his size fourteen feet from his stupid mouth, but knew from experience it was no use. At least music might be a distraction. He might regain his remaining dignity. As of right now, it looked like downtown Fallujah.

"Okay," was all Mitch could say as he found the stereo; it was her old Pioneer from her bedroom. He smiled, reminiscing about the hours they'd spent lip-syncing to her favorite bands. There were some modern bands, but most of Beth's prime cuts were from the hits of the seventies, eighties, and nineties: Heart, Journey, Pat Benatar, U2, but her all-time favorite was Norah Jones. Mitch had lost count of how many times he'd watched her croon into her hairbrush "Turn Me On" and "Come Away With Me." The happy memory swept through Mitch and brought with it a huge, barbed-wire ball of guilt.

The light blue display read, *I've Got to See You Again*, and Mitch turned the volume up, hoping it might take some of the sting out of his asinine comment.

"Ooh, I love this song," Beth said, coming back into the living room with two full glasses.

She had a smile on her face, but Mitch sensed that his bitter comment was still bothering her.

"So, hey, I really want to apologize for what I said. I had no right to say that. It was snarky and mean. I…I'm an asshole for even thinking about it."

Janis Joplin's melancholy voice testified and filled the thick space between them while Beth stared at the carpet.

Pablo howled and bayed at the snowstorm outside, and the crackling of the raging fire emphasized the awkward moment.

"You're right about one thing." Beth's chilly gaze snapped to Mitch's eyes, her mouth a thin, pursed line.

Oh shit. Way to go, Roberts. Guess it's time to go.

"You were an asshole for saying that." She kept her eyes on him and took a long, slow drink.

"Well played, Mrs. Severt. Well played," Mitch said, raising his glass to her.

The opening organ notes of "God Only Knows" took the place of Janis. It was the female version he'd never heard before. *Not now, Roberts. Can't you calm your stupid ADHD for a damn second?*

"But...I had it coming," Beth finally said, and sat down on the edge of the rocking chair in the corner. "And that's soon-to-be Ms. Connolly, thank you very much."

"Beth, I'm sorry." Mitch stepped lightly toward her, but she held her hand up. "What happened? If you don't mind me asking."

Beth stood up. "Hold on a sec. I'll be right back." She went into the kitchen and returned with a full pitcher of drinks and a pair of clean glasses and set it all down next to Mitch on the coffee table.

"Whoa, someone's thirsty!"

"Yes. We both are, old friend. Bottoms up!" Beth filled both glasses and went back to her rocking chair.

"Drink, Mr. Roberts." Beth drank again and her hard face softened. "I'm pretty sure we're both going to need it."

The distant rumble of a passing plow truck reminded him of his father. But he was certain dear old Dad was bending his elbow down at Yowner's or passed out drunk in his La-Z-Boy, snoring away to *Walker, Texas Ranger* reruns.

"Tony is nothing but a lying, cheating bag of shit." Beth's harsh words brought Mitch back to the moment.

Tears gathered in the corners of Beth's eyes and Mitch wanted to run to her and hug her. But, as always, he didn't dare. "Oh, Beth, I'm so, so sorry."

"It's okay. It's not your fault the douchebag can't keep his dick in his pants." Her words grew louder as she dabbed her eyes with her sleeve. "Right?"

Mitch choked a little on his drink. "Eh, of course not."

"How long has this been going on?" he asked, but he already knew the answer.

Beth shook her head. "Not sure, really. To be honest, it wouldn't surprise me if that's what he's always done. His job makes it easy to be out and about doing God knows what, with God knows whom, and hey, he can always hide behind his damn badge."

"Yeah, the whole cop thing," Mitch said. "I never saw him as a cop. It's weird."

"Well, after graduation, which I'll get back to, mister, he jumped from job to job. He had no college aspirations. Finally, Rob Nevelizer gave him a job at his machine shop in Arcadia Falls, but that didn't last six months."

"Wow, really? That doesn't sound like the Tony I remember." Mitch hated the guy, but they'd been tight for many years growing up, and the lazy act didn't seem right. "That was cool of Rob. He was a good guy."

"Well, it was, but thankfully, after one night of partying at Christly's Cove at Sodus Point, Tony drinks himself into oblivion and thinks it's a smart move to drive home."

"Oh boy," Mitch said. "Not good."

"No, it wasn't good at all. So, we were living down off Lake Road at the time, in this shitty trailer, and didn't he make it almost all the way home when he puts his truck through Williams Farms' pole barn."

Mitch cringed. "Jesus. Was anyone hurt?" He hated the guy, but didn't want him dead.

Beth busted out in a big belly laugh. "Ah, no. Except for a pallet of potatoes."

They both laughed loud enough to cause Pablo to join in with a round of barking.

"So what happened?" Mitch asked after they'd regained their composure.

Beth leaned forward. "Do you remember Richie Barney?"

Mitch forced the alcohol-infected brain cells aside and searched his memory banks for the name. After a few divergent alleys, his mind clicked.

"Yeah, I think so. Big jock, football player. Kind of a snob? The guy we always thought was gay, but in denial?"

"Yes. Yes, that's him."

"Well, turns out, he became a New York state trooper and recognized Tony and gave him a roadside coming-to-Jesus meeting."

"Say what?" Mitch asked.

"No kidding. Richie put him in his car, had Tony's truck towed to our house, and gave him a ride home, and they talked on the front porch until daylight. Within a week, Tony quit drinking and signed up for the Wayne County Sheriff's training academy."

"Holy crow. No way?" Mitch said, draining his glass. "That was fast."

"I know, right?" Beth nodded and refilled their glasses. "And life was great after that. He stopped drinking and threw himself into the job. But apparently, at some point, he began sneaking drinks and sleeping around with one of the slutty dispatchers." She took a long pull from her glass, staring out the picture window overlooking the snowy street. "Over and over again."

As he sat there, watching Beth fight back more tears and drain her glass as if it were a magic potion, Mitch didn't know what to say.

He had held onto so much hatred and grief since that night, yet now, it almost felt childish, selfish for him to shackle himself to such distant memories and feelings. It was a bitter poison he couldn't rid himself of.

"You didn't deserve this, you know that, right?" It was more of a statement than a question.

Beth turned to him, her face a mixture of hurt and defiance. "Oh, trust me, I know I didn't. Not one little damn bit."

"Well…" Mitch paused, not expecting the reaction he'd received. "Good. I knew he could do some pretty shitty things, but I never thought he'd stoop so low."

"I wish I'd known," Beth said.

The stereo filled the room with classic Christmas songs. While he used to love the holidays, he'd grown to despise nearly every aspect. He was fairly certain that the passing of his mom and what was happening in this living room would cement his bah-humbug lamentation.

"Me too, Bethie. I didn't see it coming either. Guess that's what happens when you trust people. There's always the chance of getting bitten right in the ass." Mitch stepped back, turning away from the window, stubbing his big toe. "Son of a—"

"You okay?"

"Yeah." Mitch looked at the culprit and discovered it was a stack of banker's boxes he hadn't noticed. *Thank you, vodka gods, for playing keep away with my brain.*

"Oh, hey, look out for those. Sorry. I meant to put them away. Told you this house was a hot mess."

Mitch noticed that he had accidentally knocked the lid off the top box and was surprised by what glared back at him.

It was a picture of him and Beth in the basement of his house with all his friends gathered around a table, playing Dungeons and Dragons. She was laying a good smooch on his bright red baby-face; he remembered the moment vividly. He reached for the picture but jumped back as Beth rushed over, snatched up the lid, and covered up the box.

"Nothing to see here. Move along," she joked.

Mitch caught the label on the box: *High School Stuff.*

"Whoa. You okay?" Beth looked at his foot.

"I'm good, Beth. I am," Mitch said, feigning a far worse limp than the mildly throbbing toe required. "I have nine spare toes. I'll be just fine." He'd always hidden behind humor. It was the finest act of self-preservation, one he'd perfected since childhood. "So, D&D, huh?"

Beth laughed, moved the lid aside, and pulled the picture out.

"Here," she said, tossing the picture on his lap as he sat on the sofa. She filled their glasses and then joined him.

"Yes. Good times, huh? So…" She leaned into him and tapped his glass. "Enough about me and Tony. Tell me about you, Mitchell. Tell me what you've been doing for, oh, I don't know, the past decade."

Mitch suddenly felt the walls closing in, and breathing became optional. A tsunami of sweat rolled down his back. He wanted to blame it on the booze, but he knew it was more than that. Words eluded him as Beth stared at him, awaiting a response.

"Oh, what's wrong, Mr. Writer? You've never been at a loss for words as long as I've known you, city-boy."

"You know how Google works, right? I'm sure you know what I've been up to. Twitter, Facebook, Google, Instagram. Hell, my ugly mug is all over the place."

"Hey, Mr. Sensitive. Take it easy. I was just joking." Beth held both hands up in surrender. "It's not like I spend my time Googling you."

"Okay, okay." Mitch took a breath. "I've mostly been focusing on my writing. Well, that and reading, and catching late-night movies down in Soho, or binge-watching the latest Netflix show du jour. Ah yes, the rock 'n' roll lifestyle of a writer."

Beth smiled. "You've been doing more than okay, Mitch. And yes, I've been keeping tabs. I've even read a couple of your books, of course." She pointed at the floor-to-ceiling bookcase, where he could make out several heavily dog-eared copies of his books.

Feeling like a giant inside a dwarven bathtub, he pivoted the conversation. "Holy crow. I'd forgotten all about this picture." Mitch ran his hand over all his old friends' faces. They were all there: Ray, Clay, Dave, Dawn, Chris, Jesse and Beth. "I remember the day. Ray's thief, Marticus, that was his name, right? That Beholder petrified him. Man, was he pissed at Dave!

"The whole campaign kind of petered out after that. You know, Ray was always a sore loser. Do you talk to him anymo—" Mitch noticed Beth's slack-jawed gaze. "What?"

"Really?" she asked.

Mitch hesitated. "Really, what?"

"Oh, I don't know…" Beth finished her drink and set it down. "You did the most beautiful sidestep I've ever seen. And, hey, I teach elementary school. Those little ankle-biters know all about avoidance. That, and the fact you played a full-out Houdini and disappeared after you walked off the stage at graduation, and you don't think the people closest to you have a right to know why?"

Despite being cornered by Beth with no escape, he continued to frantically seek a way out. Instead, all he saw was a living room inside a house that his former best friend and the love of his life lived in. The images rushed through him and twenty years pushed and pulled at him like a temporal whip that nearly snapped his neck and broke his heart.

"I…I don't know what you're talking about."

"Come on, Mitchell. It's been hanging out there for the past ten years like the biggest damn pink elephant in the history of all pink elephants!"

Mitch had been dreading this moment. All the anger and resentment. The crushing weight of betrayal had kept close, insidious company since graduation night. "No. It's okay. We don't need to get into all that old stuff. I was just hoping…"

Beth shook her head. "So, I can see you're still the master of passive-aggressiveness. Come on, Mitch. I know you're still pissed at me. It's as plain as the telltale look of anger on your face, which you've worn since I saw you at Wegmans and every second since."

He didn't know what to say. He'd run through this scenario dozens of times, but now, sitting here, staring at her pale, gorgeous face, and looking into the eyes that had melted his heart when they'd first met in Mrs. Dixon's class, he was lost for words. The hurt was still there, but he'd dealt with confrontation in the same way his entire life. Avoidance was an art, and Mitchell Andrew Roberts was Michael-freaking-Angelo. He stared into the dwindling liquor in his glass and suddenly became a huge fan of drinking.

"Well?"

Mitch sat there, searching for an answer. Yes, he was furious, but a long time had gone by. And he prayed for some divine intervention. Then, he realized he didn't believe in God.

"After all these years, do you really have nothing to say about Tony and me? About graduation night? About…us?" Beth's voice cracked.

"What's there to say?" Mitch gazed at the glass.

"Oh, I don't know, Mitch. Gee, you left the night we graduated. Not a word, a note, anything. No goodbye. Nothing."

"A note, huh? What could I have said? Oh, wait… Hey, Beth, congratulations, I'm so happy for you and Tony. I wish you all the best and hope you have the perfect life with a dozen kids and a quaint little bungalow, a minivan, and a goddamn dog. Hallmark hasn't created a card for that occasion.

He felt Beth staring at him. "Always quick with a joke, huh?"

Mitch got up and walked over to the bookshelf. He needed room to think.

"Tell me what happened," said Beth. "I know you and I were close, but I never thought we were, you know, *that* kind of close. You were my best friend. You got me through some of that nasty shit with my family and…I don't understand why you left. Why you left me here… Left me…alone."

The cruel wind caused mournful howls through the doors and windows and matched the bestial calls from the malamute in the kitchen.

Mitch found his shaking fingers tracing over his books on the shelf and closed his eyes as the alcohol fully kicked in—and he wasn't certain it was a good thing. "In vino veritas," he mumbled under his breath as the conflicting memories and shadowy emotions coalesced into finer focus.

"Mitchell!" Beth's harsh shout startled him.

He slowly ran his index finger along the spines of his books on her shelf. And with each title came an image of a pushpin and different colored string, the same kind they use on all those police procedural shows. The analogy made Mitch cringe as he pulled out the first book he'd ever published.

"You're avoiding the question, Mitch. I deserve to know why you never said goodbye." Beth's demanding tone faded to a hurt whisper. She set her drink down and came to stand next to him.

"Please don't just stand there. I know something happened, and if I did it, I am so sorry. But please, for Christ's sake, don't ignore me. If anything, what it has shown me, and hopefully you, with your mom's passing, is that life is too short to not tell the truth."

"You said I didn't leave a note or say goodbye or anything, right?"

"No. Not that I'd ever received."

"Here." Mitch handed over her beaten-up copy of *About to Rage*. He stepped away and filled his glass. "There's your goodbye note, Beth." He emptied half the glass in one pull. "I wrote the note."

Beth stepped back and sat down on the chair, opening the book. "I…I don't understand."

Mitch headed into the kitchen. "You said you'd read all my books."

"Yeah, of course." Beth continued flipping through the book for an answer.

Mitch had no clue what he was doing. He was used to making tea, not alcoholic drinks. But he followed the clues left for him on the counter and did his best.

"Mitch, I've read this book from cover to cover a couple of times, and I still don't know what you mean."

"Check the title and then think about it," he said, stirring his mystery potion.

A long moment passed as Mitch came back through the dining room to find Beth sitting on the coffee table, her face ghostly white and her eyes wide.

"I had no idea."

"Tony knew I was going to ask you out, Beth. The day before. Hell, the night we graduated, on the stage while that boring-ass basketball coach rambled on, Tony pushed me to tell you how I felt." Mitch's words caught in his throat as heavy tears rushed from his tired eyes. "He knew full well. I was crushing on you for over a goddamn year, or more. I fucking told him. Even asked for his advice."

Beth sat frozen.

Mitch leaned against the bookcase, relieved to have finally let Beth know, but somehow, it felt like a hollow victory. It wasn't as if he'd won anything. She was still married to Tony, and he was still the geeky guy standing like a goon in their living room.

He downed the rest of the glass.

The icy wind fought its way through the weak points of the house and caused the fire to flicker.

"I...I'm sorry," Beth whispered as she lowered her head, her tousled locks falling over her face. "Mitch, I told him I was interested in you, but he...uh..."

"Uh, what?"

Beth looked up at Mitch, her eyes lost in a blur of tears, and her words came in gasps. "He...t-told me you were...g-gay."

Beth's words came out in normal time, but for Mitch, each syllable seemed extended for over-annunciation and pronounced effect. It worked. After all, no matter how bizarre or unfathomable the lie had been, it made perfect sense. He felt the edges of sanity curling around him and digging in. And whether it was the alcohol or the blossoming rage,

Mitch fought back and held fast the best he could. Deep down, he heard his mom's calming voice flow through him.

"Mitch…I…" Beth reached for him, but he pulled away.

"No… No. It makes sense. It really does." His mind pitched and swerved as he reached for another drink. "Why not? In for a penny, in for a fucking pound," he mumbled to himself.

After a big gulp, he found it hard to breathe and sweat poured out of him like a drunken water sprinkler.

"I don't care if you are. Really, I don't. I thought it was the reason you left here so fast. Afraid that Tony would tell everyone just to embarrass you." Beth grabbed his arm.

Mitch pulled away and forced down another sip. "Sure. Why not? What else should a supposed best friend do for his old pal?" He moved away from the fireplace and went back to the picture window, leaning on the frame, his hot breath melting away the frost in huge puffs.

"I guess maybe I was mad that you wouldn't share such a precious secret with me."

Mitch stared out into the night. "Secret?" he huffed. "The only secret was that I'd loved you since…since…" He wiped the tears from his face. "The best-kept secret was that Tony Severt, your darling husband, was, and is, a heap of lying, conniving dog shit. And that, good lady, let me tell ya, is insulting good and kind pieces of dog shit everywhere." Mitch knew the words had come out slurred, and he didn't care. The crackling fire melded with the radio, creating an uncomfortable holiday soundtrack as they both cried.

"I know how close you guys were. I wish I could—"

"Not that asshole, Beth."

"Oh. Okay. I wish I had known, Mitch. I really do." She came to his side, and he flinched as she put her hands on his shoulders and turned him to face her.

Her wide eyes, puffy from crying, still held him entranced. And her beautiful face broke into a gentle, loving smile.

She pulled him close. He didn't resist.

"I am very sorry, Mitchie," she said. "I missed you so much."

His tears fell onto her freckled, rosy cheeks and mixed with hers.

Before he could utter another word, for once in his hesitant life, he acted.

Their lips touched, and he squeezed her tight as "Baby It's Cold Outside" played on the radio, surrounding them as they descended onto the carpet in front of the raging fire.

The warm glow of the fireplace cast jumping, flickering images onto the stucco ceiling and Mitch was awash in a euphoria of vodka, music, repressed anger, love, and pent-up lust.

Beth lay on his bare chest, and for the first time in his life, he didn't worry about his man-boobs or anything else. No. Tonight was a night for ignoring the oppressive weight of the past and for living in the moment. Tomorrow, he'd have to face saying goodbye to his mom, and the thought bored into him like an insidious virus. But he tried his best to keep it at bay. He pushed it all aside and kissed her deeply.

Beth pulled the large crocheted blanket over them as they lay on the carpet.

"So, really, what the hell is a Murphy bed?"

The storm waged war outside, while peace and growing warmth was being waged inside the old house.

INTERLUDE

Harvester of Sorrow

Karrie Wilkins ran from the house out into the blinding snow, following the screaming of her husband, Stanley, who'd been tending the livestock and the barns.

The panicked calls of the cows and horses in the two large structures awakened them minutes before.

Karrie fought her way through the deep snow, each step feeling like trudging through dense mud, while Stanley's screams pierced the night. The only light available was that of the pair of flickering dusk-to-dawn lights mounted atop the barn's peaks.

She held a hand up to protect her blinking eyes from the brutal snow tearing at her as she finally made it past the garage and saw the outbuildings, and it wasn't the ten below zero that ripped the breath from her lungs.

The entirety of their centuries-old farm—barns, outer buildings, paddock, and all—was gone.

Stanley stood, swinging widely with a shovel at nothing…but at something. The Darkness. The surrounding night? She couldn't see anything but pitch blackness.

She took a few staggering steps closer.

It was moving. That Darkness. It should have been impossible. But as tall as the barns and equally wide, it had glowing red eyes that flickered sinisterly within its twisting black form.

The woman's scream pierced the harsh night due to the long, sharp talons and rows of grinning, gnashing teeth.

This violent and unforgiving Darkness decimated everything, and the unrelenting snowstorm brutally destroyed everything in its path.

Few surviving animals escaped, jumping fences or breaking through, to vanish into the thick pines.

Then the Darkness seemed to toy with her flailing, screaming husband as he tried in desperation to protect his home. The horrid, cruel thing lashed out with two razor-sharp tendrils and pierced the man's leg and shoulder, lifting him as one would a rag doll, holding him high in the cutting air. Through the deafening gusts, Karrie thought she could hear a bone-chilling sound of laughter as the Darkness let loose a bout of slashes and hungry bites, rending the farmer into a miasma of blood, jagged flesh, and bones in a matter of seconds.

Seconds to shred Karrie and Stanley Wilkins' lives to hell.

Her mind snapped, and her bottomless, shrill scream didn't last long as the Darkness offered no quarter, relishing in each drop of blood and delectable flesh.

It was insatiable. It would easily consume all living beings in its path. Whether it be on foot, hoof, or wing, it left nothing alive.

However, something unearthly and rage-filled still consumed it.

And this otherworldly thirst drove the Darkness onward.

It would not relent until it had destroyed the human soul that had awoken it.

It followed the deep, symbiotic blood connection that now tied it to the old human.

Unforgiving. Soulless. Bloodthirsty.

22

I Think You Know What I Mean

A loud noise broke Mitch's heavy, drunken slumber. He mumbled, and tried to ignore it. But it came again. He was having an incredible dream. But more like a hazy memory. *It was his twelfth birthday. He was with his mom. They were driving in Rochester. They were talking and laughing. Memories and dreams, bright and colorful, blended like film montages. Flashbacks of better times. As old country music played inside Mitch's dream, they drove on, then stopped at a small strip mall. Three or four blurry storefronts welcomed them as his mom turned to him. A tiny, elvish woman, with long, crazy dark hair and thick eyeglasses, like those he wore. She smiled her gentle, heartwarming smile. "Happy birthday, Mitchie. Anything you want today…is yours." Mitch looked out the window of their station wagon and read the store sign:* Empire Comics & Games. *"I've heard your not-so-subtle hints." She laughed. A laugh that always made him happy. It was honest and unapologetic. "Let's go. But remember, let's not tell your father. This is between us."*

The loud vibrating buzz and piano came again.

"For all that's holy," he grumbled, blindly reaching for his phone.

"Sorry. It's mine," Beth said, rolling on top of him and leaning over ungracefully to the coffee table.

Everything came rushing back to Mitch in a throbbing haze. "Ah, should have guessed, Norah Jones," he said, praying for death—or at least a bottle of aspirin. A rush of grief and anger flashed over him. The dream. It seemed so real, yet was fleeing from his groggy thoughts with each precious second.

Beth lay naked on top of him as she answered her phone. Her beautiful alabaster skin, enhanced by a vast array of freckles, made Mitch's own skin prickle.

"What?" Beth shouted into her phone. "Hold on. Slow down. I can't understand a word you're saying when you're screaming like a damn lunatic."

Mitch tried to rub the drunk out of his puffy eyes.

"Tony!" Beth yelled. "Tony! Okay, okay. I hear you. Knock it off. Yes, yes, I will move the car. You don't need to be a psychotic asshole every day of your life." She grimaced and mouthed a "Sorry," as she slid off him.

Mitch found his phone and a different panic jolted through him as he noticed the time. "Shit!" He threw on his jeans and made for the bathroom.

"Tony. It's none of your business. Just hold on and I'll move the damn car." Beth held her hand over her phone. "Mitchie, I'm sorry. Can you move your car? Tony needs to plow the driveway, and he's being a classic asshat about it."

"No worr—" Beth cut him off with a deep, lingering kiss.

Checking the time on his cell, he pulled back. "Shit...shit...shit. I am in deep shit. I'm sorry, Bethie. Mom's funeral is in a couple of hours. I...I..."

"No, no. Go. Go. I'll see you there." Beth waved him off.

He walked to the kitchen, and the dog promptly jumped on him.

"Oh, shit." Mitch heard Beth walk in from the living room. "Pablo." She threw her clothes on and rushed to the kitchen door.

Mitch sat on the floor, covered with snow and tongue-lashed by the lovable malamute.

Beth helped him up, shooing the furry beast away, and Mitch hurriedly clambered into his boots. And kissed her deeply, holding her cellphone away from her ear.

Beth pulled him into her and nibbled on his ear.

"Guess you aren't gay. Huh. Who'd a thunk it?"

"Don't you know it." With one last hug, Mitch laughed and headed toward the door.

"Go. I'll meet you at Murphy's. If you or your dad need anything, let me know, okay?"

"You got it," Mitch said, opening the door.

"Come on, big guy. Mitchie's running late. We have to let him go before Officer Doofus buries his car." Beth lightly touched Pablo's collar, and the big hound relented and climbed off Mitch.

"Thanks." Mitch brushed off the snow, reached out and gave Pablo's fur a good tussle. "No harm, no foul, right, Chewie?"

"Chewie?" Beth asked. "Oh yeah, Star Trek Galactica."

Mitch shot her an incredulous look. "Hey!"

She shot him a wink.

A loud honk came from outside.

"You'd better go. Something tells me Tony will not be too happy to see you here." Beth kissed Mitch again.

"Oh, I'm sure. Do you think?! I'll see you later." Mitch closed the kitchen door behind him and tried to find the steps that were buried under a good foot of snow.

The soft glow of the late morning sunrise fought desperately to pierce the thick, twisting white veil of the brewing storm, much as Mitch desperately fought his way through the deep snow to his car. And trying ever more desperately to ignore Tony's searing glare as the bearded man sat inside the oversized four-by-four monstrosity, idling ominously in the partially plowed driveway.

After trudging through the heavy snow, he cleared his car off enough to get inside. The cold 4-cylinder begrudgingly fired up. He tried his hardest to ignore the large man who was staring at him, hoping that any god who might be listening would help him escape without Tony causing any trouble. Mitch felt his chest tighten, unsure if it was due to last night's alcohol or the growing fear that Tony was aware of his and Beth's actions. Despite the possibility of facing consequences, he opened the door, releasing a rush of emotions onto the once untouched snow.

Ignoring Tony, or at least pretending to, Mitch wiped the vomit from his bearded chin and quickly cleared enough of the windshield and side windows to slowly begin making his way through the snow. Tony had left the high beams on, aimed directly at Mitch's face. As he drove closer, he could see that Tony was out of uniform and wore jet-black sunglasses. Mitch was grateful for it. It was almost certain there were laser-guided hate beams firing in his direction.

When the front of his car reached the truck's driver-side door and it suddenly kicked open, Mitch barely had a second to register and slammed on the brakes.

"No!"

The driveway exit was blocked; Tony's Ford descent signaled trouble for Mitch. "Oh boy. Here we go." His breath came in a white plume.

Tony had gotten bigger, more muscular than Mitch remembered. He'd always been a farm boy, kind of big, but now it looked as if he'd been doing steroid shots and living in a gym. He wasn't afraid of his ex-best friend. Not at all. Being able to take a punch was the Roberts Family Number One Survival Technique. Especially when his dad would come home from Yowner's or the American Legion after closing. It was always an enjoyable experience in emotional and physical pain. Better him than his mom.

Tony's slow, intimidating gait caused acid to roil in Mitch's stomach.

It was a basic police technique that Mitch had learned while researching one of his novels. And very effective, most of the time. His only desire was to escape, head home, shower, and reach the funeral home before his father found him.

Tony stood at the driver's door and tapped his gloved hand on the window.

Unwisely, Mitch felt abnormally confident; this bravado would soon end poorly. Rolling down the window, he said, "Good morning, Officer. I'm certain I don't need to tell you, but it is a courtesy to lower your high beams when driving into oncoming traffic."

Tony grabbed his door with both hands and leaned into the car, nearly filling up the entire window.

"Hilarious, Roberts. What are you doing throwing up in my driveway? Regardless of how repulsive that is, I need to know why you're here."

Mitch flipped the visor down and looked at the clock radio. His already overtaxed heartbeat thrummed like a double-bass drum as the digital numbers raced forward. He was going into even deeper hot water with his father, a far worse fate than anything this Neanderthal could ever inflict on him.

"Look. I don't have time for this. I need to get home to pick up my dad. You know we're burying my mom today, right?" Mitch looked straight ahead. "You remember her, don't you?"

Tony's leather-gloved hands tightened on the door. "Yeah, I remember your mother. And I also remember all the calls we've received to pick up your old man for drinking and driving and even a few times for smacking your precious mom around. How could I forget?" He leaned in even closer and sniffed. "Whoa. You aren't planning on driving, are you, Mitchell? Are you becoming like your drunk, wife-beating old man?"

Mitch's hands tightened on the steering wheel. "I… Uh…um…I'm fine. Thanks for your overwhelming concern."

Mitch glimpsed Beth in his rearview mirror, standing on the snowy steps of the porch.

"I have to go. Can you please move your obviously over-compensating monster truck?" Mitch felt the cold jab slip through his lips and his gut clinched tight.

"So, I'll ask again… Why the hell are you at my house? With my *wife*?"

"Tony!" Beth called through the shifting, brutal lake wind.

"Tony…" Mitch turned to the overbearing man and met his steely gaze. "I'm a bit confused. Why are you the one so pissed off? Honestly, why? Aren't you the one who fucked me over?" He couldn't believe the words flying from his mouth. "You know, your *best friend*."

"It's your story, writer boy. Tell your bullshit story any way you like it. Why are you here?" Tony's voice rose to a shout as he tried to open the locked door.

"Tony! Goddamn it, stop!" Beth's yelling cut through the atmosphere. "Knock your bullshit off!"

"Get back in the house. You'll freeze your ass off. Besides, Mitchie and I are just catching up."

He glared at Mitch and stepped back. He glanced back at Beth, and Mitch saw she was still in her bathrobe.

"Oh, shitballs," Mitch mumbled, and closed his eyes and waited.

That's when Tony grabbed hold of his jacket and yanked him out of his car, through the open window.

It was a blur of motion and Mitch barely knew which way was up.

Tony pulled him nose-to-nose and Mitch could feel the man's hot breath as he tightened his violent grip on his jacket.

"You fat fuck. You fucked her, didn't you?"

It wasn't a question, as Mitch felt the first punch crunch into his jaw, sending his glasses off into a snowbank, dropping him to his knees in a desperate search for air.

Through the howling wind, Beth screamed for Tony to stop.

That's when his ex-best friend's boot lifted him a good foot off the frozen ground, stealing away any chance of breathing Mitch had.

"She's my fucking wife, asshole." Tony seemed almost possessed and lifted Mitch up by the back of his jacket.

Then he slammed him onto the hood of his running car.

"Stop!" Beth screamed into the whipping snow. "Damn you! I'm calling the sheriff!"

"Shut the fuck up, bitch! This is between me and my best friend here!" Tony smashed Mitch into the hot metal of the hood again, smearing his face in the melting snow. "I'll get to you in a goddamn minute." Then, with a sudden jerk, he yanked Mitch from the hood so violently it nearly gave him whiplash, but when Tony continued to yell and looked at Beth, Mitch saw a chance and took it.

Although he was on his knees and trying very hard to remember how to breathe, he swung upward, nailing Tony's crotch with a full punch.

It dropped the big cop to the ground.

Once free from Tony's grip, Mitch grabbed the big cop by the jacket collar and pulled back to return the violent favor.

He stared down at Tony, who was wincing in pain and grabbing his crotch.

Mitch's inner storm raged far more fiercely than the one outside.

The two old best friends, once brothers, just stared at one another, while Beth continued to beg them both to stop.

Snow pelted them both, and Mitch finally spoke.

"You were my best friend. Yeah, I slept with your wife. And I know I should feel really bad about that. Maybe later I will, but…"

Tony could only moan in pain. But his dark brown eyes held a raging, fiery storm that could melt all the surrounding snow.

"But if you remember, Tony, you told me to go for it. Remember that?" Mitch leaned in close. "I fucking do. Every damn night I had a nightmare about what you'd done. What this place had done, every goddamn, spiteful minute since I left the shit town, and you, behind."

He let Tony go to collapse into the deepening snowbank, wiped the blood from his mouth, and fished around for his glasses.

Once he was back in his car, Beth came running toward them and stopped. There must have been something in his eyes or his flushing-red face that caused her to stop dead; her wide hazel eyes glinted in the early sunlight as Mitch watched her lose the battle against the biting storm.

"Hate to run, but I have to go bury my mom."

As he pulled out onto the slippery street, he saw Beth up in Tony's face, giving him the business, and he hesitated, almost wishing the big dolt would do something stupid so he could go back and show him what a real man was. Mitch knew it was an adrenaline-filled bravado rearing its ugly head again, but luckily, Tony got up and clambered into the truck and went about plowing the rest of the driveway.

A grateful sigh escaped Mitch; his phone's ring nearly sent him leaping from his seat. It was his dad.

"Oh boy. Nice going, Roberts."

Mitch sped home as fast as he dared on the slick, snow-covered streets and prayed that his father wouldn't be out front with his M14 when he got there.

23

Kiss an Angel Good Morning

Everything was a blur. A frozen blur. It took a guilt-ridden lifetime for Mitch to get to his folks' house, ignore his father's belligerent cussing, and take a shower, trying desperately to wash the battleship-anchor-sized guilt off him, to no avail. His dad was still swearing, and he felt like garbage for being late. He got dressed in the only smart clothes he had, rushed downstairs, tried to dodge the missiles his father had aimed directly at him, and joined his dad in the car.

It took until they turned onto Main Street for his irate father to speak.

"Mitchell…" Gordon said, his voice filled with controlled rage, while staring out the passenger-side window.

The heavy snow meant that visibility was close to zero, but even through the thick veil, Mitch watched a flurry of ghosts slithering and taunting him.

"Dad… I know. I'm sor—"

His father held up a leather-gloved hand, his stony gaze never leaving the window.

"Now, boy, I don't expect you to get the way me and your mom did things around here. You've been gone so long and all."

Mitch felt a cannonball form in his gut, and he reached to turn down the heat.

"Ya know, I've never been much good at talking." His father's tone was still gruff, but softer as he continued to stare out the window. A bit of the glass misted; he absentmindedly wiped it. "Talking to you, I mean."

Mitch slowed the car as it swerved into the deep ruts.

"And I know you don't like me much and I'm pretty sure you think I never cared too much for…you. I'm goddamn sure I deserved a whole lotta your hate, boy. I…I…I'm not proud of a lot of the shit I've done in my life. Hell, never thought I'd amount to much growing up on the farm with my folks."

"Dad, it's okay. You don't have to—"

Holding up his hand, his dad said, "No. Let me speak."

Mitch nodded.

"I won't make excuses, and there's one thing I've never done, and that's lie to you, or blow smoke up your ass. I never wanted to be a father. Just never thought I had it in me. My father did well for us. We never wanted for anything. We had food, a roof over our heads. Sometimes it might have leaked a little, but it was a roof. I know you never met my folks, and, well..." He paused, smearing more fog away. "Consider yourself lucky. Now, your mother, my sweet Maggie. God bless her heart. She knew how to get me to do things sometimes. The right things, as she'd always tell me when I had my head up my keister, and I reckon that was more often than I'd care to admit. Guess now, looking back, maybe I should have listened to her more often too."

Mitch fought for something to say, but between the worsening storm and his father's words, he was floundering in empty thoughts.

"Anyway, I didn't want to go getting all maudlin and shit, but your mother's passing has made me look at things...a lot of things different."

Mitch caught his father glancing at him, then the old man turned back to the safety of his foggy window.

"No," was all Gordon said.

Mitch turned left onto Allen Street and a sudden rush of grief washed over him as he saw Murphy's parking lot and the side streets filled with cars parked bumper-to-bumper. He slowly drove around the back and Mr. Murphy met them, donned in an all-black wool coat and wearing a warm smile. He motioned to a reserved parking space and Mitch pulled in.

His dad's big blue eyes were bloodshot, he was pale as a ghost, and he looked frail. Mitch had never seen his dad that fragile ever. He was a tough-as-nails Marine, Vietnam vet, Tet survivor. Never showed a moment of weakness.

A downpour of snow immediately hit his father as he slowly opened the car door. He gave a "give me a second" gesture at the red-faced undertaker waiting coldly but patiently outside the funeral home.

"Look... Mitchie, I know I've been a miserable bastard to you and your mother. Y'all deserved much better than this old man gave you." He rested his hand on Mitch's knee.

Mitch flinched a little, then relaxed.

"I...should've done better by her...by you." He turned toward Mitch, who felt wildly adrift in this new, awkward moment. "I am sorry."

The world around Mitch froze in a bizarre, otherworldly tableau, as if he were outside his body looking in. Sweat poured down his face, and despite the brutal winter, an odd warmth fell over him. His heartbeat thrummed in his ears, and he felt drunk; surreal, as he stared at his father…his dad.

His old man coughed, abruptly wiped the tears from his eyes, and in a jerky movement, sat up straight and focused again.

"Son, I always liked that Connolly girl. I hope she was worth it. Sure, it looks like you took a good whoopin'. I hope those boxing lessons, as brief as they were, did you good. Tony has always deserved a good attitude adjustment. Your mom never liked him much anyhow." Gordon got out, greeted Mr. Murphy, and leaned back in. "We have a few minutes to say goodbye before Dave closes the casket. I'll be inside. Don't dick the dog too long now, boy. Your mother's waiting." With that, he closed the door, giving it a light tap with his fist, turned, and let Mr. Murphy escort him into the warmth and heaviness of the funeral parlor.

A sudden, violent gust shook the compact car and the high-pitched whine from the wind sent shivers through Mitch's already freezing body.

"I'm sorry…Dad," Mitch said, and he was sure the raging snow and gusting wind attacking the car obliterated his sincere apology.

"Thanks, good talk," Mitch said to the whipping snow.

Mitch wasn't much of a drinker. His father's alcoholism had caused Mitch to abstain from alcohol his whole life. Except for last night with Beth and his throbbing hangover, of course—he now truly understood the merits of drink.

Instead, he took a pull from the iced tea bottle in the console. He took a deep breath, got out of the car, and followed his livid father into the funeral home.

Looking to the north, brooding storm clouds were marching inland, and it sent a shiver down his spine.

A stifling wave of hot air greeted him as he stepped into the funeral home. A younger man, about his age, stood before him, wearing a soft, friendly smile and a flawless suit and tie.

"Good morning. Mitchell?"

"Morning. Yes, I'm Mitch." He shook the man's outstretched hand. "Is my dad in there?"

The young man shook his head, blushing. "Uh, yes. He's in with Mr. Murphy and your mom. I'm so very sorry for your loss."

His voice seemed familiar to Mitch, and the heavy fog inside his hungover mind cleared.

Mitch thanked the man, entering the viewing room, only to be gently stopped.

"I'm sorry. I know this is incredibly inappropriate, but you don't remember me, do you?"

Mitch turned to look at the man. He got a little irritated, thinking it was a fan looking for him to sign a book. He hated himself for even thinking such an arrogant thought, and any other time, he knew he'd be cool with it. But not today. Not at his mom's funeral. But, just as his hangover-fueled indignation was about to hit its fevered pitch, the man's face made sense to him.

He stood taller than Mitch. A big, beefy guy. More fit than fat, with a dark red flattop. A thick mustache adorned his pale, freckled face. It was slowly coming back to him as the man shook his hand.

"Here, let me help you out. 'By Odin's might, Thorgrim shall banish thee to the nine *hells!*'" the man said in a gruff Scottish accent. He winced at his volume. "Sorry."

Mitch's memory-flash drive scanned the years and then clicked into place. "Holy shit, Clay?"

Clay laughed, nodding. "At your service."

Instinctively, Mitch hugged his old friend and squeezed. "Sorry I didn't recognize you, man."

"No, it's okay. It's been a long time. I understand. I've put on my fair share of the Freshman Fifteen, in addition to my Senior Seventy, and I avoided suits like the plague back in school."

"No kidding." Mitch said, gently patting his stomach, "I'm right there with you. I should have remembered. I just talked to Chris, and he told me you still lived here."

"Yup. I didn't travel too far from the asylum. Man, again, I'm so sorry about your mom. She was a great lady."

Mitch nodded. "Thank you. I really appreciate it. So, you do the mortician thing, huh? Didn't see that one coming."

Clay straightened his tie. "Yeah, well. Me neither. It just kind of happened. Few career choices in the good old three-one-five, sadly."

"I get that. I do. Trust me. If I didn't have to be here, I sure wouldn't be." Mitch felt the heavy gaze of his father, who was talking to a group of people Mitch didn't recognize, except for the tall mortician who had assisted his father earlier. "Sorry. It's just, you know how it was for me." Inside, Mitch kept repeating to himself, *Shut up. Today is not about you, you selfish idiot.* It was a voice he seldom listened to.

Dropping his casual demeanor, Clay stiffened. "No. No. I

understand. I do. I'm sorry, Mitch."

"Oh yeah. Of course. Are you coming to Yowner's later? It's not really my ideal place, but, ya know," Mitch said, offering his hand.

Clay's mammoth of a hand enveloped Mitch's. "I will. Once I finish up here with um, uh, you know." His round face flushed near the color of a fire truck.

"I appreciate that. Thanks, man." Mitch put his hand on Clay's shoulder. "We'll catch up later, okay?"

"Hope so. Again, my sincerest condolences," Clay said.

Mitch turned to see Mr. Murphy standing in the viewing room archway.

"Hello, Mitchell. Your father wanted me to ask you, and I quote, *If you're done ass-grabbing, come in and pay your respects to your mother.*'" Mr. Murphy blushed. "His words, not mine, I assure you."

Empty chairs filled the viewing room. A sea of multicolored flowers surrounded the coffin, mostly purple lilacs and various lilies. Charley Pride played low through the speakers and with every note of "When I Stop Leaving, I'll Be Gone," Mitch fought desperately to keep it together.

His father stood next to the casket, heaving tears and talking to his wife. Mitch thought he'd seen him place something inside the casket, but he couldn't make out what.

Mitch couldn't see her, only the vast array of flowers and the memory boards he and his father had made hastily. But the picture was beautiful. He didn't want to go up there. He knew he had to, but every ounce of his being told him to turn around, run to his car, and beat feet back to Brooklyn.

A painful stabbing in his chest overcame him.

Hot tears formed in the corners of his eyes, and his throat constricted.

Gordon turned around, wiping his face with a handkerchief. "Mitchell. You had best come to say goodbye. Norm has to get things ready for the calling hours and all." He blew his nose and headed for the corner.

Mitch took a deep breath and whispered to himself, "Come on, Roberts. It's your mom, for Christ's sake." After a second, he approached the casket as if with every cautious step, the worn carpeted floor would open beneath him.

His mom lay peacefully in a flower-patterned dress, neatly pressed, with her well worn rosary tucked tightly in her frail, bird like hands. Tears fell from Mitch's eyes, blurring his vision. She hated dresses. Or at least she had never worn one, as far as he recalled. His father's favorite, Mitch guessed. He wiped the tears away and fought to catch his breath, and it was like being pulled by an invisible Herculean undertow from which he fought desperately to escape.

She looked far frailer and thinner than he remembered. His mind spun, grasping to remember the last time he'd seen her.

It was in a Christmas picture she'd sent him. It must've been a year ago. In front of the once green tree, lost among the sea of silvery tinsel and a lifetime of ornaments. She looked happy. Healthy. But the body inside the oblong box looked nothing like his mother. A surreal, almost mocking, emaciated effigy of the earthbound angel that had been his mom.

Mitch's body seized, and he caught himself on the stout frame of the casket.

Gathering his balance, his shaking hands recoiled from the coffin, as if it were burning his flesh away, down to the bone.

"I'm sorry, Mitchell. I truly hate to interrupt. But people are arriving. I can make them wait, but I wanted to let you know we have quite a few folks looking to pay their respects to your mother," Mr. Murphy said.

"No. It's okay. I'll be done in a minute."

"All right. That's fine. Take your time."

Mitch, after the mortician's departure, turned back to his mother.

"Hey, Mom. I love you so much. I'm so sorry for being such a selfish asshole. I...I...I'm sorry. I should have been there for you. I should never have left you alone. You needed me and I took off. I'm sorry: I wish I could make things right with you. I wish I hadn't lost all this time with you. I love you, Mom. Hope you can forgive me. Not sure how things were with Dad. You didn't deserve his abusive bullshit. I'm sorry. So damn sorry." Jolting waves of grief shook him. It took a minute, but Mitch finally composed himself and dried his tear-streaked face on his sleeve.

"I have to go, Mom. The Visigoths are at the gate. But I...I wanted to thank you for always being there for me. For always being my biggest supporter. And for seeing things in me I still struggle to recognize today. I want to give you something. Especially now that I have it tattooed on my arm." Mitch pulled out a moleskin notebook, opened it up, and pulled out a small piece of yellowing paper. He delicately unfolded it and flattened it out. "Mom, you typed this on your old Royal typewriter years ago and gave it to me. When you told me that these words reminded you of me, it changed me forever. There's no way in hell I'd be doing what I am today, no way I'd be the person I am today, if it weren't for these words—and you." Mitch kissed the typed page.

He tucked the piece of paper in her pocket and leaned close. "You and Mr. Thoreau were right, Mom. I am my own drummer. Thank you for believing in me, even when I didn't believe in myself. I love you so much. Until we meet again. I'll try to keep Dad in line. Tell Grandma and Grandpa I love them too. They're going to boot me out now. I'd best stop rambling. I'll miss you." With that, Mitch stalked away and joined his father in the shady corner of Murphy's Funeral Home.

The next four hours were a painful blur.

Unless forced to interact, Mitch's father ignored him constantly. He also noticed that Beth was conspicuously absent, and fought desperately not to let it bother him. He tucked it all away, did his duty as a son. He offered handshakes and smiles, pretending to recall everyone saying goodbye to the most angelic person Mitch had ever known.

Mr. Murphy's announcement of the spring graveside service and the family's Yowner's wake invitation (because of the season) left Mitch feeling both relieved and annoyed.

"Go warm up the car, boy. I need to take care of some things here. I'll be out in a minute." Gordon stormed over to the casket to speak to Mr. Murphy.

"Boy?" Mitch clenched his fists and headed outside. *That shit is getting old.* While shivering inside the cold car, he checked his cell and, sure enough, there were half a dozen missed calls, two voicemails, and no texts. After briefly considering tossing the phone into a huge snowbank, he listened to Beth's messages.

"Hey, Mitchell. I am so, so damn sorry. I can't talk long, but I ju—" The message ended.

That's weird, he thought, and listened to the next one.

"Mitch. Hey. I'm sorry I missed the funeral. Something suddenly came up. My sincerest condolences. Please give my best to your father… Bye." The message ended with more questions than answers, it seemed.

"What the hell was that?" Beth sounded robotic. Cold. Something wasn't right. So, he listened to it again.

At the very end, there was another sound. A voice. Deep, familiar, saying, "Hang up the goddamn phone!" Mitch squeezed the cell and nearly broke it.

"Sonofabitch! Fucking Tony!"

With each ticking second, his emotions changed. Angry, sad, happy, feeling ignored, desperate, love, rage. Round and round it went until his dad walked out of the funeral home, shaking Mr. Murphy's hand and wiping his eyes with his jacket sleeve.

"Batten down the hatches, Roberts. Your last night in hell's half-acre is far from over," Mitch said to the car's warm interior as he reached over and pushed the passenger door open. "With any hope, this snowstorm will put me out of my misery," he mumbled.

Entering, Gordon closed the door and retrieved a flask from his jacket.

"Yowner's." He cracked the lid and took a shot, avoiding eye contact with his son.

"Of course." Mitch drove out of the parking lot and tried to ignore the arctic temperatures outside the car—and the near-black storm clouds encroaching over the small town from Lake Ontario.

Appropriate, Mitch mused, then continued to the old bar.

INTERLUDE

There was never enough.

The Darkness had had far too long to fester.

Far too long to watch as the seasons came and went.

Far too long watching, waiting for its time.

For its freedom.

Evil bitterness fed the Darkness and its bloodthirsty sea of teeth and talons as it devoured and lapped up every drop and groaned in otherworldly ecstasy with every pound of flesh it consumed.

It was drawing close to the blood source. It felt it with every inch of frozen ground it rent.

The feeble human's cabin and the minuscule souls it fed upon were only the beginning.

For the Darkness sensed the human gathering ahead.

It saw the lights.

It hungrily sensed the delectable souls, every creature great and small, as it sped forward.

Its time was coming.

24

One More Ride

The snowstorm-ravaged streets of the lakeside town were quickly advancing from treacherous to apocalyptic. Mitch could barely keep the car in his lane. Only the multitudes of brake lights kept him from banging the Honda into one of the empty storefronts or the six-foot snowbanks on either side of Main Street.

He turned into a skid and righted the car. "Jesus fuckin' Christ, boy. You trying to kill me next?" Gordon shouted, fighting not to lose any of the flask's contents.

After taking a second to catch his breath, Mitch turned to his father. "Really?"

Gordon carried on drinking and stared out the snow-covered window as the wipers fought the storm.

"Kill you NEXT? Really?"

"Turn left," Gordon ordered, pointing with his deformed forefinger, which he'd damaged in Korea. A story he'd never completely told.

"I know where Yowner's is, Dad. How the hell could I forget?" Mitch gave up on getting an answer. Turned left. It was more of a fishtail pray-to-God kind of turn, but he managed and came to a slushy stop at the front of Yowner's Tavern.

"Well, well. Looks like we're being blessed by small-town royalty, boy." His father motioned for the Sterling Point Police cruiser parked smack-dab in front of the old bar.

"Who's that?" Mitch asked, parking the car.

"Oh, why, that tiny, ferret-looking guy is Mayor August 'Auggie' Van Dyne, and the cowboy-wannabe holding the older guy from falling in a snowbank is our own lawman, Sheriff Notebaert. Nice guy, but he kinda makes Barney Fife look like Rambo."

"Ah, I didn't think any small towns had their own cops anymore."

His father let out a half-hearted chuckle. "Don't let the stupid hat and dollar-store badge fool ya, boy. Sterling Point really doesn't. He's just window dressing for our loyal and brave mayor."

"Ah." Mitch had nothing to add and opened the door.

"Whoa. What are ya doing, boy? We park around the back. You know there's no parking on this side of the street," Gordon grumbled.

"I know, I know. I'm going to drop you off here and head back to the house. I want to grab something. I'll be right back." Mitch hoped his father wouldn't see through him.

The old man's bright blue eyes squinted, as if he were reading deep into Mitch's mind, and for a tense moment, Mitch feared he did. He just stared at him.

"Okay. But don't dilly-dally too long. There are folks inside that'll want to see you. Not sure why, but they will." With that, Gordon tucked the flask away and crawled out of the car, and turned quickly and shouted through the howling wind, "Don't go running off on me, okay?" Then, without another word, he made his way through the two-foot gap between a couple of snow drifts.

Even though it normally took only five minutes on a bad day to get from Yowner's to his folks' house, as the hellacious storm kicked into full swing, it took Mitch nearly fifteen. All the way, he kicked out any intrusive thoughts other than packing his clothes and his laptop, and getting out of Sterling Point as fast as he could.

Once gone, he'd never have to look back. He'd change his phone number and forget any calls from the 315 area code. This time, Mitch had no intention of returning.

While he packed everything up and dug through his closet, Mitch found his father's Ka-Bar knife. He couldn't even recall having taken it, although he was pretty sure it was during one of his many acts of passive-aggressive teenage rebellion. After all, one would not want to be too actively aggressive with a short-fused drunk with anger issues that made the Incredible Hulk look like the Dalai Lama.

Finding his backpack full, Mitch tucked the knife into an inside jacket pocket and trudged downstairs to the living room. The entire house was a time capsule. A wood-and-plaster dichotomy of happiness and despair. Mitch looked around the room and tried to memorize every inch. Even the stack of Genny beer cans beside his father's La-Z-Boy.

He walked over, kicked the thigh-high stack, sending beer cans skittering into the dining room and bouncing off the television stand. Sitting down on his mom's spot on the couch, a knife of grief punctured his heart, and he fell back and let out a bestial scream that was matched by a lone dog, barking in the storm.

"Damn it, Mom!" Mitch cried out. "Why'd you leave? Why'd you make me come back here? For Christ's sake, you know I can't..."

Somewhere in the house, the striking wind created a soulful howl to filter into the living room.

Mitch let out a cold laugh. "I know. I know." He sat forward, glasses in his hand and rubbing tears from his face.

"Fight or flight, big boy? What's it gonna be?" he asked himself and the cosmos. Something told him both would come up with bupkis.

He was snatching up his backpack when his cell rang. Fumbling into his pocket, he dropped the backpack, and it fell onto the small side table, upending it. A crashing sound echoed through the otherwise silent room.

By the time Mitch had retrieved the cell from his pocket, it had stopped ringing.

"Are you shitting me?" The screen read *Missed Call — Beth.*

"Mitchie... Don't hang up! Aw, hell. Well. I am so sorry. After you guys fought, he got really angry, and Tony grabbed my phone so I couldn't talk. It breaks my heart to miss your mom's funeral. Oh, God, I am so, so, so, sorry. I hope you don't hate me. I'll be coming to Yowner's soon. Just waiting for someone to leave. He has to work soon. With this storm, it shouldn't be long. I know this sounds incredibly insane, but please, please, Mitchie. Let me explain in person...please. Shit, I gotta go." With that, Beth hung up.

"No shit. You've got to be kidding me." Mitch's shoulders dropped, and the phone fell from his hands, rolling into the toppled nightstand.

"Oh, piss off." Mitch knelt and rifled through skeins and skeins of yarn, steno-notepads filled with afghan patterns, and a slew of his mom's creative treasures. He almost felt he was trespassing, but he had to find that stupid phone. He pawed through more yarn and some batting, and his hand landed on what he thought was his cell.

Pulling it out from the pile, Mitch discovered it wasn't his phone. No. It was his grandmother's set of antique crochet hooks. Mitch smiled as he looked them over. During his childhood, everyone had considered them holy relics, like the Shroud of Turin, the Holy Grail, or in Mitch's world, the *Star Wars Christmas Special.* After a moment of reflection, Mitch was certain he would burn in hell for such a comparison, but gave himself a pass as he gazed at the old hooks. The hours upon hours his mom had spent creating with them. And the piles and piles of beautiful afghans she'd made for all the family and friends. And all the American Legion fundraisers and giveaways she'd done for his father. How could he leave them here? Without a doubt, his dad would give them away—or worse, throw them in the trash: Gordon believed everything his mom owned was shit that cluttered up his house and should be thrown out.

Mitch tucked them into his jacket pocket next to the knife.

The old shack held a patchwork quilt of contrasting memories and emotions. Birthdays, Christmases, sleepovers, D&D games in the basement, and Mitch's most treasured memory, the long talks with his mom about the latest Stephen King—and how she did like his work, despite his odd proclivities with ladies' bodily functions.

Mitch laughed, the sudden echo startling him. He'd never had the heart to tell his well-meaning mother that King was using blood as a theme to tie the *Carrie* novel together, much as many other writers had done. And something told him his very smart and sometimes keenly coy mother had known it all along. She was just making him think more critically about the writing. Shaking it off, he wiped a cold tear, zipped up his jacket, and went back out into the raging storm.

Pulling out of the driveway, visibility had gotten even worse during his short time in the house, but something told Mitch to make a quick flyby at Yowner's. Say hello and thank you, then get out of Sterling Point before the state shut the roads down completely.

"I'd rather sleep in a damn snowbank than spend another minute here," he said, wiping the inside of the windshield with his glove.

"You are so screwed, Roberts," he said to his reflection in the rearview. "FUBAR, indeed; Fucked Up Beyond All Recognition."

The roads were even nastier now, as he hit Allenwood Street, but Yowner's parking lot was jam-packed, as was the parking lot of the church next door.

On the radio, the hometown favorite DJ cracked:

"It's your jolly li'l elf on his frozen shelf here, Dean-O's MadKidRadio coming at you here on good old 95.2 WMRK. Merry Christmas Eve, folks. It sure looks like Santa and Rudolph are going to have their hands and hooves full while making the trek around the globe tonight."

"Thanks, Dean-O," Mitch grumbled, and found a small spot between a grease trap and a dumpster. Giving himself an encouraging nod in the mirror, he grabbed his backpack and trudged to the back entrance of his father's home-away-from-home.

25

Tear Me Down

Mitch trudged through deep snow; a low growl, huffing emerged as he turned the alley corner, reaching the tavern.

Mitch jumped as Pablo startled him. This big malamute acted like a pig in mud, rolling around and burying its nose in the snow.

The dog's shaggy head perked and tilted at Mitch as he approached. The coal-black nose sniffed the frigid air, and his thick pink tongue lolled, as if he recognized Mitch and was happy to see him.

"Well, hello there, Mr. Pablo. Did your mean old master leave you alone out in the frozen tundra?" Mitch heard his thick sarcasm and hurt drip from his scathing words, and they nearly froze the second they were spat from his mouth.

Pablo nuzzled his head into Mitch's chest and gave his already wet face a welcoming lick. "Okay, boy, I best get inside before my old master does more damage to me than this hellacious storm can. You okay out here?"

Pablo's dark eyes seemed to twinkle in the bright snow, as if to say, "Hell, yes, human. This is my kinda playground!"

"Fair enough, big guy. I'll make sure your mom checks on ya." With that, he gave the dog one more scrub of the head and entered the warmth of Yowner's Tavern.

Mitch had to adjust his eyes to the cave-like darkness of the bar after the blinding white wall of snow outside. He gave his fogged-up glasses a moment to adjust to the warmth, squinting to take in the thrumming tavern.

All kinds of townspeople, dressed in various weather garb and in various stages of holiday cheer, packed the old bar as the humming cacophony of several conversations commingled with decades-old classic Christmas songs. Because of the craziness of the last few days, he had almost forgotten that today was Christmas Eve. His mom's favorite holiday.

Ahead of him, he saw the two men he and his father had seen walking in earlier. The mayor and the town cop. Glad-handing and more like opportunistic grandstanding masquerading as a Christmas celebration, in Mitch's quick estimation.

"Hey, Mitch!" Beth called out, waving a hand high over the moving crowd. Making his way through the throng of people, he noticed Beth quickly fumbling with her long blonde bangs and pulling her knitted hat over her eye. Mitch filed that away.

Beth took a shot from the bar, and she offered it to Mitch. On the other side sat his father, with two Genny beer cans and a pair of empty shot glasses in front of him. He was deeply engaged in a fiery conversation with the big cop and the diminutive mayor, along with Sal Yowner, the lanky bartender.

Mitch looked from his father to the shot glass in Beth's hand, and held his own hand up in a *no thank you* gesture and gently shook his head.

"It's about time, boy," Gordie said, signaling to Sal. "Better late than never." He patted Mitch on the shoulder. "Come say howdy to Mayor Van Dyne and Officer Notebaert."

Beth caught Mitch wincing as he turned down the shot and started toward his father. She intercepted him with a hand on his chest.

"I'm sorry. I had to run back to the house real quick," Mitch offered.

"Wait. Hold on for one second, okay? I'm so very sorry," she said.

Mitch turned his angry gaze from his father to her. "I got your message. It's okay. Unnecessary. I completely get it."

Beth paused. "You get what, exactly?"

"Well, since you asked. I got your voicemails," Mitch said. "Hey, Mr. Yowner."

The lanky bartender leaned over. "Yes, sir?"

"Do you have any hot tea, by any chance? If you don't mind?"

"Not much call for that here, son. Best I can do is some black coffee that'll strip the paint off of Gordie's plow truck. If ya give me a sec, I'll see what I can do for you," Sal replied.

"Whoa, tea? Coffee? What the hell, boy, this is your beloved mother's send-off. And you want some pansy-ass drink? Come on now," Gordie snarked. It was like tossing a bucket of gasoline on a smoldering match.

Mitch thought about the Hallmark Channel moment in the car and felt the knot in his stomach return.

The mayor and the sheriff slyly snickered.

"Mayor Van Dyne. Mitchell, is it?" The mousy man offered a weak handshake and a sleazy car salesman wink. "Great to meet you, young man."

"Mitchell." Officer Notebaert nodded sternly.

Mitch mumbled, "Likewise," noticing Beth's apologetic impatience.

"We, the town, are so sorry for losing your incredible mother, Mitchell. Sterling Point feels emptier without the saintly and loving angel who has passed.

Officer Notebaert offered a "what he said" nod and whispered something in the mayor's ear.

Gordon bellowing soon broke the reunion up from his usual perch at the bar.

"Mitchie, grab your girlfriend there and come grab a drink. The mayor's actually footing the bill. Keep 'em comin' Sal!" Gordon slurred. Beth was guessing he had milked the slimy politician's kindness a few times before calling them over. She knew the mayor all too well, and for him to open his wallet that far, something must be going on. *Wait, did he say "girlfriend"?* She hated to admit it, but she liked the sound of that.

"Ooh, an *agent*," Augustus Van Dyne cut in. His shock-white, receding hairline did little to help his thin features, which always reminded Beth of a rat, which, with his dodgy political history, she thought quite fitting. "That's quite impressive, Mitchell. Your return honors us to our humble town. We don't have many celebrities to claim as our own." He raised his glass to the not-so-subtly elbow Sheriff Notebaert standing next to him. "Here's to you, Mitchell. Congratulations."

"You bet your skinny ass, Auggie. My boy here, Mitchell Andrew Roberts, is a bestselling author!" Gordon emptied the mug and slammed it down on the bar.

He looked his son in the eyes and smiled. Beth could see tears forming in his eyes, the same baby blues as Mitch's. The old man grabbed his son by the shoulders and beamed.

"Your mom woulda been so damn proud, son, damn...proud." He pulled Mitch into a tight hug. They both let their tears win the night and the strain of Billy Squire's "Christmas is the Time to Say I Love You" played, and they both let out a belly laugh.

"Oh, I am very sorry for your loss, Gordon, and yours too, Mitchell, of course." The mayor sneaked his condolences in with the usual greasy political hackery wedge.

Beth couldn't help herself and reached out and hugged them both. Chris followed suit and joined the group hug.

"Drinks all round, Sal, my old friend. Did ya hear? My boy is a *New York Times* bestselling author. How the hell do ya like that, ya sumbitch?"

Gordon's pride grew almost as bright as the neon Genesee Beer sign hanging from behind the bar.

"No. No. No." The mayor raised his thin arm high into the air. "No, Gordon. I'm afraid that just won't do. The least our small, yet lovely town of Sterling Point can do is to spread the holiday cheer, and more importantly, celebrate the glorious life of an amazing woman, Mrs. Marguerite Roberts, and rejoice in the huge accomplishments of her extremely talented son, Mitchell Roberts."

The crowd cheered as another Christmas song played.

"Drinks are on me!" the mayor said, waving his hand in a grand flourish.

The crowd erupted in raucous laughter.

Sal's jaw hung slack, and he clapped, then reached for more refreshments—

"Right. As much as I hate to leave such a loving memorial, Gordon, Mitchell, and Mrs. Severt, Officer Notebaert and I have a few more stops before Santa Claus comes, and with the weather and streets the way they are, we mustn't tarry. Miles to go before we sleep. Once again, our deepest condolences on your loss. Wishing you all a very Merry Christmas!

Officer Notebaert nodded and led the diminutive mayor out of the bar.

"What the hell was that?" Mitch murmured.

"Never mind those idiots. Here." Gordon shoved a shot glass full of some kind of firewater toward Mitch. "Be a man. Have a shot with your old man. Don't be a limp-wristed Nancy your whole life, boy."

* * *

"Mr. Roberts," Beth said, more sternly than she'd intended.

"Nope. Let him go. Why stop him now? He's on a twenty-year run. Lord knows we don't want to screw up a good streak. Besides, one drink for Mom, then I'm out of here." Mitch accepted the steaming mug of tea from Sal. "Thank you."

"Mitchell!" Beth shouted. She knew he was angry and had all the right to be. And with the loss of his mom, this whole thing couldn't be easy. Especially after what he had revealed to her the night before. Beth didn't know what to tell him. She knew it was all over between her and Tony. Especially every time her cheek and eye throbbed. Their marriage ended long ago; Tony was irrelevant. She and Mitch shared a magical moment, regardless of the difficult circumstances. Her mind zigged and zagged, trying desperately for a thread of common sense to grab hold of.

"Come on. Follow me. No one is leaving yet." Beth pulled on Mitch's arm and directed him to a less crowded part of the bar near the kitchen. He resisted, but finally relented and followed.

Once they were away from the crowd, she grabbed him by the jacket and kissed him. Long, passionate, sincere.

He staggered into the wall behind him and blinked.

"Wow. That was unexpected," he said.

Beth leaned in, staring directly into his eyes.

"I screwed up. I'm sorry. I know I promised you I'd be at your mom's funeral. It broke my heart that I wasn't there. Especially after you and me…last night…you know."

"Yeah. Go on."

Beth gathered her thoughts. "After you left, Tony came in and went crazy. He accused me of many things, some true and some absurd."

"I wanted you there," Mitch let out. "*I needed* you there."

She pulled him into a tight embrace. "Mitchie, I'm so sorry. There's no excuse, I know."

Mitch hugged her back, and she felt his deep sobs.

"He's so angry. I don't know why," Beth whispered.

Mitch squeezed her tighter. "I know anger, trust me."

Beth understood; guilt overwhelmed her, despite knowing Tony was responsible.

"I'm sorry. Sorry for everything. I should have been there for you and your dad. It's just that Tony is—"

"Okay, okay. I've heard enough about Tony. I'm not trying to be an asshole here, but I've been as understanding as I can handle." He pulled away, holding his hands up in front of him. "I know, I know, he's your husband, and you guys have made a life here. As much as anyone can in this Podunk, regressive-gene-pool playground. But…a life, nonetheless. And I don't know what I was thinking. But I saw you and…I'm sorry to have come back here…very sorry." There was no longer a fight-or-flight response. It was more of a pure run like hell response.

Beth stepped away and mulled over his hurtful words, yet she understood his anger. "You know, Mitchell, you do a great job hiding behind your pompous, big-city, over-inflated sense of self, but at least with you, I know you're acting like a jackass because you're hurting. But let me tell you something. Your denigration of me and our hometown is not welcome. Although we may agree on some points, your arrogant psychoanalysis of my life after all this time reduces it to insignificance in just ten seconds. Absolutely no right." But, as her body shook and tears streamed down her face, she saw the look on Mitch's face turn from self-righteous indignation to hesitant, regretful confusion.

Beth sighed and slowly walked back to him.

"Beth?" Mitch gently reached up and caressed her cheek.

She pulled away—not wanting to; it was a reflex—and she lowered her head.

"Hey," Mitch said, slowly tilting her face toward the light.

Her long blonde hair slid away from her face as Mitch slowly pushed her knit cap up, revealing a swollen, purple-red bruise. Beth couldn't see it, but Mitch's wide-eyed expression told her everything.

A sharp pang blossomed in her stomach. "No… Please."

"Oh, you've got to be kidding me," Mitch whispered.

Beth had prayed this wouldn't happen. She'd gotten to be a master at hiding the bruises. This concerned nobody else. She tried to turn away, but Mitch wouldn't let her go.

"Come on. It's nothing. We were just talking, and he put two and two together. And—"

Beth gasped to see a terribly pained look on his face.

"Stop. Just stop. You've never been a good liar. Don't try it now." Mitch gently touched her cheek, and even though a flash of pain shot through her face, the warmth felt good. Comforting. She met his touch and matched him tear-for-tear, falling into his arms.

"I am so damn sorry," Mitch said.

"It's not your fault."

"What a bag of shit. How long has he been hitting you?"

"It doesn't matter. It's all over now." But Beth knew it wasn't.

"What? It sure as hell matters. The asshole doesn't get away with hitting you. He's a cop, for fuck's sake!"

"Can we please just let it go? Can we just go back to last night? Please? It won't do any good." Beth wanted to press the reset button and go back to the magical night they'd had. She'd been praying for that reset button for five years, and up till now, it had just been dreaming.

"Is this why you didn't come to the funeral?"

There was something about his face. Even when he was being grumpy, stubborn, and angry, those brilliant blue eyes, chubby cheeks, and deep dimples offered her unquestioning solace. Since school, he'd been the only person she felt utterly comfortable around. The only one she could trust. He never hurt her, nor would he ever.

"It wasn't your problem, and I didn't want to distract you. You've had enough to deal with today, and the last thing you needed was me showing up with a shiner and all my drama. That wouldn't have played out too well." Beth wiped away Mitch's tears.

"I don't care, Beth. If Captain Dipshit is beating you, you should have told someone. You're tougher than that. Hell, if I remember correctly, didn't you kick all our asses in karate class?" Mitch's hard grimace morphed into a soft smile as he brushed Beth's hair away from her face.

"I did. And still can. But this…this is different. I know it sounds crazy. But it's true. It's just…different." She nuzzled into his broad chest and waited for the counterargument, but it didn't come.

"I guess you're right. I *don't* understand."

They huddled together for what seemed like a long time, with the jukebox blasting one Christmas song after another, when suddenly, Beth reached out to one of the many shelves and produced a bottle of Irish whiskey. With a mischievous smirk, she cracked open the bottle of Tullamore Dew and took a sip.

"You realize this changes nothing? Tony needs to pay for what he's done to you. And you know I plan on filing a report once this storm clears, right? After that, I'm still getting as far away from this nightmare of a town. I need to, Beth."

INTERLUDE
Even the Losers

The Darkness' ebon form whipped and swirled, engulfing the snow-filled alley. Its sharp talons tore into the brick walls and his gnashing maw broke into a bestial grin as its red eyes watched the car drive past.

It followed.

"Are you serious, Auggie?" Sheriff Notebaert asked, turning the cruiser onto East Lake Street. "The storm is getting shitty; how long do you hope to keep them snowblind?"

The mayor poured the brandy from his flask into his steaming Tim Horton's coffee cup and sipped. He nonchalantly took in the raging storm and counted the dollar signs falling with each flake.

The thin man waved the burly sheriff off with a bony, crooked finger. "Long enough. This storm could be a game changer. We need to make certain our constituents are aware that their representatives are working for them on the streets. Besides, we don't need to go causing any extra panic now, do we? It's Christmas."

They proceeded along the snowy road that traced the lake-line.

"Okay, but I think you're playing with fire here," the sheriff said, his eyes narrowed as he looked at the road. "Jesus Christ. I can barely see through this shit. How can you tell them with a straight face that it's only another storm? Some might be that gullible, Auggie, but not all. And when this situation deteriorates, as it inevitably will, what will you do then?"

They drove along for a short time, and the weather deteriorated as they progressed eastward.

The mayor snickered and looked at the sheriff. "Ah-ha. Now you're seeing the method to my madness, dear sir." He winked.

"Are you gonna keep your master plan to yourself, or do you want to share it with the special kids in the class here?" The sheriff was growing weary of the shifty politician's cagey rhetoric.

"Okay, let me put it this way. If we play it slowly, more folks will stay home for the holiday, and when this nor'easter hits, as we expect, we can act all surprised and then hit the state and D.C. for more disaster money.

Do you get what I mean?" The mayor looked like a greedy, grinning skeleton in the white glow of the dashboard lights.

"That's really messed up. You realize just how evil that sounds, right?" The sheriff shook his head and looked ahead.

The world before them exploded in a deafening crunching of metal as deathly sharp talons and teeth decimated the police cruiser in a brutal and bloody flash.

The deathly maelstrom of ebony tentacles, cruel sharp talons, and jagged teeth surged forward, instantly engulfing the cruiser in a relentless, swirling sea of ravenous Darkness. The once-sturdy metal frame of the vehicle screeched in protest, twisting and contorting as it was mercilessly torn apart by the relentless force. The chilling air of the freezing winter night was the only witness to the agonizing screams that echoed into the void as the unrelenting, insatiable evil consumed every fragment of their flesh and bones, leaving nothing but a haunting silence in its wake.

Then, without remorse or even recognition, the millennia-old entity moved westward toward its prey.

26
Long Time Coming

"I should check on Pablo," Beth said as they made their way to the front of the bar.

"I'd be more worried about the pie-eyed patrons than your shaggy Hoth monster there."

"Funny." Beth smirked and parted the sea of jovial patrons.

The bar was packed. Loud Christmas music, singing, and laughter filled the room. Everything on the planet that Mitch hated. Yet, here he was. Despite believing Beth, he sensed something amiss. He couldn't put his finger on it. It might have been the alcohol, but he still trusted his instincts. Worst-case scenario, he'd already packed his car, and if need be, he could hightail it the hell out of town. The Storm of the Century be damned.

Suddenly a familiar voice cut through the crowded barroom. "Oh, thank the gods!"

Mitch turned to his right to see a guy barging through a pair of girls dancing to some horrific country cover version of "Santa Claus is Back in Town." Mitch was certain The King was doing barrel-rolls in his gold-plated casket.

"Who's that?" Mitch asked, stepping through the crowd. Judging by the digital camera hanging from his neck, that and being the only African American in that white-washed bar, it was Chris, heading Mitch and Beth's way.

"Mitch!" Chris belted, a wide smile bursting on his goateed face.

Thanks for coming, Chris!" Mitch took him into a tight embrace. Mitch and his best friend had been inseparable since kindergarten, when a block-stacking mishap resulted in a comical injury. Chris had never let him forget, or anyone else, for that matter.

"So damn good to see you, man," Mitch said. "Again."

Chris smiled. "Yeah, not that long ago, but I get it. Hey, let me get a pic, guys," he said, and hastily pushed Mitch and Beth together and aimed his camera, not waiting for permission.

"Well, uh, sure," Mitch and Beth hurriedly replied.

"Make sure you send me a copy, okay?" Beth asked.

"Sure thing," Chris replied, showing them the image on the digital camera screen.

Beth felt Mitch cringe as they examined the candid images.

"Good Lord, I look like Jabba the Hutt on holiday," Mitch complained.

Beth shoved him gently. "Stop it. You look cute."

Chris chuckled and coughed. "Uh. Cute, huh?"

"Shut it," said Mitch.

"Anyway, do you know if any of the others are coming?" Mitch said, shaking Chris by the shoulder. "I never thought I'd be back in this crap-hole again." He caught himself and winced.

"Sorry."

"Ah, it's okay, man," Chris said, and sipped gently from his mug.

"Yeah, not all of us can make a break for the fence." Beth hoped her words didn't sound as scathing and snarky as they seemed to her.

Why didn't I realize what an amazing guy he was back then? She thought. *It's a shame you don't always see what's right in front of your eyes.* Beth took a sip. *Christmas is the time for making wishes, right?* Mitch glanced over at her and smiled. He looked happy—something he had never really been any good at.

"So, I read it online, man. We are in the presence of a bestselling author!" Chris held up his mug. "Cheers!"

"Cheers," Beth said, snatching Mitch up in a deep hug.

She stared into his bright blue eyes, and they warmed her.

"I learned about it while on my way here. Bridget, my agent, called me." Mitch flushed and tried to break Beth's gaze but couldn't—and didn't want to.

A loud crash and wind shook the centuries-old tavern, causing shrill cries through the windows. The lights flickered, pausing the jukebox and patrons' holiday celebration. Dust fell from the rafters, and the music stopped.

Pablo pressed his massive paws against the window of the door, and his whining turned into a violent bark that broke the sudden silence. All inside Yowner's Tavern stood frozen. The lights flickered once again, and the malamute let loose a low growl that sent chills down everyone's spine.

"What's up, Pab?"" Beth called out as she ran to her dog. On his hind legs, Pablo stood, towering over her, pressed against the wooden door. His hot breath caused the window to fog up, revealing that he had bitten his lip, resulting in droplets of blood scattered on the window and streaming along the grain of the old door.

In a flurry, the front door ripped open, and a large frame burst through the opening, the howling wind bringing with it a wall of biting snow.

"For Christ's sake, close that ammonia hole. Shit!" Gordie Roberts shouted.

"It's pneumonia, Dad. Pneumonia!"

Gordie waved Mitch off and drained his beer.

A fierce snarl filled the bar, and the dog launched itself at the figure standing in the doorway.

A blur of motion ensued, and the struggle went to the floor

27

One Rainy Wish

Sheldon Hendricks shoved his "Obama" phone—as the school bullies called it—into his worn jeans, his hands stiff and trembling from the cold, his breath misting in their dimly lit two-bedroom apartment. He felt what energy he had left slowly draining away as he stood there, staring at his mom's passed-out body lying in the flickering colors of the television.

The only other light was from the rough-sawn branches Sheldon had secretly cut from Mr. Cossaboon's tree, and the lights he'd "borrowed" from the Amslers down on Marshall Street.

Their red and green lights bathed the small, sparse room in a depressing Christmas light.

Wiping his eyes as his mom snored, Sheldon caught the needle lying on the threadbare carpet, a trickle of blood mixing with the contents of its drug-filled tip.

He probably stayed there a minimum of ten minutes. He lost track.

She'd been like this since Mrs. Severt dropped him off. She spoke, perhaps two or three words, but incoherently.

Sheldon couldn't deal with the rush of sadness for too long, so he pushed play on the music app on his cellphone and Jimi Hendrix played "One Rainy Wish."

Sheldon intended precisely that. Dream his life away.

Maybe into a much happier one.

One with less darkness and shadow.

A world where he didn't have to worry about his mom.

A world where she was like all the other moms in his school.

Sheldon knew they weren't all perfect. But some were sure a lot better than his poor mom.

A new world where he felt like he had a future.

Sheldon kissed her sweat-covered forehead, checked her pulse…and was relieved to feel it strong on his fingers. He turned and plodded up the dark stairs to his bedroom.

He didn't slam the door like he used to when she got drunk or high. He didn't have the energy to deal with all this anymore.

Sheldon knew he still loved her more than anything… She was his mom. And always would be.

Snatching his guitar from its stand, he turned on his tiny Marshall amplifier. As Jimi sang in his earbuds, he waited for the guitar solo and let an apprehensive smile cross his face. He let his spirit fly as he joined Jimi soloing into the darkness of his cold bedroom.

28

Snowblind

"Aw, shit. I can't see a goddamn thing." Royce Pritchard punched the steering wheel of the Hummer as its huge tires struggled for purchase in the thick snow. Even in four-wheel-drive, the machine was barely staying between the ditches. *Wherever the hell they are*, Royce thought.

"Is it still back there?"" he asked, risking a peek in the rearview mirror.

Everyone in the back scrambled to look behind them, the sudden shift in weight causing the rear end of the Hummer to fishtail. Outside, the dense forest blurred past, trees looming like dark sentinels under the moonlit sky—all nearly lost in the blinding snow. Royce quickly compensated, righting the vehicle—for now. He wasn't sure how much more his old ticker could handle.

"Well?"

"It's hard to tell. Can't see for shit with all the snow," said Mikey Pritchard.

"Holy shit. Holy shit, man. There's something back there. Jesus Christ!" Johnny Cadigan shouted, more like a scream.

"That thing—what is it?" Carl asked, looking to see around the twitchy Johnny.

A fierce wind blast hit the vehicle, causing it to tilt.

Royce fought with what little strength he had left in his burning arms. The old man wrestled the vehicle, finally angling it into the wind, regaining control.

"We need to find a better route home," he said.

"Like what? Fuckin' teleportation?" Alicia Samms snarled from the back.

Uppity bitch, thought Royce, shooting daggers at her, then turning back to the white wall before them.

"Babe!"

Royce didn't like the sound of his son's voice. It was soft. Not in his normal, complaining way, more in the *Holy shit, I'm in bad shape* kind of way. *Closing in on FUBAR.*

"That black shit is getting closer, boss." Johnny said. "There's something inside the damn thing," his voice echoing like marbles in a metal tube.

"Boy, how you doing, troop?" Royce asked.

Alicia's cold voice rang out.

"How's he doing? Are you fucking serious?"

"Babe. Come on. I—I'm…good to…go," Denny's wavering words cut in.

The violent wind pierced through the windows and seams of the Hummer, causing haunting echoes as they drove through the increasingly impassable storm.

"Don't *Babe* me, Den!" Alicia shouted.

Royce didn't know if he should laugh or shoot her and kick her ass out into the snow.

"It's your balls-bigger-than-brains father that has gotten us into some serious shit. And look at you, you big fucking idiot. We should get your dumb ass to a hospital. Not be driving to God knows where in the middle of a motherfucking snowstorm. Call me stupid, but this shit is fucking insane." Alicia glared at Royce, who was watching her from the review mirror.

"Boss!" Johnny shouted.

"Alicia, come on," Denny pleaded.

"Fuck that, Den. Enough abuse from that old man. We need to get you to the hospital. Sodus General is close by. We can ge—" Alicia's words came to a violent halt as the Humvee slid to a stop and everyone inside the vehicle flailed for something to hold on to as they all slammed forward.

Royce turned around and glared.

"Enough of this bullshit! I'm fucking done." With that, he forced open the driver's side door and hopped out.

He let out an angry grunt as his passengers panicked. Royce pulled out his pistol and saw the twisting black clouds racing their way and pulled the back door open and grimaced, seeing all inside flinching.

"Okay, sweetheart. This is where you get off." He reached in and grabbed Alicia by the hair and yanked her backward, out of the car.

The girl kicked and punched him, and Denny frantically grabbed at her, but Royce put the gun to her head.

"Y'all are gonna shut the hell up. Let this traitorous bitch go, or I'll paint this snowbank here with her tiny brain. It's your call."

The driving rain pounded down, and the blackness was closing in. But Royce was playing to win.

"Okay, okay. Come on, Dad. Don't hurt her. Please!" Denny pleaded from the rocking vehicle.

Royce held fast, one hand holding the struggling woman's hair, the other holding the pistol to her head.

Alicia tore at his hands. "Old man. I swear I'll cut your balls off, you piece of—"

"Pops!" Denny cried from the truck. "Get the fuck off her!"

Royce let his calculating mind run the numbers, all the while relishing in the torture and torment he was inflicting. With the blackness rushing in, its long talons and gnashing teeth mixed with the battering snowstorm, he nodded to himself and let Alicia go.

"See, Denny. Daddy is a generous soul."

"Sonofabitch. Old man, I'm gonna—" Alicia stepped toward him, but Royce put a bullet into her thigh and watched her fall to the deep pile of snow on Lake Road.

With the deafening echo still caught in the thick, howling air, Royce climbed back into the Humvee.

"What the fucking hell?" Denny screamed from the back. "No!"

"I didn't kill her, boy. You should be grateful." Royce grunted and glared at his much taller son.

What Royce didn't mention was the black cloud of sharp teeth and flashing talons he could see ripping, tearing, devouring *that annoying bitch* in a blink of an eye.

He'd keep that small slice of heaven for himself.

Ultimately, his son would fare better.

"Anyone else want to complain? Speak up now!" Royce let the car door hang open. "You'll be joining her right quick, if ya do!"

A frozen, silent moment passed.

Outside, Alicia's calls for help pierced through the black storm, her horrified cries lost in the brutal gusts.

Royce fastened his seatbelt.

The slim piece of nylon offered nothing but a pathetic sliver of security.

Denny sat and cried out for Alicia and trembled in a heap.

"That's my boy," Royce said, putting the Humvee into gear and speeding away.

Once down Centenary Road, he pulled a flask from his jacket and took a sip.

As his sons and the rest wept in the back, he drove, drank, and dreamed of the riches that would come from cashing in on the prizes; although it may have cost him a life or two, that was nothing new for the old war vet. "Collateral damage," he mumbled.

He reached down into the console and felt around until he touched the comfortable, cold metal. He pulled out the revolver and tucked it into his belt. *Just in case.*

Royce paid no attention to the blur of headlights off the road to his left, accompanied by the muffled roars of the snowmobiles racing along the Centenary Road cornfield, now covered in over four feet of snow.

INTERLUDE

The Wayne County White Wave Riders snowmobile club raced along the twisting snowmobile trails that led from the eastern town of Wolcott, breaking off at the Monroe County line.

The darkening late-afternoon sky loomed more like night as its rolling clouds brought with them more violent weather.

The snowmobile club blazed through the fresh snow, hoping to make it to the final top at the Centenary Inn on the Toys for Tots Charity snowmobile run. Through the side mirror of his sled, Troy Rogers looked at the Darkness chasing them. The twisting, swiping blackness seemed…off…different. Moving too fast. Too…unnatural.

He shook it off and put it down to maybe one too many Bud Lights and Jager shots from the earlier stops.

He needed a shot of whiskey, a cold brew, and chow. And to get warm. So he pushed down on the accelerator, spitting a blinding whitewash of snow onto the rider behind him.

There were fifteen riders all heading for the Centenary Inn, whose sign—barely visible—promised warm food and cold beer.

Snow filled in the ruts as fast as the snow machines could make them as they passed houses, business, and trailer parks.

Troy looked behind them at the angry storm lurching violently on their trail.

Up ahead lay Wayne Hills trailer park. All the occupants were inside their trailers, hiding from the freezing cold and the cloying storm about to overtake them. A sea of yellow lights flashed by as the snowmobiles roared past.

Then Troy heard the deafening rending of metal and screams from the park.

Spinning the sled, he gestured for a return to the park.

They followed, and as they reached the trailers, Troy screamed.

The entire park lay swallowed up in a swirling dark cloud of blackness that seemed to have glowing red eyes, blood-slathered teeth, and gigantic talons as it ripped and rent the tin-crafted homes and humans to gore-filled shreds.

The screams of men, women, children, wailing infants, and pets filled the biting air as the Darkness devoured all living things.

In mere ungodly seconds, something consumed hundreds of people, and all fifteen riders stared in slack-jawed terror.

"Go! Go!" Troy screamed and thumbed the throttle, and the big motor roared to life, and the others followed.

It was too late.

In a bone-crunching flash, something swallowed the Wayne County White Wave Riders whole.

Human…machine. Man…woman…child… Anything that had held breath was gone. All consumed in the frozen, unforgiving wake of the nor'easter and the darkness within.

The thirsty, swelling, starving storm had only just begun.

The tiny living things offered their flesh. Their blood. Their souls. It was not enough.

Its hunger and rage were growing ever more insatiable with every living thing it devoured.

And the Darkness could smell…sense the humans that dared to interrupt its long slumber.

It would not rest until it had tasted…consumed the feeble lifeforms and punished them all.

29

Boys are Back in Town

"Enough blubbering, boy!" Royce shouted at his wailing son in the back of the Humvee. Denny had been non-stop *crying like a bitch* since he'd unloaded the extra baggage. "The damn girl was in your head, son. She ain't worth the bellyaching. Let it go, or you can join her, real quick-like!" He'd had enough and was grateful they were closing in on Sterling Point. With the lake and acres of apple orchards on their right-hand side, the old hunter knew they were back on track and sure to hit town any minute.

"But, Pops. Sh-she was my—"

The swirling black mass gained on the Humvee. Royce could've sworn there were eyes and gnashing teeth within the snowstorm. But he hoped it was the whiskey hangover filling his brain with insane thoughts.

"Come on, Pops. That shit's cold," Mikey Pritchard said.

Royce reached over and grabbed his youngest son by the hair and pulled him close.

"Next motherfucker to doubt my decisions, I goddamn guarantee you, I'll feed your ass to whatever the fuck that thing is behind us. Hear me?" Royce shoved his son against the door and turned back to the road just in time to see nothing but sheer whiteout.

Royce gripped the steering wheel and kept hitting the brakes in fear of spinning out of control.

He didn't have to worry for long. Suddenly the veil of white lifted, revealing Coleridge Marina, with the historic Sterling Point Lighthouse behind it.

The downside was that Royce was seeing it through the passenger-side window.

"Fuck me—" was all he managed before he crashed into the huge cement barriers that sat like stone guardians between the road and the frozen lake.

Next came screams, and a deafening wrenching of metal.

Then…darkness.

30
Blackout

"Run, goddammit, run!" Royce Pritchard wheezed and gasped for air as he led the way down Eads Avenue. He couldn't see two feet in front of him and hoped he was at least headed toward Main Street. There was no sign of life on the streets, and they'd shut most of the homes up tighter than a drum.

The howls had followed them all the way from the cabin in Rhodes Hollow to Sterling Point. He tried to ignore the gnawing feeling as he ran and spurred his fellow hunters onward. He could tell that the others were staying back to keep his pace. This pissed him off, but he liked it all the same.

"Pop, where the hell are we gonna go?" Mikey gasped, looking behind them into the darkness, which was beyond black. Beyond any night they had ever witnessed. It seemed to swirl and send tendrils of even deeper ebony reaching out for them. Every wisp of blowing snow seemed to have its own essence. Its own intent. The jagged wind pushed southward, ripping at their clothing and seemingly aiming to savagely rend the flesh from their chilled bones.

The streetlights offered little as the nor'easter pounded the waterfront town and the lone hunters running hell for leather through deep snowdrifts that had become one big landscape. The calling howl grew closer, and terror filled them as they searched for a haven in their whitewashed town.

They reached what they guessed was Main Street. Waist-deep snow enveloped everything and blurred their vision as though they were looking through a smeared windshield. All of them were dead-ass tired, and the wailing winds grew closer no matter how fast they tried to escape the black storm threatening to drag them back to the icy waters of the lake.

"There!" Mikey bellowed. He pointed down Main Street, the glowing *Miller Draft* and *Labatt* beer signs acting as beacons in the night. Royce caught up to his son and nearly collapsed. The rest came and joined them at the lone blinking traffic light that offered a low blip in the raging storm.

A warm glimmer of hope filled them all as Royce stepped forward and caught his breath. It fogged his glasses, and he felt as though his lungs were about to burst. He didn't care. The prize was safe, and they were about to find sanctuary—and beer.

"All right, you sorry-ass bastards, Yowner's is right there. Let's bust assholes and elbows now!"

Then the Darkness was upon them. The streetlights were gone, and even the reflective light of the snow failed to break through the veil.

"Get the hell outta here!" Royce's cries fell lost in the wintry maelstrom. They made haste to the tavern, but the black mass encircled them. Royce tried to run, but his aging legs and body struggled to respond, and he collapsed. The rest of the hunters sprinted as best they could through the muck of the snow. Twenty yards stood between them and their fallen patriarch. They didn't stop.

Mikey let loose with his shotgun; the blast fell silent within the cacophony of the storm. The rest turned back and reluctantly trudged back to his fallen father, who was flopping around in the snow, searching for his gun and trying to stand. Mikey ran to his father, and the black blur was almost upon him.

"C'mon, Pop, let's get the hell outta here." Mikey bent down and yanked Royce to his feet with one tug. Royce got his balance and pointed back down Main Street toward the fleeing hunters. The monstrous black mass rose and writhed over the rooftops and reached almost from one side of the street to the other. Its eardrum-shattering bellow nearly knocked them to their knees.

"Come the fuck on!" Johnny pleaded as he helped Mikey with Royce. The blackness reached out and grabbed Mikey by the leg, ripping his hip from its socket. The snow turned to a crimson mush as blood burst out of the fresh wound.

Royce watched his son screaming, but all that filled his ears was an agonizing, bestial howl, accompanied by the stinging wind. He watched as the immense beast pulled his son into its vast center. He turned and fled toward the tavern and prayed. Only divine intervention, from any god, could rescue him, he hoped.

The blackness formed an impenetrable wall between Royce, Johnny, and the tavern. Royce's heart pounded in his chest, and he looked for another way around.

"This way," he shouted through the storm, and they headed toward the white church, almost lost in the snow. The building occupied the long, slender lot next to Ward's grocery store and backed up against the school grounds behind it. Royce looked back at Main Street to see the blackness stop at the edge of the church property. It ebbed and flowed over it, as though it were testing the boundaries without breaching the holy ground's perimeter. He smiled, his thin, tapered mustache creating a line from his upper lip to his cheek.

"Open the fuckin' door, kid." He stood, chest out in defiance, staring at the blackness. Almost taunting it. Whatever it was.

Johnny opened the unlocked door and entered the church. Royce lit a cigar and smiled as he went inside, letting out a mocking laugh as he closed the door.

The blackness raged and fought against the *Ononciawa' ga:' Gawe:no* magical restraints cast upon it all those centuries ago.

INTERLUDE

Clayton Felton pushed up his foggy glasses as he watched Mr. Murphy solemnly close and lock the casket.

The thick, cool air inside the funeral home amplified Clay's sense of separation as he followed his boss's non-verbal direction and they escorted Mrs. Marguerite Roberts to the final room her physical body would ever know.

Sweat trickled down his back, leaving dark, damp patches on his white dress shirt and clinging to his slacks, even though a biting chill hung in the air beyond the window. He had come to terms with death as the unavoidable fate awaiting all living things, including himself. Clay had breezed through his education and exams without a hitch, his mind agile and focused. He understood that, while the idea of dying was unpleasant and the desire for eternal life was universal, such wishes didn't align with the divine blueprint. He knew that accepting this truth was a crucial step in navigating the confusing darkness of grief.

During his time apprenticing at his hometown funeral home, Clay had helped with numerous sorrowful and heart-wrenching services—for both the elderly and the young, those that were sudden, anticipated, and even violent. However, none had affected him as deeply as this particular one.

The next hour passed like a dreary dream and unwanted nightmare, as he assisted his boss with burning a woman who had been like a second mother to him.

He and his twin brother, Ray, had endured a difficult home life, and it seemed Mrs. Roberts understood this. She welcomed them as if they were her own children, consistently providing food and a safe haven for those looking to escape the troubles at home.

Clay had fond memories and would always be grateful for her. She was the only adult who knew what he was going through and would always take the time to talk to him.

"Merry Christmas!" Mr. Murphy's words hung in the arctic air as Clay donned his heavy jacket and left the funeral home behind.

The way to Yowner's Tavern was an easy one—a straight line.

His cellphone vibrated, and he checked to see. It was a missed call and a voicemail from his brother, Ray.

"Hey, bro. I'm about to hit the Rockies. I'm sure you're dealing with Mrs. Roberts' funeral. Please give them my best. I wish I could be there. Let Mitch know, if he shows up, that I've missed him and that I am so sorry. Anyway, I have to run. This weather out here sucks almost as much as they're saying about your way. I just wanted to wish you a Merry Christmas before I lose recep…"

Clay stared at the phone, silently hoping it would finish his brother's message.

After five steps into the violent, skin-biting gusts of the storm, he let it go. Instead, with each heavy, exhausting step through the deep snow, he remembered the magical moments Mrs. Roberts and Mitch's friendship had provided for him and his brother alike.

The swaying streetlights flickered, like candles blinking in and out through white curtains, as he battled his way toward Yowner's Tavern.

To fight the bitter storm, he focused on his Spotify list.

He cycled through his many lists and finally settled for Bruno Mars. He felt guilty for not playing some Charley Pride or old, crusty Christmas songs; however, Mr. Roberts had played them all day, and even a saint deserves a break.

Yowner's was only three blocks away. But in the snowy Armageddon, it might as well have been three miles.

He hoped to finally reconnect with Mitch, Chris, and even Beth. Although truth be told, he wished Beth wouldn't come. She was Mitch's weakness and the reason their friendship had suffered. The nonsense she and Tony were involved in would drive anyone away. He had tried not to blame her, but when it came to that conceited, prejudiced cop, forgiving was just too much to ask.

The plan: swift entry, swift exit. After he had said his pleasantries, he'd sneak out and head back to his dark apartment, fix up some ramen noodles, and sip wine coolers and watch YouTube videos of ghost hunting until he fell asleep. And he could put this whole depressing day—and Christmas—behind him.

Spotify began the eerie organ intro to Sinead O'Connor's "Nothing Compares 2 U" as he crossed the side street.

The snow was nearly up to his knees and the unrelenting storm promised worse as he could barely make out the flicking Yowner's sign a mere fifty feet away.

"I really need to move south," Clay uttered through his thick Doctor Who scarf as a flash of swirling darkness filled the space before him, a space that had been the snowy white sidewalk a second earlier.

Underneath the creature's oppressive weight, its slick, oily blackness stuck to him like a vile, putrid slime. As he struggled, it hauled him into a void of darkness before he could even utter a plea for mercy. The creature's talons slashed wildly, its teeth gnashing with a furious hunger, ripping through Clayton's body. His organs, from his kidneys to his bladder, were torn open, spilling their contents in a gruesome display of savage destruction.

The Darkness took its delicious time consuming him, delighting in his pain, feeding off it in more ways than one.

Then the ancient malevolence moved on. The faint stench of human souls and the blood trail of its quarry led it deeper into the town.

The Darkness enveloped the lake town with a wicked delight, savoring the torment of its prey. Its malevolent force spread throughout, leaving a path of destruction and misery, echoing with the faint cries of those it targeted. The atmosphere was thick with the odor of blood and terror as death loomed nearer.

Lost in the bloody snow, barely audible against the raging storm, the soft lilt of Sinead's angelic voice mocked the nightmarish, gruesome remains of Clayton Arthur Felton.

31

Running Wild in the Streets

Sheldon Hendricks' hands and feet were numb. The torn canvas of his sneakers let in the snow and his thin socks provided little comfort. Mrs. Severt lived nearby; a quick shortcut through Cossaboon's yard would get him there immediately. He'd felt fear before, but this was different. The snow seemed to be a solid wall, mixed with black. Almost like a concrete-colored curtain that greeted him coldly in every direction. He cupped his small hands and blew into them to warm up.

He barely discerned the outline of Cossaboon's house and moved along its side, pausing to catch his breath under the carport. There, a 1979 Plymouth station wagon stood with duct-taped wood paneling and green spray paint on the hood and fenders. The engine was still warm, so Sheldon nestled against the car, seeking warmth for his shivering body. However, the howling wind swept through the carport, stripping away any shelter the car or house might have offered.

A distant cry echoed.

"Hey, kid, get outta here!" a booming voice yelled from the puke-green house. Sheldon slipped in the snow as he saw old man Cossaboon with a shotgun through the window. He knew he had to leave fast. Taking a deep breath, he dashed for the wooden fence, climbed over, and landed in Mr. Van Cuyck's former vegetable garden. *Man, I could go for some of that hot salsa right now*, he thought, sinking into a pile of snow. Night had fallen, obscuring the yard; Sheldon double-checked his guitar and took stock of his location. He had spent most of his young life on these streets and backyards, but somehow they seemed different. It resembled an unexplored alien planet. He trudged down the driveway, trying hard to ignore his frozen feet.

His heart raced as the cloak of ebony closed in and he pushed on. He could feel something on his heels. Something unnatural. Something wrong. Dark…evil. He lost his breath but forced his frozen legs to respond and he broke onto Main Street to head for the intersection, hoping against hope of finding someone. Anyone.

Sheldon crawled through the waist-deep snow and stopped behind a covered Dodge Neon. He noticed a group of individuals having difficulty moving south along the road covered in snow. He thought he could hear screaming, and he thought he saw a spray of blood. But he wasn't sure. The wind-blown snow had created a mess of white crystal goblins and arctic demons throughout his travels, and he didn't know what was real and what were tricks of the storm. He lost his breath when a black shadow seemed to engulf the entire street and raised high above into the night sky. Beneath it, a group of people were trying to make it to the church. He wanted to avoid obnoxious drunks. Steeling himself, Sheldon charged through the deepening snow toward the Second Redeemer Church. Howling wind and soul-wrenching cries followed him.

Sheldon made it to the buried form of what he guessed was a mini-van, and he jumped behind the large snowbank. The shrill shriek tore through the heavy snow and caused every hair on his body to stand up. Deep chills ran through him, and he flattened himself in the snow. He peed himself, but he had worse things to worry about as the inhuman cries grew closer, mixed with the human shouts and what sounded like gunshots.

"All right, Sheldon, calm down and just breathe." However, catching his breath proved difficult after sprinting through the snow in the biting cold.

Suddenly another group passed by: guys carrying guns and helping a bigger guy walk. They were shouting and screaming something he couldn't make out through the powerful, howling wind. Sheldon understood only one word: *monster.*

The men stopped in the middle of the snow-covered street as one of them collapsed. Everything went crazy as the Darkness, in which Sheldon thought he saw a bunch of razor-sharp teeth twisted inside the black.

In an instant, it surrounded the men.

One turned, fired, yet it had no effect.

A bestial roar filled Sheldon's ears. He tried to cover them with his hat, but the unnatural sound only intensified as a clawed black hand the size of a car snatched the gunman and yanked his leg from his body in one horrific motion.

Sheldon turned away, covering his eyes, but not before a thick spray of blood soaked the snowbank beside him. Screaming into his gloved hand, he rolled over and tried to bury himself in the snow, and prayed.

A monstrous scream responded to the men's cries. Sheldon didn't bother to look. He silently replayed Jimi's "Angel," patiently awaiting what felt like an eternity. Finally, the men's shouts were gone, along with the monster's shriek.

Sheldon dared a peek through his hands. The storm still raged on, and he could barely see three feet in front of him. But the men were gone. A huge swath of blood-soaked snow was all that remained. He still didn't dare move, and his entire body shook from the freezing cold. He knew he wouldn't last much longer out there in the storm.

I gotta find help.

Cautiously, he rose from the snowbank and surveyed his surroundings. In the center of the street, where the men had stood, a distinct trail of blood wound its way down Main Street, appearing to end at the church. However, there was no trace of the men or the creature.

Sheldon took in the building. He needed to get warm, and fast. Everything was closed and dark. That was until he remembered Mrs. Hester's Book Store. A glimmer of hope made him smile as he trudged onto the sidewalk and headed toward it. Mrs. Hester, while very weird, loved animals and was always worried about her four-legged friends at this time of year. So she had hired someone to build an insulated winter habitat out of a fifty-gallon drum, filled with blankets, food, and water. Sheldon prayed it would be enough to keep him from freezing to death.

He located the barrel, placed on a six-foot platform to protect Mrs. Hester's animals. Sheldon climbed up and crawled inside.

Seven cats and a small dog snuggled together inside the full house.

"Hey, guys, I come in peace." The animals crawled up and joined him. He would not fight their attention.

Another horrific shriek erupted from the monster.

Reaching into his jacket pocket, he pulled out his cellphone.

He took a while to hit the buttons, but he finally dialed Mrs. Severt's number.

"Come on…come on. Please answer!"

32

Mr. Man

Pablo lay on top of the stranger, growling violently. Mitch ran with Beth to the front door.

"Pablo! Down!" she shouted.

Mitch came up beside her and caught the glint of steel underneath the fur. It was a gun.

A muffled voice shouted beneath the two-hundred-pound Alaskan malamute. Booted feet and a gloved fist struck out at Pablo.

Beth pulled at his collar. "Tony?" she said. Mitch helped tug on the pissed-off canine. "What are you doing here?"

"Get this goddamn thing off me." Tony rolled out from under the protective dog and brought his handgun up to Pablo's snarling muzzle. "Beth, best get that shaggy piece of shit away from me before I kill the fuckin' thing."

In a flash, she rushed forward, one hand smacking the large gun away and the other connecting with the startled sheriff's jaw.

Tony got up, holstered his pistol, and glared at Beth, ready to punch her.

"No," was all Mitch said as he stepped toward the bigger cop.

"I came in to tell everyone that the governor has issued a no-travel advisory. That means no unnecessary travel. Especially all you drunk bastards. And what the hell?" he shouted.

Pablo nuzzled up to Mitch, still rumbling with a low growl. "It's okay, big guy. It's okay." Mitch ran a hand through his thick fur.

Tony glared at Beth. "Keep that damn dog on a fucking leash and I won't have to put a bullet through its thick skull. Jesus!"

"You're gonna shoot my dog now? Is that it?" Beth pushed him against the wall.

Mitch saw Tony clench his hand into a fist, and he stepped between them.

"Whoa. Come on now, guys. Hey…it's Christmas. Tony just startled the bejesus out of Chewie over there. The big hound was just protecting the bar and his master." He offered a calm smile at Beth, but she wasn't having any of it. "Well…and Tony here was just coming in from that snowstorm out there and Pablo jumped him like he owed him money, so… Hey…no one got hurt…er, shot. So…" Mitch realized he was running out of bullshit and had little left in the tank.

"Get your hands off me, Roberts. I don't need you defending me." Still clenching his fists, Tony shoved Mitch away.

Mitch snapped back at his old friend and looked for something—anything—in his angry eyes. Nothing. Only pure rage stared back at him.

"Mitch, come on. This has nothing to do with you," Beth said, trying to get past him.

He stood frozen, the irony dripping in the heavy air like a joke that was too obvious for anyone to miss.

"Don't you be threatening my boy, Severt. Badge or not, this old devil dog can still stomp a size thirteen mud-hole in your punk ass," Gordie slurred from the bar.

Mitch paused in disbelief at the drunken words of defense coming from his father. "Wait… What?"

The crowd whooped and hollered, and the music resumed.

Tony's face changed for a split second. Mitch caught it and he figured now was the best time to speak, considering the effects of the whiskey running through him. He stepped forward, open-handed.

"Tony…hold on. Listen…please." Mitch offered him a smile. "Can't we just talk? It's been so damn long, man. Seriously. We were best friends, for crying out loud."

"Why do you care? You fucking left. You should have stayed gone. Nobody wants you here. What the hell could you possibly have to say?"

"Is that really the case, Tony? Or are you the only one who doesn't want me here?" Mitch leaned into his former friend. "Hell, if I'm here, that means I can finally spill the beans on why I got the hell out of here in the first place. But even with all that shit, do you really think after ten fucking years it really matters what happened between you and me?" Mitch stood strong with one hand on Tony's chest, keeping him pushed up against the wall.

"I told Beth about what you did. But that doesn't change the fact you guys were married for ten years, man."

Tony glared at Mitch, his gloved hand caressing his pistol. "That so? I know what I saw this morning… Guessing it wasn't just a Christmas party going on there, old friend."

Beth rushed forward. "Don't waste your breath, Mitchie. He's too busy sticking his dick in every high-school girl that likes his tweets or waves to him across the street."

"*Mitchie?*" Tony scoffed, pushing Mitch away. "Are you fucking kidding me?"

"Knock that 'playing innocent' shit off. You haven't been honest with me since day one," Beth said, jabbing a finger at her husband.

Mitch's head spun with the booze and the intensity of the moment.

"Oh… You're willing to believe the word of a guy who bailed on us? Really? The same old whiny, weedy Mitchell Roberts. Afraid of his own goddamn shadow and who never had the guts or the balls to tell a girl he liked her? Or any guy, for that matter." Tony taunted Mitch with a wink and blew him a kiss.

"You fucki—" The fire burning inside Mitch exploded into a raging inferno and all he could see was red. He tried to grab the big cop's jacket, but Beth got between them.

"Stop this," she demanded.

The crowd's roar calmed down to an inaudible murmur as the spat between the three of them heated up.

"Playing the 'gay card.' Nice touch. Methinks you doth protest too much, buddy," Mitch spat, fighting back tears of anger, grief, and betrayal. It was like a bomb that had been ticking inside of him since he was…since he took his first breath, he guessed.

"You know, Tony, maybe you're the one with the penchant for men, not me!" The pressure on Mitch's time bomb was at its breaking point. "All you do is lie!" He prodded his finger hard into Tony's chest.

"That so?" Tony said through gritted teeth, crushing Beth between the two of them.

Mitch, sensing she was getting hurt, immediately stepped back, but continued with his scathing words.

"Oh, hell yes. Mr. New York State Greco-Roman wrestling champ. Rolling around on those sweaty mats get you all hot and bothered, huh?" Mitch knew he was stepping far afield into dangerous territory, but his sense of fairness and the old varnish of common decency were melting away, just like the fuse on his time bomb. "So, you see, old friend, I'm not the only one with secrets. I know how to keep my promises. You sure as hell cannot say the same." The line was not only crossed, but it also exploded in a ten-megaton mushroom cloud, and things were about to go from ballistic to complete apocalypse.

Tony stood there, still as a statue, his dark brown eyes nearly disappearing into the most hateful glare promising pain and anguish; for the first time in Mitch's life, he felt no fear.

So, he poured gas on the bonfire and went all scorched earth.

"What? Are you gonna hit me? Again? Like how the big ol' badass cop hits his wife when she finds out he's banging anything with a pulse? Or will you kick a poor helpless dog? Some man you turned out to be."

Tony's normally dark complexion now burned with a fiery red-hot glow. The promise of pain and death grew hotter in his eyes.

"Shut. The. Fuck. Up," Tony sneered, verging on feral.

"No. I don't think I will." Mitch could not stop himself. "All that other bullshit aside, and there's a lot to talk about there. I am getting damn tired of hearing that I bailed on you. Sure, I left town without saying goodbye. Why shouldn't I have? After all, you were the one I trusted. *Blood brothers to the end*, right? Isn't that what you called us? I bared my soul to you, man. Told you things I've told no one else, fully believing I could trust you and that you really cared. Just like I did for you since kinder-fucking-garten. You encouraged me to ask her out. You said how *life is short, man,* and that I should *stop being so wimpy and take a chance*. You thought she would say yes, you said. Do you remember that conversation? Do you? In your parents' barn. You were working on your four-wheeler. It was a Sunday afternoon. Do you remember?" Mitch stepped closer to Tony, who backed into the wall.

Beth watched, mouth agape, staying out of the way.

"You know…the very day, no, very *hours* before I was going to ask her, and oh…how you beat me to the punch, because you got to school before me. Remember?"

"Yeah. I remember. So what?" Tony's voice sounded small. Calm.

Beth grabbed Mitch by the shoulder. "Hey…"

Mitch shrugged her hand off and continued.

"'*So what?*' Really? Is that all you have to say?" Mitch felt a painful hitch in his chest and his face grew hot. "You were my best friend. One of the few people I trusted, man. You lied to me. You…you…you hugged me and told me to follow my heart. And then, just a few hours…knowing how I felt about Beth. Knowing… How could you do that?"

Tony didn't blink or show any sign of emotion.

"Come on, Mitch. Let it go," said Beth.

Mitch leaned in. "Just when I thought you couldn't possibly get any goddamn lower. More heinous. Downright evil."

"Yeah, yeah, yeah," Tony mumbled, still staring at Mitch.

"You had the audacity to tell Beth I was gay. What the actual fuck?" Mitch held his shaking arms out wide.

The once hushed crowd murmured and gasped as the mocking Christmas songs played on.

"Well, aren't ya?" Tony smirked.

The barbed words cut deep. But nothing Tony did or said surprised Mitch. Not anymore. He just dropped his arms, then snatched Beth close. "I don't know. Why don't you ask your wife?"

Tony stepped toward them, brick-sized fist raised, as Chris stepped absently into the circle.

"Hey, man. Let's have a beer. I hear your old man is... Ohh," he said, obliviously stumbling in on the private conversation from another part of the bar.

Mitch continued to stare into Tony's unflinching eyes.

"So, what do you want me to say? What are you looking for, Roberts? A pity party? Hell, man. It was ten years ago. We were teenagers. We were fucking kids. Get over it already."

Mitch laughed. "Yeah, you know, what's a pity?"

Tony smirked. "Tell me, Tolstoy!"

"It's a pity you turned out to be a bigger piece of shit than I thought you were. After all, you won the girl, burned our friendship to the ground, then fucked anything that moved and broke your promise to her and ripped her heart to shreds. What a great guy you turned out to be. I can only imagine what a shitty cop you are on top of it all. A lying bag of shit wearing a badge and a ridiculous Smokey the Bear hat. Wonder how many of these fine citizens you've screwed over. *Protect and Serve*, my ass. The only thing you've ever served was yourself!"

"Fuck you!"

Tony shoved Mitch hard in the chest, sending him crashing into the corkboard on the wall. Business cards, notes, and various pieces of paper flew into the air. Tony swung, whacking Mitch in the jaw. He fell into Beth, knocking her to the floor.

The crowd erupted in loud hoots and hollers. The crowd's shouts of "Fight!" nearly drowned out the blaring Christmas music. And *kick his ass!*

"Stay down, Roberts. Don't make me finish this," Tony growled, standing over Mitch with his fists clenched, eyes blazing with fury. Mitch's heart pounded in his chest, a cold sweat breaking out on his forehead. Fear flickered in his eyes, but he clenched his jaw, refusing to back down.

His body trembled, yet he lifted his gaze, meeting Tony's with a defiant glare.

A low growl followed by a sharp bark broke through the din of the bar.

"Pab! No!" Beth ordered and snatched his collar.

Mitch got to his knees, dabbed his nose with his sleeve, then stood. "That it? My old man, drunk off his ass, can punch harder than that. You'll have to try a lot harder to finish it." Mitch shook his head. He didn't want to fight Tony. Sure, he'd done that twice. Once this morning, and back in school. Cornered him in the gym locker room, and Tony wanted nothing to do with him. "I'm not going to fight you, Tony. It was never about that."

"What?" Tony's clenched fists still bounced about in front of him.

"I don't care if I kick your ass or you kick mine. It was never about that, man. It was about *us*. It was about how you betrayed my trust." Mitch stepped to him, arms at his sides.

"Mitch!" Beth, Chris, and even some of the crowd gasped.

Tony staggered backward, a confused look on his face. "What?" he repeated, his back against the door.

"You knew how bad it was at my house. You saw it first-hand. Me and my mom. How many hours did we spend out in that fort we built in my backyard, hiding from my dad? You promised to have my back no matter what, saying everything would be okay. Forever." Tears flowed down Mitch's face. He let them roll. "Do you remember that?"

Mitch's time bomb slowly faded with the raging fire inside him.

Tony's fists shook, then slowly dropped to his sides. His head dropped to his chest. "Yeah. I do."

"I guess I just never knew why you did it. What did I do? Was I not a good enough friend to you? What did I do to make it so easy for you to hurt me? What was wrong with me?" Mitch said.

The room seemed to pause. To close in, as Mitch stepped closer to Tony and looked up at him.

"But ya know what, Tony?"

Tony said nothing.

"It was never about me. It was all about you and the shit you were dealing with. I was just the lucky schmuck you took it out on." With those simple words, Mitch felt a decade or more of unnecessary encumbrance lifted off him.

A collective sigh flowed through the packed bar as Billy Squire's "Christmas is the Time to Say I Love You" pumped through the jukebox.

Mitch felt his shoulders slacken, and he offered his hand to his oldest friend.

Tony looked down at it.

Mitch felt Beth's hand on his shoulder again.

"I'm sorry," she said.

"Best see what has your dog all upset," Mitch mumbled.

Suddenly, a wicked howl filled the barroom and shook the walls. The lights briefly flickered, then returned

"What the hell was that?" Chris asked.

Mitch looked around and saw Pablo glaring past Tony, out the glass of the front door, his black lips peeling back into a large-toothed snarl.

"Beth!" Mitch said, pointing at the shaking hound.

"Pablo? What's wrong, buddy?" Beth stroked his thick fur, which was standing on end.

"Come on, it's just another shitty snowstorm. Christ, we live in Western New York and it's late December. Just another walk in the damn park. Relax. Have another drink," Gordon shouted, waving all the panicked barroom patrons away.

Another shrill cry pierced the bar, freezing everyone in place, horrified. The battering winds howled outside, sounding as if the siding was being ripped clean off the frame. The bitter wind from Lake Ontario, mixed with some unholy darkness, swept away any warmth, finding every crevice, crack, and hole and spilling its unearthly chill into every occupant of Yowner's Tavern.

With the wind rattling the windows, the dim lighting cast long, eerie shadows that flickered across the room. The air was thick with tension, a palpable sense of dread hanging over the patrons. Lively chatter ceased; only nervous whispers and clinking glasses broke the hush. The scent of stale beer and smoke mingled with the cold, damp air, creating an oppressive atmosphere that weighed heavily on everyone inside.

Patrons exchanged wide-eyed glances, their faces pale with fear. Some clutched their drinks tighter, knuckles white, while others instinctively huddled closer together, seeking comfort in numbers. A few brave souls edged toward the windows, peering out into the storm with a mix of dread and curiosity. The bartender, usually a pillar of calm, stood frozen behind the counter, his hand trembling as he reached for a bottle to steady himself.

The lights stopped flickering, and the jukebox roared to life. The Eagles belted out that bells would be ringing as the wailing winds continued to pound the outer walls of the bar.

"So…it's nothing, huh, Mr. Roberts?" Beth said, leaning between Mitch and his father.

"I hate to admit it, but the old man is right. A trusted source says it's only a bad snowstorm. For crying out loud, Beth, you grew up here, for Christ's sake." Tony's look of condescension sent Mitch's temples throbbing as he reached to pat her on the shoulder. Mitch was glad as she moved away from his touch.

"It's just a snowstorm; nothing more, nothing less. There's no need to be getting your panties in a twist." His arrogant smile made Mitch want to knock his block off, and he felt Beth and his father grab him just as he was pulling back to follow through with the angry urge.

33

Castles Made of Sand

"What's out there, buddy?" Beth said, following Pablo to the door. The malamute leaped up, his hot breath fogging up the glass even more than the packed bar already had.

"It's a damn snowstorm. A nasty one. The roads are closed and it's getting worse. That's all. There aren't any bogeymen out there. Ah, come on, Beth. You know that dog's afraid of his own shadow." Tony shook his head. "I've been telling you for a couple of years now. I think the big furbag isn't right. We shoulda put him down a long time ago. He's a danger."

Mitch stepped back as Beth swung around and glared at Tony. Her pale cheeks ignited into a fiery red as she punched him in the chest. "You have no say about my dog. Got it?"

"Okay. Fine. Whatever. I'm just telling you, that thing is a menace, and a lawsuit waiting to happen." Tony backed away, holding his hands up in surrender.

"Whatever is right." Beth turned back to her dog at the window. "The best thing for you to do is leave us the hell alone."

Mitch didn't know what to do. It had already been an exhausting day. He felt everything catching up with him.

A loud ringtone rang out—"Little Wing," by Jimi Hendrix—and Beth dug through her jacket pockets for her cell.

"Sheldon? I—I can barely hear you. Where are you?"

"Jesus Christ," said Tony. "That kid. Again?"

"Sheldon Hendricks?" Chris asked.

Tony didn't even look in Chris's direction. "Yeah. One of her 'at-risk' students. Mom's a crack whore, and I'm sure he'll end up selling drugs or be dead before graduation."

"He's a good kid. He volunteers down at the animal shelter with me," said Chris. "He's had a rough life."

"Oh yeah. I'm sure he's a saint," said Tony. "The fucking kid calls her all the time. She needs to cut the damn cord. There are just some you can't save, and this kid is one of 'em."

"Really?" Mitch asked. Just when he thought things might have crossed over to being passable, Tony continued to show his true colors.

"Really!"

"But you're a cop. To protect and serve, right?"

"You bet your ass. I do just that. But come on, man. I know you've been gone a long while, but there's no way in hell you've forgotten the makeup of this county. There are a hell of a lot more of them than there are of us, and I can only protect and serve so many. Especially those who are making a career out of breaking the law."

Chris busted in. "He's a good kid, Tony. I'm telling you. I see him three days a week—have done it for four years now, and I know him. You don't know what the hell you're talking about. Not with Sheldon. No way."

"Why don't you dig your head back into your stupid pictures and comic books and keep your mouth shut? You're the one who doesn't have a damn clue. I deal with these people every damn day. I have to clean up after these animals. Not you!"

Mitch didn't want to break the fragile, silent peace, but he couldn't keep quiet. "Now look. I don't know this kid from Adam, but for fuck's sake, Tony. He's just a kid. You're talking about him like he's public enemy number one. Come on. He's just a fuckin' kid."

Tony pointed a finger at Mitch's face. "You don't know shit either. Sure, he's just a kid. His mom's a crack whore and a worthless drunk. His scumbag father is doing twenty-five-to-life for killing half a dozen other scums of the earth during a drug deal gone bad up in the city. How long before you think this 'kid' goes into the family business and turns Sterling Point into the heroin capital of Western New York?"

"Okay, okay. The pet store. Stay put. I'll be right there." Beth tucked the phone back into her pocket.

The others turned to her. "What?"

Beth pulled Pablo down off the door. "Sheldon's stuck out there and needs help. Pablo and I will find him and bring him back here," she said, zipping up her coat.

"What?" Tony asked. "It's easily twenty below. You're not going out in this shit."

Beth tilted her head. "Oh, really?"

Mitch winced. He agreed with Tony, but didn't want to admit it.

"Come on, Beth. The kid is fine," Tony added. "If he could call you, he was warm and safe enough to wait until the storm passes. You can't risk your life for him."

Beth shrugged.

"I'm not letting you go out into...*this*. It's too damn dangerous. I forbid it," Tony shouted.

The bar let out a collective wince.

"What?" Beth's eyes filled with a violent rage. Mitch stepped away.

"You heard me. You are not going out in that shit. Do you hear me? It must be at least five below out there, for Christ's sake." Tony leaned toward her.

Beth stepped forward, mere inches away from his face. "You 'forbid' it?"

Tony sucked in a big breath and nodded.

"Guess what, Mr. Officer Severt. The day you started hitting me and cheating on me was the day you lost any ability to forbid me from doing a goddamn thing. I am taking Pablo, and we are going to find that little boy and bring him back here. And to quote Mitch's amazing mother, you and your over-inflated ego can hold hands and run. I'm leaving." With that, Beth whipped the barroom door open, grabbed Pablo's leash, and walked out into the blinding nor'easter. "Or you can shoot me, asshole!"

Mitch didn't hesitate. He zipped up his jacket and ran out the door.

From behind him, he heard Chris call, "Hold up. I'm coming too!" followed by, "Ah, fuck me." Tony's words were tossed into the raging storm as Mitch heard him following behind.

This has got to be the worst rescue party in the history of mankind, he thought.

He instantly regretted leaving the bar as a violent gust of wind nearly knocked him over and pierced through every layer of clothing he had on.

To make matters worse, a savage growl filled the biting, swirling wind. He hoped it was just the storm. However, he had a feeling that it was significantly worse.

* * *

They were gone but a few frozen seconds when the interior of the bar exploded suddenly, the loud crash of glass and the snapping of wood, and they all froze as the large picture window shattered, sending shards of glass into the crowd and ushering in arctic cold winds. Black tendrils latched onto the walls and spread quickly over the bar's occupants.

34

Which Way Do We Run?

Denny Pritchard's flesh burned with the frostbite spreading on his face, and the blood from his cracking skin froze almost instantly as he entered the blackness raging in front of the church. The enormity of the storm filled the width of Main Street and swallowed up everything in its path. Along with a splitting headache and burst eardrums, he felt the pain of his joints cracking as he struggled to make it to the church. He fell to one knee and disappeared into the one large drift that was Main Street.

"What the hell is that dumbass doin' out there?" Johnny squawked from inside the church, looking through a slit in the wooden shutters that protected the stained-glass windows. The harsh wind caused the roof to creak and groan under its unrelenting pounding.

Royce stumbled to the window and pulled back the shutter just enough for a decent view. All the streetlights were snuffed out. The blackness owned the night—and, seemingly, the town. A spear-like chill thrust down the old man's spine and his eyes grew wide, his glasses nearly sliding off his nose, as he saw his son stumbling toward the front of the church. Denny carefully stepped into the deep snow, and a bullet-like wind tore at his clothing and his exposed skin. Royce pushed up his glasses; for a split second in the ripping, black storm, he swore he could see hundreds of silvery claws tearing and slashing at his son.

"What in God's name?" he whispered. He found his chest tightening again and his breath escaped him. Dizzy now, he caught himself against the wall and dropped his gun. It clattered on the wooden floor and the echo seemed to bounce around the church for an eternity.

"You okay, boss?" Johnny's voice squeaked like nails on a chalkboard as he ran to Royce and helped him regain his balance.

A loud pounding on the door almost stopped both their hearts; Royce was afraid his old ticker wouldn't be able to jump-start itself again. Johnny quickly shifted behind the old man and peered over his shoulder at the shuddering door.

"Let me in!" Denny begged, his voice hollow and fleeting on the whipping wind.

He pounded on the door again.

"Just don't stand there, ya dumbass, let him in," Royce ordered, pulling the man from behind him and shoving him toward the door. Johnny looked back at Royce, his big nose and bulbous eyes dominating his thin face. Royce pretended to kneel to pick up his shotgun, but his legs were about to betray him, and he couldn't afford to show any signs of weakness. His throbbing knee crashed down on the wooden floor and he grasped at the gun, using it as a crutch.

Using all his strength, Johnny shoved the piled-up pews out of the way. He unlocked the door, and it crashed open, sending him sprawling backward, where he crashed into a sideboard and smashed it into pieces. The fake gold collection plate clanged against the wall and landed between his spread-eagled legs.

Denny fell into the dark church and collapsed onto the floor. Jagged black tendrils and claws whipped and groped at the door and the inside of the entrance, accompanied by a shrill, mournful cry that filled every inch of the church. Royce's breath caught in his throat as the blackness coiled and whipped about as though it were searching for something, or someone. He pulled himself up to his weary feet. Spark-like pains burst down his legs with every shaky step he made toward his groaning son. Royce grabbed the door and struggled to close it, the battering winds and sprawling blackness fighting his every effort.

"Give me a hand, boy," he grunted at Johnny.

"What the f—"

"Get yer ass over here." Royce tried to shove his son's legs aside, but they were as heavy and as slack as a hundred-pound bag of fertilizer. He put all his weight into it, but the door wouldn't budge. The powerful winter storm relentlessly battered the outside.

"Move his damn legs." His heart was pounding and his blood pressure rose. *Not good.*

"Got it, boss." Johnny grabbed Denny's torn arms and pulled him deeper into the church. He dropped him halfway to the pulpit and ran back to the front door.

Johnny slammed into the door and pushed along with Royce. Together, they almost closed it as an enormous black arm forced its way through the gap. The arm, easily the size of a fifty-gallon drum and slick as oil, seemed to writhe and move of its own volition. With it came an even more violent and gut-tearing howl. The fetid breath filled the church, and burning bile rushed up the back of Royce's throat. At the end of the huge arm-like tendril was a hand filled with razor-sharp talons that looked more like scythes as they whirled about outside.

Johnny screamed and froze. Royce caught the sudden smell of urine and saw a puddle forming under Johnny's quivering legs. *Pussy!* He shoved hard again on the door as as his old knees buckled and throbbed with pain.

One of the long sickle-like claws split the night and caught Johnny on the leg. Blood gushed out of the wound and Johnny cried out in agony as his thigh burst wide open and bits of yellow fat and shredded muscle came to the surface. He collapsed on the floor and his blood was running inside the grooves of the plank floor. The guttural howl that filled their ears washed away his cries.

Royce shoved as hard as he could as the bestial arm slammed around, trying to find flesh. His head pounding with white light, his knees buckling, he could feel his strength leaving him. His feet slipped from underneath him as he hit the increasing blood puddle from Johnny's gaping wound. He let out a loud groan as he saw movement from behind him.

"Duck, Pops," Denny said, weaving with the shotgun pointed at the doorway.

35

Blind Man in the Dark

Mitch tried in vain to shelter his face from the biting wind assaulting him, pushing him backward. Visibility wasn't an option. Violent snow from the lake blotted out the streetlights. Only sporadic micro-flashes of illumination from the houses and the closed businesses cut through the wall of white. If it wasn't for Pablo's deep barking, Mitch would probably head toward Arcadia Falls. His hands and feet were numb after only a minute or two in the street. Every bit of ice that hit his flesh felt like dozens of small razor blades. Mitch fumbled around in his jacket pockets for his hat and felt something push him from behind. He tumbled hard onto the snow-covered street.

"Keep up, Roberts. Come on." Tony ran past him.

"Yeah. Olive branch, my fat Irish ass," Mitch grumbled, as he climbed to his feet and followed the deep boot-holes before him.

"Right here, man!" Chris's voice pierced through the howling winds, but Mitch still couldn't see a thing. He reached out a hand and jumped as something grabbed it.

"Just me, man." Chris laughed and slapped him on the shoulder.

"Thanks. Shitty as all hell out here."

"Welcome home, brother," Chris said.

Mitch squinted to see the faint form of Tony ahead of them and climbed through the growing snow. "Yeah. Don't miss this shit at all."

"Come on, man. The pet store isn't too far." Chris stepped through the snow as effortlessly as Legolas, the agile elf from *Lord of the Rings*, and motioned for Mitch to follow.

"Show-off!" Mitch yelled into the pitching storm. He heard a giggle ahead of him and followed it.

As a kid, Mitch hated winter, but he'd still gone out and played in the snowy streets. This was different. The snow was heavy now, and came down more like tiny barbed spears than snowflakes. Every part of his skin that wasn't covered felt the biting sting. The schizophrenic wind twisted and changed direction from one second—and one painful foot—to the next. The wind chill had to have plummeted the temperatures down to near fifteen below zero. Mitch found it hard to breathe, and a creeping numbness was spreading through his extremities. They needed to find this kid and get back to the bar before the storm took them all.

"This way," Chris called from ahead, and Mitch did all he could to stay standing. Between the thigh-high snow and the brutal, sucker-punching wind, balance wasn't easy.

Sporadic glimpses of streetlights played a mocking game of peek-a-boo through the violent storm. Pablo's sharp barks provided a much-welcome beacon and Mitch followed it, Chris's bright yellow jacket aiding his path. The frigid air was stealing his breath. Mitch's lungs burned and felt as if they were shrinking, being squeezed. A litany of second-guessing and self-loathing thoughts filled his head as he trudged on.

He slammed into something and fell backward, landing in a deep drift.

"Get the fuck out here, kid!" Tony shouted.

Beth was close behind. "Knock it off!"

A boyish voice came through the wind. "No disrespect, Mrs. S. But I don't like that dude."

"Too bad, you little shit," called Tony. "Come out now or freeze with the other strays inside your homeless condo."

"Hey, what the hell, man?" Mitch shouted. *You are such an asshole,* he thought, climbing out of his unintentional snow-angel imprint.

Once on his feet, he caught a flurry of motion and took a second to put it together. Beth had shoved Tony, and he now lay among a row of snow-covered garbage cans, flailing about like a fish out of water. The wonderful sight made the biting storm a little easier to endure.

"Sheldon. Come on," pleaded Beth. "It's not safe out here. You called me. I'm here. Come out and let's go back to Yowner's, where it's warm." Mitch finally made his way to her side.

"Is your racist cop husband still out there?" A frightened voice came from a barrel, mixed with several meows and angry barks.

Beth cut Tony off mid-sentence with another shove to his chest.

"Enough!" she snarled. Pablo matched her growl-for-growl.

"Easy, big guy." Mitch ran a gloved hand through the dog's wet fur and shot Tony a derisive look as he approached the barrel. "Hey, Sheldon. It's Mitch. I'm an old friend of Beth's—Mrs. Severt. She's told me about you." Beth quickly nodded her approval.

"Oh, yeah?" the voice replied, filled with skepticism. Mitch would've appreciated it if it wasn't pushing twenty below. "Is he out there or not?"

He looked back at the group, and they were shivering and impatient. So he focused on something Beth had told him the night before. "She tells me you're a Hendrix fan."

A long, frozen pause hung in the raging storm.

Finally… "Heck yes, Jimi is the *man*. So, what of it?"

This kid is something else. Mitch shook his head and took a long shot. "Yeah, man. I agree. I am too. You know, I have his complete album collection. All first editions on vinyl. Even the rare stuff. Killer tunes."

More chilly silence as the piercing snow peppered Mitch's face.

"Holy crap. On vinyl?" Sheldon said. "Really?"

"You bet. Even the Chitlin' Circuit stuff and the British outtakes. You come on out of there. I will be more than happy to let you have a couple."

"No way?"

"Honest. I have doubles of some of them. They're yours if you get your butt out here before we freeze our butts off," said Mitch through the piercing snow and wind.

"Hell with this shit!" Tony said, and forced his way past Beth, shaking off Chris's feeble attempt at holding him back. Mitch caught him in his peripheral vision and spun to intercept him. With all his weight and momentum, Mitch slammed his forearms into the much taller man's chest, violently stopping him in his tracks and sending him falling back into the deep snowdrift.

The powerful gust of wind silenced a booming laugh that echoed off the building across the alleyway.

36
Father and Son

Royce's heart pounded in his chest as he grabbed Denny by the arm. After the big man fired two rounds into the raging blackness tearing through the church—the slugs did nothing but piss off whatever this hell-spawned thing was—Royce knew they had to get out. He could feel the weight of the items in his coat pocket—was that what the goddamned thing was searching for? He didn't give three shits. They were his now, and he had to keep them safe, no matter what the cost.

"Move your ass, damn it!" he barked at Denny, shoving him toward the back door. Ignoring the group's screams, he pressed on. He had to focus on getting out alive.

The icy night swallowed them as they stormed through the doorway. The wind howled and snow whipped around them, but Royce didn't stop. He couldn't stop. The blackness roared in frustration behind them, unable to follow them into the storm.

"Keep moving!" the old hunter urged, his voice barely audible over the wind. He could feel the cold biting into his skin, but it was a welcome sensation compared to the searing pain of the blackness. They needed to reach Yowner's Tavern; it alone shone brightly in Sterling Point.

"We need to get to Yowner's!" Royce shouted, his voice trembling. "Go, boy!"

Denny nodded, helping his gimping father through the deepening snow. His breath was visible in the frigid air. "We'll make it, Pops," he said, more to convince himself.

"Don't leave me behind, boy," Royce threatened, and felt the weight of the items in his pocket, and the unnatural growls from the black thing were a constant reminder of the danger they were in.

They fought their way through the storm, each step a battle against the elements. The wind whipped snow into their faces, obscuring their vision, but they pressed on. Royce's breath came in ragged gasps, his old body struggling to keep up. But he couldn't afford to slow down. Not now.

Approaching the tavern, the storm worsened; darkness threatened to consume them. But they pushed on, driven by sheer willpower. Finally, they reached the door of the tavern, their bodies numb from the cold.

Royce pounded on the door, his knuckles raw and bleeding. "Open the goddamn door, you stupid fucks! Let us in!" he shouted, his voice barely audible over the wind.

37

A Stranger No Longer

Mitch turned to see a pair of eyes peering out of the barrel, quivering with either laughter or freezing chills. He was betting on the former.

"Wow. So cool!" Sheldon cackled as he pulled the scarf across his face, his dark skin turned pink and cold. A bunch of other muzzles peeked out from inside the barrel and barked and meowed.

"Roberts," Tony shouted, fighting to climb out of the snow pile.

"I don't know who you are, man, but you're cool with me." Sheldon laughed again and crawled out of the barrel.

"Get your butt over here, mister!" Beth ordered. Sheldon petted his furry friends goodbye and closed the hatch of the barrel.

"You Mitch?" Sheldon asked.

"Yes, sir. Good to meet ya."

Sheldon sized him up and gave a curt nod. He held his fist out. "Cool, man. Mrs. S. has told me a bunch about you too."

Mitch was taken aback, but was hip enough to return Sheldon's fist-bump. "Good things, I hope."

Without hesitation, he said, "You dig Jimi, you can't be as bad as Officer Adolf over there."

Mitch couldn't help but let out a chuckle and quickly regretted it as the biting snow tore into his face.

"Punk. You best watch your wise mouth, boy. You and your waste of a druggie mother are both—"

"Tony!" Beth yelled, and he drew his fist back and everyone froze in place.

Pablo leaped between them, landing in the middle of what Mitch guessed was the sidewalk. The dog's hackles stood on end and his body was a sea of tense-corded muscle and he seemed ready to attack. A deep, bestial mix of howls and growls echoed in the snowy night.

"What? You're going to hit me? Again? Been there, done that, tough guy," Beth shouted, her voice hoarse.

Terrified screams followed the bellow of gunfire that blasted through the stormy din. The storm raged outside, a furious tempest of howling wind and blinding snow. The icy gusts whipped through the streets, carrying with them a bone-chilling cold that cut through to the bone.

"What the—?" Mitch and Chris said in unison, pointing at a couple of people screaming as they fought their way toward the tavern, trudging through the snow. The storm made it nearly impossible to see the swirling snowflakes creating a whiteout that obscured everything beyond a few feet. The snow and wind created a relentless, impenetrable wall of white, reducing visibility to mere inches. Shadows and shapes flickered in and out of view, making it difficult to distinguish friend from foe.

Mitch felt his already trembling knees were like cotton wool. He attempted to shout, but all that emerged was a feeble, "The hell?"

He recoiled as someone from the group fired a shotgun at the enormous black form shifting and twisting about behind them.

Mitch, Beth, Chris, Sheldon, and even Tony turned their attention toward the swirling black cloud that was swallowing up Main Street. Within its ebony form were roving red eyes, glistening black talons, and matching maws, filled with enormous sharp teeth. It was something out of H. P. Lovecraft's nightmares, Mitch horrifically realized, and he felt not only his skin but his blood freezing. Pablo's deep growls and angry barks fought to pierce the howling winds.

"What the hell is that?" Beth pulled Sheldon close.

"We gotta go." Chris ran back toward the bar.

Tony pulled his pistol, and Mitch caught the cop's hands shaking. "You go."

Mitch stared at the churning black abattoir of teeth and talons, and something in him snapped. "No. We all go. Beth, get Sheldon out of here. Beat feet for Yowner's. Go!" He shoved Tony toward the bar and followed them southward down Main Street.

Beth shouted, "Pablo, go, now!"

The snarling malamute stayed put, his teeth bared in defense, until Beth snatched him by the collar, and he finally relented and followed her.

Heart pounding, Mitch didn't know if he could make it back to the bar. Despite the freezing cold, a river of sweat soaked through his clothes. Falling to his knees, his chest burned with pain and his lungs echoed with a searing agony of their own.

Beth and Chris turned back to him.

"Go!" He frantically pointed toward Yowner's. An electric charge shocked every muscle, blurring his vision. He sank into the snow up to his thighs.

A sudden force yanked him out of it and Mitch welcomed Beth and Chris's effort. "Thanks," was all he could afford as the black cloud bore down on them.

He regained his breath and pushed onward.

Yowner's was a block and a half away and the figures he'd spotted were almost at the door.

"Keep going!" he shouted.

Close behind the strangers from Main Street, they reached the bar door but got pushed out by an old man with a pencil-thin mustache in winter camouflage who kicked Beth in the stomach and shut the door.

Mitch would never forget the old man's evil grin.

All around them fell into an impenetrable shroud of black. Darkness devoured the snow.

Then someone screamed.

38
Act Naturally

Royce Pritchard slammed the door to the tavern and didn't give a crap about the bitch, the dog, or whoever else was with her. They'd made it. The stifling heat was a welcome sensation as the old man leaned against the door, ignoring the pounding fists and screams coming from the other side.

Every inch of Royce's body ached, and he could swear he had at least a few fingers and toes filled with frostbite. But he didn't care. He was warm, safe, and there was beer. A sudden interruption shattered his joy; everyone in the bar watched him and the other hunters.

"What the hell you looking at?" he snapped. The pounding fists jerked him forward. "Some kind of weather we're having, huh?"

"What the hell's out there, boss?" Johnny collapsed against the wall, sending a rack of coats falling to the floor.

"Shut the hell up, boy!" Royce shot Johnny a death glare. "The kid drank too much at the cabin. Pussy can't hang with the big boys. What the hell can ya do?"

"Royce?" Sal Yowner called through the crowd. "Thought you boys were down in Rhodes Hollow, hunting for Christmas. What are you doing back here? Hell, how'd you make it back with this shitstorm?"

"W—well, we decided to come home. It's Christmas, after all, and I figu—" The door burst halfway open, and with it came frenzied cries for help and entry. "Hey, looks like we ain't the only ones late to the party." Royce offered a bullshit line he was certain wouldn't fly.

"Pritchard? That you?" came a familiar voice.

"Dad!" A crazed chorus of panicked calls breached the door.

Another violent smash into the door sent Royce sprawling onto the floor.

"What have we here, Pritchard?"

Royce's gaze lifted; a grimace followed as he recognized an unwelcome sight.

Gordon fucking Roberts.

"Is that my son out there?" Gordon asked, putting down his can of beer.

The panic pounding on the door gave him the answer.

"Ya best open that damn door before I throw ya against it," Gordon winked.

"Fuck you, old man," Royce said through gritted teeth.

PART THREE

"What lies behind us and what lies ahead of us are tiny matters compared to what lives within us."

—*Henry David Thoreau*

39
What Fresh Hell

It was Chris Delaney's wide blue, terror-filled eyes, dotted with small flecks of gold, that Mitch would remember for the rest of his life—and, he feared, even long past that.

Mitch had written many graphic scenes in his fiction, but this…this was real.

He heard Beth pounding on the door behind him as he desperately held onto Chris's outstretched hand. Chris's old camera, dangling from his neck, was sucked into the dark, bloody mass, causing the nylon strap to tighten around his neck, his eyes to bulge, and his skin to turn a ghostly white.

Mitch cried out as he tugged to free Chris, but the Darkness seemed to mock him, tightening its grip and dragging his old friend into oblivion.

"Hold on, man! For the love of God, hold on!" Mitch bellowed. Chris's once-brilliant blue eyes, now dull and weeping silent tears of terror, were swallowed by a frenzied mass of razor-sharp teeth that tore through his flesh as if it were paper.

The air filled with the sickening stench of blood as chunks of meat ripped away from his body, showering Mitch and all around him in a red rain.

Everyone—no, everything screamed, lost in the lashing storm, and belittled Chris's unanswered pleas for help.

A thunderous growl pounded them, and in a flash, Chris was gone. Only tiny bits of his flesh and blood remained.

Mitch mule-kicked the door, while Beth and the rest screamed and pounded on the front of the bar.

A set of red eyes glared at Mitch as black tendrils darted all around them. Rows of blood and flesh taunted him as he stood between this thing and the people behind him, holding up nothing in defense but Chris's frozen gloves.

Mitch's entire body shook. A slight trickle of piss darkened his jeans, but he held fast, trying desperately to hold onto every scrap of reality left.

"Kick that fucking thing in if you have to!" he yelled.

"If you don't open this goddamn door, I swear to God I'll shoot the damn thing open!" Tony bellowed.

"Mitch!" called Beth.

"Get the kid inside. Break a window. Anything!" he replied, unable to turn away from the hypnotic red eyes boring down into him.

Behind Mitch, a loud crash came, then a blinding flash of warm light, illuminating the street.

Finally, the tavern door swung open, the bright lights sending a blinding flash out into the dark evening.

"No, Mitch. Come on!" Beth shouted.

He heard Tony's voice. "Go, Beth. Goddamn it, go!"

"Just go, Beth!" Mitch shouted, staring down the red glare. And now, he pissed himself.

"Mitch!" he heard Beth call. He offered a thumbs-up, but felt no better until the door closed, plunging him into darkness. He had no idea what he was doing or why. But it felt right. This storm, this thing hadn't devoured him as it did his friend, so Mitch focused on that and took a deep breath.

The large red eyes seemed to squint and slowly examined him. From his boots to his snow-soaked jeans, to his jacket and his backpack. Then they froze. It seemed the rushing talons and teeth calmed to a mere hover as the eyes grew closer to the backpack.

Every bone in Mitch's body froze, not solely because of the arctic temperatures. He wouldn't have moved, even if his body could respond. Still, something told him to hold fast.

The storm attacked the bar and kicked up enough snow to bury Mitch to his mid-thigh.

The burning red eyes finally came up to Mitch's freezing face and bored deep into him.

A strange voice pierced Mitch's frightened mind.

"For retribution, we have come. We have come for flesh and blood. We have come for what is ours. What we seek is near. You...human... You do not hold what we seek. We would smell it. Sense it on, within you." The barbed words bore into Mitch, and he fell into the deep snow in flashing pain.

A gruff sniffing sound came next, followed by what sounded to Mitch like a frigid huff in his face.

"Odd. You humans are clean. Unsullied. Hmm. Interesting."

Mitch clutched his temples, trying desperately to quench the pulsing pain.

"It is not your soul-life or blood-line we seek," the voice bayed, and then the dark cloud retreated into the swirling talons and biting teeth. "We do not wish to harm you. Alas, our wrath will not relent until we feed on those who dared disturb our darkened slumber. We will consume all living things until we have satisfied the blood debt and recovered our treasure. We will feed on the vast human souls hiding within this feeble structure. Return to us what is in our charge, and we will spare all humans. If not, we will feed."

Mitch opened his eyes and slowly staggered to his feet. Fighting to breathe, his frozen body and mind fought to find purchase on any life raft of reality.

"Go!" the otherworldly voice ordered. "Before we change our mind!"

He didn't hesitate and pounded on the door until it opened. Mitch rushed everyone inside, not knowing what the hell had just happened, but damn happy to be alive.

40

Devil Likes It Slow

The bar was in absolute chaos as Mitch slammed the door and fought to catch his breath. His body wasn't the only thing numb and fraught with daggers as the heat chased away the cold. His mind spun in a maelstrom of bizarre recollections. *Talking, dog, beast, tendrils, like snow shadows? Holy relics? Soul-life?* And he had witnessed his old friend get devoured before his eyes. What the hell was going on? Mitch's fragile brain had more questions than answers and he staggered and fell, and someone caught him, but the dark stole him away.

A warm sensation whipped his face, and a voice came to him. "Mitch?" He knew that voice.

"Beth!"

"I've got you, boy," came a gruff voice, and he felt a strong hand on his shivering shoulder.

Mitch recognized the speaker's voice before seeing their face.

"Dad?" Mitch shook his head and tried to sit up.

The lights flickered on and off and the wind slapped violently at the clapboard siding of Yowner's, and Mitch regretted regaining consciousness. His head didn't feel much better, but at least now he could inhale without it feeling like someone had parked his father's plow truck on his chest.

Beth sat next to him on a barstool and his dad sat on his left, with one of his large hands on Mitch's shoulder, the other holding a can of Genny. Mitch let a small smile slip before he saw the bloody bar towel in Beth's hands.

"Chris!" he gasped.

Beth grabbed Mitch's face, her hands trembling as she looked deeply into his eyes. "I know. It's not your fault, Mitch. It's not. You got us back here safely. That's all that matters." Her voice cracked with emotion, and heavy tears welled up in the corners of her eyes, spilling down her cheeks. Seeing her pain, Mitch's own tears began to flow, his heart aching with the weight of their shared sorrow.

Even the big dog got involved and licked Mitch's hand. His sandpaper tongue felt like a torch against his prickled, warming skin.

His dad patted him on the shoulder. "You did good. From what Beth here says, it was shitty out there. You got your friends back here safely. That's all that matters, son. Well, except for that weird kid, but you did your best."

"Gordon!" Beth said.

"What?" Gordon replied, drinking his beer.

Is everyone here?" Mitch asked, looking around the crowded bar. "Is everyone safe?"

Beth dabbed the bar towel on his face. "Yes. Thanks to you, Mitchie." While her bright smile and comforting words warmed him, it was the horrific image of Chris's bloody face and the dark words of the snowstorm that kept him chilled to the bone.

"The kid… Sheldon? Tony?" Mitch asked.

"Right here, man. That was some serious, heroic stuff right there." Sheldon peeked around Beth's shoulder.

"Yes. They're both here." Beth smiled, holding his hand.

"Don't worry about me. I don't need any help," Tony said.

"Good." Mitch forced a smile, but the grisly visuals pierced through the faux warmth and safety of the bar, and everything came back to him in a brutal flash.

"What about that asshole who slammed the door on us in the first place?" Mitch stood up on shaky legs, with a little help from his dad and Beth.

The crowd stared at Mitch, and they drew their eyes to the blood-soaked towel in Beth's hand and a wave of panic overtook them. They needed to do something before hysteria took over.

"Oh, you mean good ol' asshole, Royce Pritchard, and his rabble of dumbass peckerheads? Don't worry, boy, they're right here," Gordon said, grinning broadly. Mitch steadied himself on Beth's arm and his dad's shoulder.

Beth and Gordon led Mitch to three camouflage-clad individuals near death's door in the pool room. The one in the center seemed familiar. It was the asshole that had gleefully slammed the door in Mitch's face. He felt a deep fire rage inside his gut.

"Here ya go, son. This is the bag of dogshit that locked you guys out."

"Son? Oh, fucking great. Another piece of shit from the Roberts inbred family tree. What you got, fatboy? You gonna cry because your Big Mac-filled ass didn't make it before?"

The old man bore a resemblance to both Clyde the Barber from *The Andy Griffith Show* and Adolf Hitler. Maybe it was just the cheesy mustache protruding from underneath his crooked nose. Either way, this asshole got Chris killed. Mitch took an unsteady step back and slammed into the pool table, sending balls scurrying off the table and onto the hardwood floor.

Royce Pritchard let out a loud belly laugh, his odd-fitting dentures shifting in the old prick's big mouth. They seemed to have a personality of their own. "Oh, this is fuckin' perfect. A chip off the ol' dumbass block. Priceless."

Mitch grunted as he pulled himself up. Beth tried to help, but he shrugged her off. He watched the old man all the way. Sure, he was a tough guy, and Mitch remembered Pritchard and his dad being buddies down at the VFW back in the day, so he knew the guy had seen his share of ugliness, just like his father. But if Mitch had given his father no quarter for treating him or his mom like common garbage, there was no way in hell he'd give this abusive, knuckle-dragging redneck an ounce more sympathy.

"Funny. I'm glad you find this all so goddamn hilarious, Mr. Pritchard." Mitch looked at the other two members of the redneck club, sitting trembling on the bench. One of them seemed familiar: the big guy. It was the simple-minded, slack-jawed expression that told him exactly who it was. Denny Pritchard. Royce's dumber-than-a-box-of-rocks son, with the bleeding, bright-red face.

Mitch nodded at Denny. "We went to school together, didn't we?" he asked, his voice tinged with a hint of nostalgia, fairly certain of the answer.

Denny just stared at him. "Yeah, it was funny. You're about as soft as your drunk father over there. Ain't no use in pretending any different, boy." Royce grinned at Mitch and chuckled.

Without uttering a single word, Mitch grabbed a pool cue from the table.

He had been trying to put it all together since witnessing that black thing storming down the street. It seemed as if it were chasing the Pritchard posse. But why? Then there were the surreal moments with the red-eyed beast that had devoured Chris, talking about holy bloodlines and other crazy stuff. He'd have to log some serious couch hours with his shrink, if he lived through the night—

Loud shouts cut Mitch's internal inquiry short.

"What the hell? Put that stick down, boy. We ain't having a fucking coffee klatch here. And *you* assholes have no right to keep us penned up like common cattle. Come on, Mr. High and Mighty lawman," Royce said, turning his heated gaze to Tony. "Do your fucking job. Or did you lose that along with your ball sack in your pending divorce? It's been a long goddamn day, and with this fucking storm, getting here from Rhodes Hollow wasn't a damn cakewalk. Now, get out of my way and let me take a piss and get a goddamn shot and a beer. Capisce?" Royce Pritchard stood up and took one step before Mitch and his father rushed him.

"A beer? You killed Chris, asshole!" Mitch swung the pool cue, missing Royce's temple by mere inches as someone yanked him backward, sending him sprawling onto the hard floor and the stick skittering against the wall.

The pool room ignited with a burst of shouts and shoving. Mitch heard his father cursing and Beth calling his name and Tony fighting to save his reputation.

His body hurt. Every inch tingled with pain and the cold, but he forced himself to one knee.

That's when the lights went out, sending the entire bar into complete darkness.

41

Lights Out

All was black.

The remaining windows shattered, sending shards of glass splintering into the throng of screaming patrons, most of whom ran screaming, trying to find cover in the dark. The power was out all over town. A biting ocean of dagger-like snow flowed through the shattered windows, stealing the heat from the bar, plummeting the temperature by twenty degrees in a matter of seconds.

Mitch lay frozen on the floor, surrounded by a tornado of destruction. Like shooting stars, fragments of his shattered life covered the room while he clung to the little sanity he had left. His eyes searched desperately for something amongst the madness, and from underneath the pool table, he saw something.

People cried out for help and Tony did his best role-playing as a cop, shouting orders amongst the freezing, dark chaos. But something told Mitch the newfound object could be important. Following his gut instinct, he crawled under the table far enough to see the bag sitting between Royce Pritchard's blood-soaked boots. Mitch saw *'Property of MSGT. R. F. Pritchard''* printed on the bloody olive drab backpack.

His harried mind raced back to what Pritchard had said about Rhodes Hollow and what the nightmarish beast had said. And it all seemed like something from a satanic *NeverEnding Story*.

A deep, blood-curdling screech filled the bar as the howling wind tore through the room and the panicked patrons hunkered down, praying for help.

"Sal! Peckerhead, don't you have a goddamn generator?" From behind a post separating the pool room and bar, Gordon Roberts roared. Mitch heard his father's booming voice directly behind him, so he at least had some orientation.

"On it!" Sal called.

As if on cue, the overhead lights flickered once, twice, then stayed on. Not all of them, and there was no jukebox, no Christmas lights or beer signs. The brutal winter gale and frenzied hum of the freaked-out people created the soundtrack to the dim bar.

Gordie mocked, "On point as always, peckerhead."

"You're welcome, dumbass. Hey, everyone calm the hell down. Use whatever you find to barricade the windows. We gotta get them covered up. The generator can't run this furnace forever and we're losing heat fast."

A group of patrons hurriedly stacked tables and chairs in front of the plate-glass window at the front of the bar and the two smaller side windows.

Pablo snarled and tore off to the front door.

Mitch inched toward the bag, checking for Pritchard. No. He'd gotten lucky. Pritchard had stood and was yelling at Mitch's dad and Tony, and now the bag was behind him.

Mitch took a chance and lunged out, snatched the bag, and pulled it under the pool table.

Up close, he saw that old and fresh blood stained it. He quickly unhooked the latch on the canvas bag, fearing what he'd find inside.

While chaos reigned above the pool table, Mitch took inventory of the bag, praying to find what the murderous monsters tearing about the bar and the town wanted. It didn't take long, as something pricked his finger.

There was something cold, sharp. Even in the darkness, Mitch could make it out because of its reddish glow. It emitted enough light for him to determine that it was a handful of arrowheads. Ancient stone, yet sharp, still holding a keen edge. He rummaged through the large stash. There were coins. Old coins of various sizes and shapes. While it was too dark under the pool table to read them, Mitch guessed they weren't modern. Too big, too thick.

There were also rings and tangled necklaces and chains. It was as if old man Pritchard had robbed a dozen pawn shops or museums. Pritchard had a potential fortune here.

But what did the monster outside want?

In a white-hot flash, it came to him. "He stole all of this from that…thing." But that didn't answer the more life-or-death question. *How do we stop that thing?*

Beth called out, "Mitch?"

"Boy? Where the hell are ya?" his father bellowed.

Mitch knew he couldn't hide under the pool table forever, but his gut told him he was onto something.

"Stop dickin' the dog, boy!" Gordon called again.

Beth added, "Seriously, Mitchie."

"Mitchie? Again? What the hell is that about?"

Right or wrong, he had to do something. He fastened the bag up, took a deep breath, and rolled out from under the pool table. He hadn't imagined what had happened out in the street, or the black tendrils, so he needed to tell them what he was thinking, and he didn't care if he sounded as though he'd lost his mind. Mitch crawled from under the pool table, Pritchard's heavy bag clutched in his hand.

Old man Pritchard's eyes grew wide.

"What's in the bag?" Beth asked.

They all turned to face Mitch.

It was something out of Edgar Allan Poe's works, or from a Stephen King novel. Was his overreactive imagination being overridden by the horrific insanity of the past few minutes, hours, and even days? Had he been living the sequestered life of a self-mandated banishment? His head spun with all the impossible information and traumatic moments. Death, love, loss, every damn thing rushed before his mind as the raging thoughts inside him, as though he were in a demented courtroom where both prosecutor and defender violently, vehemently argued, pleaded their cases. And tried to make sense of it all. As messed up as it all seemed, the evidence was there.

Despite the temperature, sweat poured down Mitch's face and drenched his shirt. His heartbeat pounded in his temples.

They all needed an answer.

A scream pierced the tavern's darkness; then an outside force shattered the bar, tearing away the front wall.

"Mitch!" Beth cried out.

"Dad, Beth, I need you to follow me. Tony, grab those guys and bring them in the back. Away from these people. We need to end this now."

"What? Why?"

Tony shot Mitch an angry look, then relented.

Not waiting for an answer, Mitch stormed ahead.

"Come on, Mr. Pritchard, you guys too. Let's go."

Mitch led them into the back room. The room where he and his dad had a heated discussion not too long ago.

42
Time to Confess

"What the hell's going on, Roberts? We don't have time for your bullshit. People are dying out there!" Tony shoved Mitch in the back, causing him to stumble into the sink and send unwashed dishes crashing to the floor.

"Knock it off, Tony. That's not helping." Beth shoved Tony in return, sending him smashing into a metal shelf filled with canned goods.

Gordon Roberts yanked Tony by the shoulder. "Touch my stuff and—"

His words were cut off as Mitch spun around, glaring directly into Tony's eyes. "We have to make time, asshole! I think I know what that...thing out there is, and what it's after."

They stared at him as though a third arm had sprouted out of his forehead.

"Get on with it, then. Cut the dramatic bullshit," Tony demanded.

"Yeah, no shit. What ya doing with my bag, boy?" Royce Pritchard started toward Mitch, but a large hand jutted out, striking him in the chest.

"Easy, Pritchard. Don't go getting all froggy now. Let my boy talk. All of you." Gordon Roberts stood easily half a foot taller than Royce, and even three sheets to the wind, Mitch was certain his dad would kick the living daylights out of him. Royce seemingly agreed, halting, yet continuing his glare at Mitch and his bag.

"That's my property, kid. You ain't got no right messing with my shit." Royce turned to Tony. "Go on, *Sheriff* Severt. Do your goddamn job. That dipshit stole my belongings. Do something!"

"Just hold on, the lot of you. Roberts, what game are you playing? Is that Mr. Pritchard's bag?" Tony's shoulders sagged as he shot Mitch a "For the love of God" look.

"Yeah, Mitch, what's going on?" asked Beth.

Mitch held up the blood-stained bag. "This belongs to USMC SSG R. G. Pritchard."

Another loud crashing sound filled the bar and the entire building shook, sending pans, pots, and cans tumbling to the floor.

"Are you serious with this bullshit?" said Royce. "There's some nasty shit out there eating people, and you want to hold the damn people's court in the kitchen of a shitty bar? You insane, kid?"

"Hate to say it, peckerhead is right. Why did you bring us back here? We should be getting guns and trying to kill whatever this goddamn thing is." Gordon Roberts pulled his pistol from his belt holster. "You best get to making your point fast!"

Denny stood staring at the floor, avoiding all eye contact. But even with that odd behavior, Mitch knew he had to spill the beans, and quickly.

"Okay, okay. All right, I found this bag that belongs to Mr. Pritchard. But look at the bloody handprints. And if that's not disturbing enough, how about all the stolen treasures inside it?"

"So?" Tony said. "Wait... What?"

"What connection does that have with the thing outside?"" asked Beth. "You said you knew what it wanted. Well?"

"All right. I know this will sound batshit crazy, but—"

"Ya think?" Tony shook his head.

Mitch held his hand up. "Hold on. After king asshat there slammed the door on us, killing my friend—our friend—in the goddamn process, that thing out there, that blackness, spoke to me." The words came out in a rush, and he didn't even believe them himself.

Tony tilted his head. "Say what? Stolen treasure? It talked to you? Have you lost what's left of your mind?"

"The kid is crazier than a shithouse rat. Who you gonna believe, Sheriff? For fuck's sake. Give me our guns and my bag back and we'll go kill that sonofabitch. Easy-goddamn-peasy. We ain't got time for this bullshit." Royce turned to leave.

"Hold on. Nobody's going anywhere." Gordon Roberts yanked Royce back by his collar and the two of them locked eyes.

"You finally want to do this, old man?" Royce hissed, leaning into Gordon's barrel chest.

"Been a long time coming, *friend*," Gordon calmly replied. There was heaviness in the last word, Mitch caught. But now wasn't the time.

"Stop. Let me show you." Mitch dropped the heavy bag onto the table, opening it up and dumping its shining contents. Coins and jewelry clattered loudly, but in the end, all was silent—except for the chaotic cries from the barroom.

Their gaze fixed upon the treasure resembling museum artifacts.

"So, what does this have to do with me again?" Royce jumped in. His voice echoed with apprehension.

"Whoa…" said Beth.

Tony straightened up. "Great. First, there's been a lot of nasty violence going on tonight. That blood could be from anything. Second, maybe Mr. Pritchard broke into Godsey's Pawnshop and robbed it blind. That's tragic. But what the hell does that have to do with that thing out there?"

Mitch fought to find strength, both physical and mental, to explain his case. But somewhere in the flickering light of the bar's kitchen, he mustered the courage and ran headlong into the most improbable, surreal story he'd ever told. And he'd written some seriously twisted tales.

"It sounds absolutely insane, I know…" Mitch started. His words came out soft, apprehensive. Suddenly, he felt small, as all their eyes bore into him.

"Spit it out," Tony said.

"Well, boy?" Royce growled.

"Okay, when I was out there…" Mitch started. "That…that…thing spoke to me, as I said. It told me it was after some of us in here."

"For Christ's sake," said Tony. "You've been living in your fantasy world too long. We don't have time for your Dungeons and Dragons, Stephen King, bullshit." Tony's face grew red as the winds howled in rage outside.

They all continued to stare in disbelief at him. Even Beth.

"I know. I know. It sounds like madness to me too. But does any of this"—Mitch motioned towards the shaking building, the blood-soaked backroom, and Denny's bloody face. "Do you think what happened to all those people out there, and what happened to Denny, is all just part of my *fucking Stephen King*' imagination?" Mitch glared at Tony.

"I think this is what the creature is after. It's after whoever woke it up and stole something from it. This jewelry, the missing coins, the arrowheads and other stuff—it all belongs to that thing. But the box wasn't in the bag. So I'm guessing that someone here knows where the missing items are."

Royce Pritchard's face washed to a ghostly white.

"What the hell are you talkin' about, boy?" he shouted.

Tony turned to him and glared.

Denny Pritchard shook and mumbled something under his breath.

"You okay?" Beth asked.

Royce leaned in and whispered something to Denny.

Mitch couldn't make out the words with the raging storm and the freaked-out bar patrons.

"What is it, Denny?"

"He ain't got anything to say. Ain't that right, boy?"

Denny continued shaking and shot terrified glances up at Mitch and Tony.

His father slapped him on the shoulder and said, "Nothing at all, ain't that right, son?"

The big guy was in shock. His eyes were stuck wide open, and he was spattered with dried blood. He also had a busted lip and a swollen eye. Mitch knew all about domineering fathers; this had Royce Pritchard all over it.

"Hey, Denny. It's okay. If you need to say something, you're safe here." Mitch looked at Tony, hoping for some legal backup.

In a flash, Royce lunged at Mitch, knocking him into Tony.

"Leave him be, Roberts. You're all a bunch of damn troublemakers. Mind your own damn business. Don't you have a woman to mourn over?" Royce shouted.

That's when Gordon Roberts punched him in the jaw, sending him sprawling to the floor.

"Shut your goddamn mouth, you backstabbing son of a bitch!"

"Dad!" Mitch grabbed his father, tears streaming down the man's cracked face.

"We took all that...that...goddamn stuff from a cave up in Millstone Glenn. In Rhodes Hollow!" Denny blurted, jumping backward, as if startled by his own words.

Mitch looked dumbfounded. "Say what?"

Royce got to his feet and shoved his quivering son. "Don't say another fucking word!"

"A cave?" Tony asked.

"Boy!" Royce bellowed.

"Hey, Denny," said Beth, gently resting a hand on his shoulder. The big man jumped at her touch.

"No! Stay the hell away from me! It's that asshole. You killed A-Alicia!" Denny finally screamed. "You bastard. You killed her! Left her out there in the goddamn storm to get eaten by that...that..." He erupted in a convulsing heap of tears and rage. "Just left the rest of our friends out there."

They all stood staring, mouths agape.

"For fuck's sake, the kid is dumber than Bachman's Bitch. Can't you see that? Jesus Christ." Royce Pritchard shook his head. "The boy's lost his shit. His thick brain probably has frostbite. Come on."

"N-no. It's you who's dumb. *You're* the piece of sh-shit!" Denny hollered. "We shot a big buck and followed it into the cave. There were all these bones. Piles and piles of bones. I think most of it was animals, but now, some might not have been. The one with the bag and shit. Yeah, Mitch. All that gold and shit you see there," he said, pointing at the table, "that's only a little of it."

"There's more?" Mitch asked.

"A lot more." Denny shook as he pointed directly at his father. "He made me hide the rest of the stuff we took from the cave and that…that thing. We hid it inside the lighthouse. Dad here wanted to go back and get it after the storm passed. He called it his lottery ticket." Denny's panicked words rattled off like rapid gunfire.

"I'll kill you! You're no son of mine, you hear me?" The old man's bearded face flushed. "That's mine. Y'all hear me? Mine!"

Denny pulled his cellphone from inside his blood-soaked jacket. "It's all here if you don't believe me." Trembling, he held the cellphone up and played the video he'd taken when they'd tracked the deer into the cave.

They all watched in silence while the creaking of the building's walls against the railing storm fought to drown out the audio.

The clip started on Royce Pritchard's red face. The old hunter glared at his son, shooting the video, then down to the dying groans of a large deer and the blood trail leading to its trembling form.

And the glinting of treasure littering the floor below them.

Royce grumbled and complained about *watching out for his sector* and then—blood. Something at the end caught Mitch's eye.

"Hold on…hold on. Rewind that," he demanded.

Denny's brick-sized hands shook, but he obliged.

"What? Why?" Tony exhaled. "We get it, Roberts. They followed the deer into a bear's cave. Royce put it out of its misery. Yes, there is a mass of bones and, yes, I admit, lots of jewelry and coins, but why do we ha—"

"There! Pause it!" Mitch pointed at the screen. "There are two things. Look." Mitch pointed at Royce's face.

"Yeah, it's an ugly old bastard. What of it?" Gordon said.

Mitch ignored his father and pointed at Royce's bleeding cheek. "He's bleeding. You were bleeding."

"Yeah, my boy is as shitty of a hunter as he is dumb, so what? Damn near shot me ear off." Royce's words were still boiling with contempt.

"I'm guessing from that nasty cut, you dropped some blood in that cave, Royce," Gordon said.

"Again, who gives three shits? It was just a cut."

"Yeah, it might be just a cut, but that killing thing out there told me it wanted blood. It could sense the blood from the thing that freed it. That stole from it." Mitch's voice grew louder to fight over the raging wind and the storm outside. "You had to have spilled some of yours, Mr. Pritchard, and that's why it followed you all the way back here. Home. But there's more. Look."

A strange series of symbols, lines, or maybe words were carved into the stone walls. They glowed a bright red and continued in a flowing line that seemed to pulsate as Denny continued to record on his way around the cave.

"Whoa," Mitch said, trying to figure out what it was.

As Denny's camera phone panned around the cave, from the walls to the floor, it showed more of the odd glyphs, or symbols, not only on the walls but also on the cluttered floor—all offering the same throbbing red glow.

"It looks like writing of some kind. More symbol-based than words. I'm not sure," Mitch thought out loud.

The camera panned out as Royce began scooping things up from the cave floor. The echoing of different kinds of metal and other objects being shoved into a familiar olive drab bag.

All in the room slowly turned to Royce Pritchard, who stood rock-still and glared at them, his thin face stone-cold and expressionless.

"Keep playing, Denny," Mitch insisted.

The video played as Royce stood; his military bag seemed heavy and bloated, and hard-edged bulges protruded from the thick canvas.

Stunned gasps rose from them, clouding the room's cold air. They continued to watch what slowly came from the pitch-black darkness behind Royce as he shoved his bag over his shoulder, its weight obviously taxing on the old man's body.

"Now, we're not gonna tell any of those assholes out there what I found in here, right?" Royce stepped toward his son as the camera phone caught the audio admission crisp and clear.

Darkness accompanied him; twin crimson eyes materialized within the cave's depths.

"Oh my," Beth whispered.

"What the hell is that?" Gordon asked, squinting at the screen.

"We didn't see that when we were in there," said Denny, his voice faltering.

Royce stood wide-eyed and glaring, his hands balled into shaking fists. "Boy, I'm gonna fucking gut you, you lousy piece of shi—"

Then he lunged, punching the phone from Denny's big but trembling hands, sending it skittering across the cold, wet floor.

Mitch knew it was about to go bad. He made to lunge between old man Pritchard and his equally pissed and much bigger son. But before he got there, Tony stepped in.

"Stop, now!" Tony pushed Mitch in the chest as he pointed at Denny and Royce with the other hand.

Beth offered, "What about the video? All these weird glowing words? Those...those eyes!"

"What ya think, son?" Gordon asked. "You got all the book smarts."

"Not sure. Hell, Beth's the teacher. I never finished college, remember?" Mitch admitted, but was lost in the tangled mystery before them. "I just read a lot."

"Yeah, yeah, yeah, you've always had your head lost in a stupid book. Lost in some *Lord of the Rings* world of bullshit," Tony chided.

"Whatever." Mitch's hand absently found his own cellphone and something clicked inside him. "Ah-ha!" He nearly laughed out loud at his literal "Ah-ha" moment as he yanked out the phone from his pocket and activated it. "Thank you, Tony. You might have actually proved useful."

"Come on. We have bigger problems than playing with goddamn phones, don't we?" Tony said, his patience wearing thinner by the second. "We don't have any reception because of the storm, remember!"

"I have this useful app on my phone that I've used to translate other languages for my novels. It just might be worth a shot," Mitch said, scrolling over the multitude of apps on his phone.

"Jesus Christ." Tony turned away.

Mitch grabbed Denny's hand and held it up. "Start the video over." He held his own cellphone up with the LinguaScan app open and running, searching Denny's screen for any words or symbols.

"This is absolute bullshit," Royce grumbled.

"Shut it," Gordon shouted.

Tony shuffled on the old floor. "He's not wrong. What the hell are we doing here?"

Mitch held up his hand while his phone worked its digital magic. "Hold on."

In a flash, Mitch's phone dinged like a microwave timer. Then a smooth AI voice spoke: *"Section Scan Complete. Please press continue for your results."* Mitch's wide smile glowed in the cellphone's light.

"Okay, great. Let's see what we have." Mitch pressed continue, and they all waited. Tony and Royce looked a little impressed.

Finally, the AI voice returned, with an accompanying text read-out.

"The scanned words or images seem to be of Seneca Nation Native American Tribal origins. Please press the hyperlink for more detailed information on the Seneca Nation."

"Fuck me," Tony huffed, and started for Mitch's phone.

Beth shoved him back. "Give him one damn second!"

Tony relented, but only a little. Mitch didn't like where this was going if this whole phone thing turned out to be a wild goose chase.

"Get on with it, son," Gordon said.

"Okay, okay, I'll skip the history lesson. Hold on." Mitch pressed continue and the AI interface continued.

"Forwarding to translation: The images and symbols seem to be a warning. There is a heat-signature emanating from the words inscribed. Here is the translation as detailed as LinguaScan was able to discern:

***"Daga'nehgwa:** This word represents the concept of containment, confinement, and the restriction of negative forces within the confines of a cave or similar enclosure. It carries the essence of protection and the intentional separation of darkness from the outside world. By invoking the term 'Daga'nehgwa,' one can signify the Seneca tribe's traditional practice of safeguarding against malevolent energies by confining them to a specific space.*

"The writings on the floor seem to ward off evil spirits; they also warn that any blood tainting the holy spell would free the trapped evil creature. Beware!"

"The LinguaScan is complete. Would you like another?"

They all stood there as the room fell silent, save for the ravaging winds punishing the outside of the bar and the muddled sounds from the panicked patrons in the other room.

Silence reigned; Mitch faced a crucial decision. Taking a deep breath, he pointed toward Royce Pritchard's blood-stained bag with stolen treasure and now it made sense. Native American arrowheads.

"Pritchard, you stole this stuff from that cave. Notice the trinkets, jewelry, arrowheads." Mitch asked, but it wasn't a question.

Royce just glared at him.

"Come on, Sherlock, finish your big reveal before we all die of exposure from your supreme bullshit," Tony ordered.

"Yeah, Mitchie, spill it, please," said Beth.

"Okay. It might sound like bullshit, but, man, that thing out there, it wants something, and it ain't no coincidence that Pritchard here comes back to town, to Yowner's, leaving a trail of dead people and this monster thing on his ass. Might sound like fantasy bullshit or not. But, shit, the Darkness wants this treasure, and it wants…" Mitch looked from Pritchard to the spilled bag of artifacts, to each of the others in the room.

Inside the old tavern, the brutal wind howled and bayed, while the Darkness outside growled and called out.

They all stared at Mitch, and he truly wanted to disappear. "Guys, I know it sounds absolutely bug-nuts crazy. But it's the only answer."

A loud, deep voice broke through the growing doubt in the room.

"He's right. Dad took all of it. Wanted all of it for himself."

They all stopped.

"You motherfucker," Royce Pritchard snarled and started toward his crying son.

Gordon grabbed the back of Pritchard's jacket.

"Where is the box, Denny?" Beth asked. "Where did you hide it?"

Denny slowly looked up, his bloodshot eyes glistening with a river of tears. "The lighthouse. Dad put the box of stuff inside."

Tony glared at Beth. "We're not going to the damn lighthouse. Not now. Hear me? I don't care what we think we saw on a damn iPhone. We can't risk any more lives, got it?"

Mitch stood dumbfounded. "Come on, Tony. You can't ignore what we all are seeing here!"

Tony stepped toward Mitch, looming over him. "Enough of your *Neverland* bullshit. For Christ's sake, even after all these years, you're still living in a fantasy land and filling everyone's heads with your shit. Black demon-things talking to you. Only *you*. Why that hell is that? What makes you so fucking special?"

Mitch wanted to fade into the shadowy nothingness of the backroom. He felt his shoulders slouch, and all the wind sucked from his sails.

By Tony's harsh words.

"No! We can figure out the hows and whys after the storm passes. There isn't any use in holding court back here when people out there are in danger. But we will figure it out. Since the radio is down, for now, I'll bag all this stuff up and get back to my station and come back with backup." Tony filled the stained bag with the ill-gotten treasure, hefted it, and looked at Royce, then at the rest. "And *if* Pritchard stole all this wealth, well, then he'll have to answer for it. But all of that will have to wait until we can deal with whatever's out there."

That's when Beth slugged him in the jaw, sending him to the cold floor.

"Just like you. Big bad lawman. Always running away. Well, you know, as *Twilight Zone* as it sounds, I believe what Denny and Mitch have told us. Even someone as thick and stubborn as you are can hear what that thing is asking for. It could've killed Mitch just like it did Chris…and everyone else. But it didn't. We need to get to the lighthouse."

Tony's eyes were wide with a bonfire of surprise and rage. He scatted to his booted feet.

"And hey, if we get this damn bag and Mr. Pritchard out of here, it might lead that freaking monster away from the bar and all the people out there!" Mitch added, trying again to assemble any remaining threads of logic.

While the big lawman getting smacked distracted everyone, something told him he needed to take a piece of the treasure. A ring, trinket, anything, just in case. In a flash, he palmed an emerald necklace that lay close to the edge of the table.

Mitch held his breath. No one noticed.

A gunshot broke through the stormy din.

A blooming rose exploded in Denny Pritchard's stomach. Wide-eyed, the big man turned toward his father, mouth agape, and fell to the floor.

The snub-nosed .38 Special smoked as Royce Pritchard's eyes glared with dark hate. His cold eyes and granite-like face showed no sign of regret.

Before Mitch could move, his father shoved Royce into the wall, sending the pistol sprawling to the floor.

"What the—?" Mitch yelled, as the big man fell into him and slid onto the cold floor.

Mitch rolled Denny onto his back and his dilated pupils stared up at him. A river of blood flooded from Denny's stomach and mouth. Internal bleeding, Mitch quickly surmised, and Denny grabbed his hand, pulling him close.

"You're gonna be okay, Denny. I prom—"

Bloody air bubbles formed at the corners of Denny's mouth as he tried to speak. "I-I-I'm not stupid."

Mitch pressed on the wound, hoping to at least slow the bleeding. Warm blood shot through his fingers and onto the cold floor. "I know you're not, man. I know. Just take it easy."

"Let the lying bastard die!" Royce shouted from his pinned position against the wall.

"Shut the fuck up!" Gordon slammed Pritchard into the wall. Hard.

Tony shot Gordon and Pritchard a harsh look. "You got 'em while I call in for EMS?"

"Do it," Gordon said, not even looking at the sheriff, and keeping his harsh attention on the thrashing Royce Pritchard.

"Let me go, asshole." Pritchard tried to break free, but Gordon held him fast against the cold wall.

Denny winced in pain, squeezing Mitch's hand to where it was going numb. He then jerked Mitch close. "H-he killed Alicia. Just because she stood up to him. He never… Damn, this hurts."

"I'm sorry," was all Mitch could offer.

"Our friends too. I wanted to save them. I tried… I really did. I swear, I'm not bullshitting you!"

"I know. I know. Is all that stuff really at the lighthouse?"

The blood rushed from Denny's face, and it washed a ghastly white with overwhelming shock and pain. He slowly unclenched his eyes and stared at Mitch.

"Yes. And that thing out there wants it back. I…I…I'm s-sorry."

Mitch squeezed his hand tight, but knew there was nothing that could be done.

Tony grabbed Royce. "I tried to call for an ambulance, but the dispatcher said that with the storm, it's gonna be a long while before they can get here from Carrigan Springs or Arcadia Falls."

Mitch looked at Tony, and the big cop shrugged his shoulders while shoving Pritchard down on a chair, keeping a firm hand on the old man's shoulder.

"I doubt they can make it through all the snow," Gordon added.

"Okay. It's gonna be okay. Take it easy, big guy. It's gonna be okay," Mitch tried to reassure Denny.

"I—I am not like my d-dad. I am…not…stupid." Then he let Mitch go, violently fumbled with something in his pockets, and shoved it into Mitch's hand.

Shotgun shells.

"Take these. We shot rock salt at it. It slowed the thing down and gave us time."

Mitch's frantic mind was making connections between the rock-salt shells and their effect on the Darkness outside and what he'd been reading in the book his mother had given him.

There just might be a little hope, after all. Maybe.

"Denny, you just might be on to something there." Mitch smiled and gently patted Denny's chest.

Fumbling wildly into his own satchel, he found the book. He showed them *Mother Lorelei's Guide to the Greater World* and how to combat it. "My mom sent me this for Christmas. I've been doing a bunch of research on monster lore for my next book an—"

"Not the time, Mitch!" Tony and Beth said as one.

"Yeah, right. Sorry." Mitch hurriedly opened the heavy book and found the right page. "Here."

They gathered around the book, save Royce, whose frenzied eyes darted around the room.

"No time for a book report, boy," Gordon shouted over the groaning coming from outside.

"Okay, okay. Throughout history, salt has been used to either harm or at least repel evil beings, creatures, entities. What have you."

"And?" Tony said.

"Denny said that when they were being chased, they fired rock-salt shotgun shells at it and it actually slowed it down. Maybe even hurt it." Mitch looked up from the book.

"So, if it can bleed, we can hurt it," Beth added.

"And," said Gordon, "if we can hurt the sonofabitch, we might be able to kill the damn thing."

"Maybe," Mitch said. "Worth a shot."

"Might be the only chance we have," said Beth.

"Sounds like more of your made-up mumbo jumbo to me," Tony added. "I plan to return the bag to the station."

Denny shook uncontrollably. His bloodshot eyes grew extraordinarily wide, and he cried out in a heart-wrenching gasp, then fell still, his horrified gaze fixed on the ceiling above.

"No!" Mitch said, leaning over the big man.

"Well, *now* you can arrest someone, Tony!" Beth snarked.

Tony just stared at her. "I will." He pulled his handcuffs from his belt. "Mr. Pritchard. Put the gun down on the ground. Hands behind your back; turn around."

A blur caught Mitch's eye as Royce Pritchard moved in a flash, kneeing Gordon in the groin.

Gordon yelped, releasing Royce, who ran from the back room.

That's when a deafening pounding assailed one of the only remaining walls of Yowner's tavern, mixing with horrified screams and gunfire erupted from inside the bar.

They could hear Pablo's terrified howling, and Mitch knew the time had come to do something, anything.

Things were about to get a hell of a lot worse.

43

Stone Cold Rage

Gordon Roberts' groin exploded as if he'd suddenly been doused with napalm, followed closely by a shattering pain in his jaw. He fell backward, landing hard on something, or someone. He couldn't tell who, or what, but with the agony ripping through his body, he didn't care.

Someone helped him up and the swirling stars slowly dissipated, and he stared at the chaos inside Yowner's kitchen.

A loud howling and stinging gust hit them; he turned to see a shattered window and no sign of Royce Pritchard, except for a piece of torn cloth and a trail of blood that led out into the dark storm.

"Shit!"

"We have to go after him," Mitch said, walking toward the barroom.

"What about that...that...thing out there?" Beth asked.

Mitch turned back to her. "It could've killed me, and if my hunch about the treasure and the rock salt is right, and God, I sure to hell hope it is, it's our only shot."

"You got a death wish? The storm alone will kill you. You'll get frostbite in a matter of minutes." Tony stepped in front of Mitch, blocking the door. "And we have no idea how to fight the goddamn thing!"

Pablo lurched forward, growling.

"There are innocent people getting slaughtered out there. You know, the same people you've sworn to fucking protect!" Mitch drew deeply from within and shoved the handful of shotgun shells into Tony's hand. "Here. You must have a shotgun in your precious cruiser. Use it. Unless every oath you take means absolutely nothing to you?" Without waiting for a response, Mitch shoved the door open and ran into the barroom.

And before he had a second to enjoy his small yet meaningful victory, the moment turned into a bloody nightmare, and he wished he'd stayed in the kitchen.

44

Grinder

Red. All Mitch saw was red.

But despite the blood, the savage, swirling Darkness was gone. Only the horrific apocalyptic scene stood before them.

The entire front of the bar was torn to shredded kindling, and an uncountable number of eviscerated bodies lay tossed all around like rag dolls. The surviving patrons were hiding somewhere in the darkest shadows. Their collective cries created a tortured wailing that filled Mitch's heart and made his head pound.

But the raging Darkness was gone.

A violent gust whipped away the feeling of relief as Mitch remembered—

Royce Pritchard.

Shit! The lighthouse. Fighting to catch his breath, Mitch kicked open the door to the kitchen and ran inside, yelling.

"That thing is gone. Guessing it followed Pritchard. Lighthouse! Let's go."

Beth shot him a concerned look.

"How bad is it…out there?"

Mitch shook his head.

"Sh-Sheldon. Did you see him?"

He didn't know what to say. How could he have had any idea? There were bodies, there were parts of bodies. A sudden wash of acid rolled inside his stomach, rushing a wave of bile into his throat. He forced it back down.

"I don't know. But I'm betting he's okay." Mitch didn't believe the words for a stone-cold second, but he couldn't tell her that.

Mitch pulled Beth back as she ran for the door. "You don't want to go in there. There's a chance he's hiding somewhere, just like he did before."

"I have to make sure he's okay," she rebutted. "Come on."

"No," said Gordon. "You need to go find Pritchard. The kid's a survivor. 'Sides, he was with Sal when we went back. Now, I ain't promising he's okay, but judging by what he's done so far, and he's with good old Sal, I'm betting on 'em both. My boy is right. You need to go." Gordon stepped through the gaping hole in the front of Yowner's Tavern and out into the raging snowstorm.

"Where you are going, Dad?" asked Mitch.

Gordon gave a weary, crooked smile before pulling his camouflage balaclava down over his wrinkled face. "If the Pritchard boy and your mother's book were right, I might have a plan of my own, son. But first I'm gonna find Peckerhead Sal and the kid. You best get going."

Gordon Roberts vanished into a room beyond the bar, where the sounds of suffering pierced the icy darkness.

Mitch took a deep breath and turned toward the shattered door of Yowner's Tavern. "We have to go," he said, then ran for the snowy exit.

The deep drifts and ocean wavelike blankets of snow hid all the parked vehicles, leaving them as lost white shapes.

From behind them, Gordon Roberts shouted against the storm. "Found 'em. Peckerhead and the boy are scraped up, but right as rain. Now get your asses going. And don't worry, Mitchie. You're not the only Roberts with an imagination. See y'all at the lighthouse."

Beth seized Mitch; they struggled for a view of the three figures at the tavern's ruined entrance. After a blurry moment, Gordon, Sal, and Sheldon waved at them from the bar.

"Thank God," Beth said.

"Told you," Mitch said. "Now let's go."

"I'm sure he'll be okay," she said. "But you're right. We need to get to the rest of the treasure before Pritchard does, or this entire town is screwed. If we don't appease that thing, none of us are going to live."

"Hell no!" said Tony. "You're all idiots. You really think there's some mysterious monster out there and that we must return its ancient treasure or it will destroy Sterling Point? Are you both mad? You're not going out. Now, Mitch, if you and your drunk father want to get your foolish selves killed, by all means, go for it. But I sure as hell won't let you get my wife slaughtered. Hell, the wind chill alone..."

Mitch could tell his old friend was trying to keep up his usual asshole demeanor, but there was a definite concern in his dark eyes.

"Hey, watch it, Tony. If you're not careful, you just might have a beating heart in there." Mitch tapped him on the chest.

Beth looked at Tony, deep into his dark brown eyes. For a long moment.

That's all Mitch needed to see, as he slung his bag over his shoulder and headed out the door.

He didn't get too far when he heard Beth shout at Tony.

"I'm not your wife…not anymore! You can choose to come and help us or stay here. But I will not allow you to control me anymore."

Then came a wild howl from Pablo.

He didn't look back. Climbing through the rough hole in the wall, he was uncertain if Beth and the dog were closely behind him as he stepped out into the raging snowstorm.

The wind was brutal and tore at his skin, and he questioned his disunion with every difficult step. Ignoring what he thought was a voice from behind, he pushed his way down the street.

45

White Din

The entire town of Sterling Point was lost in a blinding whitewash.

What looked like burnt silhouettes jutted out from the thigh-deep snow, which was threatening to bury everything. While visibility was near zero, the reflective wash from the snow cast the town in a haunting light, while the dark buildings and houses looked like cold, dead fingers.

Mitch saw a dark figure in between the swelling hurricane-strength gusts and the momentary pauses of the whipping snow. Then it disappeared altogether.

A mailbox whipped past Mitch's head as he lunged out of its trajectory just in time.

Ahead, he saw Royce Pritchard, heavy bag and pistol still in hand, trudged through the snow. The old man didn't look good. He was slowing down and had one arm slumped to his side. It amazed Mitch that the guy was able to keep going.

"Pritchard!" he shouted uselessly through the hurricane winds. "Stop!" Mitch prayed the man would listen. His legs tingled and burned as the sub-zero temperatures caused a painful mix of sharp needles and thrumming numbness, which was slowly progressing through the rest of his body. But he had to catch Pritchard before he could reach the lighthouse. A cold jolt through his already exhausted body pushed him forward.

"Wait!" Beth called from behind. In the madness of what had happened back at Yowner's, Mitch wanted to ignore her, but stopped still when she called his name.

"Have you seen my dad?" he asked as shrapnel from the town's buildings tore through the street. The cries of the people inside joined the sadistic cacophony of the chaotic storm.

Mitch fought to catch his breath as he watched Royce Pritchard round the corner of Wood Street and Haynes.

"N-no. He headed south, away from the bar. I-I lost him in the storm. Can't see a damn thing," Beth said. "I'm sure he's okay."

"Shit!" Mitch shouted. Even though he'd been gone a long time, he still remembered that Haynes Street led down toward the lighthouse.

"You're probably right," he said. "Let's go."

Mitch followed the old man desperately as the winds pushed him back with every step.

The bestial cry was at their heels as they hit the main drag of Cadigan Street.

"How in the hell did it get behind us?" Beth shouted. "I thought that thing left the bar after Pritchard and his bag."

Mitch felt a powerful tug on his arm as Beth caught up with him. "I don't know. We've got to get to the old lighthouse," he replied, his voice growing hoarse.

They stalked through the deep snow, trying to ignore the whirring razor-claws and snarling, gnashing teeth of the Darkness ravaging the town behind them.

The historic lighthouse, once a source of inspiration for his childhood writing, now loomed dark and foreboding in the Christmas Eve night sky as snowflakes fell in frozen torrents in the blustery winds. He shivered as he stared at the silent silhouette of the icy pier, which jutted out into the frozen waves of Lake Ontario.

"Pritchard!" Mitch called. But the old man didn't answer. Mitch felt his chest tighten, and a knot formed in his gut.

The storm was the worst he had ever seen, even having been gone for nearly ten years. In the northeast, winter was nearly seven months long. One got used to the lake-effect snow, the Alberta Clippers, and the occasional brutal nor'easter. You didn't like it, but you grew accustomed to the seasonal abuse from Mother Nature. Not Mitchell Gordon Roberts, though. No, he'd despised the snow since taking his first walk outside as a toddler.

His mother had taken him sledding out on Goat Hill, at the back of the high school. The sledding aspect was fun; it was when his foot found a slippery patch of ice and he went ass-over-teakettle, as his father so compassionately put it, that things turned sour. Young Mitch landed headfirst on the ice-covered blacktop and lost all memory of that day. He'd gotten a concussion and stayed home from school for two days. Which turned out not so bad, because that meant his mom made him sit on the couch, watching television or reading, and would feed him bowl after bowl of tomato soup and elbow macaroni. "The cure for all that ails you," his mom always touted. Mitch didn't argue. He knew that once he was old enough, he'd never spend another winter in Sterling Point.

Something, someone screaming, punched away suddenly at his memories. "Mitch!"

He heard Beth's call. It sounded like she was screaming into a pile of sand: muted and futile. Then another voice came.

"Beth!" It was Tony Severt. "Roberts!"

"Screw him. Come on. We need to get to the lighthouse. Let's go!" Mitch turned back toward the lighthouse, fighting to ignore Tony—and the Darkness barreling toward them.

The old murderer, Pritchard, had left deep, telltale trenches, but the unforgiving blowing snow filled up the hunter's tracks nearly as fast as he left them.

They were getting closer to the pier that led to the lighthouse, and while that might have been a good thing for Mitch and Beth, it meant the psychotic Pritchard was even closer to the box of artifacts.

That made Mitch push on harder. He didn't know why. He hated this town, and almost everything it stood for—

A sharp, agonized cry pierced through the din of the storm.

Mitch spun, nearly falling, and Beth did the same.

Behind them, Tony lay prone, flailing, gun in hand, firing into the whirling Darkness. It was spreading now, enveloping the entire street.

Its many ebony tentacles and sharp talons thrashed in a blinding, chaotic blur, trying to devour the burly, screaming sheriff.

Mitch stared, frozen, as he watched the man he used to love as a brother lying helpless in the snow.

"Mitch!" Beth called to him, and she ran to her ex-husband.

Growling, Pablo hurled himself at the cloying Darkness attacking his master.

Mitch's small town felt besieged by the world and the encroaching Darkness.

The Darkness swung its tentacles at Beth as she grabbed Tony and fought to yank him free.

Behind him, the killer, Pritchard, made his way closer to the artifacts.

Before him, the love of his life and his former best friend fought to get free from the storm and the swallowing Darkness.

Fuck me running, Mitch mouthed and found his body moving without his having a say.

Beth screamed a bloodcurdling scream as the ravaging Darkness tried to tear Tony's legs from his body.

Against the brutal, stinging wind, Mitch fought his way through the snow to get to Beth and her fighting dog.

Once there, he pulled Beth back, and yanked Pablo away from the storm.

"Now, you take Captain Courageous and go find Pritchard, okay? Tony needs help. I'll be right behind you." Mitch nodded. "I promise. Now, go!" He flinched in disbelief as he heard himself utter the words. "Then we'll catch up, okay?" Mitch tried hard to believe the lie that dripped to ice as he spoke.

Beth stood in place, her face a picture of concern.

"Go!" Mitch's shout pierced the relentless storm's clamor. "Please! I've got this!" He pivoted, eyes fixed on the landscape ahead, but what should have been a street had vanished. The snow had ascended to the first-floor windows, and where the unforgiving wind had assailed, drifts had reached the second-story facades lining Main Street.

"You'd better make your way to the pier, Roberts. Don't you dare run off again. Do you hear me?" Beth demanded as the biting snow and the relentless, red-eyed blackness whipped around them. She locked eyes with Mitch, and before he could react, she embraced him fiercely, her lips meeting his in a desperate kiss, then dashed toward the lighthouse as the tentative hint of sunrise unsuccessfully battled the thick ebony storm engulfing Lake Ontario.

Tony's cries for help grew more desperate with each gunshot.

Mitch pivoted and pushed forward as best as he could through the thick snow toward Tony's frantic pleas.

Then the gunfire fell silent in the howling wind.

Mitch didn't check to see if Beth had followed Pritchard. He didn't want to know. But Pablo's echoing barks suggested they were headed to the lighthouse.

Tony had rolled to his stomach and was crawling through the snow, creating deep trenches as he fought to escape. A long, bloody trail lay behind him, soaking into the white.

His Smokey-the-Bear hat had long gone—likely torn to felt and cardboard threads and blown away in the arctic winds.

He stared at Mitch with bloodshot eyes, begging and pleading for help, all his macho bravado washed away in the torrential winds.

"Please," he mouthed desperately.

"Go!" It was all Mitch said, not even looking at him. Instead, he glared up at the raging Darkness that promised nothing but a bloody nothingness.

Tony didn't say a word and staggered northward as fast as his torn body could manage.

Mitch didn't know what the hell he was doing. The wind had gusted away all common sense.

He stood statue-still amidst the raging snowstorm.

"Hey," Mitch shouted into the void. The Darkness froze and hovered, as if confused.

As if analyzing this idiotic human daring to stand in its way.

He had no clue what he was doing. All he could do was stall and pray he'd give Beth and Tony enough time to stop Pritchard before he reached the artifacts.

What he knew was that he wanted to keep Beth and his dad safe. Including Tony and the rest of this town.

In a sudden flash, a mass of sharp, barbed tentacles lashed out and snatched Mitch off the snowy street.

The Darkness tore deep cuts into Mitch's body as it pulled him in close to its snapping maw. Burning crimson eyes glared at him as a sea of snapping teeth bit at the arctic air all around his quivering body.

"Do not try trickery on us, human. We have given you a chance. Yet the thief still lives. Our patience is waning. Do not stand in our way." The words dripped icy daggers.

Razor-sharp claws gripped Mitch's throat and squeezed.

A violent coughing fit shook him as he fought for air. In his peripheral vision, he saw Beth and Tony disappearing toward the pier, into the whiteness of the storm. He struggled to reach his jacket pocket; the blackness sending dark tendrils to secure his errant hand.

"No! I...I h-have—" Mitch's words were a tangle, cut off by the black.

An instantaneous fire erupted in his right hand, but he screamed and continued to dig into his pocket.

The sea of blood-stained teeth snapped at Mitch's face as the matching livid eyes bore into him, drew back, and snapped.

"We grow tired of your interference."

In a desperate flash, Mitch yanked free the beaded necklace and several of the arrowheads he'd filched from Pritchard's bag and held them up.

"H—here!" he cried, his shaking, outstretched arm burning with frostbite.

A long, cold moment passed.

"I told you...I-I'm not..." Mitch heard himself speak, but he didn't feel in complete control. It was all a horrific nightmare that showed no sign of ending.

"What is this?" the blackness coldly stated. Not to Mitch, but to someone—something—else. Something...otherworldly. Its attention swayed away from Mitch, allowing him to breathe.

The blackness let loose its strangling grip on his burning throat, dropping him back to the snow.

As he rolled and kicked away from the beast, he desperately tried to find his breath. The backpack slumped forward over his shoulder, knocking him in the face, sending his glasses spinning off.

"No!" He dug into the pile of snow. He finally found them and put them on. After wiping the snow from the lenses, through the smeared glass, he spotted the backpack. Some of its contents had spilled out.

Mitch grabbed the old book from the snow, tossed it and other items into his backpack, then struggled upright.

The blackness hung in the air, not paying him any heed. Mitch thanked God and tore off, as fast as the snow would allow, toward the pier.

The abomination behind him continued slaughtering everything in its wake. Mitch's frenetic thoughts twisted and made obtuse connections as he raced through the snow. His chest pounded like a jackhammer, and his throbbing, overworked lungs exploded with pain. For a split second, he was grateful for not being able to feel his hands or feet.

A sudden deafening roar from the black beast behind him shook the snow from the nearby rooftops.

He didn't dare look, but prayed his father was safe. Maybe he was back at Yowner's with Sal. Mitch knew better, but kept trudging through the difficult terrain.

Up ahead, the sound of shouts and gunshots rang out.

Ignoring the screaming warnings from his overweight body, he pushed himself and rounded the corner, leading to the pier.

The lighthouse seemed to glow against the pale-blue light of the snow. But Mitch's already taxed heart nearly exploded, and he heard himself scream as he saw old man Pritchard shoot Beth, and Tony jump behind a pickup truck.

"No!" Mitch's cry became lost like a shattered whisper in a frozen hurricane.

The unearthly scream of the blackness returned behind him, bringing with it a dark promise that he was nearly ready to embrace.

46
So Weak So Strong

An opaque white veil covered the pier ahead of Mitch as he ran headlong into the violent storm. His run became more of a clumsy, awkward climb as he struggled through the snow-buried street. Tears froze as they escaped his aching eyes, as the desperate cries from Beth, and other voices he couldn't make out, tore into his heart. Maybe he was wrong. The situation could be playing tricks on his eyes. Or on his mind. Maybe. Either way, that cowardly prick, Tony, would pay. Just standing there, watching the old man shoot Beth. What the hell? Mitch's frantic mantra kept repeating as he trudged his way toward the lighthouse: "I'm gonna kill him."

To make matters worse, the snow grew even deeper the farther along the lane he went. It was up to his waist, and the nor'easter was continuing to dump white hell as he climbed through the drifts.

"Hold on, Beth. I…I…" The subzero temperature stole his breath, and his heart felt as if it would erupt inside his heaving chest at any second. While the deadly snowstorm guaranteed a painful death on the outside, the unbearable rage tearing at his insides was more likely to drop him from a height, leaving him to die out here in this ungodly storm, in a town he despised.

"I'm coming, Beth. Hold on. I'm coming," he shouted into the brutal white din of the storm, and pushed on.

Up ahead, Mitch lost sight of Pritchard. There was no sign of Beth or Tony. *Lucky for Tony,* Mitch thought, and despite his aching body's raging defiance, he continued, almost making it to the truck Tony had ducked behind like the lowly prick he was.

The lighthouse's light hadn't worked in decades, but the gaudy strings of red, green, and white Christmas lights still cut an eerie glow.

Five feet might as well have been five miles as Mitch kicked and dug his way through the snow. His body was numb except for the pinpricks shocking his hands and legs. The sudden growl penetrating the wind caused his heart and body to move faster.

No sign of Tony. Mitch fought on.

He'd gone only a short distance when he noticed bloodstained snow. "Beth?"

A roughly-hewn trench cut through the snow, leading to the entrance of the old lighthouse. Mitch rushed toward the door, more bestial barking and growling cutting through the storm as he drew closer. Harsh shouts and the sound of fighting came with what he could only assume was the gigantic malamute's fierce growl.

Mitch finally made it to the lighthouse. Collapsing against the cold metal wall, he tried to catch his breath and looked back up the street toward town. The writhing blackness was fast approaching, its ebony tentacles blocking out the whitewash of the storm, swallowing up the remaining sliver of the town. Time was running out.

The blood trail on the surrounding snow stopped at the door, covered with several bloody handprints.

Inside, more angry voices. But then someone else spoke. It wasn't Pritchard. It wasn't Tony.

It was Beth.

Mitch took what breath he could and kicked the door open.

An explosion erupted in his arm. A sudden force sent him sprawling back into the door, sending him into a pain-filled whitewash as he fell to the floor.

Someone screamed.

Beth!

Mitch shook his head to clear the shock from his mind.

"I fuckin' told you assholes to leave me be, goddammit. Sonofabitch. Why did ya have to follow me? This here shit is mine! Every fucking piece of it. And there ain't nothing you can do about it. Understand me?" Royce Pritchard aimed the smoking pistol at Mitch's face.

"Please. This isn't about you!" Beth begged.

Pablo stood between Beth and the batshit crazy old man, the enraged dog's teeth bared in a bestial rage, not unlike the blackness closing in from the pier outside.

Mitch held his hands up in defense as he looked around the sparse room for the source of the blood. Beth seemed to be fine. Blood splattered on her right side, but she didn't seem hurt.

"You...you...okay?" he wheezed, feeling his shoulder and putting pressure on what he hoped was a flesh wound.

"I'd be more worried about your own fat ass, Roberts!" Royce Pritchard's gun hand shook and waved wildly while he fumbled through a stack of boxes with his other hand.

Beth shot Mitch a reassuring look, then discreetly pointed to the floor beyond the crazy old man.

Tony lay still. In a pool of blood.

Pritchard laughed as he kicked over a box and shot Mitch and Beth a death glare. "Don't move, either of you." He squatted slowly and groaned as he opened up a large box. He quickly snatched a large sack from beside it.

"We don't have time. It's coming! You need to give back that treasure you stole!" Mitch shouted. "It's coming for you! Keeping that shit isn't gonna save you, dumbass!"

"I heard that nasty motherfucker talk to you, boy. Why you? It won't hurt you, right? Hell, son. If that's so, then your fat ass is my get-out-of-jail-free card, huh? Come on, Roberts. Your whole useless family just might prove useful for a change. Get up. Let's go!" Royce Pritchard motioned toward the door with his pistol, while clutching the sack over his shoulder.

"Hold on. You don—" Mitch's words were met with a brutal pistol-whip across his temple that sent him spinning, and he collapsed into the door again.

In a sudden rush of movement, Tony was on his feet and rushing toward Pritchard. A deafening gunshot echoed off the metal walls.

"Tony, no!" Beth screamed.

Mitch forced his eyes open, only wide enough to catch two forms rush by, out the steel door and into the raging storm.

The pier vanished into the swirling, hungry darkness; only a small, rusty railing remained.

Another gunshot shattered the cold, and soul-wrenching screams followed.

Mitch searched for the source in the blinding and howling din of the snowstorm.

47

When I Stop Leaving I'll Be Gone

It had been one hell of a day. Christmas Day, to be exact.

It was hard to believe that only a few hours ago, Gordon Andrew Roberts was saying goodbye to his beloved Marguerite. After drinking about two gallons of Genesee beer and ten shots of whiskey later, he was clumsily climbing into his town plow truck, determined to save his son and his ill-deserving town from whatever godforsaken creature had destroyed Yowner's and their hometown of Sterling Point.

When this entire world of crap had hit the fan back at Sal's, Gordon had first thought he'd finally drunk too much and his entire lifetime of bad choices had finally caught up to his old ass, and he'd lost his damn mind. That black death cloud or whatever the hell it was, and the tavern getting beaten to hell and back. To his old friend-turned-spiteful-stranger nearly getting Mitch, Beth, and other folks sliced and diced. But when Mitch told them all about what Pritchard and his redneck hunting party had done, it all started making some kind of *Twilight Zone* sense. Then, that stupid-ass Pritchard had gone and killed his own son. Well, if that shit wasn't real enough, Gordon was damn sure the rubber hit the goddamn highway then.

He'd left Mitch and that Connolly gal, the one that Maggie had always known was the one for their boy, but early on, the cruel hand of fate surely had its middle finger up for the boy and his unrequited love. What a cold, nasty bitch fate could be.

"But, by damn, Maggie, my beautiful, sweet darling girl." Gordon sniffed. "Once again, you were right."

They left with that dumbass lunkhead of a cop and Beth's dog, chasing that even dumber ass, Pritchard. "Hope they got you, asshole!" Gordon said.

With the Hendricks boy safely tucked away with Sal—Gordon had one last job to do.

The old war veteran-turned-plow-truck-driver thought they were all screwed, seven ways from Sunday. That no-good, lazy-ass son, who'd run away from Gordon and his mother, turned out to be a good kid. That damn Mitchell ended up being damn smart and might just be able to do something good.

His son gave him an idea that didn't stand a snowball's chance in hell, but the rock-salt story Mitch had told them all gave Gordon an idea. Probably a stupid idea. Not his first. But it would certainly be his last.

He had done two plow-and-salting runs before the funeral services earlier that morning, and returned to the town barns, where he'd had the boys load the big rig with fuel and a full load of rock salt for the next run.

But for some reason, his punk of a boss never called him out. Maybe the greedy bastard had finally had his Scrooge moment and given Gordon the day off. Who knew?

Funny how shit works out sometimes, he thought.

And that was another reason he knew he didn't feel that way about Mitch. His son was the brightest one out of all of them. The old Marine had many regrets, and he never blew sunshine up his own ass, and knew damn well why he'd never been given a *World's Greatest Dad* mug.

Never deserved it. He nodded to himself in the side-view mirror and glanced away, despising the man he saw glaring back at him: drunk, bloodshot eyes, and more of a ten o'clock shadow than a five.

Never would have accepted it.

Gordon allowed a somber smile at the comforting sound of the engine roaring to life and shoved the defroster on high. He absently reached into the cooler he had hidden behind the rarely used passenger seat.

He found a cold 50-ounce Genny Cream Ale and cracked it open. "Ah, yes. Come to Papa."

Gordon pushed play, and Andy Williams sang "It's the Most Wonderful Time of the Year." He watched the wipers struggle to clear the windshield, but they finally shoved the thick ice and snow from the frosted glass. He took time to inspect the sawed-off shotgun behind the cooler. Then, it had become a comfort. He couldn't explain why, but just knowing it was there made him breathe a little easier. Old habits die hard, he'd guessed.

With half the beer gone, he reached into the cooler for another, cracked it open, stowed it away in the cup holder, and found the cigar that Sal had slyly given him.

Staring out into the blinding storm, he drained the old can and tossed it onto the passenger-side floor. After taking a puff on the stogie, he let out a huge smile as Charley Pride's "Christmas in My Hometown" came through the speakers.

He turned the volume up, took a quick sip of the Genny, and nodded to the changed reflection in the frosty side mirror. That guy had a plan.

"Semper fi, Devil Dog," Gordon said to the smirking man in the mirror.

Dropping the truck into gear, Gordon aimed the plow toward the ominous black cloud that hovered over half of Sterling Point. The center seemed to be gathered around the pier.

Oh, the Christmas chimes are ringing in the tower
Jingle bells can be heard all around.
Time for all to go and wait for Santa's comin'
'Cause it's Merry Christmas here, in my hometown.

Gordon took another sip of beer, a pleasurable puff from his cigar, and stomped on the pedal, leaving piles of snow in the truck's wake.

"I'm coming, Mitchie. I'll be seeing ya soon, Maggie-girl."

48

Temporary Saint

It all happened so fast; Mitch's near-frozen brain could barely comprehend what was in front of him.

He expected to be torn to shreds, but the massive black form twisted at the last second, and someone shot at it from entering the lighthouse.

Beth's scream pierced the bitter air. But it wasn't her holding the gun.

Mitch stood, squinting to see. *Tony.*

He held a pistol out in front of him and fired again into the swirling, deadly mass.

The Darkness swiveled toward Tony and the lighthouse, leaving Mitch shivering on the pier, holding the heavy bag.

"Shit. No!" he bellowed.

Caught in a complete, paralyzing oscillation, he stood frozen, unsure what to do.

"Run, Roberts, you dumbass," Tony shouted, firing into the flowing Darkness. "Get out now!"

It was when he heard Beth calling from inside the lighthouse that Mitch snapped out of his impotent stasis and trudged forward.

He shouted at the swirling black cloud that bore down on Tony.

"Hey, asshole! Here. I have your magical shit. Come on. Come get it! Hey, hey!"

The wavering Darkness ignored him, and Mitch cried out as Tony disappeared into the rush of teeth and barbed tentacles.

"Son of a bitch!" Mitch yelled, continuing to the lighthouse.

Pablo's ferocious bark did little good against the monster, and Beth fought to hold him back from a guaranteed death.

Blood erupted from the center of the Darkness, coating the Christmas snow.

Mitch dropped to one knee, the frigid temperatures and waist-deep snow taking their toll on his hefty body.

All was lost. How the hell could they stop this monster that was hell-bent on destroying every living thing in Sterling Point? Mitch's troubled mind tried to answer the unfathomable question.

Nothing came as the Darkness assailed the lighthouse. Its talons and tentacles ripped shingles from the roof, shattering the large panes of glass at the very top and battering at the outer metal shell.

"No! Wait." Mitch heard himself screaming. Crying. Begging. Anything to distract the monstrous creature.

"I have your shit. Here!" Mitch's hoarse plea disappeared into the storm, and in final desperation, he threw the bag of ill-gotten gains into the swirling form attacking the lighthouse.

"But I know these trinkets aren't what you're after." Mitch fought to breathe and prayed he was right. "You want the blood of the one who set you free."

The raging dark cloud rose high above the pier, destroying any appearance of the winter storm coursing all around.

"We have what you want!" Mitch shouted. "You can have it."

"Fuck you!" A demonic growl, guttural, burst from the dark lighthouse; then a figure rushed out.

Royce Pritchard.

The mad old man leapt on top of the bulging duffel bag, screaming incoherently.

Pritchard and clutched it to his chest, his face twisted into a terrifying mask of rage. A pair of crimson eyes blazed, burning like twin fiery beacons in the black night.

The Darkness let out a chilly, otherworldly howl that curled its massive tentacles around Pritchard's head. A surge of razor claws ripped through him while countless sets of lethal, dagger-sized teeth sank deep into his skull. Hot blood gushed from his scalp as the cruel fangs tore him open; still, he couldn't bring himself to relinquish his prize.

Mitch's burning stomach roiled. He fought back the bile surging in his throat as he watched the man's exposed brain until an enormous claw punctured it and it burst open in a gush of crimson and gray matter. His arms and legs followed next; with a sudden, forceful wrench, their limbs were yanked from their sockets, the sound of tearing flesh and snapping tendons echoing in the air. All that remained were raw, dangling stumps, swaying slightly with the motion. Steaming blood sprayed into the pre-dawn sky and fell like a nightmarish rain onto the deep snow of the pier.

Tears filled Mitch's eyes, and his stomach burned, then he vomited the day's contents of booze and terrible food onto the untouched snow.

The thrashing black waves of death lurched and surged as the Darkness devoured Royce Pritchard's twitching, lifeless body.

A deafening shriek erupted from within it, the sound echoing and rolling through the air, overpowering even the howling winds over the lake. Mitch's heart constricted in terror as the immense shadow loomed closer, shifting with an almost sentient malevolence. He wanted to run, to escape, but terror held him rooted to the spot. Mitch was paralyzed, powerless.

Looking around for an escape. Nowhere to go. But Mitch moved backward until his back struck the cold, hard metal railing at the end of the pier.

Mitch fought to speak. He tried to scream, but nothing came out, only a hollow, desperate gasp, as he frantically gripped the railing.

Although dawn was nearing, the lake offered nothing but a soulless blackness, and Mitch knew there was nowhere to run. Nowhere to hide. Not anymore.

What a great way to end a novel, he thought, then his heart pounded like a million drums in his chest with the realization that this was not fiction.

The demonic growls drew closer, and Mitch heard Pablo barking and Beth Her voice raw, panicked. calling out his name. Cold tears ran down his frozen cheeks, and a fit of sobs shook his body. He was out of options. Save one.

Spitting out burning bile, Mitch Roberts made a choice.

Letting go of the railing, he stared into the monster's hateful red eyes once more. One last time.

Mitch prayed it would give Beth and Pablo enough time to escape.

He smiled…and waited for the end.

49.

I Shall Be Released

A horn blared, followed by a loud, low growl cutting through the din of the storm as a set of blinding headlights appeared out of nowhere and grew closer, shaking Mitch from his reckless martyrdom.

As the familiar guttural growl of a diesel engine punched a widening hole in the nor'easter's hold on the lakeside town, a roar came from the Darkness.

The distinctive horn blew again, and in an instant, it took Mitch back to his childhood. A flood of vivid images of his father taking him for a ride in the town's humongous plow truck. He must have been nine years old. It was just before Christmas. His dad's smile was nearly as bright as the car-high snowbanks they had driven by on the way out of the hospital in Sodus. And he was smiling from ear to ear. It was an exciting memory that Mitch silently cherished. A dark memory he tried to keep even from himself. There couldn't be any way he'd had a happy, fond memory with his stoic, volatile father.

Could there?

Mitch had always allowed himself to recall a portion of that day. It was the latter half that turned ugly and painful. The morning was filled with Christmas magic, and his dad was so happy and fun. That was until he told Mitch he had to make one stop, and if he was a good boy, he'd let him have all the soda he wanted and would let him play video games. He just had to promise not to tell his mom.

He was beyond ecstatic. Free Coke and video games. Heck yes. Christmas was the time of year for miracles after all.

That was when Mitch spent Christmas Eve at the American Legion, high on sugary soda, playing video games and turning to the dog-eared copy of *I Am Legend* as his once jovial and kind father got a different kind of plowed.

That sunny, fun day turned into a dark, violent one when his mom ended up coming down to the Legion and grabbing Mitch, and it turned out to be one of the worst fights his parents ever had.

That Christmas, he received drawing supplies and Dungeons and Dragons and *Lord of the Rings* books, while his mom got a black eye and a fat lip. And for his brooding father, a brooding hangover.

Merry Christmas to the Roberts family.

The piercing air horn blew again, jolting Mitch back to the moment.

Dad!

Mitch's mind screamed as a scorching pain surged through his left leg. He reached down and found that one of the talons had pierced his thigh, resulting in a deep cut that was gushing hot blood into the snow below.

He fell to one knee, gripping his leg, and cried out as a row of gory teeth bore down on his face.

The familiar horn blasted again. This time, Mitch saw his father's plow truck and fought to tether himself to any reality he could as the ten-foot-tall plow blade smashed into the Darkness, pushing the massive beast forward into the railing.

In the massive truck's wake, an immense wave of rock salt filled the air, and the Darkness seemed to recoil and screech in agony as the millions of tiny, jagged salt crystals exploded into its swirling form.

Although the storm was waning, the Darkness fought to keep its grip on the town, but the brute force of the ten-thousand-pound truck sent it through the steel railing, obliterating it and sending the unnatural, bestial entity crashing into the thrashing waves of Lake Ontario below.

As the truck sped by, it continued sending large sprays of rock salt from the massive bed. Through blurry, pain-filled eyes, Mitch glimpsed his dad, still in his suit from his mom's funeral, chomping on a burning cigar, a can of beer in one hand, the other on the steering wheel. But even in that fleeting moment, Mitch caught something he hadn't experienced in a long time.

A stream of tears rained down from his dad's craggy face, and Mitch could've sworn his father smiled, took the cigar from his upturned mouth, winked, and mouthed the words, "I'm sorry, Mitchie. Love ya!"

Then, the massive snowplow slammed full-speed into the Darkness. The scratching and clawing blackness let out a soul-wrenching scream that sent frozen shockwaves over the entire pier.

Its writhing black tentacles wrapped around the body of the truck as the razor-sharp teeth and talons punctured the metal, shredding it into ribbons.

The truck bed blasted open, releasing a shower of rock salt that flew like shrapnel. The crystals shimmered in the air and sliced deep holes into the massive shadow of tentacles and teeth, which howled out in pain.

Mitch gasped as his father's truck sped past them toward the pier, the writhing Darkness wrapped around it, dragging the two underneath the pier. Then they were gone, vanishing beneath the unforgiving, icy waves.

He screamed out, his body shaking in frozen spasms, staring wildly at his father's sinking truck. Its red and white taillights glowed in the depths before finally disappearing into the swallowing waters.

His father was gone. The truck—the monstrous Darkness. All gone.

As the truck disappeared in an enormous splash of white foam, Mitch heard someone's muffled scream, as if miles away.

Mitch desperately grasped at the bent and broken metal railing and collapsed onto the snow. The cold was nothing to him anymore. Just another numbing feeling. Even the talon gash burning in his leg meant nothing—

Mitch stared as something jutted out of the depths. He saw the black tentacle, frantically traced it back to the pier, then to his leg, and that's when a new, searing pain jolted through him. The Darkness bored into his leg, then violently yanked him into the frigid, pitch-black water.

Mitch couldn't feel anything but the biting cold and hundreds of daggers digging into his body.

For a split second, he thought he glimpsed his dad's yellow plow truck. If it were possible to cry underwater, he was surely doing it. Mitch wanted to fight. To keep living. To make it to the surface. But the demons of doubt filled his tired mind.

Why should he fight? Why should he get to live?

The cold took him, and even though something was tugging on his leg, he didn't care anymore and let himself go.

50

Santa Claus is Coming to Town

It was early Christmas morning, and young Mitch was awake so early the sun wasn't even a thought yet, but he didn't care.

He swore he'd heard reindeer hooves on the roof and the telltale jingle-jangle of sleigh bells above him.

He slowly got out of bed, barely able to control his growing excitement at the thought of Santa being downstairs at this very second. Mitch fought to keep quiet.

Running to the wall between his parents' bedroom and his own, he put his ear to the cold plaster and listened, hoping, praying, for any sign they might be awake.

His shoulders slumped when the empty sound of silence came through the wall.

Should he knock? Call out to them? Nope, his father would be grumpy, he arrived home late the previous night.

But Mitch's excitement and waning patience wouldn't hold up much longer.

What would Dr. Strange do? Yoda? Dr. Who? These were all valid questions, but none of those guys could help Mitch now.

He stood there in silence.

Then, a familiar smell wafted under his door.

It was warm…like roasting peanuts, but…darker.

Mitch ran to his door, gripping the cold knob. He pressed his ear to the wood. This time he heard something.

A low mumble of voices and soft laughter came from downstairs.

His young heart felt as if it would tumble out of his chest, and he jittered all about the room, waiting. Hoping for the second, his parents called him down to see just what magic and miracles Santa Claus had brought him.

After what felt like a torturous, taunting eternity, a comforting call from downstairs finally came.

"Merry Christmas, Chief Thundercloud. Come on down. It's all clear. Santa is gone!" His mom's words filled him with overwhelming love and excitement.

"Yeah, boy, what's taking you so long? If ya don't get your butt down here soon, I'm gonna keep all the good stuff," his dad called up the stairs, his words filled with a rare, playful tone.

Mitch's entire body felt so warm and filled with such joy and happiness, he thought he just might burst.

He whipped the door open with a creak and darted down the stairs.

Christmas music welcomed him as he reached the landing that led to the last three steps into the living room filled with a twelve-foot, fully lit, decorated tree, surrounded by brilliantly colored gifts and bright red, blue, and green lights.

"Merry Christmas, Mitchie," his mom and dad said with gentle, loving smiles.

But something was off. Something was different.

Mitch nearly fell onto the hardwood landing in his stockinged feet.

Before him, his mom and dad stood in front of the tree, flanked by an epic pile of presents. But—

Their smiles…their faces were wrong.

Mitch expected them to be younger. Fewer wrinkles, less white hair.

"Merry Christmas, Mitchie." The wave of warmth engulfed him as a distant voice called out to him from somewhere far away.

"Mitchie. Mitchie."

Mitch's vision blurred. His parents swirled and blurred. Their flickering image washed into a kaleidoscope of colors as all went dark, and the distant voice drew him closer, as though someone was calling him home.

51
Happy Christmas Day

Something shook him as shards of sporadic light splintered the darkness.

"Come back to me, damn you!" A different voice came from the spreading light. A woman. But not his mother. Yet familiar.

Mitch heard more muffled cries. It was a different voice.

Not his own this time.

Mitch understood the words—barely. But he couldn't identify the speaker. His leg throbbed, and his lungs burned as he felt himself throwing up a swimming pool's worth of water.

With closed eyes, he still could sense light. A flashlight, maybe? Headlights? No… Sunlight.

Something wet lapped at his cheek.

"Mitch. Can you hear me?" The voice came again. This time, it was becoming more familiar.

"It's me." The voice was far away and dreamlike. *"Your Bethie."*

Those words caught him. He opened his eyes to see Pablo licking his face and panting.

"Hey! There you are," Beth said, tears flowing from her watery eyes. A mile-wide smile crossed her exhausted, beautiful face.

Mitch coughed up what felt like a gallon of freezing lake water as he woke from his dream.

"Mitchie. I'm here," the soft, enticing voice called again.

A bright white light blossomed in his eyes. Starting with a tiny speck of golden yellow, slowly widening like a brilliant iris as a warm, welcoming voice filled his mind.

"Can you hear me? I'm here." The voice was closer now.

He felt someone sitting next to him. The warmth of their bodies pulled at the tether that sought to bring him back to consciousness.

"M-Mom?" He reached out as he tried to open his eyes. But something tugged at his arms, pulling him back.

In a blinding, disorienting flash, Mitch shouted and awoke in a bright white room.

It was Beth sitting on the edge of the hospital bed. The light coming in through the large windows by his bedside softly illuminated her radiant face.

It took a long while for him to navigate his dream and the waking world before him.

"I…I…" was all he could muster.

"Focus on me, babe," Beth said.

Focusing his eyes, the face came into view.

"Beth!"

Finally shedding the disorienting dream, Mitch took inventory of his new surroundings.

"Oh, Mitchie!" Beth grabbed his face, but he pulled away.

Beth put her hands gently on his chest. "Oh, I'm so sorry. I've got you."

In the distance, many shrieking sirens pierced the early morning air.

* * *

The room was blindingly bright. Too damn bright.

Mitch felt a dull ache in his leg and closed his eyes, trying to find an anchor between his dream and now, hopefully, his waking world.

"It's okay. Stings, is all." Every inch of his body ached with a dull, cold throb. What felt like a dozen angry ice picks bored into his temples, making him feel as if his head was about to explode.

"Am I dead?" he said through panicked breaths.

Beth shook her head, and her wide, welcoming smile took a tiny scratch of the pain away. "No!" She kissed his cheek. Her full lips were warm and wet, assuring him he was indeed alive.

"You're not leaving me ever again," Beth said, wrapping him in her arms. She smelled of campfire and cinnamon, mixed with the strong disinfectant smell of a hospital.

"You got that?" She smiled wide, her rosy-apple cheeks and heart-stealing hazel eyes calming him, as they always had.

"My dad?" he heard himself ask. Mitch swallowed hard, as he already knew the answer.

She just shook her head and kissed him. The salt from her tear-covered lips still stung a little, but he didn't mind.

They hugged for what seemed like a long time as Mitch slowly found solid footing and a way to shake the thick cobwebs of sleep.

"I'm so sorry," Beth said, her eyes glistening with tears.

His mind reeled as the thick veil of webs slowly parted, and he struggled to piece the horrific memories together.

He wanted to stay in her arms forever, but the world swirled around him. As the memories of the past two days came flooding back, turbulent visions of chaos and bloodshed mixed with snowdrifts in his mind.

Mitch held onto Bethel Marie Connolly as tightly as he could with what little strength his battered and cut body kept.

He realized he'd traded the biting storm for this alcohol-sanitized hospital.

"I'm so, so sorry, Mitchie," Beth whispered in his ear, her breath warm against his skin.

He spent a long, desperate moment painfully calculating what had happened, trying desperately to piece together the bloody, violent images populating his mind like cuttings from a nightmarish scrapbook.

Mitch abruptly pushed away. "Tony… Sheldon?" His mind felt like a hazy jigsaw puzzle as he hurriedly tried to find the missing pieces. "Pablo? Is he okay?" He looked around the sterile white room for any sign of the dog.

Beth gently grabbed his hand. "Sheldon is safe. When that…*thing* attacked the bar, Sal grabbed him, along with some others, and hid in the beer cooler. And Pablo is fine. He's with Sal too. They're all probably a little frostbitten."

"Yeah. Know the feeling." He gripped Beth's hand tight. "That's pretty fast thinking for an old bartender," he said, squinting as he looked out the window to the parking lot, which lay buried in an ungodly amount of snow. Long icicles on the upper part of the windowsill dripped as the sun was finally working its magic.

"So…" Mitch started, "Tony didn't make it?"

She squeezed his hand tighter and shook her head.

What was there to say? It was all so confusing. A numb, open wound that stung like fire when he thought about it. The unforgiving hands of fate tore open a decades-old scar and left it splayed open. But despite the hell he'd gone through—all they'd gone through—Beth was here. By his side. Where he needed his sweet darling girl the most.

In a jolting flash, as if she had remembered something, she went to her ripped jacket on the chair beside the bed and took out a pair of weathered old photos.

"I found these in the snow," she said. "I thought I saw your dad throwing something out of the window of the truck."

Mitch's hands trembled as he looked at the first of the old photos: he and his father inside a Wayne County plow truck, when they were both so much younger.

"Look at the old man," he said, running his thumb gently over the worn image.

"I know. He was actually smiling."

"Bigfoot and Elvis were harder pics to capture." Mitch forced the joke. "But good old Gordie had his moments. Few and far between as they were."

"He was proud of you. He loved you, Mitchie. You know that, right?" It wasn't a question.

"I suppose." He shrugged.

His mind went back to the last conversation he'd had with his dad in the car. The old man's awkward yet sincere apology.

"He sure had his way about him," Mitch said.

Beth kissed his cheek. "He sure did."

The second photo captured his mom and dad on their wedding day at that small church in Ontario. His mom would always go on about that, saying it was too hot and too small, but that it was still one of the most magical days of her life. That, and naturally, when he was born. She was always quick to add that.

He lingered a long time at his newlywed parents. They were so young. So happy.

"Wow," was all Mitch could muster. His breath caught in his throat.

"I know. Your mom was so beautiful. And I hate to say it, but your dad was quite the looker too."

"A whole lifetime ago," he said.

"Sometimes, when one of the gang's games was going on, I'd sneak up to chat with your mom, and she would often talk about their wedding day. She was definitely happy as she looked at the picture. Her face would brighten up the room when she talked about that day and your dad."

"Yeah, I remember too. Life's a funny thing. You never know what's going to happen. We start off thinking we know exactly what we want. And then life, fate, takes its own chaotic path. Guess we try to control our lives, but all we can do is try our best."

Mitch gently kissed the pictures, and then kissed Beth on her cheek, then rested his head on her shoulder and wept.

"Thought you'd want them, Roberts."

He pulled her close. "Thank you, Bethie." He smiled. "Forgive me for leaving. I'm sorry."

Mitch sat up and smiled at the view through the hospital window. A beautiful Christmas morning in Sterling Point, and the wind-ravaged Lake Ontario and the lighthouse beyond. This time, he let himself live.

"Merry Christmas, Mom. I love you," Mitch said to the bright blue sky, finally sending the fading snowstorm away. And turning his tear-drenched gaze to the rippling waters, he said, "You too, Dad."

The storm had shifted off to the east, but Mitch was certain he would never forget the brutal Christmas storm and the Darkness that would take the town decades to recover from. If ever.

He stared deeply into her breathtaking hazel eyes as all traces of the cold fled his body and soul. With a bandaged hand, he caressed her cheek.

"Hey..." he said.

"Yes?" Beth beamed.

"Hey, so...what are you doing for New Year's?"

-END-

EPILOGUE

The frigid waters of Lake Ontario were as still as glass—the deadly storm had moved far to the east, leaving a frozen and chaotic aftermath. But deep beneath the now calm waters above, no fish were stirring, no ship sat on the horizon.

The 30-ton snowplow now rested on the dark bottom of the lake. Its plow, like a great shovel, had dug into the earth and lay buried deep within the mud.

Gordon Roberts' body floated to the top of the cab. His well-lived face wore a strange, yet peaceful smile.

Perhaps the frozen water had captured his final moments in life, as he and his son finally understood one another, at least to the best they could. Or perhaps he reunited with the one true love of his life, Marguerite, in a heaven he'd sworn never existed. Either way, Gordon Andrew Roberts was at peace.

Although the frigid water was dark as pitch, something far darker writhed slowly from the depths, engulfing the monstrous dump truck.

In mere seconds, the truck was gone.

All the while, the blackness swelled.

HUZZAHS AND THANK YOUS!

(Spelled this way on purpose!)

Jonathan Maberry – You have encouraged me to write *Snow Black* for over a decade. Even more than that, you've been a steadfast mentor, friend, and continuous inspiration. The words *thank you* just don't seem like enough—but I am, and always will be, eternally grateful.

Linda Nagle – My amazingly talented, honest editor and Literary Lumberjack. Thank you for gently—and honestly—showing me the forest for the trees. You rock!

Gord Rollo – Your ongoing support, encouragement and friendship has been a huge part of me keeping on writing and striving to get better. Thank you, brother!

David Moody – Your writing inspiration, encouragement, and support have been so important to me. Thank you!

Kealan Patrick Burke – Your words, both written and spoken, have been a great inspiration. Thank you and Slainte.

J.T. Patten – Thanks so much for the writing mentorship and advice and ongoing encouragement. Here's to mucho more words.

Sheldon Higdon – My friend, my writing compadre, con-goer, and brother. Thank you so much for all the years of inspiring and uplifting conversations and amazing friendship.

Bridget Manns – You've been a huge supporter and faithful beta reader. Here ya go, kiddo—it's finally done. You keep reading, and I'll keep writing.

Holly Zaldivar – Your steadfast support, encouragement and editing have been a godsend. Thank you.

Greg Hookstra – My fellow jam brother and loyal, patient reader. Here ya go, brother. I hope the long, long wait was worth it. See you in *Sterling Point!*

Scarlett R. Algee and **JournalStone** – Thank you for finally bringing this deeply meaningful story to life.

GOV'T MULE – *Déjà Voodoo and all their other albums.*

This album was a huge inspiration and my writing soundtrack.

(See the complete soundtrack and scan the Spotify QR code to listen while you read.)

Cover Image Contributing Artist: Drew Brayshaw

ABOUT THE AUTHOR

Thom Erb is a genre fiction writer, editor, and artist from Newark, NY, celebrated for his immersive explorations of horror, fantasy, thriller, weird western, and science fiction. Refusing to be confined by genre conventions, Erb's stories consistently blur boundaries and probe the definitions of heroism, shining a light on unlikely and flawed protagonists who overcome adversity. His bibliography includes *The Last in Line* (Book One of The Eternal Flame Trilogy) and *Heaven, Hell, or Houston*, alongside numerous short stories and anthology contributions. In addition to being a writer, he is an illustrator with credits for book covers, comics, and murals. Erb is a lifelong comic book enthusiast, drummer, and gamer, active in promoting speculative fiction through podcasts and collaborations. He is deeply engaged with the creative communities of Upstate New York and continues to create for both adult and young readers, always seeking new ways to challenge and entertain through the written and visual arts.

More about his work and upcoming projects can be found at www.thomerb.com.

SNOW BLACK:
THE SOUNDTRACK

https://open.spotify.com/playlist/6Wntqai1cCIv1D1GtMo2c9?si=d06c7
99bb06941f0

Music has always been—and will always be—a huge part of my life. My Grandma O'Brien gave me my first Elvis Presley record. (Yes, vinyl. And yes, I loved it.) My mom sang Charley Pride constantly while going about her daily routines around the house. Then, in junior high during the early eighties, I discovered RUSH and Iron Maiden. From there, it was the Allman Brothers, Government Mule, and so many more.

Music inspired me to teach myself drums at sixteen and sparked a lifelong passion for jamming. It has also fueled my other creative outlets—whether I'm drawing comic books, crafting Dungeons & Dragons characters, or setting the soundtrack to my writing adventures.

Dear readers and listeners, I offer you the sonic inspiration behind *SNOW BLACK*. Use the QR code to explore the incredible music that inspired me throughout nearly a decade of writing this story.

The music—and this story—mean the world to me. I truly hope you enjoy them both.

Live Life Full,
Thom Erb